Emma's Journey

and

Emma and the Leprechauns

Elizabeth Daish spent some of her childhood on the Isle of Wight, trained as a nursing sister at a famous London hospital and became a theatre sister.

She married an accountant and has two children, a son who is the clinical research administrator for a large pharmaceutical company and a daughter who has graduated as a medical scientist. She now lives on the Isle of Wight with her husband, and her hobbies are sailing, walking, cooking and entertaining friends.

Emma's Journey

and

Emma and the Leprechauns

Elizabeth Daish

Pan Books

Emma's Journey first published 1999 by Severn House Publishers
Emma and the Leprechauns first published 2000 by Severn House Publishers

This omnibus edition published 2001 by Pan Books
an imprint of Pan Macmillan Ltd
Pan Macmillan, 20 New Wharf Road, London N1 9RR
Basingstoke and Oxford
Associated companies throughout the world
www.panmacmillan.com

ISBN 0 330 39878 4

A CIP catalogue record for this book is available from
the British Library.

Printed and bound in Great Britain by
Mackays of Chatham plc, Chatham, Kent

Emma's Journey

One

"You must be really thrilled, Sister." Eileen fi.[ ] the tussore silk and lace angel tops and sighed.[ ]

"I find it hard to believe that Bea can go into a shop in Washington and buy whatever she wants for the twins, and presents for us." Emma Sykes put the rest of the small garments on the highly polished chest of drawers in the bedroom and handed a smaller parcel to Eileen. "She sent this for you," she said and smiled, hoping that her face didn't look as stiff as it felt and that her voice was warm.

Eileen tore off the wrapping paper and held up a garishly embroidered dress, perfect for a baby girl – if one wore dark glasses and lived in the hotter parts of the United States of America. "Mrs Miller, you are a lovely lady," she breathed, looking heavenwards as if in prayer. Eileen glanced at her employer and seemed embarrassed. "Are you sure you wouldn't like to exchange this for one of yours? It's so beautiful." She hugged the dress as if she couldn't bear to part with it but thought she must try to be fair, as the plain and elegant cream tussore silk seemed to her to be dull against the bright embroidery.

"Quite sure," Emma reassured her firmly. "Mrs Miller

1

knows that you like bright colours." She could imagine
Bea choosing the clothes, knowing exactly what each
of the young mothers would prefer, and trying to hide
her own preferences. The bright dress must have caused
her some misgiving, but seeing Eileen's almost tearful
eyes, Emma knew that as usual Bea had got it just
right, however much she might have shuddered when
she bought the gaudy dress.

"I wish she would come back," Eileen said sadly. "We
all miss her, don't we, Sister?"

Emma's tense face relaxed. She had forgotten that it
vasn't only her who missed the friend who had played a
major part in her life for several years; they had trained
together as nurses during World War II at the Princess
Beatrice Hospital – Beatties – in south-east London. There
was so much that was both good and bad to remember of
that time, and later, during their fairly light-hearted period
as private nurses. That was before Bea had taken her twins
and followed her husband Dwight to America, then had
another son Mark; and before her own little Rosamund
had been born at Beatties over two years ago.

"I'll get Mick to take a snap of Jean in the dress. It's a
bit big for her now but she'll grow into it soon and it will
last all the summer. He can take one of Rose as well,"
Eileen offered. "That new camera is wonderful and he
fancies himself as a photographer."

"I'll go up to the consulting room while you find Mick.
I promised to sit in when Esme Bolt is under hypnosis.
She should be gone by four and we can have tea and buns
at half past."

Almost wearily, Emma climbed the stairs and tidied the

2

large airy room where Paul saw his psychiatric patients. She picked out two wilting daffodils from a vase and smelled the earthy fragrance of the tiny iris bulbs in the wide blue bowl. Spring again and Rosamund was a potent reminder of new life and growth, but Emma was tired. On the way to help her husband she had looked in the nursery and gazed down at the sleeping child, now quiet but gathering energy for the next burst of fun and games. Such energy, and Emma found it difficult to keep up with her now that she was walking and eager to explore.

"Is she having her nap?" Paul asked and grinned.

"At last! I nearly climbed in beside her. I had no idea that one small girl could be so exhausting." Paul regarded her with a wry smile. "I know I should be glad to see all that activity, or so my psychiatrist husband told me, but compared with Jean, Rose is hyperactive." She smiled and glanced towards the door as if she might be overheard. "Not that I'd change her for Jean. She's prettier and so healthy that I want to eat her at times."

"You need a rest. You help in the clinic and do nearly everything for Rose as well as organising the house. We must find a girl to share the load. No, don't protest! I don't want a wife who is limp and sad. Now tell me what is wrong; not Rose or the hard work but something more."

Emma moved away restlessly, almost upsetting the flower arrangement. "It's nothing, or almost nothing. I find that spring is always a trying time, and this year it's worse, now that we are emerging from winter, and yet it's not warm enough to let Rose play in the park."

"Is that all?"

Emma looked uncomfortable. "This may sound as if

3

I'm envious, and I suppose I am. Bea sent one of her in-between-birthday presents and a very good letter and I suddenly felt low. There is nothing I can send her that she hasn't at least two of and the shops here are so lacking in goods. Will these shortages ever go away? She casually talks of treats that the twins enjoy as routine and Mark has so many toys that Bea gives away those he discards when he is tired of them. They have this wonderful nanny who wants to stay for as long as Bea needs her. It's a bonus that Bea says the girl is partly British and she has no really sharp American accent so the twins still sound at least half British." She saw Paul's quizzical expression and sat down heavily on the leather chair by his desk. "All right Doctor, I confess. I have a fit of the blues. I miss Bea as much now as I did after they went back the last time that Dwight brought her over here."

"So you need more than pink pills for pale people," Paul said.

"I don't need a tonic at all." Emma yawned. "I just want to walk up the road and see food shops with no anxious women holding saggy string bags outside the butchers and with newspapers ready to wrap up the bread. It's become a habit since they rationed bread for a while after the war. We thought that once it was over we would be back to what we knew, but there seems to be a kind of grey apathy as if we have shortages and must put up with them for ever. Bread rationing is over now thank goodness, but when that happened I thought we'd really reached rock bottom! We didn't even have bread rationing during the war when the convoys were bombed and our own farms produced less grain than we needed." She shrugged impatiently. "I know we did well and we had a supply of flour from one of your farmer friends, so we could make soda bread and scones and real bread when I could find yeast; but most people had so little and I felt guilty accepting extras that they couldn't obtain or afford."

"So you made soda bread for the cleaner and most of her large and hungry family." Paul laughed. "I noticed that the whole house smelled of baking for weeks, but it was a good idea."

"It was the least I could do." Emma brushed aside any hint that she was too generous.

"Bea misses you, too," he pointed out. "All that luxury can never take the place of friendship, but Bea is in the right place," he added firmly. "She couldn't settle here again as her life is with Dwight and the babies and she does enjoy the American way of life, but there are times when Dwight is worried and wishes we were there." He eyed his wife thoughtfully. "I worry about you at times but you are in touch with your roots and can talk to Aunt Emily and Janey and visit places you will always love. I know you couldn't tear yourself away from all that and we couldn't be apart for more than a holiday." He put a finger under her chin so that he could see her eyes and looked serious. "Could we?"

Emma put his hand to her cheek, felt the flow of love between them and shook her head. "I *am* happy, but sometimes I know I could do more. Not more in the house, sitting in the clinic or looking after Rose – that is true fulfilment – but I have other talents and they are a bit rusty."

"You said you couldn't go back to Beatties, even after being asked to do so several times."

"Not that, but I miss the sensation of being able to make someone better, or at least to bring relief and hope to ill patients. Wasn't it Milton who wrote about 'Having one talent that is death to hide, lodged with me useless . . .'"

"You do enough here, but I know what you mean." Paul glanced at the wall clock. "Miss Bolt is late but I think I hear Mick with her now. We must talk again later, Darling. I get far too absorbed in work and time flies, but I do have an idea or two that might help. I don't think it's Eileen's evening for the flicks so we can go out to Mario's and talk seriously over a meal and a bottle of wine. Mario said he'd save a bottle of Rioja for us."

"Lovely." Emma's cheeks dimpled and she was relaxed. "I promise not to leave you alone with Esme Bolt; that's if she hasn't seduced Mick on the way up."

"She *is* getting better, but please don't leave me."

"Some men would enjoy having half the nymphomaniacs in London chasing them."

"Very funny!"

"She's very pretty."

"Too many men have thought so. I have the result of the Wassermann and it's positive."

"Syphilis?" Emma whispered and he nodded.

"I want to find what triggered her obsession with sex so we'll have a fairly deep session today and then I have to tell her what's wrong clinically and refer her to Davies in 'A' Block at Beatties for treatment."

Emma giggled, remembering the uncompromising attitude of Dr Davies and his thick Welsh accent imbued with the disapproval of generations of Welsh Chapel. "What a challenge for Esme!"

"Quite a challenge for Davies! I almost believe that he does that particular job with venereal diseases to punish himself for something."

"Maybe he needs a good shrink," Emma whispered as the door opened to admit Esme. Mick Grade hovered behind her ready to escape as soon as possible, his face slightly red.

"Ask your wife if we can have tea in about half an hour," Paul said solemnly, to impress Esme with the fact that Mick was married and unavailable.

Esme stared at Mick and smiled. "I do hope you haven't married a *good woman*. What a waste of a good strong body," she purred and Mick nearly fell backwards from the room.

"I hope you've kept the diary up to date," Paul said. She nodded. "And the drugs?"

"I've been quite good, but I know you won't think so," Esme replied sulkily. "That medicine tastes absolutely filthy and makes me so sleepy that I don't feel like having any fun."

"That is the idea," Paul said simply. "You lost two very good jobs because you embarrassed your employers, and your own doctor asked me to help you. I need to find out what caused your condition, so that you may be able to control your . . . urges."

"It wasn't fair. I ran that shop well until the wife of a customer complained that her husband was meeting me after work." Esme was the picture of innocence.

"And the other job?" Paul asked.

7

"That was a bit naughty I suppose, but it takes two to tango."

"On the office desk?"

"It's so difficult, Doctor. I seem to have wonderful jobs offered to me as I *am* pretty and very efficient but there are a lot of very attractive men about. I can work really well unless I'm distracted."

Paul consulted a folder on his desk and Emma saw that Esme was eyeing his well-set shoulders with far too much interest, so she led the woman to the couch and helped her off with her shoes and jacket before settling her down comfortably.

Paul held a syringe up to the light and expelled a small bubble of air from the liquid. "Just to relax you into a light sleep." Emma rolled up the loose sleeve and swabbed the patient's arm with a wad of gauze moistened with surgical spirit and then held the hand steady while the needle slid smoothly into the vein. A piece of sticking plaster was placed over the syringe to secure it in place and allow the plunger to be depressed whenever Paul needed more thiopentone released into the vein.

Esme smiled. "This is wonderful. A sort of floating feeling almost as good as gentle sex."

Paul refused to have eye contact and told her to take three deep breaths. "Just think back to when you were completely happy as a child."

Esme closed her eyes and relaxed her grip on Emma's hand. "It was so long ago. It was before I went to school."

"Were you happy on your fifth birthday?"

Esme giggled. "Had a party and we all played sardines.

I hid in a cupboard and my uncle found me and said he wanted a reward for being clever in finding me so quickly. He said we must keep quiet and he gave me a big hug." Paul put her slightly deeper and she sighed. "He had soft hands and he stroked me all over, then kissed me. He was kind and said he loved little girls." She wriggled lower on the couch. "Daddy never said he loved me, not once, and when I was all spotty with the measles, he pushed me away when I wanted him to hug me and told Mummy to keep me away from him as I was hot and smelly, but Uncle Robbie said he'd sit with me and read a story while Mummy went to the shops, and he took off my nightie and rubbed me all over with scented powder. It was lovely and my skin was cool."

"You loved Uncle Robbie?"

"Yes but Daddy was nasty to him and he went away."

"What happened?"

"It was Christmas and we'd undone our presents and I went to sit on Uncle Robbie's lap but Daddy said I mustn't."

"Did Uncle Robbie live with your family?"

"He stayed with us very often and always brought me nice presents and we had a secret." She laughed. "He was silly, really. I liked what he did to me but he told me that if I said anything to Mummy, she'd be cross and he'd go away and never come back."

"Did he ever hurt you?"

"Not really hurt. Only once after he'd given me some nice orange juice and I couldn't really stay awake. It hurt a bit but after that once it was nice and I asked him to do it again the next time he came to us." Esme began to cry.

9

"But Uncle Robbie went away. Why did he go away? I tried to snuggle up to Daddy as I did to Uncle Robbie but Daddy pushed me away and asked me whether Uncle Robbie had touched me and hurt me. I said I loved Uncle Robbie and he loved me and I hated Daddy for being so nasty."

Emma saw the tension in Paul's face and she held the patient's hand gently. "So Robbie went away," Paul said softly.

"Daddy hit him and I was frightened and tried to hug Uncle Robbie, but Daddy smacked me and sent me to bed, and the next day Uncle Robbie was gone and there was nobody to make me laugh and to love me. Daddy said I was wicked and I must never let anyone do those things to me again or God would punish me."

"So you tried to find Robbie?"

"I ran away three times but I never saw him again. I looked everywhere and tried to find someone like him but I never did."

Paul injected a little more thiopentone and Esme breathed deeply. "Think about later. Were you happy at school? Was it a girls' school?"

"Yes. I was quite clever and good at sports. When I was twelve we had a new games master. He was like my uncle. He had fair hair and his eyes laughed and made me want to be near him." Her voice became more adult. "He was a creep. He said he loved me and we did make love but he was no good and he went with other girls, so I wouldn't let him do it again, but I was so lonely, until we had to join the boys at the grammar school for science, and I tried to find someone like Robbie there."

"And you've never found anyone like him?"

Esme gave a shuddering sigh and tears fell again. "Sometimes it's very good and I'm happy but afterwards I feel so lonely that I drink too much and I have bad dreams."

"When you wake up you will take your medicine and enjoy being sleepy. You will think of good things that have nothing to do with sex and the next time someone wants you, be sure that you really like him as a person and not just for the act of sex."

Esme sighed and yawned and slowly sat up. "Was I asleep? It was good. What happens now? Do I go on with that horrible medicine? Someone told me it was like the bromide they gave to the soldiers when they couldn't have women."

"It is a bit like that," Paul admitted. "I hear that you have a new job?"

"Another shop. At the trial interview they liked the way I dressed and my easy manner with customers." She grinned. "Not the male customers, and I'm being very discreet. I'm glad you told me that I am sick, Doctor. I thought I was a freak who ought to have been a prostitute. I do draw the line there. I sleep with men who are clean and nice-looking." She glanced up and saw Paul's expression. "What's wrong?"

"One of your men wasn't clean. I had the result of your blood test and you have a rather unpleasant sexually transmitted disease." Paul spoke seriously and without emotion and Esme stuffed a handkerchief into her mouth to stifle her sobs. "I shall write to a colleague at the Princess Beatrice Hospital who will treat the disease. If you have any regard for others, you will not have

11

intercourse with anyone until you are cured. This is a notifiable disease and the law could intervene if you knowingly infect another person."

"What can I tell my friends? I'd hate to have this made public."

"You will attend a clinic but your name will be confidential and you will answer to a number. If anyone asks if you are receiving treatment there they will be unlucky as your name will be only in the records and not on your chart."

"One of those VD clinics? It sounds like prison. Must I go there?"

"Now you have been diagnosed, you must be treated. The sore that you reported to your doctor is highly infectious and the sooner you have drugs the sooner you and any sexual contacts you make will be safe, but the fact that you can be cured fairly easily now with antibiotics, compared with a few years ago when the treatment was tedious and often took several months, does not mean that you can never be re-infected. This is not an immunisation against further infection."

Eileen tapped on the door and Emma asked her to come in. She put the tea tray on the desk and eyed Esme with interest before leaving the room again. "Why didn't you want to take the tray, Mick?" she asked when they went down to their own apartment.

"Go near her? Not on your Nelly, and you'd better be careful when you do the washing up."

"What a thing to say! I thought she looked nice but a bit shocked. She was very clean and smartly dressed, Mick. She doesn't need a doctor for something catching.

Dr Paul isn't that kind of doctor. He treats the mind and the nervous system." She smiled. "That suit must have cost a lot. Did you see that lovely scarf?"

"I saw her notes," Mick said briskly. "The blood test was positive."

"What test?"

Mick regarded his wife with pity mixed with amusement. "A blood test to see if she's been a naughty girl and caught syphilis."

"Who could do that to a nice woman like her?"

"The doc will be more concerned as to how many she's given it since she got her dose," Mick retorted severely.

"I don't believe it." Eileen's eyes widened. "You don't mean she's a prostitute?"

"Na! Nothing so common! She just likes sex and they don't need paying if she fancies them, which is most of the time."

"I can't think that I'd fancy many other men," Eileen said. "I find you quite enough!"

"You'd better keep it like that, my girl," Mick said grimly, but slapped her bottom gently, and she giggled.

Two

M rs Coster was, as usual, washing the hall tiles when Esme left.

"She can't bear to miss anything and she seems to know when there's any drama in the consulting room." Emma laughed. "I think she'd love to listen in to your hypnosis sessions and she tries to winkle out details from Mick if he's been sitting in as chaperone during a consultation."

"She probably thinks she knows as much about the human brain and its functions as I do, but she does push her luck at times even though her rather earthy common sense is impressive." Paul poured more red wine into Emma's glass and smiled. "She's been with us ever since we came here and we'd be lost without her, so I hate to upset her. What was her diagnosis this time?"

Emma sipped her wine and then looked roguishly over the rim of her glass at her husband. "She told Mick to watch out as 'that one' was a right tart. She'll probably warn you too, given the chance."

"She knows better! As Mick is ex-service, Mrs Coster takes it for granted that he was tempted by women who haunted the camps and probably slept with one or two, but I doubt it. Mick came from a poor background

14

but had enough sense to distance himself from such entanglements. His sister was an example of what he might become if he stayed with his family and played the black market, or worse. It took a lot of hard work and dedication to become a sergeant with a lot of authority."

"He was much more help to us when he was in a wheelchair than any of the orderlies, and he took over a lot of our paperwork as he does here."

Paul looked pensive. "We depend on him a lot, and he handles the office work better than most trained secretaries."

"I'll never forget how he managed my mother's affairs when she died and I had the flu and couldn't cope with the funeral," Emma said fervently.

"I want to make clear what our future will be here with Mick and Eileen," Paul said.

Emma looked startled. "They haven't hinted that they want to leave? Eileen is happy as our housekeeper and they both love their nice comfortable apartment. Little Jean is sweet and is company for Rose and we share the baby-sitting so that Eileen can indulge in her twice-weekly visits to the cinema and I can feel free to leave Rose in safe hands whenever we need to be away for a few hours."

"Don't panic," Paul said mildly. "I admit that life is orderly and good but there comes a time when we have to do other things. I have been unwilling to alter anything, but as you know, I have turned down a few offers of lecture tours and decided that it would be impossible to leave here for a long holiday or business trip."

Emma sat very still, aware that something momentous was about to happen.

15

"I want your help and honest opinion before we decide anything. If you want to stay here and go on as we have done, I shall say no more about it." He laughed, suddenly boyish. "But I think you will find my proposition interesting, Sister!"

If he was Guy, Emma thought suddenly, recalling her lover who had died helping the survivors in Belsen, he wouldn't have asked me or considered my opinion on anything important – he would have *told* me after he'd arranged it and expected me to agree. "What is it? And what have Mick and Eileen to do with it?" She smiled. "You bring me to Mario's and ply me with delicious food and wine and soften me up for what?"

"Would you like to visit Bea? Take our time over there while I do two lecture tours?"

Emma burst into tears and Luigi, Mario's son, hovered anxiously by the next table. "Tears of joy I hope," Paul said hastily and Luigi beamed and rushed away to the kitchen. "You do realise that he is telling his wife that you must be pregnant again?"

Emma laughed through her tears and took a deep breath before drying her eyes. "Luigi is convinced that tears of joy must mean another *bambino*, but usually it's the wife who knows first, not the husband, and I'm not."

"Very coherent," Paul said. "So they might just be tears of joy?"

She nodded and her voice was husky. "It's a dream. I hoped it would come true but at times I couldn't think that far ahead and it made me sad, but is it any closer now or is it still a dream? There's the clinic and your patients, the house and Rose."

16

"A hundred things," Paul said happily, "and we have enough help and support to see to everything."

Luigi glanced disapprovingly at the wine in Emma's glass and Paul held out the empty bottle. "If you have another like that, we'd like it. Join us if you have time, Luigi. My wife is *not* expecting a baby but we do have something to celebrate." Luigi's face cleared and he came back with a fresh bottle and sat with them, hoping to hear more.

"America? I have a brother in New York who wants me to go there and open a restaurant with him but I am here with an English wife who hated the Yanks during the war." He shrugged. "I am content and I think she would not like my brother, or I would not like him looking at her as he does with other men's wives, so I stay here where I am not jealous and you bring all your friends here, yes?"

"If we go away, I'd like you to have some money to pay for anything that Eileen orders if they have to feed visiting doctors. She will have enough to do without catering for parties. When the money is used up ask Mick to pay you, as he will handle the day-to-day expenses."

"Will there be visiting doctors?" asked Emma. "What about the clinics? Where will your patients go and who will look after them?"

"The clinics will continue with a locum psychiatrist in charge, and possibly an assistant."

"Have you brought him here to eat, this new doctor? Is he *comprensivo* . . . sympathetic and easy?"

"That's a problem I have to face. I have two men in

mind who are clever and seem very well qualified, but I haven't decided which one to approach first."

Luigi grinned. "Invite them to eat here and my wife will tell you who is the right one."

"I think I need another opinion, Luigi, and there are things such as qualifications and references to check," Paul said lightly. "You can't judge a psychiatrist by the way he holds his fork or drinks his wine."

Mario chuckled. "My wife would know as soon as he lights a cigar or cigarette. There was a man who wanted her, before she married me, and she said he was charming and wanted to be *amoroso* but as soon as he struck a match and lit his cigarette she knew him to be bad and dishonest with women."

Paul roared with laughter. "She was joking, Luigi. I have never seen that one in any of my textbooks. How could she know?"

Luigi looked deflated. "She would never say it to me."

"But she married *you*, Luigi," Emma said consolingly. "You can tell her from me I know exactly what she meant. I saw a lot of men in hospital who gave a clue to their real characters over quite small mannerisms."

The two men stared at her in disbelief. "What a good thing I don't smoke," Paul said cryptically. "What happens if I bring him here and he doesn't smoke, either?"

"Then you leave him to me and Aunt Emily."

"The lady from the Isle of Wight who visited you and showed my wife how to make light, light cake?" Luigi kissed the tips of two fingers and sighed. "A wonderful lady who told me I would have a son, and Antonio was born safely after much labour."

Paul tried to be serious. "I don't think that this is the way to appoint a senior psychiatrist for six months, with a view to a partnership later." He began to laugh again. "Poor man, if I confronted him with you and your wife Luigi, not to mention Aunt Emily, and, of course, our Mrs Coster who cleans the house and makes spot judgements on all who pass her over the wet hall tiles."

"Don't forget Mick and Eileen and *me*," Emma retorted.

"Maybe I should leave you to it for a week and come back when you've made a decision," Paul said dryly.

"You would want to book a table, Doctor?"

"I'll let you know!" Paul replied weakly. "I wish I'd never mentioned it here."

Luigi helped himself to more wine and filled the other glasses. *"Salute e fortuna."*

"And may he be acceptable to our loyal friends, Mick and Eileen," Emma added.

"Who are at this moment in charge of our daughter and may want to get to bed. Stop dreaming and get your coat."

"I take it that you have put in a toe and found the water not too icy?" Emma said as they walked home.

"If you mean, have I made any progress towards finding a suitable locum, yes I have, and I was surprised that at least four people showed an interest. Two have wives and children and might be bad choices as far as Mick and Eileen are concerned. The children in both families are at least ten or twelve years of age, and noisy. I dropped in to see them casually and quite honestly I'd hate to let

19

them rip in our house. Both of the doctors believe in self expression and I'd not want them expressing themselves all over our drawing room."

"Mrs Coster would leave at once! What about the others?"

"The others are both unmarried and younger. One said he was now in Dublin, after having worked in Edinburgh for a year or so, but some of his family live in Surrey so he'd like to be near them for a while. Half a year would be fine for him, living in the house and carrying on the practice very much as I run it as far as psychoanalysis is concerned; but he isn't a neurologist. He was with a group of doctors at the last meeting we had at Tommies but none of the others knew him when I tried to find out more about him."

"And the other?"

Paul glanced at Emma and hesitated. "He's ex-service – Navy – and has done locum jobs for the past year. He's met your cousin George and likes him."

"I'm not surprised. George is a very likeable man," she said firmly. "He is going to be married again. Remember the nice Wren officer he met in Inverness? Aunt Janey says that she gets on well with George's son Clive and she wants more children to make a complete family. It's what George needs and I have great hopes for them."

"Will she leave the service and take care of Clive?"

"Not really. I know that Clive is very young but George thinks he's nearly old enough for boarding school and he wants to go away. Living with his grandmother all the time and attending a very small school where they don't have decent sports fields can't be much fun for an active boy. George has very limited time with him as he's in the Navy, so school is the answer and it will give George and Margaret time together. Until he is ready for boarding school, Clive will stay with Janey as he is now, and then come to her for holidays and half-term breaks later when George and Margaret will be able to see him there."

"As Clive doesn't remember his mother and has been secure and loved living with Janey and Alex since just after he was born, the future looks good for him, with few hang-ups," Paul said, drawing on his professional expertise.

"Margaret and George have mutual friends and she knows the Navy, which helps. Poor Sadie was out of her depth with George's friends and homesick for America and her fashionable life there."

"And George was still in love with you, Emma."

Emma brooded for a full minute then said quietly, "I think he's forgotten me but I'm not sure. As there was never anything going between us, at least as far as I was concerned, and we are first cousins, he had to find someone to fill his life after Sadie died and I married you. If we are really truly going away I want to miss their wedding. I have no intention of being even the faintest of spectres at the feast. It's only fair that Margaret can have her husband to herself and wipe out any thoughts of me for ever."

"Wise girl." Paul tucked her hand into his and kissed her on the cheek.

"So when do I meet the candidates?"

Paul frowned. "I hate to make it difficult for you but when we were all talking and George was mentioned,

I asked Commander Forsyth to come over for dinner, purely for a social occasion as I knew you'd be interested in meeting him."

"And what happened?"

"Dr Allen was listening and asked if he was included as he definitely wanted to be interviewed for the possible locum job. I told him that this was not an interview but he said that he'd need to come to see me soon to discuss the possibility as he was very keen to join us. He hinted that I was giving Forsyth an advantage because we had a mutual friend." Paul looked embarrassed. "He made it sound as if I had rejected him before he had a chance to tell me about himself and was, I thought, a bit offended. I remembered that we invited Catharine and her husband to dinner and you said you might ask the Sister from Beatties so I thought that he could be invited to make the numbers even. He has a certain charm and socially would be fine, but if both candidates were there together with me, a perfectly good social evening might become nothing but shop talk."

"Is he professionally sound?"

"Who can say on such a brief meeting? But as I felt obligated, even though I haven't advertised the post as yet, I've asked Martin Allen to dinner tomorrow if that's okay. The ex-naval type can wait until the later date I arranged with him and maybe the others could come to that party, too."

"Fine. With Robert and Catharine and Sister Joan Bright from Casualty at Beatties, that will make a good mix. Joan can look them over. She's a great judge of possible talent, medical and romantic. I'd better make

22

sure she can arrange to be off duty to come to dinner with the other one too, so that she can compare."

"Why not just line up the Inquisition and parade the candidates before them? I'm glad it isn't me! Imagine Mrs Coster's beady eyes boring into me while Eileen and Mick mutter between themselves and Joan Bright asks awkward questions. Terrifying!"

"I'm not terrifying and I'll make sure he feels at home. He might terrify us. If he takes the practice I hope he likes Victorian beds with brass knobs."

"You'd put him in Bea's old room?"

"We'll be coming back and I want our rooms left as they are. He can have that bedroom and the dressing-room for a private sitting-room and a spare room for guests, but leave our rooms alone. The office and consulting rooms will be enough as they are and Eileen will still queen it over the kitchen and allow him to use the drawing-room if he wants to entertain, with food brought in from Mario's or whatever he likes to arrange, so long as she is not over worked. As it is, Eileen and Mrs Coster will have to do the shopping that is normally my job. I wonder what Mick will say?"

"He will look after our interests and I trust him completely to handle the financial business and the bookings. In the old days on large estates, he would have been the steward and have a lot of power. Maybe we are not so big a concern, but the idea is the same – steward, keeper of the keys, major-domo? Which do you think he'd like to be?"

"They will need a rise in wages."

"That's easy. We are quite well off now and the

offers I've had for the lecture tours are very generous."

Emma slipped out of her winter coat as soon as they entered the house and warmed her hands by the sitting-room fire before checking that Rose was asleep.

"The scourge of physical examinations is cold hands," Paul said. "Rose wouldn't appreciate being held unless your hands were warm. That should be taught as priority to every eager student and embryonic nurse."

"I learned the hard way," Emma admitted. "We had a convoy of six old people bombed out of a Home, and when they were put into bed, hardly knowing that they'd been moved, let alone bombed out, I thought one of the old dears was dead as she was so pale and limp and I could see no chest movement. I put a hand under her nightie to feel her heart and she slapped my wrist and said very crossly, 'Take your ruddy cold hands off me!' I was very embarrassed, but not as much as the chaplain who came in later to set their spiritual minds at rest and who was asked in ringing tones for the piss pot, my lad, and be quick or I'll do it in the bed."

"Nursing lets you meet such refined people."

Rose was asleep, her small fingers curling over the sheet and her mouth slightly open. Emma brushed aside a heavy lock of dark brown hair and kissed her gently. Not light brown hair like Paul; but her eyes had his steady gaze and were as tawny as his, the slight gold flecks making them bright; yet people seeing her for the first time said she was like her mother.

Mick answered the in-house phone, connected at night to buzz quietly and flash a light instead of tearing away the

24

silence and disturbing the whole house. "Good grub?" he asked. "There were a couple of calls for himself. Nothing urgent except that a Dr Martin Allen said he could manage to come to dinner tomorrow but would like to come over a bit early before dinner to discuss the work here."

There was silence for a few moments, then Emma asked for details of the other call.

"What's up, Sister?" Mick asked bluntly. "It sounded as if Dr Allen wants to work here. Is there something I missed? Going away and selling up, are you?"

"You'd be the first to know if we had to do that, Mick," Emma said tactfully. "Nothing like that; in fact we might have to expand and have a locum to help out if Paul goes on a lecture tour, but it's pie in the sky as yet and I heard about it for the first time this evening. Nothing has been discussed and certainly nothing will be decided until we have a meeting with everyone connected with the clinic. We'd want to know a lot about anyone we had to trust to take over any of our clinics and our home, so we may invite a few likely candidates socially to assess how well they'd fit in here."

"I knew that the doc wouldn't pull a fast one, but I was a bit worried. This Dr Allen is to be given the once over? Sounded as if he already had his feet under the table."

"Paul will assess their capabilities as psychiatrists but we'd depend on you and Eileen to make your frank assessments as anyone working here will affect you. However skilled they may be, the one who comes here must be, as Mario or Luigi would say, *sympatico*, and a warm person. I hope that Dr Martin Allen isn't taking too much for granted as at least four people were interested when Paul mentioned it at the last congress in London, even though he told them that there is nothing planned for the immediate future."

"That's why he was so keen and a bit pushy," Mick said. "Wants to get his foot in the door first. How long would you be away? If the lectures didn't take a lot of time, he could live out and come in for clinics."

"I really know as little as you do, Mick, but I was given a hint that we might go to America."

Mick gave a low whistle. "What a turn up! But about time. I'll keep it quiet and not tell Eileen tonight, as she will worry, but you know that we'd sort out any problems from our point of view. Tell the doc I'll come up to the office after breakfast before I do my phoning. I'll chivvy up the plumber. That tap in the cloakroom is still dripping and it looks bad if patients want to use it."

"Thanks, Mick. Quite frankly, I don't know what I think of it all. I'd love to see Bea and the family in their own surroundings but I would have to leave a lot of friends if we decide to go, and Rose and Jean would miss each other."

"Not to worry. It will all come out in the wash."

Emma went to the kitchen smiling. "Cup of tea?" asked Paul and looked at her quizzically before handing her a mug. "Did Mick have anything to say?"

"Dr Martin Allen rang up and accepted the invitation to dinner but wants to come earlier to discuss the work here."

"Really! I invited him to dinner, not to join the firm."

"Mick was a bit upset, as our guest seemed to think he had his feet under the table already, and Mick thought him pushy."

26

"That's one valuable opinion. I suggest that we say nothing more about the appointment but listen carefully to what the others think of him, and the other candidate too, when it's his turn to eat with us. If we don't care for either, we can look again or abandon the project. People are more important than a moment of professional glory, but I really want to do this and so do you."

"Eileen will meet them when she serves dinner and Mick will be available to give them drinks. If he's coming here about six o'clock maybe Mrs Coster would stay to open the door to him while I am busy with Rose. Eileen and I will have to bath the children early and hope they settle quickly with no long stories read to them." Her face clouded. "I hate being rushed."

"Save your opinion for later. It isn't fair to form a prejudice before you meet the man. Remember, he has no wife or child so he can't know what problems they bring! Sorry," he said hastily. "More tea?"

"Did you like him when you first met?"

"Yes I did. He's bright and ambitious and said that he'd already written a very good treatise on memory loss and the value of hypnosis."

"But you want to meet him as an ordinary person and a possible friend?"

"Exactly. He'll be on his best behaviour tomorrow; good bedside manner and all the stock-in-trade of the successful shrink, and that goes for us too, I suppose, but the party is big enough to make him unwind and show his real nature if we're lucky."

"I'll put on some music and ask what he prefers."

"Just put on mild background music. I couldn't stand it

if he opted for an evening of Wagner or pizzicato piano if that's what he likes."

"Now who is showing his prejudices?"

"Come to bed Emma. I need to hold you and keep away the ghosts of 'what if' and 'perhaps it isn't wise', and tell you how much I love you."

Three

"Having decided to do the lectures, I'll have to organise a locum soon," Paul explained. He regarded Mick with a slight smile. "Don't look so worried."

"What if he wants to change things here? Bring in staff of his own? Where would that leave Eileen and me? With Sister going away with you, he might want a qualified SRN or assistant nurse to help him."

"You know the routine and have enough experience with sterilising syringes etc. to do what is necessary. We do no surgery here so we have no theatre apparatus and techniques to concern him. Whoever comes here must understand that you are in complete charge of the office and the finances of the clinics and he will have a salary payable monthly into the bank of his choice. Eileen is officially our housekeeper and you must make sure she has a realistic amount of time off duty. Mrs Coster will come in when necessary for as many extra hours as you think you and Eileen need and you both get on well with her. Of course, he may prefer to have his own accommodation elsewhere but this place would have to be run as it is now in the interests of all of us and the patients. A lock-up consulting room and office would not do for this kind of practice. I am convinced that the warmth and pleasant atmosphere does a lot towards a patient's trust in me, and the ultimate recovery." Paul Sykes drew some papers from the drawer. "I have mapped out the details of your stewardship and your future salary to fit in with the extra responsibility, and Eileen's job as housekeeper must be seen to be on a regular basis." He pushed the papers over to Mick, who read them carefully and then gave a low whistle.

"Making sure we aren't going to leave you now, aren't you, Doc? Sure you want me to take all this power?"

"We need to come back and find everything in order," Paul stated. "Also, you need to feel secure."

Mick grinned. "Eileen had better watch her step now and not get above herself! She'll be wanting a chain with keys round her waist."

"She may need one if she has to lock up the larder! Dr Allen has a lean and hungry look. It's time you had your own refrigerator in your own quarters so that you are self-sufficient. Will you get that done, Mick?"

"Eileen and I can go to the Co-op tomorrow. She'll like that and she can have the divvy if that's okay with you. It mounts up and she looks on it as her perk. She's bought quite a lot with the Co-op dividend. She'll be excited as she doesn't know anyone apart from you who has a Frigidaire, but they say that nearly everyone has one in the States."

Emma called. "I'll start preparing for tonight while Eileen takes the children out to the local shops. Mrs Coster knows I'm going to be busy, and will open the door to patients. She says she'll be pleased to stay on to let in our guests then she'll be off to see *Me and My Girl* with her husband."

"Gawd help us! She'll sing all day tomorrow once she gets the hang of the tunes." Mick sniffed. "Well, I've a lot to do with the monthly accounts, so I'll get stuck in."

Emma made pastry and flavoured it with cheese that had become too hard to eat in any way but grated, and cooked a mixture of diced potato, swede, carrots and sliced onions in water flavoured with two Maggi stock cubes of mushroom flavour. She thickened the vegetables with cornflour and filled a large dish lined with the pastry, covered it with more pastry and decorated it with pastry leaves. The large boiling fowl that the butcher had saved for her had been simmering in a stock made from more vegetables, bacon rind and herbs and to Emma's relief the rather adult flesh was now tender and flaking from the bones. Cut into neat pieces, the chicken, with cooked rice in a parsley sauce, would be enough for six to eight people and the pie would make it go even further.

Young pink rhubarb cooked and set in raspberry jelly would have to do for pudding, she decided, if she spared some ginger biscuits to go with it, and there was a bag of coffee beans left over from an earlier gift from Bea's father.

Paul joined her for mid-morning coffee and looked in the sideboard for drinks. "We've enough for tonight. Grateful patients have the impression that we wallow in gin and we have two bottles of quite acceptable red wine."

"I saved a lemon but it's a bit dried out. We can use orange concentrate for the mix. Gin and orange made

31

with the kiddy stuff is very good and I think there is enough vermouth left if anyone prefers gin and it. Do you know? I'm quite nervous about meeting Martin Allen and I haven't even thought about the ex-naval man. He'll have to eat boiled gammon and butter beans and like it, but Mrs Coster said she can get me some spinach when her boy goes to the market, and he can buy some more carrots too. We've used our meat ration and I had to sweet talk the butcher to get a joint of ham."

"Forget the real reason for asking Martin to dinner and enjoy a party. It could be fun."

"Everything will be prepared in advance and heated up, so I can join you for drinks and chat, and Eileen won't be needed to help so she can look after the children."

Eileen brought Rose into the kitchen and gave her a cardboard box and some small patty tins to amuse her. She banged them with a wooden spoon and smiled at the sound. "Quite musical," Eileen announced.

"So long as no heartless friend gives her a drum for a present! Are you going to cope with two of them this evening, Eileen?"

"I'd like to bring her in to say good-night when she's ready for bed."

Emma looked puzzled. "You've never done that before. We look in later when she's drowsy or asleep. Fortunately she isn't a clinging child and accepts you as readily as me at bedtimes."

"What if he doesn't like children? If the new doctor just came in for the clinic he need never see Jean or Rose, but living here, he's bound to notice and hear them. I can't keep Jean quiet all day long. I take her with me when I am working up here and she is very good at wandering out to see Mrs Coster who thinks she's lovely. Jean shouts with delight when she tickles her."

"You must carry on as you do now, Eileen. We never find that the children interfere with serious business and they are remarkably well behaved for such tiny tots." Emma laughed. "Your real reason for wanting to bring Rose to say good-night is to see who my husband wants to appoint and have a good gossip about him with Mick!"

Eileen blushed. "That too, but when I think of you going away my stomach churns and I'm frightened."

"No, Rose!" Emma pulled her daughter from the vegetable rack and put the earthy potato back with the others. "We'll make it as easy as we can, but Paul has to choose someone who will be efficient in the clinics and good with patients and not ruin the reputation we've built up here. If this one turns out to be really unsuitable, either professionally or as a human being, we shall think again." She saw that Eileen had doubts. "We have already crossed two off the list," Emma reminded her. "Would you rather have one bachelor who will obviously spend a lot of spare time away from the house and may not even sleep here, or a family with two large ten- and twelve-year-old boys and a big shaggy and noisy dog?"

"Crikey!" Mick said from the doorway. "As bad as that, was it? Something smells good." He looked serious. "We'll have to come to terms with whatever the doc decides. He's bending over backwards to make it easy but he has a clinic to consider first. Most people wouldn't study the hired help and just push on with whatever was right for the firm." He grinned. "We'll manage. Now that

I am really in charge of everything but the consulting room, I shall make sure that this place is run well and if necessary, I can grass on the new bloke if he is a bastard. The doc knows I'd never lie to him and he'd want my opinion."

"Time we had something to eat, Mick. I want to tidy the dining-room this afternoon while Jean has her nap. "I'll put out the big damask tablecloth and the serviettes, but one of them is a bit frayed so I'll slip stitch a new hem. I'll fetch Jean and take her down to our kitchen if Mrs Coster can spare her."

"Take a jug of chicken broth," Emma offered. "Just thicken it, and there are lots of vegetables so it will do for Jean too."

"What is so amusing?" Paul looked up from his diary.

"I sense a new aura of responsibility. Eileen has avoided mending linen for months but now everything has to be just right and we'll be overwhelmed by crisply starched table linen with not a hole in anything."

"Even if we cancel our plans to go away, I think we shall gain a lot. Everyone gets into a rut at times and we can do with a shake-up. I just hope that Allen is compatible and agrees to our terms. I have consulted the British Medical Association and have their guidance about salaries for locum consultants and Beattie's unit will help if there are hitches with appointments or referrals for obstreperous patients. We have never taken patients in here but sometimes we do need access to safe beds for special cases needing restraint and supervision."

"When do I pack?"

Paul kissed her. "It may never happen," he teased her. "I think you will hate it."

"You can't upset every one and then drop the idea now." She held him close. "Oh Paul, it's going to be wonderful. Imagine it. Do we go in through New York? I can't wait to see the Statue of Liberty."

"You've been to America."

"Only when I went with Bea in an Air Force transit plane and saw my Uncle Sydney, Emily's brother. We flew direct to an Air Force base and didn't see the statue."

"Do you want to fly or go by liner?"

"Do we have a choice?"

"A plane would be quicker but a liner would give us more of a holiday and we could take more luggage by sea. I'll need books and papers and case histories for the lectures and you will need a lot of clothes if we are to stay away for a some while."

"When can I tell Bea?"

"Leave it for a day or so until we have a clearer picture or she'll have a nanny lined up for you and want to arrange lots of visits to her friends."

"A nanny? I shall look after Rose myself and feel very idle with no house to run."

"You will need help at times. There will be official dinners and functions where a baby would be out of place and bored, but where I shall need you to charm a lot of people. Think about it, as our life there will take a similar course to that of Bea's. She found that a nanny was essential and I'm sure we can leave that to her."

Emma looked uncertain for the first time. "You may

have to go away alone to be with members of university faculties and Rose and I will have to cope without you."

"As Bea does when Dwight has official duties," he pointed out. "You can stay with her if I am away, and the tours are in two different groups of States, which cuts travelling down." He grinned. "Knowing you I have no doubt that you will fill your time and as they say over there – have a ball."

"I shall be fat and lazy."

Paul regarded her slim figure with approval. "Fishing for compliments? You look wonderful, but you'll need to buy a few new clothes. They wear a lot more glitter over there and postwar England is not very bright unless you buy couture clothes like some of my wealthy patients."

"With a small child it's too easy to dress in jumpers and skirts and low-heeled shoes, but it would be nice to dress up a little where it wouldn't look out of place."

"Promise me you will not go with Eileen to the Co-op to buy clothes when she buys their new refrigerator."

"I promise. I have no intention of looking like a Russian peasant. I saw Margot the other day and she looked like that. Very leftish and feminist and ready to start World War III if she could find a suitable enemy. She wouldn't approve of high fashion. The New Look made her speechless. She agreed with Mr Wilson that long skirts wasted too much cloth."

"Wear something pretty tonight," Paul suggested.

Emma's eyes widened. "I suppose I could. Do I seem dowdy, Paul?"

"Never that, but you do have pretty shoes and dresses that you seem to have forgotten."

Emma opened her wardrobe and took out an armful of clothes. She put them on the bed and examined them one by one. The ageless turquoise silk suit that Bea had exchanged for something that fitted her better at that time, looked as fresh as it had done a long time ago when she had flown to the States with Bea to see Dwight and to visit an uncle whom Emma had never met, only to find him dying of tuberculosis after a lifetime as a film actor.

"What was good enough for Uncle Sydney is certainly good enough for an aspiring psychiatrist."

"I like it too. You had a necklace of pearls and marcasite, didn't you? I recall that you wore it with the suit."

"Look in that box, Paul. I'd almost forgotten it."

"It's here. Decide to wear that suit then, and come away. There isn't time for you to get dreamy over old times. Rose is calling."

"Rose will have no problem with clothes. So many friends and clients have brought presents for her, and Bea is overwhelming with gifts as if she thinks we dress her in old potato sacks. I've reminded her that clothes rationing is over but she turns up her nose at the lack of pretty designs for children and the often skimpy finish to seams and hems."

Paul laughed. "Bea likes to think that she finds more exclusive garments but she still sends measurements of her twins' feet so that you can send her Clark's sandals."

"I must make a list of what she can't get over there. They don't do everything better than we do in spite of shortages."

"Children's feet grow fast. Stock up on several pairs

of shoes to fit Rose as she gets bigger. You are going to be busy! No time to be fat and lazy," he added with satisfaction.

Emma heard Paul greet a man and take him into the consulting room. She pursed her lips. It was earlier than she'd imagined for Martin Allen to arrive but for the moment that was Paul's problem. The last patient had left only fifteen minutes ago and Paul liked time to write up notes immediately and consider what he should do during their next appointment before other matters blurred the interview.

She bathed Rose and took her down to Eileen and Jean for a story before bedtime. The dinner was keeping hot and the drinks tray was ready, so Emma showered and changed and wondered if Paul would manage ten minutes to himself to get ready for the evening, before their other guests arrived.

Emma listened to the stranger's voice, with Paul interjecting monosyllables, and knew that she must give her husband a few minutes respite and allow him a restoring gin and orange.

"Still chatting?" she said brightly. "I'll get Dr Allen a drink while you change, Darling."

"But we have a lot more to discuss," Allen said.

"We have other guests coming," Emma said briefly. "They will be here very soon and Paul needs to get ready. It's time you both forgot work for a while," she added sweetly. "I hope you like the others. They are pleasant and humorous and we're looking forward to a good social evening."

"See you later," Paul said, and escaped.

Dr Allen watched him go with a hint of resentment but Emma led him firmly into the sitting-room. She handed him a drink and motioned towards a comfortable chair. "Are the others who are coming tonight candidates for the post?" he asked after sipping his drink and trying to look relaxed.

"No. We try not to mix business with entertaining. Paul likes to give his full attention to each situation and was rather surprised that you wanted to come here before the time we expected you for dinner, just to talk shop." She eyed him seriously. "I think you've both talked of that enough, in what should be leisure time. The others would be bored stiff to have to listen to accounts of other people's obsessions and paranoia, as they are not medics, except for the Sister I invited from Beatties who will want to talk of anything but work."

"I want to come here and I know I can do the work."

"You wouldn't have been given an invitation to apply for it if Paul thought he was wasting his time and yours, but he is just compiling a shortlist and we aren't in a hurry to leave until we are certain we are ready."

"Some people think I'm brash and pushy. You don't think that, do you? It's just that I am anxious to get on and have to get in before the opposition."

Emma was saved from replying. Rose was laughing and trying to run away from Eileen to hug Catharine, who was one of her favourite people. Dr Allen stared as the child rushed into the sitting-room and flung herself onto a low stool. She was pink-cheeked and tendrils of curling hair fringed her face. Emma smiled tenderly and glanced at Allen to see his reaction to the lovely child but he seemed unmoved.

"Come here!" Eileen grabbed Rose and held her high in her arms. "Say good-night and God bless and then it's time for bed." Emma kissed Rose and Eileen turned away towards the door as there was no sign that Dr Allen wanted to speak to Rose or for her to look at him. The door closed behind Eileen and the others, who went out to take off their outdoor clothes.

"She'll go with you to America?" Dr Allen asked hopefully.

Emma half smiled. "Of course, but Jean, who is about the same age and belongs to our housekeeper, will be here to liven the place up. This house isn't just part of the business, this is home to two families."

He looked puzzled. "How does that fit into a psychiatric clinic?"

"Paul believes that patients who are disturbed need to feel comfortable in their surroundings. He never lets our family life interfere with clinics, but when patients need just to talk of everyday matters, we give them tea and biscuits and perhaps more of our private time than is usual." Dr Allen seemed doubtful. "It works," Emma said briefly. "I think the others are all here now, so would you mix a jug of gin and orange. I've diluted the orange as it comes in a thick syrup, but it's really very good." She laughed. "We have more gin than suitable mixers and lemons are still difficult to buy."

Catharine took Emma to one side. "I wanted to bring something but the off-licence had only that awful British sherry that you don't like so I brought something above the price of rubies!"

Emma took the paper bag, tied up with an incongruous bow of blue ribbon and opened it. "Bananas? Can you really spare them? I managed to have some about two months ago and I haven't seen any since. Oranges are more plentiful now, but bananas! The babies will love them mashed with custard."

"A friend came off a boat from the West Indies and brought a lot of fruit with him. Some were a bit over ripe by the time he got home, but most were edible and there were fruits that I had never seen, like mangoes. He bought unripe bananas, so they travelled well and would you believe, my darling daughter who had never seen one, tried to eat it skin and all when I handed one to her to look at before I skinned it for her."

"Did she enjoy it?"

"I was glad I gave her a small piece to try. Ungrateful child spat it out and refused any more, so we ate the rest when she was in bed."

"Do you remember that during the war a famous doctor appealed on the wireless for anyone who had bananas brought home by soldiers and sailors on leave should hand them in to feed children with coeliac disease?"

"What's that?"

"Babies are born with a digestive problem. They can't eat anything with wheat in it, and when you think about it there wasn't a lot of food that had no bread in it in wartime. In Holland, after the Germans took all the wheat harvests to Germany and left the Dutch starving and trying to use potatoes and even flower bulbs to make up for wheat, they found that the coeliac babies no longer died, but thrived, so they discovered something useful through what was for most people a tragedy."

Emma thought of George, her naval officer cousin who had a talent for bringing back otherwise unobtainable presents such as bananas and oranges from abroad . . . Dear kind George who had been in love with her and who deserved to find happiness and make a home for the small son left to him after his wife Sadie died of meningitis.

"I hope Dr Allen's made the drinks strong enough," Emma said. I think there's a streak of the puritan in our maybe new doctor."

"Or plain selfishness?" suggested Catharine.

"This is the first time I've met him," Emma replied.

"Me too, but he isn't as nice as Paul."

"Who is?"

"I would never feel that I could tell Dr Allen about my hang-ups and I doubt if he'd understand."

"Let's see how we feel about him after this evening," Emma suggested. "I wanted you two here tonight as we can use a few unbiased opinions. You are coming to dinner again if you can bear it the day after tomorrow, to do the same when we have our ex-naval type for an evening."

"I can hardly wait. I love being nosy."

Four

"Ⅰf he comes here, he'll want to be waited on hand and foot," Mick warned his wife.

"He's very good-looking and he enjoyed his dinner," Eileen said. "He was ever so interested in where he'd sleep and things like that, as if he knew he'd be coming here."

"Maybe," Mick said cryptically. "I want to see who else the doc has lined up."

"You didn't like him."

"If the doc says he comes here, then I'll put up with it but I can't say I'd be thrilled to have him about the place all the time."

"I'd rather he slept out," Eileen agreed, with conviction.

"Now who doesn't like him? I thought you lapped up the nice things he said about the way the house was cared for, and wanted to know if you'd be cooking his meals," Mick said dryly.

"I wouldn't want someone who didn't enjoy his food." Eileen sounded defensive.

"He'd want to know all that, but mark my words, he's all for number one. I bet he works by the book and would finish with a patient so that he could have his dinner. Doc

43

never does that and sometimes he misses a meal if he thinks the patient needs more time."

"He had his eyes on the bananas they brought, and I think he'd have pinched one if I hadn't taken them down to our kitchen. Cheek! I told him that they were for the children and he said he hadn't had a banana for ages and really liked them. 'What the children haven't had they'll never miss,' he said, so I told him that goes for us too, and him! You like banana custard but you won't have any until we can buy them easily. We had some once when a pal of yours came home on leave, do you remember? That was before Jean was born so we made pigs of ourselves over them and didn't have to share with anyone, but now Jean comes first and we wouldn't dream of touching anything that would do her good."

Emma, who had come into the kitchen, caught the last of the conversation. She handed Mick the list of goods they needed to replenish stocks of food ready for the next dinner party. He thought that he might be lucky enough to find some things in the street market. "I'd hoped the shortages were lessening, even so, we can't get some things unless we queue for them," she said. "See what's available and I'll use whatever you order. I need cooking fat today. That pie was good. I'll make another like it as it goes with most dishes and will help out the gammon. My cousin George kept Aunt Janey supplied with bananas for a time and she sent me some but he gave the next lot to the hospitals when he heard that babies were dying of a wasting disease because they couldn't absorb gluten in wheat. He made sure his men gave up the fruit they brought home, too."

"Now he's what I call a really nice man."

"You've seen him only once or twice, Eileen." Emma told her.

"He made me laugh and was ever so friendly."

"Yes, he's a good man," Emma said slowly. "I hope he gets married soon and Clive has a happy home with his new mother. My Aunt Janey says she's lovely and very fond of Clive."

"Will you be here for the wedding?"

"I doubt it," Emma replied lightly. "We may be in America if we have found someone to take over the clinics. I have to go to see Luigi and Mario in the restaurant." She went into the consulting room. "Do you need me?" she asked her husband.

Paul frowned. "We have half an hour before the next session and I've been thinking about one or two snags. Having Allen here made a lot of things clear. "I have no intention of anyone taking over my private clinic, although he seemed to think that he would manage. I stressed that the appointed locum would be salaried and would cope only with the National Health Service list and emergencies. He was put out and said I must learn to trust him."

"That was a bit of a nerve."

"I've already mentioned to Shilton that I'd like him to follow up any private patients who need help so they would see him at his home and not come here. In fact, the workload here won't be excessive. Just the general patients according to my Health Service contract and emergencies. For a start, Allen hasn't done any hypnosis and isn't as well qualified as I'd been told. Analysis is

45

about his level and any neurological disorders he finds should be referred to Beatties or St Thomas'. He's more a psychotherapist than a psychiatrist or neurologist as yet and the danger would be that he might think himself more clever than he is and try to be too adventurous." Paul looked pensive. "I picked up more than he seems to know just by watching Shilton and a few others, and yet he gives the impression that he knows it all, which I distrust. On paper he has an impressive list of names with whom he worked in Edinburgh."

"Why not pass all the work over to Dr Shilton and start up again after we return?"

"I need continuity here and must provide a locum for the National Health clinics. Even if we engage someone to live out and come in for set sessions, Mick will have a lot of paperwork to do and Eileen will have to provide meals and keep the consulting room clean and efficiently run. That will take a lot of time when you aren't here."

"We'll see what the other doctor is like this evening. I know that Eileen is anxious to see him. Mick is resilient and has had to deal with all kinds of people but Eileen would be thoroughly miserable with an unsympathetic doctor here. Looking back to the time when we first employed them, Eileen was very withdrawn and a bit helpless, as she has never trained for anything. Full marks to her and to the safety she feels living here and being married to a strong character like Mick. It has allowed her to be more assertive, but I could see that she was very worried when Dr Allen took no notice when she brought Rose in to say good-night, as if Eileen and children were of no importance and could be ignored as a necessary evil."

"He made a point of talking to her later when she brought in coffee," Paul conceded.

"He was anxious to find out if he would be well looked after!"

Paul shrugged. "No decisions until tomorrow. I'm fairly sure that Martin Allen isn't who we want and if I'm not satisfied with Commander Forsyth, we try again."

Mick called through on the intercom. "Call for you, Doc. Dr Allen wants a word."

"Tell him that I am busy and have patients to see all day. He can leave a message if he has anything to add to what we talked about last night but I shall not be in touch with him until I have interviewed everyone on my shortlist."

"Fair enough, Doc." Mick sounded pleased.

"He'll enjoy telling Dr Allen that he must not ring again," Emma said. "What do you need for the next patient?"

"Not even a chaperone. Why not take Rose to the park for an hour? It's a lovely morning."

"I'll take the pushchair and her reins. When Eileen or I take both the children it's wise to strap them into the big twin pram that Bea left us as they are so active. I can manage one if I take reins to stop Rose darting away and the pushchair is handy if she gets tired. See you for lunch."

"There's a pretty girl," Mrs Coster said as Emma pulled the pushchair from the hall cupboard. "It's warm out there now and the grass is dry. Have a nice walk." She swept Rose up in a firm hug and kissed her cheek.

"Bye," Rose said and waved as Emma led her out through the doorway.

"Don't let her learn too much American," Mrs Coster said and shook her head. "I don't know why you want to go away. It will be very dull without you, and little Jean will feel it very much."

"We haven't decided when we are going," Emma reminded her, and left before Mrs Coster could go into details about the terrible things that happened in New York. She knew it was all true as she'd seen it in the cinema.

The air was warm, and fresh green softened the gaunt trees. Soon there would be no clear view across the park when the leaves burgeoned and shaded the paths. Rose made a rumbling sound with her lips as the pushchair went over the rough side path, then wanted to walk when there was no sound from the wheels and they joined the well-paved lane to the statue of Peter Pan. Rose laughed with delight and struggled against the reins that Emma insisted that she wore to restrain her if she suddenly saw something exciting and tried to investigate.

"We'll take a picture of Peter Pan to Aunt Bea when we go to America," Emma said almost to herself.

"Bea-Bea," Rose said and chuckled. "Peter."

The statue was badly marked with pigeon droppings but the carved animals were enough to satisfy a small child and Rose was, as always, fascinated by the monument to eternal youth. They walked until Rose demanded to sit in the pushchair and Emma took her to the row of local shops that had sprung up at the end of the war and now seemed as if they had been there forever. Mario, Luigi's father, brought out two bottles of wine that Paul had asked him to save if there were enough to spare from the restaurant and Rose graciously accepted a biscuit covered with hard white icing.

"When you give her a little brother?" he asked as usual. "Maybe not yet until you come back from America? You don't want him to be American." He tapped his very Italian chest. "You want him to be British like me."

"I'll think about it, but just now all I can manage is another dinner party for a colleague of Paul's."

"Maybe he will not find a good man and you will stay?" He asked hopefully, and Emma felt a surge of misgiving. What if there was no likely candidate? She realised just how much she wanted to go to America and she hurried back, willing the ex-naval officer to be right for the clinic and for the house she loved.

"Do you want me here when the doctor arrives?" Mrs Coster asked.

"No, I think he is coming at the appointed time for the dinner party and not earlier to talk about work with my husband first. Eileen can put the girls to bed and we can meet our guests when they arrive. Don't look so disappointed. Eileen will no doubt tell you all about him, and if he comes to work here you'll see enough of him later."

Mrs Coster looked at her employer and then away. "I was saying to my Maureen . . . no, it's none of my business."

"What were you saying?" Emma asked politely, knowing that Mrs Coster had every intention of speaking her mind.

"Well, the truth is that I said I didn't care for the doctor who came here and I can't see him getting on with the patients we have here."

49

"He is qualified as a doctor but hasn't a lot of experience of neurological conditions or psychiatry, or not as much as we had hoped, but he's very keen to come here."

Mrs Coster sniffed. "He wanted to know who would do his laundry."

"Not you, and we haven't appointed him or anyone. We have to see at least one more doctor, and probably we may advertise."

"Did he do his training in London? I can't see him as a Beatties man. All my family go to Beatties and I know a doctor from there a mile off."

Emma frowned. "I think he trained in Ireland but when Sister Bright asked him, he changed the subject and said that Paul didn't want him to talk shop. That was after he'd been trying to do just that all through the first course!"

Mrs Coster looked complacent. "What did I tell you? He isn't one of ours."

"You look a bit pensive," Paul remarked, meeting his wife at the doorway of his office.

"Mrs Coster seems to think that Dr Allen is less than human because he didn't train in London. I told her that other medical schools did wonderful work and had worldwide reputations but she sniffed in the way she does when something smells bad or doesn't come up to standard."

"I must telephone Shilton and ask if he knows of Allen."

"Does he worry you as much as that?"

"It's being surrounded by suspicious women that makes me anxious! Or I hope it is." He sat down at his desk.

"Was that call for me?" he asked Mick who was sorting the mail.

"Someone checking the time of an appointment. All okay, Doc."

Emma followed Mick to the kitchen where Eileen was making pancakes for lunch. She heard Eileen giggle and the couple stopped talking when she came past them to fetch a drink for Rose.

"Who rang, Mick?" she asked. Mick turned on the tap and filled a tumbler with water, drank it and made for the door. "*Mick*!"

"It was Dr Allen again, Sister." Mick looked suspiciously innocent. "The doc told me he didn't want to speak to him again until he's seen some more possible shrinks."

"So what did he want?"

"He asked when Commander Forsyth was coming to dinner as he met him at the conference and wanted to meet him again. He said he could meet him here for a chat; as if he owned the place," Mick added.

"That's not his business! And this isn't a social club."

"That's what I thought, Sister, and I didn't want to worry the doc," Mick said virtuously.

"So what did you tell him?" Emma distrusted the self-imposed halo and waited for Mick to reply truthfully.

"I said the Commander was coming here tomorrow."

"Oh dear, I thought we were having a party tonight." Emma laughed. "Why did you tell him the wrong night?"

"Don't want him walking in on us tonight, do we? Might want another meal and a good look at the opposition. And he tries to pick the doc's brains as if he knows very little himself; but as he thinks he's one of the anointed he thinks he can take liberties."

"That's ridiculous," Emma replied but could think of no other reason for Dr Allen's curiosity."

Mick grinned. "Better have baked beans on toast tomorrow for supper or fish cakes from Lyons."

"I don't like fish cakes," Emma replied, then smiled. "If he smelled the gammon boiling, he'd have his table napkin under his chin before anyone. I did find him pushy," she admitted.

"It's not just that he wants to be fed and have a comfortable billet. That is what we all want but I hope the doc has checked his qualifications."

"What do you mean?"

"I've been here long enough to have memorised a lot of what is said and done in there." Mick looked serious. "At a pinch I could talk to patients as the doc does and know what I was talking about." He grinned. "Maybe I'll set up on my own. It's wonderful what you can pick up from just listening and from books."

"That's ridiculous. You may be a genius Mick, but some things must be beyond even you."

"That sex-mad woman and psychotics would be."

"Glad to hear it," Eileen said primly.

"The butter beans have soaked all night and I've put them in the oven on a very low heat," Emma said. "We can cook the spinach at the last minute and I think the carrots would be good mashed with a little orange juice."

"I can see I'm not wanted," Mick said.

"Have your lunch, Eileen. I'll see if Paul has finished with the last patient. I think I have time to take some polish into the office as there is a dark patch where a vase overflowed by the bookcase."

The smell of wax polish was friendly and reminded Emma of the days long ago when the pupil probationers in the Home on the Bristol Downs had to polish the rows of leather cases stored in the luggage room that was a haven for junior nurses, where they could escape the rasping tongue of Sister Cary. She rubbed the patch until the dullness disappeared, then noticed some dust inside the glass doors of the large book cupboard. She looked again and saw that there were gaps among the books. Two large books on psychoanalysis and one on schizophrenia were missing.

Emma looked into the consulting room and saw that Paul was alone. "Lunch is ready when you are free," she said. "I didn't know that you were selecting books for America. I suppose we have to take some but those ones are very heavy."

"Which ones?"

"Two on basic analysis and one on delusions."

Paul looked into the bookcase. "I haven't touched them for ages. Those are fairly basic and I don't need them now. I was considering putting them into the medical library at Beatties but it seems that someone got here first," he added dryly.

"Mick often reads medical books but he reads them here and puts them back," Emma assured him.

"I was thinking of our visitor. After the dinner party, he made an excuse to come back to the office to fetch the briefcase he left here and then hurried out."

"He worried you?"

"I've been telephoning a few people. Nobody remembers who brought him to the congress or knows where he trained, but Maurice thought he knew the name from Dublin. He said he'd find out more and ring back."

"Did you think he was well qualified to take clinics?"

"No, and until I know more about him I shall not encourage him. I wish I'd not invited him here but it was awkward. I invited George's friend for a purely social evening and at that time, the possibility of a locum had been mentioned only in passing. I said nothing about interviews. Allen on the other hand took it that I wanted to see both men as possible candidates and was hurt that I gave an advantage to a friend of a friend." Paul shrugged. "The dinner was a success and I hope you enjoyed it but he pressured me and wanted to sit in with me on some cases almost as if he was a student."

Emma hesitated. "He rang again today."

"The hell he did!"

"He wanted to know when Commander Forsyth was coming here as he wanted to meet him again to discuss a couple of things."

"Did you speak to him?"

"No need. Your steward takes his duties seriously. He told Dr Martin Allen that we are entertaining the Commander tomorrow, but said nothing of them meeting here."

"Tomorrow? They are coming today."

"Exactly. Mick suggested that we have fish cakes for supper tomorrow when we are alone in case he arrives expecting to be fed!"

"Good old Mick. The effrontery of the man amuses me,

but this could be serious. I see a lot of innocent-looking charmers in there and they are often the worst kind of con men."

Mick poked his head round the doorway and raised an eyebrow. "A Dr Maurice Flynn is on the phone."

"It's, okay, Mick. I am expecting this call."

"Did you tell him the other one called, Sister?"

"Yes and he approves of what you said."

"Thank Gawd for that."

"Paul?" the caller enquired.

"Speaking."

"I spoke to a friend." There was silence for a few moments and Maurice Flynn coughed.

"Tell me, Maurice. I have grave suspicions about Allen and need to know the worst."

"He was a medical student in Dublin, fluffed his exams and wangled a course in Edinburgh by pleading ill health after being bombed as a youth during the war. He was no good and it is rumoured that he stole money and books from other students, but he escaped prosecution. They were glad to see the back of him, so pressed no charges. Since then he has been a medical orderly and came south where nobody knew him."

"Thank you very much. I have a feeling that this is serious from several points of view. Not only is he passing himself off as a fully qualified medic but he has grandiose ideas that he can safely treat psychiatric patients."

"You have to alert the police, Paul. He is a menace and a criminal and I think in need of treatment in an institution. I've sent you an account of his history and you can pass it on to the authorities."

"I'll be in touch, and thank you, Maurice" Paul replied soberly. "I hate to do this but I think he's ill and must be stopped before he does harm." He replaced the receiver, deep in thought.

"Everything all right, Doc?"

"No." Paul told Emma and Mick of the telephone conversation.

"You'll have to wait until Dr Flynn's letter arrives, possibly tomorrow morning, with documentary evidence, so you can't go to the police today," Mick said firmly. "He can't do much harm for a day or so but if the letter arrives tomorrow, we know where he'll be tomorrow evening. I know a bloke at the local police station. I'll go round tomorrow. If they want to arrest him they can pick him up before he comes here. At least we know his address."

Emma bit her lip. This was so like the time when Bea had to report a German officer who thought she couldn't understand German and said obscene things to her in the ward of German prisoners of war. It was all said with a broad friendly smile. The other prisoners laughed and showed signs of being difficult. The military police took him from the ward as soon as they knew and the other men in the ward were very well behaved after he had gone. The military policeman had reassured Bea when she said she felt guilty, that she had been sensible to report him. He said that one rotten apple in a barrel destroyed the good fruit and the men would be very co-operative in the future.

"I hate this," Emma said, "But I know it has to happen. What will they do to Dr Allen?"

"As soon as they have proof that he is posing as a doctor and is a fraud, he will be treated – but not by me," Paul reassured her.

"Let's hope the Navy is okay." Mick grinned. "I have a better feeling about this evening."

Five

"Is this a bad time to call?" asked Emily Darwen anxiously.

"No, Aunt Emily. We do have people coming to dinner in half an hour but everything is ready and Eileen is seeing to the drinks tray."

Emma told her who had been invited and when she mentioned Commander Forsyth, Emily said, "That's a friend of George. He was in the Navy with him but now he's Dr Forsyth. George told me all about him. He was a very good naval officer, but took the offer the government made to officers in the services, to go to university when they left for civilian life. Robert's ambition was to be a doctor."

"You've met him?"

"When he was in Portsmouth after he had come out of the Navy and had his medical degree. George stayed with him for a weekend and brought him over to the island. That seems a long time ago but I'd like to meet him again. I gave them a meal. You'll like him," she said firmly as if Emma would not dare to doubt her opinion.

"It's good to have an unbiased testimonial," Emma said dryly.

"I suppose he ate everything in sight and drank your strong whisky tea after the meal."

"Of course he did, but apart from that, George said that he is a very good doctor and is now involved in the same work as Paul."

"How is George?"

"Janey is very happy about the future for him and I can't see much wrong either. Just you keep away until he's settled into marriage and he'll be fine."

"We shall be in America when he is married."

"Good girl."

"You want to get rid of me!"

"For a while. Bea needs you and I think you need her, and Paul has work to do, so go now and enjoy America, then come to stay and bring my great-niece to see me."

"Give George my love."

"I'll do no such thing. I'll say you rang and that Rose and Paul are well. George will always love you, Emma, but he will be happy. His fiancée was engaged to be married but he was drowned in the Pacific, so she and George have every chance of understanding each other. Personal tragedy for both of them must smooth off a few rough edges and make them softer, unless they go the other way and close up. I think they are strong enough to make a good life together. They'll be fine," she added.

Emma told Emily about Martin Allen and was amused when Emily promised to write a testimonial for Robert Forsyth to make sure he became Paul's locum.

"You've fallen for him."

"I like a nicely set up young man," Emily replied coolly.

"I may be an old woman but I still know an attractive and good man when I see one."

"That gives me courage. I was dreading Paul having to advertise and see lots of strange people coming here to be interviewed."

"Are you going by ship?"

"We've made no plans but I've never been on a liner. Paul needs a holiday before he starts his lecture tours so a few days being pampered would be lovely."

"I'd rather you went by sea."

"Why?"

"Just a feeling. I can wave as you pass down Southampton Water. I spent a day at Cowes with Clive. He knows all the shapes of the big liners and adores the sea. Give my love to Rose and Paul and get back to the kitchen. What's for dinner?" Emma told her and Emily approved. "I've a bush of parsley that needs picking. It would have gone well with butter beans to make parsley sauce. Wilf sowed it in the conservatory and I have it all through the year now."

Joan Bright arrived and was very curious to hear about Martin Allen. "We had no time to chat after dinner but have you heard anything from him? I wangled another evening off as I just couldn't miss seeing the next man on your list. I hope that Paul has gone off the idea of taking Martin into the practice?"

"Paul never had that idea. It was Martin Allen who tried to make Paul see him as the only one for the post, but he will be lucky not to be arrested."

"Real trouble? I'm not surprised. I caught him out on one or two clinical things when he was rabbiting on about what he had done and who he had worked with."

"He's not qualified as a doctor, even after two attempts. He had a doubtful reputation in Edinburgh as a student and he was a medical orderly before he came south."

"He must have read a lot to think he could cope with psychiatry."

"So I believe and he does have a great opinion of himself. He walked off with two or three of Paul's books without mentioning them, so I can't see him bringing them back. Paul thinks he needs treatment and may be schizoid. Whatever he is, he isn't fit to be released onto the public as a shrink."

"There's a grey area here," Sister Bright said. "If he claimed to be a qualified doctor, he is in trouble for that, but if he just says he practises psychoanalysis, he may get away with it, as anyone can say he is a psychologist. Aren't we all? We need to be, to deal with some of the devious characters in the wards or who come to Casualty hoping to get a bed for the night on the strength of an imagined ailment." Joan laughed. "We sort out a lot of them by producing a large tray of instruments, which I must say are never used, and a large syringe which we say we need to take blood for tests. The Casualty technician asks if the patient needs to strip completely for the examination, and surprise!, the condition is suddenly non-existent and the cubicle is empty as soon as my back is turned."

"What if you miss genuine cases?"

"I don't think we do. They stay and are eager to be helped. I'm sure you have ideas about who is a sham?"

"I do, and so do most nurses and doctors. It didn't take any of us long before we labelled Martin as an attractive fraud, but Paul did a lot of careful checking." Emma smiled. "It was hardly necessary. Mrs Coster, our cleaner, didn't like him, Mick and Eileen hoped he would not come here again and you decided that he wasn't genuine. Go into the drawing-room while I bring the others up for drinks."

The handshake was warm and firm, the eyes glinted with humour and the mouth was as Bea would say, just full enough for interest and not too outrageous to be a threat.

"It's good to meet you at last," Robert Forsyth said. "I've heard a lot about you from George."

"I've just been speaking to my Aunt Emily and she asked to be remembered to you," Emma said demurely, avoiding any reference to her cousin. "Come and meet the others. Paul will be here as soon as he's finished in the office."

If he was Martin Allen, he'd have been in the office after Paul, eager for what he could learn of the practice and making Paul late to meet the other guests, Emma thought, and sighed with relief.

"I loved it there when George took me to lunch with her. She's a very good cook." He laughed. "I'm glad she liked me. I had the impression that if I fell short of her high standards she'd give me no pudding."

"Did she make you drink that awful tea with lots of whisky in it?"

He shuddered in mock alarm. "That habit doesn't run in the family, does it? I was glad not to be driving that day and I had a terrible hangover, but I could forgive her everything for that wonderful apple pie. Do you think she'd invite me again?"

"I'm sure she would." Emma's lips twitched. "She said you looked more like a sailor than a doctor and being an islander, she likes sailors."

"I heard that not all islanders feel the same," he said, solemnly. "By the way, George is very well."

"I know. It's wonderful that he is engaged. Clive needs a full family lfe." He gave her a keen look and nodded approval and she knew that he could delve into minds as Paul did, gently and relentlessly, until the patients involved told the truth and eased their minds in a process of self-healing.

"What a lovely house. It must make a lot of difference to patients to come in here and be surrounded by what is so obviously a friendly and comfortable home."

Emma smiled. "Sometimes too comfortable, and they try to persuade Paul that they need treatment here for a couple of weeks, but we never take residential cases."

"Very wise."

Joan Bright handed Robert a drink and gave a thumbs up sign to Emma when his back was turned to greet the other guests. "All right, just don't eat him before dinner," Emma whispered.

"I thought I'd pop up to see if you wanted any help." Eileen said, appearing at Emma's side and taking in every detail of the doctor, from his well-polished shoes to his silk paisley tie and shining hair. "Mick is downstairs so he can keep an eye on Jean. She's not settling and I think she has another tooth coming through."

"You've seen him now – satisfied?" Emma teased. "Oh

dear! I think your door is on the latch again. Someone has escaped."

"You little devil," Eileen said as Jean waddled in, wearing a bright pink winceyette nightdress and trailing her small 'comfort' blanket.

Robert saw her and laughed. "You look like my brother's infant." He bent down and smoothed her reddened cheek. "Where's your teething ring?"

Eileen was enchanted. She brought a large silver spoon which Jean seized and rubbed against her inflamed gums, beaming up at the kind face that gave her confidence, just as her father's did.

Eileen picked her up and carried her downstairs where Mick stood by the door to their apartment. "You'll have to get that door fixed," she said accusingly.

"I did it yesterday but I knew she'd want to have a look at the new man so all I did was to shoo her upstairs and say go and find Mummy, and she thought it was fun."

"Oh, you are awful, Mick Grade!"

"Well what did you think?"

"Nice! He has good hands and is ever so nice-looking."

"Right! That settles it. We can't have him here if he's going to make you all of a tizzy!"

"Then why do you look so smug?"

"I asked if I could put his car away when I happened to see him from the front porch, and he was pleased, as he didn't want it left on the road. He looked up at the house and grinned at me. 'Posh aren't you?' he said. Reminded me of my old CO. No side and lots of laughs with him even when he was telling you off. Never said a word unless you deserved it and then you never felt put down, if you know what I mean? But whatever it was you did wrong, you never did again. You can tell he's used to Navy discipline."

"You were Army, Mick."

"Same thing really. A good'un never loses it."

"Sailors are tidy. Not like that other one would have been."

"Doc might not decide on him, or Sister might not want a friend of her George here. What if he asked him to stay?"

"When he's married it won't matter and the family will be away, silly."

"Jean's getting drowsy. I'll put her in her cot if you make the tea. What's for our supper?"

"Mrs Coster's Alfie got a pint of shrimps for us and some crab claws so we can have a treat. I made some bread for us when I made it for Sister upstairs and it's nice and fresh.

Mick came back into the room after settling his daughter and raised his beer. "Cheers. I have a feeling that once again Mick and Eileen Grade are going to land on their feet. If our Jean likes him and you do, we are halfway home."

"Mrs Coster will want to hear all about him. She was dying to stay tonight to see him arrive."

"Tomorrow will be soon enough for her and tomorrow night I'd better be around in case there's trouble, unless Mr Allen has been warned off or picked up by the law."

"He wasn't really bad. He was polite and he wanted to come here," Eileen began.

"Look at you! Making excuses for him. Just like you

65

to be brought round by a few sweet words. He knew he could charm anyone if he tried long enough, but not Sister, that's for sure."

"Dr Forsyth met Sister's Aunt Emily," Eileen said with deep meaning.

"If *she* approved then we needn't worry about him," Mick replied. "Come on, Girl, let's do the washing up and listen to the wireless."

Paul ground the precious coffee beans and put them to steep in a large earthenware jug of boiling water and Emma set out a plate of biscuits on the sitting-room table. The aroma of good coffee by the wood fire made Joan Bright sigh.

"This is like home used to be," she said. "I remember that smell in my grannie's kitchen and cried when they told me that she had been bombed out and it was all gone."

Emma felt nostalgic too but not for family comfort. Her memory was of a small instrument steriliser bubbling gently, with a jug of coffee simmering and ready for theatre staff and surgeons to drink after the cases were done, or when visitors came to brighten the long night-duty hours when the ward on which she was working was slack. "It's good to have the excuse to use the good coffee beans," she said when Robert remarked on the flavour. "It takes me back."

"I think I told more personal secrets to near strangers over cups of steriliser brew than I'd dream of confessing to another living soul," Joan Bright said. "With so many different medics coming to Beatties and Heath Cross in

Surrey, we saw a lot of new faces and most of them felt fed up, far from home and ready to talk to anyone who would listen."

"So you gave what the textbooks never tell us, essential tea and sympathy and friendship?"

She looked at Robert sharply. "All that at times and it was difficult to remain professionally aloof when they were a little . . . overwhelmed."

He smiled. "I doubt if you knew just what an impact you all made on medical students, and patients who were suffering but were emotionally mature men."

Emma giggled. "We had our moments and at times had to take avoiding action. It was convenient to have both Beatties and Heath Cross hospitals, as our friends could say we had been transferred to the other one if an ex-patient was too pushy and tried to contact us after they'd been discharged."

"I had letters." Joan smiled. "Some were pathetic but it wasn't a good thing to reply. More seriously, some were the moral blackmail sort . . . If you won't see me I'll kill myself."

"What did you do about them?" Catharine was fascinated as the only time she'd been in hospital was when she had had her tonsils removed as a child.

"We handed over the letters to Admin if we were alarmed and they referred them to their own doctors. We heard no more from them."

"So you emerged unscathed?" Robert regarded her with more interest than might be expected during a casual dinner party date.

"Pretty well," Joan said enigmatically and refused to

meet his gaze. She looked at the ormolu clock on the mantelpiece, a gift from Emily Darwen brought from the house on the Mall where Emma's grandmother had lived. "I'll have to go," she said. "Is that the right time? That's a lovely clock."

"My aunt had it cleaned and overhauled with a few other nice pieces that my grandmother left and it keeps perfect time."

"It *is* late," Robert agreed. He stood and gave one last look at the glowing fire. "No wonder your patients want to stay here." He handed Joan her small evening bag. "Come along. I can see you safely home." Emma gave Catharine a warning glance. After the last dinner, she and her husband had driven Joan back to Beatties. Catharine smiled and sat back again, and Paul rang for Mick to bring Robert's car from the garage.

"More coffee, Catharine?" Emma asked.

"We haven't talked shop," Paul said as Robert followed him with Emma to fetch his coat. "I'd like to see you again as soon as possible." He raised an eyebrow in a silent question and the two men smiled.

"Come again soon," Emma added. "After all, before Paul asks you to join us we must see what our very perceptive Mrs Coster thinks of you." Her eyes sparkled. "Mick and Eileen have given you the all clear, especially as you seem to like children, so come to coffee tomorrow if you have the time."

"What about other candidates? You must have a shortlist of very well-qualified men."

"If you find us bearable, we'd like you to come," Paul affirmed.

"Thank you," Robert said simply.

"I'll ring you tomorrow, Emma," Joan said then whispered, "Do you think he'll want a part-time Sister? I could fit him in during my spells off duty."

"Hush! He'll read your mind. In that respect, he's rather like Paul."

"Nice car," Mick said after the guests had all departed and Emma had offered him some coffee. "Is he coming here, Doc?"

"I hope so. He's very bright and has the right manner for this work."

"Where is he living now?" Emma wanted to know.

"He has a small flat near Covent Garden which he will keep as a permanent base and live here for some of the time. He needs to be further into town for some things but wants to use a room here when he is busy. I don't think he'll be too much for you and Eileen to cope with."

"He mentioned a married brother who has a small child. Is Robert . . . attached?"

"There's hope for Joan Bright yet," Paul said dryly.

"They got on very well," Emma agreed.

"I'll tell Eileen the good news. She can't sleep until she hears the gossip. Good-night all." Mick took his leave.

"Let's sit by the fire. It's still warm in there," Emma said. She looked amused. "Do we employ Eileen and Mick or do they rule us?"

"Neither. We have an arrangement and a mutual respect. We are so lucky."

Emma snuggled into Paul's arms. "So very lucky."

"Tomorrow, you can ring Bea and say that we have

definite plans to visit them if they can suggest a simple bed and breakfast place."

"That will send her tearing about finding somewhere like the White House for us if she doesn't completely disrupt their own home just for three extra bods."

"I expect that Emily will know by now, so there is no need to ring *her* to tell her," Paul teased her.

"I'll have to go down to the island before we go away. Emily has several pieces of crochet that she's made for Bea. The Americans go mad over them and she could sell them for a lot of money but she likes to give them away to Bea and me and a few chosen friends."

"We must take them presents. What can't they get over there?"

"Not much, but Wilf makes wooden toys that are rather good and if we go by boat, we can take a lot of things that we couldn't manage by air."

"A few rolls of films are a good idea. Bea loves London and we can take snaps of improvements made since she left England.

"I wanted Wilf to make a rocking horse for Rose. If he started it now it would be ready for her in a year's time, but Aunt Emily was against the idea, so I didn't suggest that he made one for Bea's twins."

"Why was that? I had one when I was very young and loved it. Maybe we should have one in the consulting room for patients who had been deprived of rocking horses in childhood." He laughed. "The action is very soothing and nearly everyone loves them."

"When I asked what she had against the idea, Aunt Emily told me about a child in the family who had

70

been nearly killed when she fell off a wooden horse. I believe she was disabled for a long time but recovered eventually."

"So rocking horses are out. Wilf could make a horse on wheels to be pulled along on a rope. Not as exciting but still satisfying." He grinned. "I think that the advantage for the child is that an adult has to be there all the time to pull and push and give undivided attention."

"Last week, I thought of the day-to-day problems and made short-term plans," Emma said reflectively. "Now I am beginning to take a longer view and I am halfway there to the States."

"Don't go too fast. We have a lot to do: banks to visit and visas to get and presentable clothes for the more social occasions."

"Much of that?"

"On board the *Queen Mary*, and in Washington, and on the lecture tours."

"The *Queen Mary*?" Emma's eyes widened. "I've watched her often enough in Cowes Road and waited for her wash to come over the beach there, several minutes after she passed, but I never dreamed I'd sail in her."

"She's back to her pre-war state, with all that grey camouflage paint covered with shining black and gleaming funnels again. They say that she looks like a completely different ship. It seems incredible that she was stripped down to be a troop-carrier during the war, and it was a miracle that she escaped German bombs."

Emma yawned. "You're right, we have a lot to do. Tomorrow we have invited Robert to coffee while you make plans for the clinic and I start to search the West End for presents. I shall enjoy that."

Paul switched off the office lights. "Don't buy the whole of Liberty's, and try to get tickets for Miranda's latest play. Bea is hoping that it will be transferred to America and she can show off her glamorous stepmother."

"I'll need a lot of spare time. I hope that Eileen can cope with Rose for the day."

"Tomorrow," Paul said gently. "Leave it for now."

Six

Emma stared at the slim back of the woman disappearing into the theatre. She hurried forward and called, "Miranda!"

The woman stopped and turned. "Emma? It's good to see you. What are you doing here?"

"Shopping, and booking for your play. That is if there are seats left for Tuesday night."

"Wait here. I'll check."

"Please don't bother. I can ask. I'm sure that you are in a hurry."

"I want to talk to you, so don't go away." Miranda smiled and went into the booking office and returned quickly. "Here. Two dress circle tickets with my compliments."

"I didn't mean . . ."

Miranda waved away her thanks. "Just as well we met. I'm pleased to say we are sold out and my own personal tickets are the only ones left for that evening. Come and have coffee. I have a meeting in half an hour but if I don't have my mid-morning calories, I shall be in trouble with my husband." She gave a happy laugh. "He's a tyrant and makes me keep to the diet rigidly. Rehearsals take a lot of energy so I have a small amount of carbohydrate now and balance it with slightly less at lunchtime."

It was obvious that Miranda was contented in her marriage to Bea's father and from the bloom on her cheeks and the sparkle in her eyes, Emma could see that the diabetic condition was under control.

"You can tell Bea that her wicked stepmother is being very good." Her expression showed affection for the woman who was so many things to her. "I owe Bea a great deal. I remember only too well that she nursed me when I was badly in need of stabilising on the newer types of insulin, read the riot act about my future, and put me on the way to self-discipline." The wide blue eyes were serious. "She also brought her father to see me again after we'd been apart for too long, and so I live happy ever after, with even more success in my career."

Emma glanced round the elegantly draped dressing room and smiled. "You were a success before Bea took you in hand."

"I am an actress." Miranda shrugged. "I was able to show the public a better face than the one I wore backstage. I was sad inside, I was sleeping badly and I felt my stamina slipping away, but now I am fine."

A girl brought a pot of coffee and a plate of biscuits which Miranda offered to Emma. She took the two biscuits from the other small dish that made up her own allowance and sipped slightly milky coffee.

"Bea enjoyed working with you."

"She was surprisingly tough and I suspected that if I didn't do as I was told she would ask to be given another private patient to look after."

"Rubbish. She was doing that for your own good and had no intention of deserting you. Private nursing was a different world and we had to take a lot of initiative in strange surroundings." Emma looked pensive. "We didn't do it for long but it was a very interesting time."

"So I heard," Miranda said dryly. "I was talking to one of your patients last month and although he is happily married with three infants and a new hunter of which he is very proud, he had a certain look in his eye when we mentioned you."

"He must have forgotten me by now."

"No. He is full of admiration for your help and gentle encouragement when you nursed him, and for pointing out very tactfully that you could never be happy as lady of the manor with horses and dogs . . . and his mother. I think you saved his dignity without giving in to what must have been a temptation – wealth and position and the love of a very attractive man."

"I didn't realise that you knew him well enough to tell you all that! It was rather sad, as I grew really fond of him but knew that I could never marry him. Can you imagine me on the hustings speaking up for him as a future Member of Parliament? His own personality and his war record were enough and his wife is perfect for his way of life."

"I meet a lot of people in politics now that I'm married to a Member of Parliament myself, and one with a knighthood." Miranda giggled. "Makes me doubly famous and the theatre puts a bit of icing on the dull politics, or so I'm told." She looked at her watch. "I'm due at rehearsal in five minutes, but I wanted to ask if you are going to see Bea within the forseeable future? She hinted that you are considering it but hadn't done anything about it, to her disgust."

"Nothing settled but we are working on it."

"Which could take for ever." Miranda sighed. "What I really need is a friend or a nurse companion to come with me to America to see to my diet on the voyage, my injections and my general comfort. When I get over there I shall have my usual dresser, who is flying over a few days later, and she knows all about me and is as strict as my lovely husband, but until then do you know of a nurse who would like a paid working holiday?"

"When are you going and why now?"

"The play is going to America soon. I take the leading role to get it started, then if I tire of it, someone else carries on for six months and I come back here." For a moment her face clouded. "I shall have to go alone. When I'm there, I shall be okay but I dread the voyage as I shall have no protection from the press or the public on a liner. I can't stay in my cabin for five days and I could eat the wrong things and have a blip in my health. I'm very good now, but if I am depressed I am not so strict and might eat comfort food."

"Why not fly?"

"I hate planes and I am air sick."

"But not seasick?"

"Not that I know of, as yet, and the complete rest for four or five days on board the *Queen Mary* would be a blessing, if I had a companion who would not indulge me in a weakness for cake, and was amusing!"

"I doubt if it would fit in with your arrangements, and I'm not sure when we may go, but Paul is busy choosing a locum to run the practice so that he can fix two lecture tours in the States."

"Darling! Ring me tonight when you've talked to Paul and if we can't go at the same time, at least give me a name or two if you know any private nurses who are in between jobs."

A muted bell reminded Miranda that she was due on stage for rehearsal and Emma made her way to the West End shops, but her mind was not on skirts and dresses and blouses. She wandered into the huge offices of the Cunard Line and asked for brochures and timetables of Atlantic crossings on the *Queen Mary*.

"There are other sailings in many of our ships if you need to leave sooner than the *Queen Mary*'s next sailing," Emma was told.

"We did want to go on her, and a friend might want to come with us so there would be three adults and one small child."

"There is a large suite available on the next voyage, a few first-class single cabins and some doubles, but for your party, the suite might be more suitable and would cost little more than separate first-class cabins." The clerk was persuasive. "We can guarantee privacy and extreme comfort. Many famous people use that suite and none of the other ships have anything like it."

"When would you need to know by?"

"A week before the sailing for confirmation, but we shall be booked up long before she sails in about six weeks. Renovations and redecorations have to be done between sailings and there are still some things to be done now that she is out of wartime camouflage. We try to make a quick turn around, but there are bound to be times when people have to sail in other ships. You do need visas and up-to-date passports for the States," he pointed out. "May I pencil in your names, Madam?"

"Just Dr Paul Sykes for now. You can have the other details if we decide to book." She thought of Miranda and the need to shield her from unwanted publicity on the voyage and wondered if Miranda would have to say what her stage name was as well as being Lady Shuter.

The urge to save money was deeply rooted and Emma found it difficult to spend on luxuries, although wartime limitations were gradually giving way to more plentiful and sometimes frivolous goods in the shops.

The House of Liberty in Regent Street had always been her favourite store and she recalled with pleasure a time when as an impoverished nurse in training, she had rather diffidently asked about an offer made in the store. If a customer bought dress material, then on coupons and very precious, and bought the pattern for the dress at the same time, an expert would cut out the garment, taking into consideration the exact measurements of the person hoping to wear it, and would add hints as to how it should be sewn. Emma had done this when she saved up to buy some fine pure wool that draped well; the result had been a perfectly fitting black dress that looked as if it came from an exclusive couturier. Dressed up with pearls or bright beads, or sometimes with sprays of felt daisies or swathes of turquoise tulle, it had been her mainstay for social occasions for most of the war.

No such offers today, but Emma bought several lengths

of very fine printed cotton that was famous in the store
and used for dresses and blouses for people living in,
or visiting, hot countries. Bea would have them made
up and would revel in the fact that they were unique
and very 'English'. She bought silk too, printed with a
special design of poppies and cornflowers, a design that
she had wanted but never afforded until now.

Muted colours in matt silk and discreet patterns made
her smile. These neckties would be perfect for Dwight,
who assumed a very British appearance when Bea wanted
him to tone down the more brash American clothes that
he favoured for casual wear.

After buying shirts for Paul and underwear for herself,
the pile of goods became bulky and she treated herself to
a taxi back to Kensington.

Mrs Coster greeted her with a hoarse whisper that
must have resounded up the stairs to the office. "He's
still here, Sister."

"Who is?" For a moment, Emma thought that Martin
Allen had surfaced again.

"The doctor who is coming here," Mrs Coster announced
with great conviction. "Took to him the moment he came
through that door," she added dramatically. "I shall tell my
Maureen that he's a real gentleman and I'll have no trouble
from him. We'll get on well."

"That's a relief!" Emma smiled. Mrs Coster sounded
as if she had fought off a psychotic rapist and found a
knight errant to save her.

A flood of comment threatened and Emma hastily said
that she must grab a bite to eat and then go out again.
She carried an armful of shopping up to her bedroom and

said she'd come for the rest later, then hurried up to the kitchen.

Paul and Robert were sitting on kitchen chairs eating bread and cheese. A good smell of fresh coffee made Emma glance towards the stove. "We thought you might be back soon," Paul said. "Hungry?"

"Starving. I had a full morning and there's more to find but I can go out again as soon as I've had something to eat."

Robert laughed. "We haven't eaten all the cheese and I brought this. You need a good ham sandwich."

"Lovely." Emma cut bread and made a thick sandwich while Paul poured coffee. "When can we leave for America?" she asked, and brushed away a few crumbs.

"As soon as you like."

Emma told them the date of the next sailing of the *Queen Mary* and both men nodded. "She's in dock having repairs but will be ready in six weeks." She looked uncertain. "You did say we'd do it properly and go first-class, but it's expensive."

"I know."

"He pencilled in your name but I didn't mention Miranda."

"Miranda? What has she to do with our going to America? I hope you managed to get tickets for her play?"

"That's when I met her and she insisted on giving us complimentary tickets. The play is being transferred to America and she is going by sea as she hates flying, but dreads being alone. Her husband is tied up in the House and with his job on the War Graves Commission, but her dresser will fly out to meet her."

"Could she go on that date?"

"Any time within two months. If she is there too early she will visit some friends in New York."

Paul grinned. "You really have got the bit between your teeth." He looked at Robert Forsyth. "Is that too early for you?"

"Suits me very well. It gives me time to meet a few patients and build up a rapport and give you time to see to your plans."

"That would help a lot. Move in a few things whenever you like and take it that you are in business! I'd better arrange time off to settle our passage." Paul smiled. "What did Miranda really want from you?"

"Not me in particular," Emma replied defensively. "She wanted the names of private nurses, one of whom might like a paid passage in return for caring for Miranda's diet and injections."

"So when you ring her before her matinee, she will know that one very skilled Sister will be there to do everything."

"She's fun," Emma retorted. "It will be a pleasure and she can share the expense of our suite."

"Suite? And do we dine with the captain?" Paul asked with a hint of irony.

"Oh dear! If Miranda is recognised we might get more attention than we want."

Robert laughed. "I'd love to be a fly on the wall. How do you feel about full evening dress every night, Paul?"

"I think I could hate you, Robert! You are a bad influence. You are jealous because you aren't going to

escort one of the most beautiful actresses in London."
But Emma was smiling.

"I have other plans closer to home."

Emma remembered the spark of electricity between
Robert and Joan at the dinner party and wondered.

"But that's wonderful, Darling. I shall give an inspired
performance today, now that I know you will be with
me on the ocean, and a private suite sounds really nice."
Miranda wrote down the date of sailing and said that she
was sure that her husband would have time to see them
off on the ship.

"So it's another visit to the Cunard office today," Paul
said. "Only two patients this afternoon and neither of them
very serious. Is that all right, throwing you in the deep end,
Robert? Mick will see to the notes and be around in the
office if you need him. He knows the patients and will
be able to tell you as much about them as I can. You'll
find him indispensable and very shrewd."

"It's a good start and I'm very pleased to be available."

"He's going to set your mind at rest," Emma said when
they got into the car. "What a relief."

"Now to business," Paul told her. "Visas will be needed
and I hope we have time to obtain them."

"What it is to have important friends. Miranda said
she'd ask her husband to get ours when he asks for
hers."

"Good." Paul handed her a list of things to do. "Our
passports are not out of date and Robert can give us medical certificates to say we have no infection or dire diseases.

We need no jabs against typhoid or cholera for where we are going and Rose has had her immunisations done."

"She enjoyed the anti-polio sugar lump. Quite a surprise treat as she is not allowed sweets between meals."

"Here we are. I hope they still have that suite available. Have you thought what we call Miranda?"

"I asked her and she wants to be incognito as Lady Shuter."

"That will save a lot of confusion as that is her name on her passport and if it is on the passenger list, the press might just miss the fact that they have *news* on board."

"She will have to be interviewed before we reach New York as her agents will insist that she gives publicity to the show opening in America, but a private suite will protect her from casual encounters. Famous people such as Noel Coward sail on that route frequently and they say that the Queen Mother has a great affection for the ship and her crew."

Paul filled in forms and asked questions and Emma made sure that the booking clerk made a note that Lady Shuter was a diabetic and that she would give a diet sheet to the catering department to be followed rigidly. "We shall also need sterilising facilities for the needles and glass and metal syringes used for insulin injections as Lady Shuter will not bring an unlimited supply of sterile material with her."

Nothing seemed a problem and they emerged from the office with a sensation of achievement mixed with a slightly guilty feeling that they were going to move in very expensive and elevated circles.

"I shall grow lazy, surrounded by luxury, and I may

even be able to wear that gold watch and chain from my grandfather. Up to now I haven't had the paunch to show it off, but I intend to eat everything that's fattening and expand into a dignified figure."

Emma gave him a dirty look. "I believe that Dwight had all the latest gymnasium equipment installed to make sure that he stays slim."

"Good, we don't want you to lose your lovely figure."

An air of light-hearted independence made them laugh as they made their way back to the car. Nobody would recognise them as an eminent psychiatrist and a skilled nursing sister with a family and responsibilities. They looked young and very happy.

"It's so exciting," breathed Emma. "Until we really signed and booked our passage, I only half believed it would ever come true, but now I shall plan, make endless lists and I can't wait to tell Bea the news."

"Most of the shopping and arrangements will have to be your duty," Paul reminded her. "I have lectures to assemble and contacts to make in the States. I know the outline of my itinerary but it needs firming up and suddenly there is no time at all to do everything."

"You have masses of material. Your collection of case histories alone, and the results, are proof of your status."

"They need reviewing and making sure that real names and locations are not used. Some of the earlier cases who have responded well want to forget that they ever had the stigma of mental illness, however much we reassure them that they were ill and not mad."

"The functional disorders which were just a resistance to the trauma of life? like Dwight's conviction that he had dropped the bomb on Hiroshima and therefore should not have children? I think that the medics in the States will learn a lot from your wartime cases of battle fatigue."

Emma did more shopping and Paul bought several latest editions of textbooks that he wanted to show to his contacts in America, and they arrived home as Robert was putting down the phone and pushing his notes together.

"It went well," he announced with satisfaction. "Mick is helpful and isn't afraid to give his private opinion to back up my diagnosis." He grinned. "Very pungent, some of his remarks, but relevant."

"Any calls?"

"Two new appointments made through local doctors and one call from a woman who wanted to speak to you personally. She refused to give a name and sounded cross that you were not here, but when I asked if she was a patient, she sounded as if I'd suggested something obscene!"

Paul shook his head. "Could be anyone. If it's urgent she'll ring again."

"You'll stay and eat with us?" Emma suggested. "You are a part of the establishment now."

"Not tonight. I must clear up in my flat and bring more things over. See you tomorrow." He gathered his papers and briefcase and they heard his car start. "I must baby-sit for Eileen," Emma decided. "It is her night for the cinema and I think Mick wants to see the film too. We can have omelettes and salad and fresh fruit after I've put the babes to bed."

"We'll wait until it's reasonable to ring Bea. I think the

last time we called, we woke her up. The time zones take a bit of getting used to."

"She was glad to hear from us. One of the twins had a bad cold and she was sitting with him and was very bored."

Paul glanced at the notes that Robert had made and was satisfied. Everything would be safe in his hands and even Mick had been impressed.

He selected twenty case histories that he would need to monitor if the patients were to remain incognito and began the work to retype them under new names. Mick would do some of the work if he had the pencilled alterations to follow and with luck the work could be done quickly.

The phone rang and broke his chain of thought. "Dr Sykes."

A female voice sounded cautious. "You really are Dr Sykes?"

"Of course."

"What I have to ask is confidential."

"May I have your name and do you wish to make an appointment to see me?"

"I'm not coming to you as a patient. All I want is information about a friend."

"Unless I know who you are and what your authority is to ask details of what is a private matter between doctor and patient, I can't help. I'd rather not be told the name of the patient but is this person a patient in this clinic?"

"So I hear." The voice was spiteful. "And not only your patient if what I hear is true."

"You really must not ask about anyone who comes

here," Paul pointed out again. "Why not ask the person concerned?"

"She refuses to tell me, but I know that she has been to see you and she was seen coming away from the Princess Beatrice Hospital one morning."

"Hundreds of people go there for a variety of reasons," he said gently.

"Not through that entrance."

"What entrance?"

"The one that leads to the block where they treat prostitutes." The venom was even more pronounced. "The one by the side gates."

"The one marked Medical Unit?"

"Yes," she said eagerly.

"Have you read the whole notice there? It also leads to the X-ray Department, Skin Unit and Physiotherapy, if I remember rightly."

"They treat venereal diseases there and I know that she is a dirty little whore."

"That is a serious accusation."

"It's true. My brother went about with her and now he's got syphilis."

Paul felt cold and in a quandary, torn between his vow of patient confidentiality and his public duty to expose the source of infection. "I can tell you nothing about any patient who attends my clinics. I have no idea why you ask me, as I do not treat venereal diseases. Anyone attending the clinic you mention is protected against casual enquiries, but they are treated, and contacts are found and warned or treated if infected. Your brother must tell his own doctor if he is sure of the source of his infection but there is no way that a third party can obtain such information from me or anyone else involved." He hesitated. "It would have to be established that she was the only one who could have given him the condition. Do you have proof that she does have the disease? A man who takes a lot of partners must be careful who he accuses, as must you."

"There have been other women but I just know it's her and not one of them. Thinks herself somebody special and he is nuts about her, but once I've found out the truth he'll never want to see her again."

"You must speak to your brother and he must tell his own doctor, but I cannot help you."

"I'll see her damned! You doctors are all alike, you gang up with each other and tell what lies you want but I'll get even with her."

"You'd better tell me her name," he asked reluctantly.

"Not likely, now that I can see you all stick together." She slammed down the phone and Paul sat heavily in his leather chair, more uneasy than he'd been for months over a patient. He was sure he knew who the patient was and he had heard from 'A' Block at Beatties that she had admitted a string of names who might be infected. That was under control. What scared him was the anger and venom that came over the telephone line and the feeling that violence could be in the air.

Seven

"What's up, Doc?"
        "Did you take a call from a woman yesterday who refused to give her name?"

"Yes. I handed it over to Dr Forsyth, who told her you were away. She wouldn't leave a message as she said you were the one who knew about the case. A bit fishy I thought. Like that man who wanted to know what was wrong with one of his employees so he'd have an excuse to sack him."

"This was worse. Be extra careful if she rings again. She was very angry and might cause a lot of trouble. I must put Forsyth in the picture when he comes in. I have a shrewd suspicion that she is trying to find out about the lady I referred to 'A' block."

Mick whistled. "No need to worry about her, Doc. She'll make her own bed of nettles if she can't control herself, but when she comes here again you can only repeat your warning to be careful, if that's possible for her. That's all anyone can do."

"She's much better now that she is lightly sedated and she knows about her uncle and her childhood and I think she's beginning to control her passions. In a way she is fastidious, and the thought of disease horrified her."

"Like everybody, it couldn't happen to her!"

"She is responding to treatment in 'A' block and will come here for only a few more sessions of analysis. Forsyth can cope with them. She was very upset when I told her what came out of the hypnosis and genuinely wants to put the past behind her."

"I bet she's scared. Maybe that's her cure. Like in the Army, nobody thought they'd get a dose and it couldn't happen to them, and when it did there was hell to pay when they went home and had to tell the wife." Mick grinned. "Some poor bastards thought that having an FFI examination when they came back from a night out waved a magic wand and was a treatment in itself, so they couldn't get anything really bad wrong with them for sleeping with a dirty woman."

"The Free From Infection inspection is still valuable, if only to diagnose the conditions that can now be treated with penicillin."

"A real miracle drug, Doc, but I'm glad I never chased skirt. I wouldn't have Eileen and Jean if I had."

"We have work to do." Paul handed Mick a sheaf of papers. "Use your imagination and type these again using fancy names and placing them firmly in Dundee or Belfast, Timbuktu or any place far from here."

"I'll ask Eileen for names. She has a fancy for double-barrelled names and I'll have to watch out that she doesn't suggest the names of her favourite film stars. We don't want Ronald Colman accused of being a psychopath," he added cheerfully.

Paul went to see his first patient and was joined by Robert an hour later while Emma looked through the clothes that she hoped would still be big enough for Rose when they went to America. The boxes of bright new sandals were ready to be packed and would fill a small case, as Bea had sent the outlines of her children's feet so that Emma could buy some for them too.

Emma laughed. "Red sandals seem to be the fashion for the very young. Rose said that the other colours hurt and Bea asked for red, too."

"I bought some pretty pink shoes in the market," Eileen said, "but they rub Jean's heels and Mick was ever so cross when I told him, so I had to buy some like you did, and the lady in the shop measured Jean's feet and put them under some kind of X-ray machine. They look too big to me, but she said they were her right size and I suppose she thinks she knows, but the pink ones are so pretty."

"Mick is in the office by the phone and the doctors are busy and don't need us, so let's take both the girls into the park and they can wear their new sandals."

Emma could ill afford the time, as she had many things to do, but she wanted to make sure that Eileen allowed Jean to wear the right shoes. Eileen was only too eager to make her child look pretty, and sacrificed comfort and practicality for her idea of glamour. Shades of Shirley Temple and the other early child stars, Emma thought. How many unfortunate babies had suffered their bouncy hair to be tortured into stiff ringlets and made to wear short white socks meant for sunny California, even when the weather was cold in an English spring breeze?

Dressed in a warm coat of cream wool, edged with a

pale blue velvet collar and trimmings, tailored in a version
of a double-breasted adult topcoat, Rose looked smart and
very sweet. Her gloves hung from a cord threaded through
the sleeves and behind the neck so that she couldn't lose
them and the red sandals were almost over bright over
the warm, cream stockings.

Eileen looked at her own daughter with reservation.
"The sun is warm, isn't it? I did want her to look nice
and wear that woolly I knitted but the last time she went
out without a coat, she cried and said she was cold."

"That child will have another cold if you don't watch
out," Mrs Coster said accusingly. "Run and get a coat for
the poor mite while I get out the pushchairs."

Emma gave her a pleased glance as Mrs Coster had
voiced her own thoughts but she tried not to find fault
with anything that Eileen did for her own child.

The red sandals were a great success once the little
girls had overcome their distrust of the first stiffness of
the soles and Eileen forgot that Jean was muffled up in
a brown jacket and couldn't show the orange jumper,
lovingly knitted but quite hideous.

Luigi, as usual, gave each child a biscuit when they
passed the restaurant and as usual asked the mothers when
they would be producing more children. "They both need
brothers to keep them in order," he said, and lightly boxed
his son's ear for stealing a biscuit.

"He is awful," Eileen giggled as they pushed the now
silent, biscuit-chewing chidren home. "The nerve, talking
about such things. It's none of his business, but Mick
would still like a little boy so that he can play at trains
and aeroplanes."

"What do you think of it?"

"I'm not keen. I love my Jean and if I have another I hope it will be another girl, but I don't want to be fat and ugly again for months and months, so I keep putting it off."

Emma ignored the glance that said that she was doing the same as Eileen. "You looked very pretty when you were carrying Jean."

Eileen blushed. "Mick seemed to think so. He kept saying that I looked like that Italian film star with the big bust and he was quite disappointed when it all went after I finished feeding the baby."

"Men like curves and you still have a good figure."

"That's as maybe but I told him he'd have to wait for a son until you and Dr Paul come back from America."

Emma smiled. Eileen had made every excuse possible to avoid having another baby and this was the best line she had managed for months, but was she any worse than Emma? There was no real reason why she should wait if she wanted more children. A chance meeting with Stella, the obstetrician who had delivered Rose had made Emma realise that too great a gap before she was pregnant again mightn't be good for Rose.

What had Stella hinted? That an only child could easily be spoiled and be too demanding. Looking at Rose's smiling and contented face, Emma dismissed the idea, but she noticed that the two little girls now played far more self-centred games and had begun to share less of their toys.

"Help me go over Rose's clothes," Emma suggested. "If we are away for a long time, she will grow out of a lot of what fits well now, and the climate over there is different so you must take what will be too small for her shortly and let Jean get the benefit from them."

"Do you want to keep that nice dress?" asked Eileen. "You never let her wear it and it's ever so pretty."

Emma bit back the remark that it was not right for Rose and unfolded it. A patient who said she was a dress designer and loved making children's clothes had brought it and insisted on seeing Rose in it. The harsh yellows of the fabric decorated with green leaf sprays had robbed the child of all her vibrant colour and the lace dripping from the collar and cuffs was limp and reminded Emma of pictures of consumptive Victorian women.

"You really like it?" she asked, unable to hide her disbelief. Hastily, she added, "It's too big just now but if you want it, take it and keep it for Jean."

"It's brand new!"

"So is this but Rose doesn't like it." Is Rose being allowed to have her own way too much? she wondered.

Eileen went off happily hugging a bundle of clothes and Emma packed up the pretty, smocked Vyella dresses and smooth pastel knitted cardigans that would suit any climate.

The long evening dresses that Emma had worn a few times seemed to belong to a make-do-and-mend era. The inventiveness that most women had shown when clothes were rationed and supplies of cloth were scarce was now unnecessary. She looked at a picture in *Vogue* magazine and caught her breath. The crimson silk dress with masses of material in the skirt and the high ruched bodice and tight waistline that accentuated the model's bosom would be perfect for use on the *Queen Mary*, and for Washington if what Bea had told her was true.

"Buy it," Paul said when she showed him the picture. "It says there which shops have that model, or there must be many similar styles that would suit you." He grinned. "How am I to live up to having two glamorous women with me?"

"I need a tailored suit more," Emma said reluctantly.

"We have money, and you have money of your own which you never spend on yourself. Why not see Miranda after the play and ask if she can go with you on a day when she has no matinee?"

"I'll be delighted," Miranda told her, in her dressing room. "I need some cocktail dresses, and a suit if the weather is cold there. I shall have to travel to promote the play and I've been told that I may have to be filmed for television. Can't say I want that. A friend who was interviewed said that they made her up with terribly thick cream and she felt as if her skin would crack when she smiled. She had to wear green eyeshadow that made her look, as she said, as if she had two newt's armpits above her eyes. The very bright lights make complexions look like dingy leather unless they pile on the make-up and the American actresses favour much heavier mascara and very bright red lipstick. My husband says that he could never kiss a woman with all that mess on her face, so maybe I shall make him come to America where he'll be safe from temptation."

She turned from her mirror, the last vestiges of the cold cream that removed her stage make-up glowing on her smooth skin. She wiped it off with a soft cloth and applied a light vanishing cream and a dusting of powder.

"We won't keep you," Paul said. "The play will be a great success everywhere you take it but it wouldn't be the same without you. You were superb."

"Thank you, Darling." Miranda kissed Paul and hugged Emma. "See you on Friday," she said.

"Shopping with Miranda is like being taken along in a whirlwind," Emma said as she sank into a chair surrounded by her packages. We went to five major stores and a boutique."

"She looks so fragile," Paul said with a grin.

"It helps to know what you want and not to be intimidated by snooty saleswomen. She sat on a gilt chair and demanded what she wanted without stirring a finger and let everyone else do the panicking. Surrounded by lovely clothes I was confused and I had to feel fabrics, wonder if the garment would fit me and try them all on before deciding, but she had a list of measurements and colour preferences and made it clear that she was not going to waste time trying on anything that she didn't choose. Finally, she gathered what she wanted and fitted on a few while I tried not to be persuaded to buy a dress I hated but which the saleswoman said would be *divine* with my colouring."

"You seem to have bought a few things all the same." Paul eyed the pile of bags with mock alarm. "Are we going to afford America after this?"

Emma laughed. "Bea once told me that Miranda would be wonderful haggling with Arab traders. She bought three dresses and I bought a long evening gown and a short cocktail dress, then Miranda calmly asked what discount they would give us as if she expected one as a matter of course. 'Don't pack the dresses until I know what I am paying,' she said sweetly to the girl. 'Ask your superior and tell her that at least one of the dresses will appear when I take the play to the States, that is if I decide to buy.' She then looked at her wrist watch and declared, 'We have other places to visit. I think that Harvey Nichols will be good for suits.'"

"What happened?"

"It was so funny. A very stiff and smartly dressed woman came and tried to look very formidable but Miranda smiled and looked at her watch again, saying that she really didn't have all day to waste on a few clothes. Almost meekly, a generous discount was offered, and Miranda said she'd call back for the clothes when they were parcelled up."

"So, what are you going to do next? I can see that you are restless and if you pack and unpack too many times you will have to press all the clothes again!"

"It's all very well for you, as you have to tell Robert so much and tie up the loose ends with the others who will help with your private patients, but Mrs Coster's Maureen helps Eileen now, leaving me a lot of time for Rose and myself."

"When you thought you'd be busy preparing for the voyage you decided you'd be overworked," Paul agreed, "but we should have realised that your normal efficiency would mop up any extra work quickly and here you are, twiddling your thumbs!"

"What do you suggest? I'm too restless to start sewing again and we've given dinner parties to everyone we like, saying we are going away."

"Go down to Emily. Don't say that there isn't time for that. You have a couple of spare weeks and could go for a long weekend or even a whole week. Take Rose and relax."

"Aunt Emily would be thrilled, and Rose adores her."

"Wilf can leave your old car at the end of the pier for you and you have a spare key."

"The car might be a bit reluctant to start after all this time."

"Actually . . ." Paul began.

"You've already spoken to Aunt Emily!"

"I did talk to her last night. She said that she lent your car to George when he came to her a few weeks ago with Clive. He changed the oil and saw to the electrics and it is as good as new, or almost."

"So when is she expecting me," Emma asked dryly.

"Tomorrow? Ring tonight and tell her you'll be on the late morning ferry. Rose will like going by train. I wish I could come too."

"It's a very good idea. Eileen has to get used to me being away and she can be really in charge of Mrs Coster and Maureen and everything for a while, but still be able to ask me anything that puzzles her when I come back and before we go away for a long time."

"Daddy come too?" Rose asked for the third time the following day.

"Not this time, precious. You are going on the train

98

and Aunt Emily will be on the island to see you and let you play with Noah's Ark."

"All the animals?"

"All of them if you are careful. Poor Wilf had to make another sheep as you lost one the last time you played with them."

"He ran away," Rose protested.

"Perhaps you'll find him this time, Little Bo Peep!"

Mick drove them to Paddington Station, bought a platform ticket from a penny-in-the-slot machine and settled them in the train with their luggage, which was decidedly less than when Emma had nappies and cot blankets to take with them. By the time they reached Portsmouth Harbour, Rose had looked at three books, drawn an animal that she said was a horse and drunk a small bottle of orange juice.

Emma put reins on the excited child when the train stopped, opened the pushchair and loaded the case onto it, and they walked to the ferry terminal. Rose almost fell over, trying to look up at the wheeling seagulls and when they were on the ferry demanded to be released from the reins, but Emma firmly kept her well under control and after a few minutes Rose found so much to see that she forgot that she was tethered.

The last of the rusting iron sea defences had gone and the buildings on the seafront at Ryde were sparkling with new paint to spruce up the town, ready for summer visitors who now trickled back as the dinginess of the war years was put behind them. As Emma drove to the house near Shide where Aunt Emily lived, she passed several houses with bed and breakfast signs in the windows. She sighed with pleasure, remembering the hordes of holiday-makers who came to the island before the war. Everything was recovering and the future looked bright.

Wilf, Emily's handyman waved to Emma to stop at the corner of the path that led to her own cottage. "Thought you'd be on that ferry," he said, as if he had seen her very recently and her arrival was no surprise. "Miss Darwen has a full house so you'll be staying in your own place this time. I've lit a couple of fires and the beds are made and there's milk and bread in the larder with some eggs and things for breakfast. Miss Darwen wants you to go up to the house for midday dinner and she'll tell you all about it."

"Who is staying there?" Emma called, but Wilf waved her through the gateway and walked away behind the coal bunker.

"I expect that Aunt Janey is with Aunt Emily," she said to Rose. "I wonder if she's brought Clive with her?"

"Clive!" Rose darted away in the direction of Emily Darwen's house and would not come back when Emma called. Emma shrugged and returned to her unpacking. Rose would come to no harm and she was very fond of her big cousin. Bad luck to Rose if Aunt Emily had other guests. She couldn't take it for granted that they were the only people to descend on her at a day's notice.

Emma banked up the fire in the small sitting-room so that it could be stirred into flame when they returned from the house. The smell of burning applewood was a memory of other visits to the island and her expression was soft when she strolled up the lane leading to the home of her favourite aunt.

"Mummy!" Rose ran to meet her and hung on to her hand. "Come and see Clive. I want a spade."

Clive was digging potatoes from the clamp at the end of the garden and from the state of Rose's shoes, it was evident that she'd been helping him.

"Have you said hello to Aunt Emily?"

"No." Rose stood uncertainly by the pile of potatoes, torn between her desire to see her great-aunt and to stay with Clive, who was surprisingly tolerant for a young boy and was really fond of his little cousin.

"Go on," Clive said. "I've finished now and I want to come in for some milk."

Rose ran to the house calling for her Aunt Emmy in a loud voice, and Emma followed her into the kitchen.

A masculine voice said, "You can't go in there yet. Take off those filthy sandals and let me clean them. Now you can go," he added and Emma saw her daughter dance away in stockinged feet while George held her muddy sandals. He grinned. "I think I recognise you but it's been so long since we met that I'd almost forgotten how pretty you are . . . almost."

"I didn't expect to see you here," Emma said. "When do you get married?"

"Soon." His smile was softer now. "It's about time, or so they tell me. You will like her, Emma. She has a certain smile that dimples one cheek, just as your smile does."

"Let me take those shoes," Emma said, forbidding the treacherous dimple to appear.

"I'll do these. You are in charge of cabbages. Aunt Emily needs two as they are small and I'll help Clive bring in the potatoes."

"Where is she?"

"In there with my mother, talking as usual. You'd think they never saw each other from one year's end to the next." He bent foward and whispered. "Go and see her or they'll think I've abducted you."

"Idiot," she said, her dimple showing, and left him staring after her.

Eight

Emma prodded the potatoes and said that they were done and Emily basted the joint of pork for the last time. "Did Dr Sutton have another grateful farmer patient?" Emma asked.

"I'm glad you are all here. I'd never have finished it on my own and Wilf doesn't like pork." Emily laughed. "I know who will have some cold. Dr Sutton gives me too much on purpose as he likes coming to supper to have cold pork and home-made chutney."

"You should have married him years ago," Janey said. "I suppose you made extra stuffing for him too. Does he eat all that?"

George looked at his mother with a wicked smile. "Why not make Mother happy and we can have a double wedding. She hasn't had a good cry at a wedding for ages."

"That will be quite enough of that kind of talk," Emily said sternly. "You can all go back over the water if you go on like that. Emma and I can have a bit of peace."

"Not with Rose around," Emma said. "Where have they gone?"

"Turning out the play box," George said. "Clive found a very dirty wooden sheep in the potato clamp and they

103

are putting it back with the other animals, washed and a bit blackened but otherwise none the worse. Leave them while we eat and they can have something when they are hungry. They may need drying off as Wilf gave Clive a model boat that they found fascinating. They sailed it in the bath with a lot of splashing to make-believe rough seas."

The tension that Emma had expected when she met George again wasn't there and he seemed very much at ease with the cousin he had been in love with for so long. They talked of his coming wedding and he showed no sign that he was relieved or disappointed when Emma told him that she would not be there but would be in America.

"I must try to think of a suitable wedding present," Emma said. "Perhaps I'll leave it until I am in America unless you can tell me what Margaret would like?"

"We like surprises," he said and grinned. "I must give Paul a few addresses of naval friends. America is a big place and a few widely scattered contacts can be useful," he offered. "Margaret will have to meet you later, when we come to London."

"Robert Forsyth will make you welcome if we aren't there. He is moving in this week and it's as if he's been working with us for a long time instead of a few days. It's such a relief for Paul as the other applicants for the job were not suitable at all and we were afraid we'd lose Mick and Eileen if the right person wasn't found. It was a shattering experience to find that one applicant isn't even a qualified doctor but was so pushy he hoped he had convinced us that he could do the work. Why not arrange with Robert for you to stay at the house for a while when you come back from your honeymoon? There's masses of room."

"We'll bear that in mind but I have to get back to work and so does Margaret. She will stay in the Navy for a while and Mother is going to carry on looking after Clive."

"Clive is no trouble at all," Janey said, with an air of defiance, as if someone had doubted her abilities to cope with a lively small boy with an enquiring mind and loads of energy. "I love him dearly and dread the day when you will take him away."

Emily brought in a steamed pudding with golden syrup and Janey served it, but her hand was weak and she spilled some hot syrup on the tablecloth. Quietly, George took the serving spoon and finished filling the dishes and Emily looked worried.

"Emma and I can wash up," she said firmly. "I want to talk to her as it's been months since she was here."

"We'll go for a walk as far as the station," George said. "Is that too far for you, Mother? I can handle the children and they both love the trains."

"Nothing wrong with my legs," Janey retorted, "just my hands."

"Her arthritis is very bad," Emma said, as soon as she was splashing hot water into the sink and swishing the cotton head of the washing-up mop through the water. The mesh container filled with scraps of soap that Emily used to soften the water for washing up was a remnant of wartime frugality and Emma was amused to see the bar of soap for hand washing had a backing of silver paper to keep one side of the bar from dissolving when in use.

"Janey's hands are getting worse. I had a touch of

rheumatism but nothing really bad, but Janey has a lot of pain and can't hold heavy dishes. She's afraid of having an accident but she's too proud to ask for help."

"Is she able to look after Clive? She sounded as if someone had told her that she can't do that for much longer."

"That was her nosy neighbour who is liable to rub anyone up the wrong way, but Alex told her to mind her own business, which is a surprise as he is such a mild man. He is very good to Janey and helps her a lot. Alex retired and sold the marine instrument firm so that he can be with her and take his part in looking after Clive, and they have a nanny and help with the cleaning, so she can manage and I never hint otherwise. Clive is a big boy now and does a lot for himself." Emily Darwen laughed. "As one door closes, another opens, or so I've always believed. George is lucky to have Margaret. Next year when she has her first baby, she will leave the service and take over making a home for George, Clive and the baby brother."

"A baby boy? So soon?"

"Yes. They will want a child quickly to make their lives complete and it will be a boy. Margaret is a very wise woman. She knows that George has a dread of losing her as he lost Sadie, and she knows about you," she added with a wry smile. "Both of them have loved and lost or not been able to have their heart's desire and even if Sadie died of meningitis and not in childbirth, the dread is still there for him. He has lost too much in life. If she is to have a husband who looks at her and no other woman and feels secure in their marriage, she must make it happen." Her eyes were dark, as if she saw visions. "She will care for Janey too, which is a blessing. They really like each other and Margaret looks on Janey as her own mother, as her family died in the Blitz and her only relative is an ancient aunt by marriage who lives in Scotland.

"What about Alex? Does he miss the business?" Emma asked quietly, sensing that once again Emily knew the future.

"Alex will be busy turning one very big house into two apartments. He is good at that and renovation of property has always a been a hobby when he had leave from the Navy. He spoke to me about it last month and has a house in mind. I saw it coming. Either they will live in one half and let the other, with a lot of help in the house for Janey, or Margaret and the children will live in the other half ready for George when he is home on leave and yet have a care for Janey. They will have a willing child-minder if they want to go away."

Emma watched the thin hands wiping the dishes. There were more liver spots than she recalled but the fingers were flexible and strong. "You don't have arthritis," she remarked.

"I get the screws in my knees at times but nothing much." Emily shrugged. "I've never been able to sit still for long enough for my joints to stiffen."

"It's the hard stuff that keeps you going." Emma said, giggling.

"You may laugh, but I know it does me good and it helps Janey's hands to hurt less when she has some in her tea. She hates taking medicine for her rheumatics and I've been making an ointment that my mother used to make for a friend with bad rheumatism."

"Is that it?" Emma bent over the iron pot on the stove. A thick, almost solid concoction was warm and fragrant with herbs. "Smells good enough to eat."

"I need some more bark and leaves. There's a copse by the mill and we could walk down and get some. Put on gumboots as the sides of the stream are marshy. You can help me pick some but we'll leave the children with George and Janey when they come back from their walk as it's far too muddy where we are going and they've got wet enough for one day, playing with that wretched boat. I'll have words with Wilf over that! We'll slip out the back way without the children seeing us."

Emma knew that her aunt wanted to be alone with her as she would miss her when she was in the States, so she pulled on the pair of wellingtons that almost fitted, and followed Emily out into the back garden, through the bushes to the lane and down to the mill.

"It's never used now is it?" Emma asked, gazing up at the tapering ivy-covered walls and the remnants of the upper storey where once grain had been stored and the miller and his family had lived.

"The force of the water grew less with the years as the stream silted up and the last miller died in my mother's time. We came here as children to play in the stream and to pick watercress if the gypsies left any. They hawked the bunches in Newport and sold a lot to our shop. I heard that the floor was rotten and that it all had to be boarded up to prevent anyone from falling through, but tramps do get in and use it for shelter sometimes. They'll set it on fire one day if they try to keep warm and use the dry floorboards for fuel. Otherwise they do no harm and the police take no notice."

"What are we trying to find?"

"Willows by the water. I want leaves and bark to grind and slim stems which I can peel and steep the scrapings until they are soft, then I boil it all up and add it to the lanolin base."

"Is that all?" Emma said dryly. "It sounds like hard work. Can't you buy an ointment?"

"There are unguents but this will do better. I add rosemary and lavender to make it smell sweet which in itself is soothing and a few leaves of bay and some other things that Mother said were good." She giggled. "My trade secret, and when it's put through a strainer and is smooth and set, nobody can tell what goes into it. Dr Sutton says I ought to patent it. I don't think he admits where he gets it, but it has done a lot of good to two of his patients."

"Willow?" Emma thought for a moment. "Of course. Salix! Salicylic acid . . . aspirin for rheumatism."

"Probably. Nothing to get excited about," Emily said composedly. "Whatever it is does some good."

Emma stripped long, pointed leaves from a tree and picked twigs but left the remains of the willow catkins as Emily didn't need them. They gathered bay leaves from the bush in the garden and she wondered who had discovered the healing properties of herbs years ago.

"You must look at my Culpeper. That book has a lot of sense and I've used it several times over the years and especially during the two wars. Men came home with wounds that didn't heal properly even after they'd been in hospital and yet the men were better in every other way. I helped a good few old wounds, just with honey, and others with seaweed," she said quietly. "Doctors don't know everything as I tell Dr Sutton sometimes when he gets on his high horse about some folk remedy or other."

"Does he know you are a witch?"

"Stop teasing me and put the kettle on. I need a cup of tea after all that walking."

"Where did you go?" Janey asked.

"I needed some herbs and Emma doesn't mind standing in mud if she has gumboots. I'm afraid I'll slip so I try to get someone else to pick my leaves."

Janey stirred the iron pot. "Is it ready?"

Emily tossed in the torn bay leaves. "Not quite. Here's a job for you, George. Mash the willow leaves and scrape the twigs and add all that to the pot, and leave it to simmer while we have tea. It will be ready to take away tomorrow morning when you go home, Janey."

The children played happily with Noah's Ark and a book about cats and after tea Rose was sleepy enough to want to go to bed. Emma put her in the pushchair and said good-night.

"We have to go back in the morning," Janey said. "Alex will need me and George has to go back on duty."

"Come to breakfast," Emily suggested. "You can drive them to the ferry. What about supper? If Rose is in bed, you can't come up here and leave her but I can send something down."

"I don't need anything," Emma assured her. "I have

those lovely fresh eggs and bread and cheese that you left in the cottage and I'm a bit tired too."

"You can move in here when the others are gone," Emily suggested. "If Rose goes to bed early and you are in the cottage, I'll see nothing of you unless I come down there and I like my own fireside."

The cottage was warm and the fire needed only a touch with the brass poker to ease it into flame. The smaller grate in the little bedroom that Rose used gave out enough heat to take the chill off the air and Rose was almost asleep when Emma undressed her and tucked her up in bed with her favourite knitted cat.

Outside the back door, a hen, escaped from the neighbouring farm, made self-satisfied crowings and pecked at the cabbage leaves that Wilf had left on the compost heap. Emma smiled. Even the hen would be safe here and find its way home when it was tired of rummaging, unless a fox was about at night.

London faded from her mind as she slept and the absence of traffic made the night soft.

The friendly sounds of the country woke her early and she listened to the awakened world of small animals. It would be wonderful to live here, she decided, then heard Rose talking to herself in the next room. When small arms hugged her and a moist kiss on her cheek said good morning, she knew it could never be true until Rose grew up and Paul gave up his work in Kensington, but so long as they were together, it would never be a problem where they lived.

"Anyone awake?"

Emma looked out of the bedroom window and waved. George sat on the broken bench by the kitchen window and Clive trailed a stick along the railings by the path, making a very satisfactory metallic drumming noise. "We'll be ready in five minutes," Emma called.

"Clive! Clive," called Rose and impatiently tried to help Emma dress her but made no fuss as her arms were thrust into garment sleeves and her shoes were buckled firmly.

"Now you can go," Emma said and Rose ran out into the garden to see Clive.

The hen had decided that Emma's garden was more peaceful than the farm and sat on a pile of dry leaves by the flower-bed. George put a careful hand under her and laughed. "For my next trick! Ta-ra!" He brought out an egg and handed it to Emma. "I think she's getting broody so we'll take her back to the farm in case she is lost. Put Rose in her pushchair and we can go while you help the others with breakfast."

With amusement, Emma watched the strange little procession: Clive pushing Rose in her stroller and George with an unprotesting hen under his arm and an egg in his hand walking slowly with the two children. A wave of affection made her want to be with them but she held back and went to the house knowing that George was being wise. He kept contact with her to a minimum even now that he had Margaret to love and to marry soon.

Emily gave Emma a sharp glance. "Where are they?"

"Taking a hen back to the farm," Emma replied. "No need to look at me like that. I have done nothing to inflame old passions. He thinks that a broody hen is far more exciting than Emma Sykes."

112

"I'm glad you came," Emily said. "He needed to see you just once more in familiar surroundings before he marries Margaret and both Janey and I think he's almost over you. Not entirely," she warned, "but enough to set him free."

"Paul likes him and I am very fond of him. I feel a real sense of family now and I think he is beginning to feel the same, as a cousin, so we hope to see something of them after the wedding."

"I've looked out the lace for Bea and her mother-in-law. In her last letter she said that the Americans go mad over handmade lace."

"And you took the hint!"

"Bea is all right," Emily said, as if she needed to justify the deep affection she had for the ebullient and beautiful woman. "I'd love to see you meet again, and you can give my love to Dwight. He's all right, too."

"Praise indeed," Emma replied dryly.

"What are you taking over there?"

"Dress material from Liberty's and sandals for the twins and Mark. I wish I could take more but those are the things I know she needs and can't get over there. Miranda bullied me into buying some rather nice clothes for myself and it will be fun having her with us on the voyage."

"Have you decided on which boat you sail?"

"The *Queen Mary*. It's all arranged and you can wave if she goes out on this side of the Solent."

"I'm glad. Somehow she is a part of the life here. I saw her when she started on her maiden voyage in the thirties. Hundreds of small craft sailed round her and followed her as far as the Needles, and the men in the

113

docks went nearly mad with pride. She looked really grand and somehow even during the war when she was used as a troop-ship in dangerous waters, I knew she'd come to no real lasting harm."

"She's back to her normal colours now they say. The grey camouflage paint was useful on the grey Atlantic but I want to see her gleaming with red and white and black paint again. I must see if I still have the brooch you gave me that you bought in Cowes on that occasion. Maybe I should wear it or pin it to Rose's coat."

"I'd forgotten. Your mother bought one too but of course hers had to be bigger and brighter," Emily said with a sniff.

"I wore it pinned to my beret and tried to look like Jean Harlow." Emma giggled. "I wonder what film stars Rose will find as fascinating in a year or so."

"So long as she doesn't fall in love with one of those boys who wear clothes copied from the Edwardians. What started as an elegant fashion is becoming common, with the wrong sort wearing it now."

"You are a snob, Aunt Emily. I met some of the Teddy boys in London when I went to Beatties to see Joan Bright and most of them are only showing off. Everyone has to have someone to admire and they try to be different. Some of the clothes are really expensive and when they keep them clean and well brushed they are really smart."

Emily looked disbelieving. "I heard that they have gangs who fight and do a lot of damage."

"That happens in every generation and now that most of the young men have been demobbed they are bored. Cheer up! By the time that Rose gets interested in boys, something else will be the fashion and we may find that the next lot are very staid and good."

"You are too optimistic. Be careful when you are in America. I hear it is a very wicked place, with people being robbed in broad daylight."

"Confess. You don't see anything bad for me, do you?" Emma asked gently.

"No, that's true, but it doesn't mean you can run risks. I could be wrong, you know."

"Not you. Where would I be without your second sight?"

"You don't need it. You can now make your own good fortune. I worried a bit over Guy, although I liked him very much, and wondered if your mother would strip you of your energy and humour. They were both selfish people but Paul is your salvation and he'll be like a rock for you and your family."

"I know." Emma turned away, her eyes damp, and when she turned back Emily was busy sorting oranges in the fruit bowl. Family? Emma thought. I have my family. Paul and Rose are enough, aren't they? We are complete.

As if she had heard Emma's unspoken thoughts, Emily looked at her with a gentle expression, the fruit spread over the tablecloth and the one 'specky' orange she had found set aside on a plate. "Rose isn't enough," she said. "Don't leave it too long or she'll lack something she needs, and so will Paul."

Nine

"We *are* going for several weeks," Emma said when Paul looked aghast at the number of cases lying ready to be packed.

"There are such things as dry cleaners and laundries," he said mildly.

"There will be so many different places where we'll need clothes to suit the occasion. Bea said, in her new American phraseology, that we have already been invited to some very prestigious tables in Washington and Dwight wants us to go to the main American Air Force base near Boston when you go there for the Harvard lecture tour. I remember the wonderful clothes and make-up the women wore when they came to England and we had parties with Bea's godfather, the General. We had to try very hard to keep up with them when clothes were rationed." She laughed. "The men looked good too, so you must pack an outfit for every occasion." She kissed him and ruffled his hair. "You are so good-looking that I shall be very proud to be seen with you whatever you wear."

"I refuse to wear a checked backwoodsman shirt and go duck shooting."

"What about ice skating? Bea is very keen just now."

"No ice skating and no barn dancing."

"Spoilsport. Nobody has suggested that."

"It's only a matter of time," he replied darkly. "I'm beginning to distrust all things American and our dear Bea Miller in particular."

Emma giggled. "She's so excited and she wants us to see and do just about everything."

"Crikey!" Mick's head appeared round the door. "You really are leaving."

"Anything urgent?"

"No, Doc. Just that Eileen said that she's making the tea and there's hot apple cake waiting in the kitchen. Oh, yes . . ."

"What is it?"

"What's-his-name Allen rang. Would you believe he wants you to give him a reference to begin a course in psychology at the Tech. Doesn't give up, does he? I referred him to the probation officer as they said we must if he contacted us when he didn't go to chokey for impersonating a medic."

Paul sighed. "If he rings again I'm afraid he's Dr Forsyth's headache now."

"No need. I sorted him out, Doc, and he sounded as if he took the hint at last but he hates having to report to the probation officer."

"I feel rather sorry for him and I hope they follow up his case and give him psychiatric help. He does have a certain ability but not enough, as two medical schools found out. With his vanity and ambition he could do a great deal of damage if he worked without proper training. I no longer feel responsible for him and I still have work to do before we leave, but Dr Forsyth seems to have everything under control as far as the clinic here is concerned and I know that you will tie up any loose ends, Mick."

"I finished the case histories and included the notes you left with them. I thought you might need more than one copy in case you lose them or are robbed in Central Park or down some dark alley, so I made three carbons."

"I think you ought to come with us," Paul said.

"Not on your Nellie. I've had enough of overseas and Eileen would kill me."

"Why does everyone try to frighten us about America? Bea has never had trouble and Dwight thinks that New York is safer than London or Paris."

"You aren't going to New York," Mick said cryptically as if the rest of America was very dangerous. "Eileen made me get rid of my old gun or you could have that."

"No guns!" Paul said firmly. "Come on, I can smell apple cake."

"If Eileen feeds me like this I shall be one obese psychiatrist by the time you come back. How do you manage to stay so slim, Paul?" Robert Forsyth took his plate over near the fire.

"Self-discipline," Paul said, taking a large slice of apple cake. "I'll have to stay slim. My darling wife has crazy ideas about what the modern man is wearing in the States. What is more, she has already bought me some clothes and I suppose I have to wear them."

"Such as?"

"Coloured silk waistcoats to wear under dark suits, a silk umbrella because my old brolly is splitting at the seams and a bowler hat to impress our ex-colonials."

Robert choked on a crumb. "I thought we were entering an era of freedom where men never wear hats and they are allowed to have hairy tweeds and yellow ties with foxes all over them."

"They are there too, for the country, complete with leather patches on the elbows."

Emma feigned indignance. "I bought those because Bea wanted some for Dwight who fancies himself as a country squire or whatever they call them over there. She thinks it might make him spend some time in Texas at the family ranch, but he seems tied to Washington and the White House staff, sometimes in uniform and sometimes in formal office clothes."

"It was easier when we had clothes rationing. I had the choice of one good dark suit from pre-war days and a series of sweaters hand-knitted by aunts and grateful patients and a blazer passed down from my father. Now I have three suits and can never decide what to wear," Robert said. He laughed. "I don't envy you, Paul. When do we see you with a Tony Curtis hair cut?"

"On the day you see me with a shoelace necktie and velvet lapels on my jackets. I am rapidly trying to find excuses to stay here. We even bought some Frankie Laine records for Bea and a terrible one of Johnny Ray where he cries as soon as the song gets a bit sentimental."

Eileen was cutting apple cake to take down to her own quarters. "Johnny Ray is lovely," she said as if defending a dear friend. "I cry too when he starts and it's really moving. He's so sincere."

Emma took a cream-coloured raincoat from a hanger by the fire and shook it briskly. "This seemed like a good idea in the shop. Everyone is wearing belted raincoats with rubberised linings but they do smell at first and I am hoping that a warm kitchen will take away the smell before Paul wears it."

"Yes, the smell of rubber in a warm room isn't very good. I'd rather it smelled of roast beef or chocolate cake," Paul decided. "I hope it doesn't attract more odours or I'll have all the dogs in Washington following me." He tried it on. "Isn't it a bit on the military side for me, a dedicated civilian?"

"Fashion still says uniforms and broad shoulders," Robert assured him. "I suppose that the lads now doing National Service are used to wearing uniform and may even like the trend. I think we shall see clothes like this for years in the future, unless the Edwardian influence catches on with the general public and not just with the few rebels who want to be different."

Emma consulted a list. "I have a few more bits and pieces to buy for Bea. She wants school blazers for the twins. I did ask if she was serious and she said that when the children have to go with her and Dwight to meet important people she wants them to look very smart and very British. Besides, blazers are very useful at any time, but even Bea draws the line at the type of caps that boys wear at school here."

"There's still a lot to do and I seem to be making new lists all the time to make sure everything runs smoothly for Robert and Mick," Paul sighed.

"When I was in America visiting my uncle, we were treated to every luxury possible," Emma said. "I tried to think of something that we didn't have there that I could take over for Bea. Not easy as they seem to have everything but I remembered that one morning I asked for a boiled egg for breakfast and it came sliding about already shelled in a small dish with a spoon but no egg cup. The waiter didn't know what I wanted when I asked for an egg cup and from his expression he thought I was a very strange female, so I've bought half a dozen china egg cups to take over with us. It will be a talking point if nothing else."

Rose was given a small attaché-case to pack a selection of her favourite toys and soon the nursery was strewn with everything from her toy box and the case was already full to overflowing. Emma left her, as she was absorbed, but decided that the case would not be packed until the evening before their departure and the lid could be closed when Rose was asleep.

As the day of their leaving drew near, the telephone rang incessantly as more and more of their friends heard of the lecture tours and those who had met Bea wanted to send their regards.

"He insists," Miranda said, when Paul tried to refuse her husband's offer of a huge limousine to take them all to the docks. "Don't say no as he really wants to help and wishes he could come with us on the *Queen Mary* but he will come with us to the ship and see me installed safely. He fusses over me as if I might break in the middle," she added happily. "We shall need that car, with all our luggage, and we might have to be followed by another smaller car with the excess. I took a look at my cases and I can't believe that I have so many clothes! I couldn't travel by air. They'd forbid me to take all that on a plane."

"Have you everything you need for your injections?" Emma asked her.

"My own doctor has been in touch with the shipping office and we shall be able to use their sick bay for sterilising the syringes and giving the injections. Once I am in the States my dresser will cope with all that as she will have a small electric steriliser with her and all the testing equipment. She is a gem and did a lot of VAD work at the end of the war so I trust her implicitly."

"We'll be ready for the driver to collect our luggage in plenty of time to embark at Southampton." Emma told them. "If we are early, we can see the docks from the ship and listen to the band they have there to send off the liners going to America or South Africa. I've told Rose that we can take coloured paper streamers to throw from the ship and she is enchanted as she is not allowed to spread bits of paper around the house!"

"Emily was a bit too generous," Paul said dryly, "but I suppose we'll have to take every one of the dozen packets of streamers. I asked where she bought them and she told me about the local annual carnivals they have on the island, where streamers are a part of each parade."

"I remember them," Emma said dreamily. "The red ones were my favourites, but I was allowed only one packet. A lot of my school friends saved theirs and had fights with them in the recreation field and were told off about the mess, but I used all mine to throw at the various floats and wagons."

"I must have had a very deprived childhood," Paul said, and his smile was teasing. "I love you when you go all soft about the past. I wish that I had been brought up in a smaller community. I think you had more fun than I did."

"The summer visitors made a difference. The town councils arranged fêtes and carnivals to attract money to the island and we were a part of it as we belonged to a sports club and the Girl Guides. I was a flower fairy, shivering in a paper dress on one float and another year I was a Dutch girl on the wagon decorated with artificial tulips. I bought a pair of wooden clogs for that but didn't realise that we had to walk in procession in the main arena. My feet were covered with blisters after that and I never wore them again."

"What it is to be a star."

Emma gave her husband a dirty look. "I suffered!"

"It sounds lovely." Eileen sighed. "I can just imagine my Jean as a fairy."

"She could be if you take a holiday with my aunt on the island next year in the middle of August. She has invited you, I know, and maybe even Mick could be persuaded to go then. Jean would be too young to enjoy it this year, but next year would be fun as she would be old enough for the junior parade they have one afternoon during the carnival."

"Meanwhile," Paul interrupted, "there is a little matter of America on which to concentrate our thoughts. That is if you are not planning to be a majorette over there. Do you realise that we leave tomorrow?"

"I'd drop the batons," Emma chuckled. "You are quite safe. I have no more ambitions to cavort about in fancy dress, and we are all packed up ready to go."

"You asked me to hide the big bear," Eileen said. "Rose

saw me put it in the cupboard and she pulled it out at once and has played with it ever since. Sorry about that."

"We can't take that huge thing with us," Paul asserted. "I think that Teddy is about to have a nasty accident."

"And have your daughter needing a psychiatrist?" Emma laughed. "I'll let her make pastry. The birds will have bent beaks when I tip it out but that's their worry."

"I'm getting good at pretending to eat her masterpieces," Paul said. "I found a large lump of iron-hard stuff in the pocket of a coat I put out for cleaning last week."

"While she's busy I'll take the bear down to our flat," Eileen promised. "Now that the weather is fine I'll take her out to the park with Jean and that will tire her out tonight."

"Good. We have an early start tomorrow and we need her to be wide awake when we get to Southampton."

It was strange to think that they wouldn't see the house or the practice in Kensington for a very long time and Emma had last minute misgivings. Suppose she hated America? Suppose Paul worked too hard there and gave in to far too many requests for his time and expertise? Suppose she found that Bea had altered and was now a stranger?

"Cold feet?" Paul asked when they were ready for bed.

She smiled wanly. "I don't think I need a hot-water bottle."

"That could be remedied easily, but you do look a little fraught."

"Just a little."

"I feel the same."

"But you are so calm and organised!"

"Not inside. I see dragons round every American corner and I know they'll hate me!"

"They'll love you almost as much as I do. I do love you, Paul."

He held her close and caressed her in the way she needed to be touched, and made love gently. "That's all that matters," he murmured. "The next time we make love we will be far away in a strange country."

"But we shall be together," she said, softly.

As if she knew that something very exciting was happening, Rose pulled Paul's hair to wake him up at six the next morning. Emma was wide awake and had crept into the kitchen to make tea. All three of them sat on the bed, Rose with a beaker of orange juice and Paul holding the hot mug of tea between both his hands. Emma looked yet again at her list of last minute things to do and sighed.

"I know I have forgotten something but I have given up trying to think."

"I've packed," Rose said loftily.

"Your case is down with the others," Paul assured her, hoping that she wouldn't want one last inspection of her case of toys.

"And you have a new coat to wear," Emma reminded her.

By the time the car arrived, with Miranda and her husband seated in the back and an alarming number of suitcases in the boot, Emma was dressed in a new suit with a pulled in waist and padded shoulders and a silk scarf that filled the neckline but made no bulk under the close-fitting bodice. Her high heels and sheer silk stockings made her seem tall and slim and her leather handbag was the same tobacco brown of the shoes.

"You all look lovely," Eileen said with satisfaction. "Give my love to Mrs Miller and himself and a kiss for the children."

Emma's eyes were moist and she found it difficult to say goodbye. Even Mick's voice was husky and abrupt as they packed the luggage into the car and onto a large roof rack. They turned away from the house where they were all so happy and wondered why they were foolish enough to want to leave, even when they knew they would return.

As the car drew away from the drive, Emma had a sense of déjà vu. When she had left home for the hospital where she was to train, she had felt she was free, but when she returned on holiday, leaving her work and friends behind her, she had felt a sense of dread because she was going to be with her demanding mother again. Now, she just felt a dull ache. She glanced at Paul's set face and knew he was having the same experience. Miranda on the other hand was bubbling over with excitement, and her husband smiled indulgently as she prattled on about the wonderful letters she'd received from her agent and producer in America.

"I'm so glad you are going to be with my wife," he said. "Give my love to Bea and tell her that I will try to come over quite soon as I have to see a minister in the White House and can make it coincide with Miranda's debut into the American theatre."

Southampton was bright and the sun shone on the huge liners in the various docks, as if, finally, all traces of war and privation had been thrust away and there was an uplift to life; only a few empty shells of buildings gave a hint of what had happened in the war years. At last, Emma felt a rising excitement, and Rose couldn't sit still.

"Look Rose! That's the ship we shall be in tonight," she pointed out and suddenly the *Queen Mary* seemed almost too big to be real.

The luggage was seized by an army of skilled handlers and disappeared into the dark interior while passengers walked up the sloping gangways to be greeted by the ship's personnel and escorted to their cabins.

Although Miranda was travelling incognito, one or two people nudged each other as they recognised her and Paul wondered if she would be allowed to remain just Lady Shuter and not the glamorous actress who had made such a success of her career in the West End of London.

Once on board they heard the music from a Guards' band and found their way to the ship's side overlooking the dock. Uniforms of red and black with fur-trimmed cockaded hats made a patch of colour against the grey stones, and the silver trumpets gleamed in the sunlight. Tunes from popular musicals hung on the air and the engines of the huge ship began to throb into life.

Rose wanted to sit on the rail but Paul held her firmly and she was soon absorbed by the sights on the shore, the sounds of music, and the seemingly never-ending trail of passengers coming on board.

A siren gave a signal that the ship would leave shortly and a voice over a loudhailer called, "ALL ASHORE

127

WHO'S GOING ASHORE. ALL PASSENGERS ON BOARD. ALL VISITORS LEAVE NOW. ALL ASHORE WHO'S GOING ASHORE."

Miranda clung to her husband for a minute; he kissed Emma and Rose, shook Paul's hand and hastily left the deck, his face showing deep emotion, as if the temporary parting was too poignant to prolong.

The atmosphere must have been like this when troops left for foreign waters and the unknown, Emma thought, but then there would not have been coloured streamers to lighten the leaving. It was electric and exciting but somehow sad. The band struck up again. 'Will ye no come back again?' and tears began to fall as coloured streamers were unrolled into the air and the thin bands of colour flew in wide arches to beribbon the sides of the vessel and land on the quay. Rose was enchanted and threw her steamers, some unfolding and some leaving her small hands still in tight rolls, but her face was alive with wonder as the rainbow of colour became a dense cloud of farewell.

The hawsers were stowed and the vessel left the moorings; the streamers broke as they were pulled from the shore and the symbolic severing of contact was complete.

The *Queen Mary*, now pushed by fussy tugs, was pointed in the direction of the open Southampton Water, the Needles on the Isle of Wight, and then the wide open sea, towards America; the ragged remains of the streamers were torn away in the wind as if the passengers had indeed severed all contacts with home.

Ten

Emma rang for the steward and asked to be shown where the ship's sick bay was situated. She regarded Miranda with some anxiety as she looked flushed and overexcited. "It's time for your evening injection," she pointed out.

"I'm not really hungry." Miranda said firmly. "I could miss this one and not eat this evening."

"You know better than that," Emma replied, and although Paul said nothing, Miranda sensed his disapproval, lowered her gaze and shrugged. "You really do intend to make me be good. You are right, of course, and it's nice to know you care enough to bully me."

"Come on, the steward is waiting, and this isn't going to take long." Emma picked up the case containing all the equipment that Miranda needed for injections and urine testing for her condition.

The small clinical room was well equipped and Emma looked about her with approval and interest. Only a faint humming from the distant engines, and the small round porthole windows, made it apparent that this was not on land. A nursing sister greeted them with a welcoming smile and was obviously impressed by the fact that a very famous and beautiful star of a long-running play on the stage, and soon possibly of the screen, was in her domain.

She took the specimen of urine that Miranda produced and tested it for sugar and acetone, then charted a drop of blood to start a blood sugar curve as an extra precaution in case Miranda was careless in her diet. The atmosphere of the room, smelling of disinfectant, calmed her and when they returned to the suite, Miranda was relaxed and said she thought she could manage dinner.

"We'll eat here tonight," Paul insisted, then added, as if to make sure that Miranda didn't feel that she was the only one to be considered, "Rose is overtired and I don't want to leave her with a stranger tonight while we are in the dining-room."

"That's good. I don't want to have people staring at me and wondering if I am who I am," Miranda agreed. She examined her reflection in one of the mirrors in the suite. "I feel a bit tired but I certainly don't look it." She stared at herself in the mirror. "I'm amazed at how well I look."

Paul walked over to stand behind her and smiled above her head into the mirror. He laughed and Miranda turned to look at him then back at the mirror. "I think we should have a looking-glass like this in our clinic," he said. "Very flattering and good for the morale. Patients would go home convinced that they were very much better just because they saw their faces in a flattering reflection when they tidied hair and fixed make-up before leaving the clinic."

Miranda put a hand up to the glass, then smiled. "What

a mean trick. We all look better in this mirror and I can see now that the glass is tinted peachy pink. What a good thing I brought a glass that shows up every blemish. I couldn't face the photographers, believing that I looked this good after seeing myself in this peachy glow. The camera they say never lies but I would blame the photographer if I appeared badly on film after putting on my make-up in this mirror."

The suite of rooms was spacious and well appointed with solid and handsome furniture and pastel shades over the small lamps dotted about in useful positions by the inviting deep armchairs. Rose made no fuss about sleeping in a tiny room with a porthole window. Her favourite toys were scattered on the floor and she hugged a smaller version of her bear.

A handwritten invitation came for Miranda and her party to dine at the captain's table. She pleaded exhaustion but told the messenger that they would be pleased to accept the invitation for the following night.

"We are on our way," Emma whispered, as they prepared for bed after a wonderful meal brought into the suite on a wide trolley that doubled as a table. Suddenly, she was very tired, the tension of the past few days catching up with her.

Paul yawned. "Tonight I shall hear nothing but the sea and the distant engines, if I hear a thing," and they were fast asleep when the steward brought early morning tea and the ship's newspaper with details of all the activities available for passengers energetic enough to sample them, and details of the daily gamble over the speed of the ship that day and the sea miles covered.

131

In a simple beige trouser suit and dark glasses, Miranda was sufficiently unrecognisable to venture into the dining-room for breakfast after being given her first injection of the day and she read for a while on a recliner on the promenade deck while Emma and Paul took Rose to explore the ship.

Slightly overawed by the immense funnels and the wake of white foam that thundered after the ship, Rose was quiet and content to walk with her parents, Paul's hand held tightly in hers for reassurance, but later, she was persuaded to join several other children in a nursery filled with toys and exercise equipment, including a rocking horse, and Emma was free to enjoy the ambience of the voyage.

It was strange, after a lifetime of caring for others and working so hard, to be at leisure, on call to nobody except Miranda – who was little trouble – and every wish immediately granted, or in some cases, anticipated. Hot bouillon appeared when they joined Miranda to sit on the deck recliners and she was able to drink some as it was safely free of carbohydrate, but stimulated her appetite for lunch.

"I needed this time away from everything," she said and sighed with contentment.

"I think we all needed a break," Paul agreed. "After this I shall be ready for work again, but it will be nothing so taxing as life in the clinic in London."

The steward took away the evening dresses and Paul's dress suit for pressing and Emma was free to do as she liked all day. Rose was very busy with her new friends and Paul took pleasure in walking the decks and exploring the ship's library. They dressed for dinner early as they had been invited to a cocktail party before they ate at the captain's table, and Emma was impressed by the almost pre-war elegance of the guests and the magnificence of the cut glass and ancient silver in the dining-room.

It was hard to imagine the ship divested of all that luxury, and stripped of everything moveable that could be stowed safely during the war and not brought out again until it was safe to display them again. She tried to visualise the public rooms filled with iron bedsteads and bunks to accommodate thousands of soldiers during the war. The *Queen Mary* had not sailed the Atlantic proudly, as a queen of the sea, but had been forced to take avoiding actions and steer devious courses when enemy submarines were suspected to be within range with torpedoes.

Emma looked about her and wondered if all that drabness could ever have existed, and after dinner sat in a comfortable plush-covered chair to listen to a concert of light music, played by a well-known dance band that she had previously heard only on the wireless.

The four days passed in a kind of indulgent dream and Miranda valued the private suite. Having appeared at dinner with the captain and other important people, Miranda was unable to remain incognito. At dinner, she was beautiful, dressed in a slim, silk dress and high-heeled sandals, her skin radiant and her hair loose as she wore it in the latest play. In the suite, she could relax and avoid the few pushy fans who tried to dog her steps. Emma and Paul kept a protective eye on her and she made full use of the hairdresser, the beautician and the Swiss masseuse on board.

Refreshed and bright-eyed, they packed ready for dis-
embarkation; Rose said a tearful goodbye to the nursery
nurse and the little girl who by now was her very best
friend in all the world, and Miranda posed for the press
and photographers.

On deck as the great ship eased her way into New York
Harbour, the passengers crowded the rails to catch the first
glimpse of the Statue of Liberty. Emma was overwhelmed
by the dignity, style and impressive size of the famous
edifice and many of the passengers had tears in their
eyes when they saw it for the first time or felt they were
returning home to familar sights after being abroad.

Gulls wheeled above *Queen Mary*'s funnels, and sirens
from the shore and the many tugs easing her into harbour
made her arrival an occasion for welcome and anticipation. The smartly uniformed pilots were piped aboard at
the harbour entrance as soon as the ship's speed reduced,
and eventually the docking was made fast, as the hawsers
were tied to the quay side.

Music from a brass band was as bright and foot-tapping
as the music at American forces' dances in London, Emma
recalled, and the irreverent strains of 'The American Patrol'
belted out over the sea. Paul grinned. "Now I really believe
I am in America."

Everything was well organised. Miranda was greeted
by her dresser, Doreen Birch, and Emma passed over the
diabetic equipment that she'd used on board. "I shall see
you when we come to Washington," Miranda said and
kissed Emma with real affection.

"I have a car waiting, Lady Shuter," Doreen said, then
conceded, "you look really well," as if she expected the

worst when her charge was out of her vigilance for five minutes. The slightly angular, plain woman was obviously fond of Miranda and scooped her back into her care as soon as the luggage had been taken to the car. "You'll have a rest as soon as we get there. I've arranged it, and a little light lunch, but I made it clear that you would not want to meet any friends that your hostess has invited to meet you until you have recovered from the voyage, and then only those who were connected with the theatre," Doreen said firmly. She sniffed dismissively. "Social climbers! They are as bad here as they are in London although they boast that America has no class system."

Paul exchanged amused glances with his wife and wondered if Doreen had taken over the whole of their hostess's house. He decided that in any argument Doreen would come out victorious and would protect Miranda's interests beyond the call of duty.

When she hugged Emma, Miranda whispered, "She bullies everyone including me but she's quite indispensable and I love her."

A limousine took the Sykes family smoothly to the airport after they passed through immigration, and a small executive plane, gleaming and new, was waiting on the tarmac.

"Is this an Air Force plane?" asked Paul.

"Seconded to Mr Miller," the steward told him. "In fact it is for the private use of Mr Miller and his party and a few other diplomats and senators. Champagne, Mrs Sykes?"

Paul raised his eyebrows. "Dwight must be really important," he said.

"I hope not *too* important," Emma remarked. "I remember him as a fairly simple man whom we all loved."

"He hasn't changed," Paul said warmly. "When I speak to him on the phone he sounds just as we remember him."

"That's the private man," Emma remarked shrewdly. "He must be very disciplined and more formal in his work and we have never seen Dwight Miller, the diplomat."

"With Bea as his wife, he would never have a chance to be pompous and overbearing as some important people become. Remember Dwight with a clothes-peg on his nose, changing a nappy? Bea stood over him and told him that if he didn't want to do it, he should never have been so potent as to sire twins."

"Dear Bea, that was when his morale needed a boost after he thought he might be unable to give her babies. She took every opportunity to make him believe that he was very important and virile." Emma giggled. "After the next baby was born, Bea decided that enough was enough and told me that she'd said 'Whoops, down boy!' and gone back to wearing a diaphragm."

A late lunch was served during the flight to Washington and once again, Emma was intrigued by the imaginative presentation of American food but thought that Aunt Emily would turn her nose up at the bland flavour. Prawns from the warm waters of the Pacific had the texture of cotton wool and were rather tasteless. She could smell no hint of the sea like the shellfish off Bembridge on the Isle of Wight and those from cooler northern waters, when served on ice.

"Don't say it!" Paul cautioned. "You are in enemy

territory and we like everything we are offered," he added, as if reading her thoughts.

"I hope that Rose is as tactful." The remains of a discarded creamy dessert of bright pink with curls of chocolate and a badly chewed cookie showed that Rose had not as yet been converted to what she saw as strange foreign food. Everything looked appetising and Rose was a greedy little girl but as Aunt Emily's Wilf would say when anyone left food, 'Your eyes were bigger than your belly!'

The long distance between New York and Washington made Emma aware of the immense size of the country and she knew that they would not be able to see even a fraction of it, but the important thing was that she was going to see Bea Miller, the girl who would always be her spiritual sister after all they had shared during hospital training: sadness, anxiety and great joy. She smiled and the corners of her mouth trembled. Paul held her hand. "Happy?"

"I can hardly believe it." Emma glanced at Rose who was busily drawing an aeroplane to show Dwight. "He'll like that. I don't suppose he's ever flown in one quite like it," she said, observing the peculiar set of the wings.

"I think the pilot might need a parachute," Paul whispered but promised to fold the paper carefully and carry it in his pocket, ready to give to Dwight.

The exclusive area of the airport away from the main terminal was reserved for government planes, diplomats and high ranking service personnel. It was bare except for two small planes similar to the one in which they had just flown, but from the main runways came the sounds of sirens, heavy engines and the swish of luggage vehicles.

Paul looked out of the window as their plane taxied to a halt. "There they are!" He was as excited as Emma and picked up Rose, ready to leave the plane at the first possible moment.

Bea stood by a large limousine, looking relaxed and nonchalant as if it was an everyday occurrence to greet her friend from England after such a long time away from each other. As usual she was dressed in elegant clothes and her blonde hair, now shorter than Emma recalled, was as smooth and shining as burnished white gold against the dark blue coat and multicoloured scarf. At Beatties Bea had had a reputation for appearing aloof, and she appeared so now, until Emma put her foot on American soil and ran forward.

The cool illusion vanished and Bea rushed to meet her with tears running down her cheeks. "About time! What kept you?" They hugged and Paul felt a lump in his throat as he greeted Dwight.

"Paul! You are handsomer than ever," Bea said and was kissed with great enthusiasm.

"You limeys! Emma and I will get on fine if you have to keep on hugging each other. I think she's prettier than you, Bea." Dwight kissed Emma and stood with an arm around her shoulders. She sensed his genuine pleasure and they all started to talk, stopped and then interrupted each other as words tumbled out in an unintelligible tangle of excitement.

"Take no notice of my husband," Bea warned Emma. "He is too big for his boots these days. I hope you didn't pack any presents for him. Don't encourage him."

"No children?" asked Emma. Rose was looking about

her and walked over to the motor car to see if they were inside.

"We left them back home so that we could have a little conversation without them hogging your attention," Dwight said. "Gee, it's good to see you," he repeated for the third time. "Now I can get Bea off my back. Right up to yesterday she worried in case you didn't come."

"You didn't get excited, I suppose," Bea retorted. "Who rang the chauffeur twice to make sure the car was 100 per cent ready?"

"That's not just any old car, and I wanted to drive it today," Dwight said and Paul inspected the huge Cadillac. "It isn't one of the official fleet. I've begun collecting vintage cars. This is my best so far and belonged to Douglas Fairbanks, but what I really want is a Silver Ghost Rolls Royce and an early Bugatti."

Bea smiled. "Fairly innocuous, but expensive," she said. "A lot of sugary sentimentality that does nobody any harm. I've a better feeling about it than the one we went around in during the war," she added softly. "Remember the terrible car with curtains and soft cushions that was a passion wagon belonging to that assassin Goering? I wished that the boys had never 'liberated' it. I hated it and could imagine shocking things happening in it and not all were to do with sex."

"If you are determind to go down memory lane take another turning," Paul advised them.

"Quite right," Dwight agreed piously. "Keep Bea off the war. She swears she never talks about it but as soon as some brainless idiot with more fat on his butt than sense, mentions how he did very well out of munitions or food supplies to the Allies, she loses her cool and tells him a thing or two that he doesn't want to know. They'll deport her one day," he added cheerfully.

In the car, Bea took Rose on her knee and pointed out another little girl with two dogs on leads in a park bordering the wide road. "I want a puppy," Rose said, and Emma wondered if a dog would be an adequate substitute for another baby.

"We have a dog," Bea told her. We are lucky to live outside the city where there is space for dogs but you are surrounded by houses and busy roads in London so it would not be easy to cope with a puppy."

"Does your dog bite?" Rose wanted to know. "What's his name?"

"He only bites his dinner and dog biscuits," Dwight said. "He licks a lot and likes little girls. He's a spaniel with floppy ears and a waggy tail."

The few miles of well-washed streets and fine buildings gave way to a more gentle scene with avenues of shady trees and warm red-brick edges to the grass verges. A party of children on ponies, led by a woman in smart riding breeches and a well-cut jacket, made slow progress along the road ahead and drew closer to the verge as the car passed them. Bea waved and the woman saluted with her riding crop.

"Do you know her?" asked Emma, and Rose stared wide-eyed at the disappearing procession.

"She gives lessons to the children, and they are really keen to learn. Her stables are quite close to our house and we can take Rose along to look at the horses later."

"Rose has only sat on a donkey a couple of times when

we went to the island to see Aunt Emily. Wilf keeps one in his field to keep down the thistles and he's amiable and slow, which is wonderful for small children."

"A small pony on a leading rein will give her confidence," Bea suggested and laughed. "It's a wonderful time-consuming pastime and children do get very absorbed with riding and everything to do with horses."

The one-storey house sprawled across a wide patio and looked out onto a very English-looking lawn, with flower-beds and a hedge that separated the garden from an orchard and a vegetable garden. A glass conservatory with a raised ridge of Victorian wrought iron on the roof was full of leafy plants and garden furniture. A gardener straightened his back to watch the party go into the house.

The cool blues and greens of the window drapes in the main sitting-room and the spare use of furniture was refreshing and attractive, but Bea took them along a corridor to a small suite of rooms that she explained would be for their use all the time they were in America.

"Not that you will be here much during the day. We have so much to do and many people want to meet you. The children can play in their own nursery, and thank God for good nannies."

"We'll fit in with any plans you have and make ourselves scarce when you have official visitors," Paul said. "I'll let you have details of my own itinerary which will take a lot of my time, but I hope we can do a lot together."

Eleven

"Oh, there you are. I think she's still asleep so be quiet, children!" Emma opened her eyes and saw three solemn faces staring at her over the bed rail. The voice behind them was soft and the dark face laughing. "I'm sorry if they woke you, Madam, but they have been awake for hours, wanting to see you, and they escaped me."

Emma struggled into her dressing gown and swung her legs over the side of the bed. "I'm awake," she said and smiled. "Hello, you three, where's Rose?"

"Dr Sykes took her to see the garden and the fish pool. I'm Ellie and I look after the children for breakfast when they've had their baths, while Mrs Miller gets herself set for the day and writes letters."

"We wanted to see you," Johnny said and Avril nodded vigorously.

"I want to play with Rose," Mark added plaintively.

"Later, Honey," Ellie laughed. "Yesterday he fell in the fish pool and Mrs Miller said he must stay away from that part of the garden for three days."

"Mark likes water," Avril said. "He dunks himself in any he can find and Mother gets mad at him."

"Leave Mrs Sykes to get dressed and we'll go find Rose for breakfast. Mr Miller had to go out early but you and your husband and Mrs Miller can have your breakfast in peace on the terrace."

The children left with Ellie, and Emma was impressed by their acceptance of what they were told. They were lightly disciplined but obviously not repressed. Emma laughed softly. Bea had not lost her touch. Strong men had obeyed her slightest order and there had seldom been a time when she was confronted by mutiny from any of the patients on her wards of orthopaedic Army casualties at Heath Cross and Beatties.

The suite of rooms was neat and pretty, with just enough muted elegance to show the care that had been taken with the decor. Expensive without opulence, Emma decided, and luxuriated in the shell-pink shower room and the huge matching towels and bath soap.

"You conscious, Sister Dewar?"

Emma draped herself in a bath towel and brushed the damp hair from her eyes. "Quite decent and almost human."

"I hope you like American breakfasts?" Bea was cool and immaculate in a shirtwaister dress of soft yellow with gold buttons and a simple chain at her throat.

"Not dieting?" asked Emma.

"Never!" Bea twirled to show her slim hips and trim bustline. "I have far too much to do to put on weight. The kids keep me like this and wear me ragged." She sat on the bed while Emma dressed. She eyed the full navy blue skirt and pale blue blouse with amusement. "Almost a uniform, but nice," she announced. "I suppose you really do work

143

in the clinic, and it shows. All you need with that skirt is a wide blue belt with a silver buckle and then you'd really look like a Beattie's Sister." She laughed. "We'll soon change all that. This morning we show Rose the horses and maybe sit her on a fat old pony we keep for timid visitors. It's useful having a stable close by where we can leave our own horses and have them to ride whenever we want them, but we let Eve, who owns the stables, use them when we are away. That pays for their keep and exercises them." Bea sighed. "I'm really happy here but I wish we had more time to visit Texas and let the children ride in a more free atmosphere. Here we trot along established bridle paths and along the side of the exercise field and it's a bit like riding in Rotten Row, at home."

"They really enjoy horses?"

"Love them, but Mark is a little bit of a trial as he makes them canter when we are in a zone reserved for more sober riding. He's adventurous like his father."

"Who are the twins like?"

"A mixture. Avril looks like me, thank God, and not Dwight's sister who is a bit butch, and Johnnie is like Dwight with a bit of my father thrown in. Mark will be a tearaway or a film stuntman, or maybe a future President of the US of A, or an explorer."

Emma laughed. "From what Ellie said, he might even be a deep-sea diver."

"Ellie does the early stint and hands over to the nanny at ten. She gives them small jobs to do and makes them read for half an hour, mostly English favourites and less of the *Little Black Sambo* and *Uncle Remus* kind of books. Stop looking quizzical, Dewar. I take care to give them the best of both countries, with no prejudice, and if I lived in a country where the local language was foreign to us, they would be bilingual." She shrugged. "I sometimes think I'm losing a battle over diction but on the whole they are not terribly Yankie, wouldn't you agree?"

"I think they are wonderful," Emma said simply.

"C'mon. I'm starving. Paul is on the terrace taking photographs of the house and Rose has deserted you for Mark who she kissed twice as soon as she saw him, little hussy!"

"He should feel honoured. It isn't every boy who gets that treatment."

"He's going to be like his father," Bea said dryly, "but where did Rose get that flirty look? Not from you, and Paul hides his libido under that wonderful sexy calm. Do all his female patients fall in love with him?"

"I keep him well chaperoned but you should see the malicious glances I get when I sit in with him on analysis sessions. They make every excuse to get me out of the room, so I send in Mick who can sort out threats from both sexes."

"Both sexes?" Bea giggled. "For a man like Paul the odd queer must be far more terrifying than an army of nymphos."

"Giggling already? I should have known that you'd take over where the last bit of conspiracy left off," Paul said, joining them.

"Only talking about you, Sweetie," Bea said. "Take a picture of Emma and me before we get mussed up by the children and then we must introduce you to Hickory-smoked crisp bacon, maple syrup and pancakes."

Coffee arrived in a silver pot, and dishes covered with silver domes gleamed on the table in a patch of sun on the terrace. In the distance the hum from the expressway made a background reminiscent of the whine of trams from the hill up to the park near Beatties, and yet there were no really intrusive noises.

"We're very lucky to have this house," Bea told them. "Masses of rooms for visitors and a staff annexe where Ellie and Nanny and other female staff live, and an apartment for the gardeners and male staff if they want to live in."

"This is much too relaxing," Paul said as he poured syrup on another pancake. "No thanks, I've had enough scrambled eggs and I must make a few phone calls, if that's okay?"

"There's a private line in your apartment and Emma and I can look over the garden unless the children are ready for Eve and the horses." Bea peered over a clump of bushes. "The car has arrived and Nanny is putting the kids inside, so we'd better be on our way before World War III breaks out."

Paul walked with them to the car and was introduced to Jan, the nanny, who had been with Bea for a year and was happy to stay with the Miller family. "We passed that stable on the way here," Emma said. "Surely we could walk there? Even Rose can manage that far."

For a moment, Bea looked bleak. "We drive the children everywhere. If we walked, the police would stop us and want to know where we were going and even if they know us, they caution us that it isn't wise to be walking along a public highway even for a couple of hundred yards."

Jan gave a nervous laugh. "You get used to it, Mrs Sykes. We are pretty safe living here, with security gates and alarms, but this is an area where a lot of important diplomats and senators hang out and it attracts a few nuts from time to time."

Bea gave Jan a warning glance. "I'll tell you more later Emma, but we keep a low profile with the children so no more for now. Let's get to the horses."

Johnny struggled out of the car to show Emma his new shirt and Bea gave a sigh of resignation. "I know, it's awful! He chose it and his dear daddy approves and says he looks a real regular little guy, so what can I do?" A smile curved her lips and she hugged him and shooed him back inside the car. "He'll be fit for a lumberjack and nothing more," she asserted. "Try not to think of him as a walking chequer-board and wear dark glasses if you can't take all the colours."

"I think he's cute," Jan said warmly, and Emma agreed.

Jan drove the car, after making sure that the children buckled up their seat belts and that the doors were locked from the inside, making Emma aware that this was routine and a serious precaution against, as Jan said softly, "Being jumped at the lights."

The field into which Jan turned the car was green and well kept and ringed by high, creosoted fences. The outside world seemed cut off and Emma lost her feeling of formless apprehension. Timber stables with rough shingles on the roofs and stout open half-doors through which horses of various sizes peered over the locked lower doors gave an immediate impression of the countryside, and memories of the rides on Epsom Downs in England were vividly reflected.

Rose jumped up and down. "Is there a nice donkey?"

Jan took her by the hand. "Let's just look at them first," she said wisely, and when Rose saw a large horse led out for a woman to ride, she clutched the friendly hand and drew back.

"Maybe this one," Jan said softly and Emma saw a Shetland pony that looked as if its back had bowed under the saddles of many fat little children.

"There are two," Bea explained. "Sugar and Spice, and Mark likes to ride Spice, so you can try Sugar and ride with him." She laughed. "Now you know why I insisted that you bought cotton trousers for Rose. Avril wears them but the boys have heavier denims like the ranchers wear. They think they are tough guys!"

"He looks easy to ride." Emma smoothed the shaggy coat and brushed the unruly mane away from the pony's face.

Rose beamed, her cheeks warm with excitement. "Funny saddle, Mummy."

"Clever girl to notice. All the saddles are American which is fine for the kids when they need to have confidence, but I think they'll have to learn to ride all over again if they want to ride in England. No armchair saddles there," Bea told Jan and left her to sit Rose on the padded leather seat and urged her to hold tight to the pommel.

"Better keep a leading rein on for the first time," Eve smiled. "Not that he has the energy to run away with her but it's a rule and she must begin the right way."

"You okay? I'll take Emma to see the tack room and all your trophies. See you all later. Have fun."

Bea led Emma away. "It will be good for Rose to be without you for a while and I'd better put you in the picture about Washington."

"So far, I've been very impressed."

"I know the house is sensational and all that goes with it. You'll meet some very nice people while you are here and a few that I can't like and would prefer not to meet, but I have to bite back a few caustic remarks and smile at times. Dwight tries to limit such meetings, but you know how it is."

"In ideal times, as Aunt Emily says, you wouldn't cross the road to give them the time of day. Does it worry you? We had plenty of practice in hospital. I've wanted to slap down a few and so have you, but we knew we couldn't."

"And sometimes got misunderstood when we made efforts to be pleasant."

"Saturday nights in Casualty were the worst. I can't believe that you have anything as bad here?"

"Not here, but you saw how careful we are with the children outside the gates. They *are* safe, so don't get anxious. It just means that we take precautions. In cars, always lock the doors from the inside, even if you want to travel short distances and think that nothing can happen. All the motors have childproof locks so that even my little fiddle-fingers, Mark, cannot open a door from the inside.

149

Emma regarded her with interest rather than anxiety. "I suppose many people would consider London unsafe, but we get about freely and have very little to scare us. Is some of this American hysteria?"

"Never say that again. The country is full of ex-service men living on state handouts or nothing, and crime has escalated since Korea. Jan was set on by three men who stole her purse but she was wise and did nothing heroic and they didn't hurt her. The police took notes but they have many such complaints every week and seldom arrest anyone."

"Not everyone has a car, so how do they manage?"

"The buses are good and cheap and we lend Jan a car if she needs to go into the city. She prefers to live in and sleep at nights," Bea added dryly. "If you want to explore Washington, downtown, we'll have a man to drive us. I wear no jewellery in the city and carry only what cash I need for that day." She gave Emma a bear hug. "Cheer up, you are safe with us and it's just wonderful to have you here. Let's see who has fallen off what!"

Mark was fighting back the tears. "Tell me," Bea said gently as she wiped them away from his dirty cheeks.

"Nasty horse," he mumbled.

"What did you do to him?"

"Nothing."

Bea sat back on her heels and inspected the grazed arm. "Nothing?"

His defiant expression wavered and he grinned. "I hit him with a stick to make him gallop and he tossed me."

"He had every right to do that. Spice is a civilised animal and you did wrong, Mark. Go into the house and ask Alice to put something on that graze and then sit out here and wait for the others to finish."

"I want to ride!"

"You'll ride again when you've learned to treat Spice with respect. You may feed him when the morning session is over. Make a fuss of him and say sorry, but you do not ride again today."

Mark kicked dirt as he went into the house but obeyed his mother and came back with a clean face and a plaster on the graze. Rose sat sedately on Sugar and the twins trotted along the sides of the field and back to the stables when Eve called them.

"They are very good," Emma remarked, looking at Mark who bore no resentment against his mother's order.

"They have to be," Bea said firmly. "They meet a lot of important people and the Americans love the twins' good manners. Mark could be a problem when he is older as he has a lot of my bolshie attitudes and hates to be held back. I almost wish he'd been a girl like Rose, but not quite. He's afraid of nobody and I hate to disillusion him and say that many people are not good and he must learn not to speak to strangers, but it's difficult to draw a firm line beyond which he must not go."

"He's little more than a baby," protested Emma. "Rose is very trusting too and I worry about her sometimes but she is never away from me or Eileen for very long and she is shy of complete strangers, so that problem doesn't arise."

They watched the children hold buckets of pony nuts for the Shetlands and Mark made a fuss of Spice and said he was sorry he hit him. Spice nuzzled his neck and

151

crunched the food, obviously not upset and convinced that he'd applied his own effective brand of punishment.

"Home for milk and cookies." Jan packed the children into the car and Bea came away from Eve's office, after arranging another ride so that Rose could be included.

By the corner of the main road, Emma noticed four men lounging by a hydrant, watching the passing cars, and she felt uneasy. Bea saw her expression and smiled wryly. "You'll get as bad as me if you stay here. I try not to condemn every layabout I see but I have to be careful since Jan was attacked. If I had them in a ward I'd get to know them and find out if I could trust them, but here, there is a certain us-and-them feeling which is wrong but necessary."

"Do they ask for casual jobs?"

"Frequently." Bea frowned. "We ask for references when we want to employ someone new and we have an ex-naval overseer who knows what to do if he thinks that a man is unsuitable, and never allows anyone inside the main gates without a pass. Mark loves to watch the passing traffic and the arrival of visitors in flashy cars and Jan has her work cut out making sure he doesn't go near the main gate. The nursery nurse should be with him if the twins are visiting their friends but when he runs down to the gate to see if they are coming back she finds him difficult to catch." Bea sighed. "She is a great pudding of a girl and slow moving but she's kind and loves the children, so I suppose I have to put up with one or two faults. You'll meet her tomorrow when she comes back from a few days off."

"While Rose is here Mark will have someone of his

own age to play with, and that may make him more amenable." Emma watched the two youngest children laughing together. "They get on so well!"

"She could be very good for him," Bea admitted. "I'd hate to pin him down too much but he does need to learn self-discipline, even at his age. Never too early for the influence of a good woman! What am I saying? I'll be planning their wedding soon!"

"Don't!" Emma shook her head, laughing. "They need to go to school before that."

"I know." Bea regarded her son with wry affection. "What do they have in store for us, Dewar?"

Emma glanced at her sharply. Bea called her Dewar less and less and only when she felt something deeply. "With you as parents, none of them can be bad. I see normal healthy tots who are a credit to your upbringing and love. It shows Bea, and Dwight is very proud of his family."

"What does Aunt Emily say about them?"

"Not much. She loved seeing the twins when you brought them over but she hasn't seen Mark. No shadows in her mind about the twins but she laughed at some of the things you say about Mark on the phone and says he needs watching. That's nothing bad," she added hastily. "We all gather that he is the active one with too much imagination." She saw Bea relax and changed the subject. "Talking of weddings, I have to buy a present for George and his bride. I thought we could find something over here. Any ideas?"

"Something that Margaret will love and yet not be so personal that George will treasure it and think it's for him?"

"Something like that. Something impersonal for the home."

"I hope you've brought me something personal from Emily?"

"I think she burned the midnight oil finishing the last one for you."

"Bless her. I am very lucky with my relations," Bea said airily.

"Whose relations? You merit lace cloths and doilies but she hasn't made you a whole bedspread," Emma said smugly. "And I've known her for longer."

"I shall telephone her late tonight to thank her. You may have a word too if you are good and haven't drunk too much wine."

"What had you in mind?"

"Dwight really dropped me in this one, and you and I share everything don't we, Ducky?"

"I think this is the night I wash my hair."

"C'mon! You've done it before in England. Remember the Italian officers we met at the General's house in Epsom?" Bea's laugh was malicious and very amused.

"Oh, *no*! Not again. I was pinched at least five times and I couldn't avoid noticing that one was getting very excited when we danced."

"You were much too young and inexperienced to know that such things came up during a purely social occasion," Bea spluttered, then looked dreamy. "Did you know that Dwight wore a cricket box when he was pursuing me so that he could control his pants and appear normal? Poor lamb. I couldn't think what was in there and it wasn't something that one asked while Joe Loss was playing a

154

rumba or one of the big bands was playing something very cheek to cheek."

"I had forgotten what a bad influence you are. Tell me what the evening will bring. At least we have stalwart husbands now to protect us."

"This is a mixed diplomatic bag; some French, some Scandinavian and a few Americans and Canadians. They all speak English but I do make an effort to talk to the French in their own language as they are a bit touchy that French is no longer the main diplomatic language worldwide. Pa taught me that one, and I have been given some very nice French perfume on occasion as a result of my tactfulness," Bea said complacently. "Cocktail dresses and welcoming smiles, but not too welcoming as my husband will begin to mutter and threaten an international incident." She sighed, theatrically. "The demented creature thinks I am still the lovely girl he married."

"You know damn well you are and he adores you."

"Nice, isn't it?" Bea seized her arm. "We can have fun being beautiful but correct. They find it a 'real turn on' as they say over here. We must count the times we are called, 'jus wunnerful' and 'formidable'. I don't know what the Scandinavians say, but it will be fun finding out if they are as dour as they look."

Twelve

"My, my, you surely are a couple of handsome beaux. I sure will enjoy being danced by you'all," Bea said with a heavy Southern drawl.

"Less of the Scarlett O'Hara," Dwight said but his face was aglow with approval and affection. His white tuxedo was immaculate and the row of decorations in miniature showed just what he had done in the American Air Force and how important he was now in diplomatic circles.

Emma smiled at Paul and her eyes sparkled. Bea wasn't the only one to have such a good-looking husband. Paul's well-cut but more sober black dinner-jacket and neatly tied bow-tie contrasted with the pleated white shirt, and the lean cut of his trousers showed the firm but graceful lines of his thighs. His eyes showed the golden flecks that indicated that he was happy and relaxed and Emma knew that he needed this break from patients and their worries and the strain of being responsible for the well-being of sick minds.

"No dancing yet and you will have to join the line up," Bea said. "I shall be very picky tonight."

"Right! First you smile but not too much and be nice to

156

the ambassadors but not too nice. I'm fresh out of duelling pistols," Dwight said dryly.

Bea giggled. "Steer me in the direction of the Scandinavians. They might be less volatile than the French. Bad luck, Ducky. You take the Latins and the French and one lecherous husband of a very good friend who deserves better. The blood won't muss up Paul's nice dark jacket if it comes to blows."

"Behave!" Emma whispered as they came closer to the row of distinguished guests.

The introductions over, the guests mingled and Bea introduced Emma to some people she knew well, including the lecherous husband of her good friend. "You can't keep her to yourselves," Dwight warned. "She is on duty tonight and I expect her to charm Monsieur Martine."

"That's real mean," Jepherson Pyke said and held Emma's hand firmly for a full minute. Emma let her hand stay limply in his, having found from experience that if she seemed to have no reaction to his touch, the man would soon release her, embarrassed by his lack of success.

Bea grinned, knowing exactly what was happening. "I see that you remember Heath Cross dances," she said, and Jepherson looked puzzled.

"Hospital dances, but not ones as glamorous as this evening," Emma said hastily. "This is fun," she added now that at least a few feet separated them.

Paul raised an eyebrow and came to her side. "Sorry to drag you away, Darling, but the group over there are waiting to meet you, Dwight told me."

Bea had deserted her and was deep in conversation with an elderly Frenchman who, having kissed both her hands, now stood and looked at her as if she was a piece of delicious meringue that he wanted to eat but had no means of doing so.

"You look far too pretty for this crowd," Paul whispered. "Shall we run away together?"

"Too tempting but I have work to do," Emma replied sternly. "Besides I'm enjoying myself. Go and chat up a few American matrons. They'll love it."

"Just watch that dimple. It's showing, and isn't good for local morale. There will be others apart from me who want to kiss it."

"Stop flirting with your wife and let Emma come with me," Dwight growled. "I'll find you someone who I think needs a psychiatrist! I didn't ask you over here to slack off and hog one of the only two pretty women here." He held Emma's arm in a proprietorial way. "Get lost, Paul. Emma's dress goes better with my tuxedo than it does with your mortician's black."

"Now what?" asked Emma.

"You wanted to meet the Swedes and I'll feel safer if you and Bea stick with them this evening. They are solemn and take life seriously. My wife needs a slap on the butt when she looks at men in a certain way."

"She likes to be friendly," Emma asserted. "And she is only doing her duty by being charming to her husband's diplomatic contacts. Both of us are here to please, Sir! We are willing to work really hard for you." Her lips twitched. "You know it means nothing."

"I know it, you know it and Bea knows it but the poor guys who see her smiling at them don't know it."

"She can handle men," Emma said briskly. "You didn't

see her with thirty healthy earthy types with nothing wrong with them except for broken limbs which did nothing to dull their libido!"

Dwight grinned. "I can imagine. C'mon and meet some real people. This only needs my godfather here to make this one of the parties we had at Epsom."

"It's better." Emma spoke softly. "I have Paul now."

He glanced at her and nodded, his expression gentle. "He's good for you, Emma."

"I'm starving." Bea stood near the huge buffet decorated with exotic flower arrangements and spotless damask table coverings. Delicate porcelain and colourful linen napkins grouped round champagne flutes and wine glasses where people were helping themselves to lobster, prime beef and lamb and various intricate dishes and salads. Bea's Frenchman handed her a glass of champagne and an empty plate. "Thank you." she said and put the glass down on a table. "I'll choose some food first as I can't handle a glass at the same time."

Dwight casually changed the champagne for a glass of white wine and gave Emma the same. "Can't have you two getting the blues," he whispered. "Bea is fine most of the time but with you here she might go down memory lane and find it strewn with weeds."

"You are an angel," Emma replied and knew that he recalled the time when champagne reminded them both of the death of a dear friend in the Blitz which made it the one wine that for years they had been unable to drink with any enjoyment.

The Air Force dance band played softly in the background and when the guests moved away from the food into the parquet-floored arena, changed tempo and played the latest dance tunes. Saxophones brought haunting memories but these were good memories and the dancing couples made a rainbow of colour as they moved across the wide room. Emma saw her reflection in the long mirrors on the panelled walls, and the bright expensive clothes of the other guests, and was glad that she had spent far more than she had ever done on clothes for this visit.

"You dance very well," said Hans, the fair-haired Swedish diplomat who Dwight had brought to meet her, thinking that he was harmless but possibly boring. Dwight was conscious of the fact that Emma and Bea were making a very definite impression on men who were vulnerable to the charms of fresh British complexions and bright interested eyes.

During a pause in the dancing, Bea whispered, "Aunt Maggie, alias my dear husband, is the perfect chaperon. He steered me away from an absolutely divine Spaniard who looks like a matador and has the most heavenly wicked mouth."

"Remember you are a godly and sober matron with three children," Emma retorted. "What happened to that demure expression you promised to wear tonight?"

"We dance again," Hans said when the music started once more, and Bea looked amused, then mildly puzzled, seeing the solemn Nordic face.

"I like this tune," Emma said. "I once had the record and we wore it out at hospital dances, using it until it was too scratched to play."

"I, too, remember it."

"Where did you hear it?"

"In hospital, in England. When we were convalescing, we were invited to what they called the 'hops' and they played this tune very often, but this is the first time I have danced to it."

"And did you have to listen to 'An Apple for the Teacher?'"

Hans looked animated. "And 'Who's taking you home tonight?' when there was nobody for us to take home," he said eagerly.

Emma experienced a sharp vision of déjà vu and saw an emaciated pale-faced man with unkempt blond hair and dark shadows under his eyes, sitting apart, away from the rough splintery dance floor of the recreation room at Heath Cross, the military sector hospital attached to Beatties. Elbow crutches rested against a chair and by special request, Edith Piaf's throaty French voice came over the slowly dancing crowd of nurses, students and doctors with a sprinkling of nearly healed patients, passionately asserting that she regretted nothing. At the time there had much to regret and Emma had been lonely, too.

"Where was this?" she asked but she already knew. "Were you in Nurse Shuter's ward?"

Hans stumbled and lost his achieved American nonchalance, with a very American and un-Nordic expletive. "I thought it could not be her." He stared at Bea who was laughing up into the face of her Frenchman. "Nurse Shuter is Mrs Miller?"

"We all looked different then, in uniform after hectic days of anxiety and hard work," Emma said gently. "I do remember you with elbow crutches and a plaster cast on

161

one wrist. There was no doubt that you were a patient as you wore hospital blue to mark you as an ambulant service patient who had recovered sufficiently to be allowed out on buses and into the local town and pubs. As I recall the locals were generous and let you travel free most of the time and gave you good service in cafés."

"Why did you remember me?" His eyes gleamed with pleasure. "Why me when there were so many there?"

"There were only five patients there that night and Bea was in charge of seeing that they had their fair share of the curled-up sandwiches and cider before the ravenous students hogged it all. I helped and kept an eye on your group as I thought that two of you might faint with all the excitement of one of our dances," she added dryly.

He laughed and he lost the air of polite formality. "I thought that life was bad, but looking back it was good, a little more than I knew."

"And now you are completely better?"

"Most of the time, when I am back in my own country."

"And at other times, when you are in America and England?"

"I mourn for the destruction of beautiful buildings in London and here I mourn because many people have not seen what others have seen and suffered."

"The war is over, Korea is over, and you are an important man," Emma said gently. "All this is on the surface and hides a lot of feelings."

"I know that now. Were you here for Memorial Day on May the thirtieth?"

She shook her head. "I have a lot to learn about

America. I know about Thanksgiving and how that originated when the first immigrants had a safe landing and gave thanks, but what is Memorial Day?"

"I was out there on the plaza by the White House this year and the edges of the sky were purple as they had been the day I was wounded in France. There were thousands of people, listening to speeches and hearing patriotic tunes and many men were crying. They commemorate all the wars from the War of Independence to the present day and have much memory of recent wars when their own people were killed. I realised that under some of the less pleasant aspects of this country, there is real feeling and memories of sorrow. It was good for me. I come from a less spontaneous people, but on that day I wept, too." He laughed uneasily. "I am boring you."

"No." Emma blinked to hide her own emotion. "I would have joined you."

The last triumphant chords of 'Yes Sir, that's my baby' crashed to a noisy conclusion and they walked across to Bea and her partner. Bea held out a hand and smiled at Hans. "Complicated fracture of tib and fib and a Colles' fracture of one wrist, plus shrapnel in the chest," she said briskly. "I knew I'd seen you somewhere."

The Frenchman looked very confused. "*Comment?*"

Bea gave him a ravishing smile. "Dance with Mrs Sykes, monsieur. I have met an old friend."

"This tib and fib is a joke?"

"Not exactly; an old war wound, but it's better now. Hans promised to dance with me when he was better and he never did, so now I demand my rights."

"*Formidable,*" the Frenchman said, looking after Bea.

163

He held Emma lightly and she found that he danced well, and the lack of communication between them due to her not speaking much French was hardly noticeable.

Dwight and Paul did their duty, dancing with wives of the various diplomats and as Bea remarked, totting up points for America. "And Britain," Emma insisted.

"Who told them I was a psychiatrist?" Paul asked when at last he sank onto a chaise longue in a glassed-in annexe with Bea, who had seen that he was being pursued by a determined lady of vast proportions and had rescued him. "You are a genius, Bea. She was impressed when you told her that I was wanted on the phone and I hope I never shall discover why she hated her father and wet the bed until she was nine."

Bea giggled. "I didn't exactly say that the President needed you but I did murmur 'White House'. I'm afraid the staff here are far too meticulous. One of the aides made a list of guests and their occupations and you were billed on it. Cheer up. We can go home soon. Dwight looks exhausted after trying to speak and understand Spanish. Maybe now he'll take a few lessons. He's put it off for long enough and the Hispanic influence is growing all the time."

"I've been amazed at the many different faces and cultures here. America really is a melting pot of every nationality," Paul declared.

Bea looked sad. "The original promises have been watered down a little. All those hopeful immigrants coming here under the shadow of the Statue of Liberty must have had high hopes of a wonderful future and a good living, but so many faced poverty and disappointment." She shrugged. "I don't know the answer but I do see a lot of suffering when I go into the big cities."

"I haven't seen many signs of depression among the crowds in the shops. Maybe they are philosophical about their lives."

Bea smiled slightly. "One good thing is that they have a more optimistic view of poverty here. It is not a sin to be poor and they believe that every American regardless of race and penury could have the opportunity to be President if the cookie crumbled their way. Personal merit and hard work is valued over wealthy parents and family history. The son of a tramp is respected if he pulls himself up by his bootlaces and becomes a captain of industry. Such progress is a cause for pride. They see no need to hang fake portraits of 'ancestors' on their walls to prove how highly born they are."

"It's what you have done personally, not who your ancestors were that counts," Paul agreed.

Yellow taxis and private vehicles took away the guests and Dwight and his party went home in a official limousine.

"You can stay with us as long as you like," Dwight said. "You were a real hit tonight and I had to fend off a string of invitations that I don't think you'd enjoy."

"Including, I hope, the lady with the purple feather boa and enormous caftan?" Paul asked hopefully.

Bea laughed. "I thought that she would engulf you under that caftan and carry you off to give her a *very* intimate consultation."

"She hinted that she needed at least six consultations

to sort out her wounded libido," Paul said wryly. "Next time I go to one of your parties, Dwight, I shall wear dark glasses and a heavy black beard."

"They'd love it, and take you for Dr Freud." Dwight grinned, but Paul knew he was serious when he said, "You should come here for keeps, Paul. You are just what this mentally unstable country needs and you could make a fortune in private practice. Analysis is a very fashionable must for film stars and important people, as a necessary addition to life, and we need good men like you to drive away the charlatans."

Paul shook his head. "We have enough inadequates at home to keep me busy for years and we like London, and of course we need Aunt Emily and the Isle of Wight.

"Don't," Bea said pathetically, "You make me homesick for her apple pies and lovely bread." She glanced cautiously at her husband. "If Dwight gets a posting to Whitehall you might see more of us than you want."

"Is that likely?"

"Not for years," Dwight said firmly. "I just keep the idea in her head so that she thinks we are nearly there, but there's a lot to do first." He led Paul away to look at a modern painting and asked what he thought of it and Emma was left with Bea for a while.

"Would you really come back for a while? What about the children's education?"

"We talk about that but can't decide what we want. My father would like the boys to go to his old school and a British university but I am not so keen. I've seen some of the dimwits and crooks they turn out in the dear old school."

"Your father is a successful businessman and a Member of Parliament," Emma pointed out. "He also has great charm and a famous wife, so the school can't be all bad."

Bea screwed up her handkerchief and frowned. "He wasn't like that at one time. He sowed enough wild oats to supply a porridge factory and do you remember my cousin, dear Major Ripley who had charm, a marvellous war record and a snake-like fascination for little rabbits, and tried to rape you? He went to the dear old school too."

"If Dwight was posted to England, you'd have to decide on somewhere."

"Not for ages yet," Bea said comfortably. "All I want for the babes is a peaceful, safe and happy childhood, with visits to you sometimes, and then the miracle of the perfect school wherever it might be, here or on the other side of the drink."

"Does Dwight want them to board? George is sending Clive away as he will need a certain continuity if his parents move around in the Navy." Emma laughed. "At least that's what George thinks but, of course, Emily has other ideas – Margaret his new wife will have a baby as soon as possible after they are married and stay in Hampshire until the baby is old enough to travel around, and if Clive isn't to feel unwanted and shunted off to school when the new baby is born, I can see little Clive attending the local day school for a while."

"What does Emily see for my infants?"

"Nothing bad," Emma said hastily and tried to forget that her aunt had suggested that little Mark might need care.

As if sensing what was in Emma's mind, Bea gave her a hard look. "I worry about Mark at times. He's so tiny but as Emily would say, he's a wilful child and difficult to keep in one place, like a ball of mercury. I'm glad you brought a set of reins for him, and he wanted to wear them as soon as he saw Rose wearing hers. He pretends to be a horse but they just might keep him from running off when we are in a big store."

Dwight kissed the back of her neck. "Bed and a busy day tomorrow, Honey. I'm all tied up with official business here but I've told Chris that he must be ready to drive you wherever you want to go and suggested he make a tour of the Capitol. Why not leave the children with Nanny for the morning and see the sights in peace?"

"Count me out too," Paul said apologetically. "I have to see the Harvard people and plan the tour, so I shall have to catch up with you later for dinner."

"Just you and me, Emma. What fun! Nobody to tell us not to linger in the dress shops."

"This is a cultural tour," Dwight admonished.

"We need to know what's being worn by the great and the good," Bea replied sweetly. "We can have lunch and go to an exhibition that I've wanted to see but I knew would bore Dwight as it's very modern art."

Thirteen

"Just drop us off by the park and I'll call you when we are finished with shopping, Chris. That will be about four. In fact let's make it four p.m. outside the plaza gates and we can be home to play with the children for an hour after they have tea."

"Yes, Ma'am," Chris replied and asked if there were any errands he could do on the way back to the house.

"Go home first, then collect the bundle of clothes for dry-cleaning and take it along, and take this message for the stables. There will be a waterproof jacket for Mark to bring back from the saddlery shop, but you can leave it in the car as he will want it when we go down to the river. That's all. You are free until you pick us up later."

"This is like old times," Emma said with satisfaction. "Our precious day off from Beatties was something to fill with anything more exciting than work and today feels like that. We can do as we please!"

They strolled along the wide road edged with well-tended trees fronting smart dress shops, and saw so many wonderful creations that it was impossible to choose which was more attractive than the others and would be perfect for them.

Elizabeth Daish

"I want something smart and practical," Bea said firmly. "I don't think we'll find it here. These are marvellous and completely impossible, and designed by someone who has never had a child within a hundred yards of her or him, and very expensive." She sighed. "Just as well to move on. Dwight would have a fit if I bought that one," Bea told her, pointing to a gauzy creation that might look good on a skinny model on a catwalk but would not stand up to sticky fingers and pony hair. "The sacrifices I make for my children," she laughed.

"And worth every bit," Emma said. "I can't think how I existed before we had Rose, but I know how couples without children must think we are a bit biased and far too absorbed by our own tots."

"It's good that you have joined the club and understand about colic at three in the morning and tantrums when bedtime is imminent; at least we have them with Mark at times, but Rose is so good I don't believe it's true."

"Next time have a girl," Emma suggested.

"You're the one who should be having morning sickness. One little girl is nothing," Bea told her.

"I'm thinking about it," Emma confessed.

"Ask Emily."

"No! She might make me feel guilty."

Lunch in a salad bar was good and the food imaginative. "Reminds me of the Quality Inn where we ate in Leicester Square during the war. That was the first American place we found and the food was always good, if a trifle odd at times. I'm still not sure if I like goat, but we ate it as it was off-ration." Emma looked thoughtful. "It was where

170

your cousin Eddy Ripley appeared and you tried to brush him off."

"My completely evil but nationally heroic cousin. Do you still have his cap badge?"

"Somewhere tucked away in a drawer. I couldn't throw it away, could I?"

"No, Ducky. He was a part of your education and a grim warning about men, but I'm glad he died." Emma looked shocked. "Not just because of what he tried to do to you, Emma. If he had lived he would have ruined a lot of girls and become a real menace to society, once the war was over. Cheer up! I don't have any more awful cousins and my father is now a pillar of propriety and besotted with Miranda, so he's no threat to young virgins."

"He is coming over to see Miranda's first night in New York, isn't he?"

"Soon, and he'll visit us here with her for a weekend when the play has settled down and she can leave the cast for a night or two."

"Is it time to get back?" Emma asked.

"There's a café by the plaza where Chris will know where to find us, so we'll wait there. I need to sit down. We've walked for miles and these shoes are killing me."

After a second cup of coffee, Bea glanced at her watch for the third time and Emma saw that it was twenty past four.

"Not like him to be late," Bea said, and looked worried.

"Maybe we should wait outside," Emma suggested.

"Yes." Bea stood up and walked out into the sunshine. She waved to a car that was driving slowly along the

171

edge of the walkway and the driver stopped when she saw Bea. "What's wrong?" By now Bea was running towards the car and Emma followed closely, Bea's apprehension making them move urgently. "Jan? Where's Chris and the limo?"

The children's nanny looked pale. "Chris told me to collect you. I can't manage the limo, so I drove this smaller car."

"Why?" Bea's voice was low and yet seemed to be under a desperate control. "It's one of the boys, isn't it?"

"Mark is missing." The girl burst into tears and Emma saw that she was in no fit state to drive.

"Move over," she said briskly. "I'd better drive."

Bea nodded wordlessly and climbed in beside her, leaving the now incoherent girl to sit in the back seat.

The road signs were clear and Emma gritted her teeth and drove carefully, trying not to think of a possible accident as she had never driven an American car before now, or on the right-hand side of the road.

"Where is Chris?" Bea asked. "Snap out of it girl, I need to know."

"He's looking for Mark. We saw him this morning and then Karen, the nursery nurse, said he didn't come in to lunch."

"She was supposed to be with them all the time," Bea said bleakly. Emma recalled the overweight and rather offhand girl who Bea suspected didn't do her duty very well, but as she was amiable and liked by the children she was kept on the staff to double up for the real nanny when she needed a break or was absorbed by the twins.

172

"Did Mark play her up this morning?"

"He ran down to the gates three times and hid behind a tree to scare her and she brought him back each time then told him to stay indoors until she fetched him for lunch. She was grumbling that he was being tiresome and had worn her out."

"Where did she go?"

"She helped Chris put the clothes in the car for the dry-cleaners and then I think she sat on the swing couch under the awning until it was lunchtime. I saw Chris return from the stables and put the car in the driveway, after he'd taken some gear out of the trunk of the limo and he'd gone to close the main gates."

"He left the gates open?"

"Only for a minute or so," Jan said quickly. "The gardener was nowhere to be seen when Chris drove through and sounded the horn. It's his job to close the gates, but when Chris noticed that he didn't arrive he hurried back to close the gates himself."

"It takes less than a minute," Bea said worriedly, "Mark is like an eel. He could be anywhere."

"Karen is very upset," Jan ventured.

"So she should be! If anything happens to Mark I shall turn her over to the police and say she is responsible." The passion and grief in her voice was terrifying.

Emma parked behind the big car that Chris had as yet left in the driveway, as he'd expected to use it to pick up his employer and her friend.

"Where are the other children?" Emma had a lump in her throat. She was desperately worried about Mark too, but a guilty tinge of relief persisted that Rose wasn't involved.

"Rose is having a nap and the twins are playing in the walled garden."

Bea frowned. "Mark has his nap now and if he doesn't sleep for an hour he is impossible and naughty. If he has wandered out through the gateway and been picked up by someone he could be at risk, as he might be very difficult." She hid her eyes for a moment then braced herself and said firmly, "What's been done? Have you alerted the police and tried to contact my husband?"

"Chris is out on his motorcycle, touring the streets and park and one police car is already here and there is another coming up the drive. Mr Miller has been contacted and should be on his way."

The police officer was brisk and wasted no time on pleasantries. His business-like manner had a calming influence and Bea was glad to let him take some of the strain. "Who had care of the child and where was she when he was missed?"

Jan told him the bare facts.

"I want to see her *now*. How long has she been employed here and has she been efficient in the past? Any boyfriends, any relatives calling here? Anything like suspicious characters in the grounds? Any spooky phonecalls for anyone?"

Karen was still in tears and the officer viewed her with ill-concealed contempt. "Cool it, Lady. I need to know what happened. What is your part in all this?" He regarded her with great distrust and she sobbed and couldn't speak so he turned away muttering, "Fat, useless broad."

Two of his men waited for instructions.

"You don't know if he left the estate so let's start right here. You go down to the gates and ask anyone including the bums by the wall over there if they've seen the boy." Jan handed over a picture of the child to one of the policemen. "You search the house," the officer ordered the other man, and told Jan to go with him. He half smiled at Bea. "You'd be surprised, Ma'am, how many times we find missing persons inside. I had a dog once, scared of thunder, who went missing and after we searched the woods we found him hiding under a bed."

"We'll look in the outhouses," Bea said, obviously relieved to have something to do.

"Maybe the gardener knows something. You said he was on gate duty?"

The boy who helped in the vegetable garden shook his head. "He had to go to bed a while ago as he had the gripes. Something he ate, he said."

"Where is he? I want to speak to him. Maybe he has the gripes maybe not." The officer's voice was grim. "Take me to his quarters and I'll judge for myself how bad he is."

A distant droning became louder and they looked up at the helicopter circling the house. "They got in touch with Dwight," Bea said with relief. "I thought he might be at the old airport and he got my message."

A flurry of dusty air made them turn away until the rotors stopped and Dwight flung open the door and hurried over from the helipad. He saw the tense faces and knew that no progress had been made. Bea rushed into his arms and he held her tightly, his face drawn and anxious.

175

Bea pushed him away gently. "I'm okay. We were about to search the outbuildings. You take the path behind the swimming pool and we'll go that way."

"The pool?"

"Not there. They looked there first. The men are looking over the house and asking passers-by, and the last ones to come are going to join Chris in the streets."

"Let's go." Dwight touched her cheek and smiled. "That's my girl. Chin up," he said and sprinted along the path to the patch of woodland behind the pool.

An eerie silence was broken only by the sounds of feet trampling the long grass behind the pool and the clunk of doors opening and shutting as the outhouses were searched. Bea sent Jan to telephone Eve at the stables in case Mark had wandered that way. He knew where to go and was fascinated by horses, but Jan shook her head and said that Eve had seen nothing but would watch the road in case she saw him.

Karen seemed in a kind of torpor unable to move and unable to speak coherently and everyone ignored her.

The searchers gathered by the front entrance for further instructions as no trace of Mark had been found except for one small scuffed sandal that Bea found behind the limo. She held it tightly as if to absorb his vibrations and prayed that Aunt Emily had been right and that nothing terrible would happen to any of her children.

Emma recalled that her aunt had remarked that Mark needed watching but had given no hint from her fey mind that any dark cloud hung over him.

"What now?" Bea sounded fraught. "Mark has eaten no lunch and must be hungry and very tired. "I should have been far more strict and made sure he never speaks to strangers, but he likes people and I couldn't make him suspicious of everyone who comes here."

Emma went into the house to see if Rose was awake and hoped that she had not been frightened by uniformed policemen with guns in hip holsters, looking in her room.

Rose held out her arms and her face was pink with sleep. "I want to play now," she said. "I want Mark."

Emma hugged her, revelling in the softness and sweet smell of flower-scented talc and she kissed the dimpled cheek, so like her own and promising the same beauty. "Not now, Darling. Mark is . . . isn't here just now."

Rose chuckled. "He's hiding." She struggled out of bed and handed Emma her sandals. "Help me, Mummy. I want to find Mark."

Emma buckled the leather sandals and thought of the one that Bea now held so tightly as a kind of talisman.

As soon as she was dressed, Rose ran from the room and avoided Emma's restraining hands. She blinked in the bright sunlight and regarded the group of solemn grown-ups with reservation, her normal shyness asserting itself, then she sidled over to the limo and stood by the tailgate of the trunk.

"When did you see Mark?" Emma asked.

"Not telling. He's hiding." Rose giggled and pushed a fist into her mouth.

"He didn't have lunch. Did you see him after lunch?"

Rose shook her head vigorously. She liked this game.

"Before lunch, out here?" Emma forced herself to be calm but wanted to shake her darling daughter and she could see that Bea had the same urge. Inspired, as she had a feeling that Rose knew more than anyone there, Emma said with a lightness that she didn't feel, "Count up to three and call him and then go and find him. Show us where he's hiding."

"Close eyes first?" Rose suggested. "Everyone close eyes?"

Later, Bea dissolved into tears of a kind of irritated joy as she described how three tough policemen and a sprinkling of staff put their hands over their eyes on the orders of a three-year-old.

"Mark!" Rose bellowed and tapped on the door of the car trunk. Bea ran and opened the stiff door and almost crumpled up on the rough tarmac, then stood and reached into the large space and picked up a sleepy and rather cantankerous boy.

"I'm hungry," he said, fighting off Bea's tight hugs. "Someone shut the lid and I fell asleep but I've had my nap and I want some fried bacon."

Dwight came running and Emma could have wept to see the relief on his face, but he said gruffly, "Boys who hide and worry people do not have bacon and pancakes. They have bread and cheese and milk." Mark turned away from him and ran into the house to find the cook and Dwight grinned weakly. "Do we beat him or love him?" he asked. "Just now I want to do both." Bea clung to him and their relief was full of tearful laughter. Chris appeared with a tray of bagels and sandwiches for the policemen and Dwight went in to fetch Coke and root beer and fresh orange juice.

"Nobody was really to blame," Emma said. "Don't be

too hard on Karen. I think she has had a very bad shock and you may find that she is almost too careful in future if you give her another chance."

"I'll think about it." Bea sounded grim and Emma wondered if Karen would ever be trusted again. Jan fetched the twins from the small garden and they took Rose with them to find strawberries in the kitchen gardens.

"If you sack Karen, you still need a nursery nurse," Emma pointed out. "It means getting used to a fresh face and another unknown person to care for the children. At least you know the worst of Karen now. She's honest and she is very upset."

"I need some coffee," Bea said. "I feel as if I've been kicked by a mule." Chris brought a tray out to the terrace and Dwight hastily drank a cup of coffee and took a large bite from a bagel. "Gotta go," he said and ran towards the waiting helicopter. "Maybe they will still be chewing the fat over minor details and I'll not have missed anything."

Emma poured coffee and looked at Bea's pale face. "What a lot can happen in an hour."

"What a lot could have happened in five minutes if . . . if—" Bea burst into tears."

Fourteen

"I envy you Boston." Bea looked sad.

"I'd rather stay here." Emma glanced out at the wide garden. The scent of freshly cut grass filled the air as the gardener swept past the terrace on the sit-on mower and the air stirred.

"It's going to be warm and that means that Mark will be fractious if last year is any guide. Washington in summer is humid and hot and even though we are above the city, we still feel it."

"It's only pleasantly warm as yet," protested Emma. She glanced at Bea's set face and shook her head. "Come on now, we shall only be away for a few weeks and then we all go to the mountains. Your father and Miranda will visit you while we are away and it's time that you realised that Mark and the twins are safe."

"I know, but that scare really threw me even though nothing happened. I saw the expression on that officer's face when he spoke to Karen. He had her labelled child molester or worse and I knew that he must deal with dozens of cases where children are hurt or killed. Sometimes I hate America and everything in it."

"No you don't!" Emma spoke sharply. "It's because

180

you are so happy here that you reacted as you did when something threatened to spoil it for you. You love it here; you have Dwight and the children and a good life, Bea, and Dwight is far too busy to need you throwing a wobbly."

"Yes, Sister Dewar." A slight smile began to spread into a chuckle. "You are right of course. When were you ever wrong, but I hate to see you go away. See what a spoiled bitch I have become. I might have known I'd get no sympathy from you. I hear Jan calling the twins, so we'd best go down to the car and hopefully wear them out on the horses before they go to bed." Bea glanced at her watch. "Dwight said he'd be home early and wants us here, so we have only an hour or so to spare."

Eve quickly allocated the ponies to the children and two stable girls took Rose and Mark on leading reins round the exercise yard and into the paddock while Emma and Bea sat in the shade and drank freshly squeezed orange juice from tall glasses filled with ice.

"I admit that America has *some* advantages," Bea said, topping up her glass with more juice. "When did you ever have unlimited juice back home?"

"One orange is a treat at home," Emma agreed. "And the rest?"

"Good coffee, wonderful steaks and corn meal muffins, lobsters flown in from Maine and friendly people," Bea allowed. "Just one thing missing . . . the Sykes are not here forever."

"The Atlantic has shrunk since you came over, Bea. I shall never think of you as far away again. Admit it, you feel the same and we both know that at any time we can cross over and never feel isolated."

"If we decide to have the children educated in England, it will make a wonderful excuse for me to visit you several times a year." Bea looked better, without the tightening of her mouth that showed she still suffered from the effects of Mark's escapade. "The trouble with me," she said slowly, "is that I had such a lousy family and a lot of emotional neglect that I want everything now and can't get enough of friendship – real friendship – and love, and I shall make sure that the children have it all."

"They do have it all," Emma replied softly. "It shows, Bea, but don't overdo the material things. They don't need that."

"I suppose you are about to tell me how you had nothing but a bouncy ball and a set of playing cards when you were little and were blissfully happy," Bea reported tartly.

"I wasn't blissfully happy and I wasn't allowed cards. My mother said they were the work of the devil," Emma said mildly. "You and I have a lot to forget about our families, and now is the time to enjoy life."

Bea looked almost accusing. "You have Aunt Emily and Janey and your precious island with all those noisy seagulls and damp grass!"

"And we both had Beatties and Heath Cross and so much fun in between the hard work and sadness. We probably had more experience of real emotion than most people have in a lifetime."

"I know. Take no notice of me; I see it all the time and know that I am really, really lucky. Some people have such empty lives. It's just that . . . since we nearly lost Mark, or thought we had, I wonder about the future." She cast her eyes up and her hands supplicated in a mock dramatic gesture. "Aunt Emily where are you when I need you?"

"Eve is waving; time to collect the children and get back. Dwight wants us there as he has something for us, or so he hinted."

"Mummy, look at me," Johnny called. He had a scarf round his neck and a battered hat over one eye. "I'm Roy Rogers and this is my horse Trigger. I want a real Wild West hat and spurs."

"Ask Daddy when we get to Texas," Bea suggested. She helped her son down from the saddle and hugged him. Time to go, Cowboy."

"I *do* want a real hat."

"First, you must ride a lot better and be more like Roy Rogers," Bea teased him. She whispered. "We are all going to the cinema tomorrow to see Trigger, but don't tell Mark yet."

"Are you going to buy him the clothes?" Emma asked.

"Certainly not!" Bea laughed. "I've already told my father that if he buys a few Wild West duds for the two boys he will be their friend for life. Funny! Pa never bought me the right presents but he has changed a lot over the years. Miranda has a lot to do with that and I have shown him the folly of his misspent youth."

"You have?" Emma's disbelief was comical.

"I told him that if I hadn't gone to Beatties and met some soul mates who had a few morals, I would have been as bad as he and my mother were, sleeping around and never really knowing love." She chuckled. "He looked shattered and said he had no idea that I'd ever known what he did, swore he'd always cared for

183

me and been proud of me and actually asked me to forgive him."

"And now he is the perfect father, grandfather and devoted husband."

"Come on, we can't wait all day," Dwight called as he opened the car door.

"Yes, *Sir*. See, Emma, I attract bullies. What is it now? An inarticulate corn-bred senator to smile at and give him English tea?"

Dwight glanced at his watch and hurried them into the house, leaving Jan to take the children. "Hector assured me the time would be right and being the perfect public relations officer he's usually right. Because of the congress, the overseas calls have had to be stacked all this week, but there he is and as far as that man can smile, he's smiling. I tried to reach Emily a few times but even she has to sleep. She should be drinking that god-awful tea by now and stirring the fire ready for the day." He took the receiver from Hector. "Hi there, beautiful."

"Let me," Bea begged and he laughed, said a few more words and handed the phone over to the two women. "I suppose you'll pull rank, Dewar. Be quick, I want to speak to her."

"What a nice surprise. I can hear you as clearly as if you were in this room."

"It's almost as good as that. How are you – and Aunt Janey?"

"Is everything all right with you and those youngsters? I had a bad head a few days ago and I couldn't shake off a feeling but it went all of a sudden and I think they are fine now?"

"Nothing bad happened but Mark hid and gave us all a scare," Emma said. "We can't have long on the line and Bea wants to talk to you."

"Good. I think she's worried so I'll say goodbye to you and give my love to the children and Paul."

"Aunt Emily?" Bea sounded like a child asking an adult for a favour and Emma saw how much her contact with Emily meant to her.

"I hear that Mark is giving you trouble. Don't lose any sleep over that rapscallion. My mother would have said he was like my brother Jack, as slippery as an eel, in and out of trouble and never a scratch on him."

"It made me edgy," Bea admitted.

"And so it should. Being as you are, in a foreign country with all that crime, you need to be careful, but I see no real harm for you and yours. One thing that may be not important, but came to me. Have you a man who does work for you? Younger than middle-aged and a good worker, who works outside, but I am sure he comes into the house when you are out?" There was a pause and Bea knew that Emily was being fey.

"We have an undergardener who's been with us for six months and we like him."

"That's as may be. Be careful of your nice things. He's a bit light-fingered. Did you have references?"

"I'm not sure. I think he's a relation of the gardener, so he might have vouched for him. I'll get the office to check him out."

"Just as well to be careful. You need to be a bit more careful locking up drawers, my girl. What's that noise?"

"That's to say we must ring off. Bless you, dear Aunt Emily. I can afford to lose a brooch or two, but not my children."

"Everything okay?" asked Emma. "Next time I'd like to talk to her," she added dryly.

"You are safe and healthy. It's my mind that needed sorting out."

"And did she do that?"

"Of course."

"But there was something?"

"Do you remember me asking if you'd seen that turquoise scarf pin I wore last week?"

"You left it on your dressing table after you changed for that cocktail party and we were in a hurry to leave."

"I said I'd lock it away later," Bea said bleakly, "but I forgot and now I have no idea where it is."

"Have you asked the cleaner?"

"She looked everywhere and said I must have put it away somewhere safe, and I let it ride as she hates anything that might accuse her of stealing."

"Has the oracle spoken?" asked Dwight.

"She suggested that we beat our children every day and give Mark to a home for bad boys."

"Liar! What did she say?" Dwight eyed his wife and grinned. "She told you that all is well with the Miller family and you can rest easy."

"My, you are as bad as Emily!" Bea kissed his cheek. "Thanks Pal, I needed to hear her voice."

"So I can eat dinner and not have to wonder if you are okay?"

"There was one thing."

He sighed. "If the kids are fine, I can take it. Tell me the worst."

"Emily described Greg Nolan and hinted that he needs watching. Did we get a run down on him from the agency?"

Dwight frowned. "He came to us when we were away in Texas and was cleared, as he was a relative of the gardener who came here four years ago, before I was appointed. Maybe I'll see his references and I can have a quiet word with Chris to see if he's kosher." He laughed. "Does Emily think he steals our roses? He's strictly outdoor staff and doesn't come into the house."

"Wanna bet? I know it's my own fault for leaving things about, and I dismissed them as being mislaid for a while, but I have missed a rather nice scarf pin and now I think of it, maybe other small trinkets and a new leather purse."

Dwight rang for his secretary. "I need to see all the files on our personal staff," he said. "I think Chris needs upgrading and there might be other changes so to be fair I'll see them all."

The girl beamed her wide toothpaste advertisement smile. "Do you want me to go through them? There's quite a pile."

"No, just stack them here and go off duty. I'll have them put away when I've glanced at them."

"Oh dear!" Bea was shamefaced when the files were put on the wide desk. "I didn't mean to make a lot of work for you, Darling."

"For me?" He smiled sweetly. "Them who stirs a hornets' nest flushes out the critters and clears up afterwards. I'll let you eat dinner first and then you can get stuck in,

187

but you need only look at the ones who have been here for less than a year."

"We could do with Mick here," Bea said with a sidelong glance at Emma.

"Don't you dare! Mick and Eileen are ours and they actually enjoy working for us." Emma grinned. "America is far too strange and dangerous for Eileen, and Mick doesn't like 'abroad'."

"I admit I tried to outbid you but they are a boring couple who don't know what would be good for them." Dwight chuckled. "They looked at me as if I was asking them to stab you in the back and I backed off sharpish."

"Remember how we did most things together, Sweetie?" Bea dumped a pile of folders in front of Emma and began to sort out the individual dossiers. "Most of them have been here for years and Dwight trusts them, but there were seven new appointments this year, mostly outdoor staff, since we needed a helipad, and extra fences round new ground that was requisitioned for a pool, and changing rooms and extra quarters for male staff if they live in."

"Is this the one we want?" Emma held up a slim folder with 'Greg Nolan' written on the cover. "Lovely name. Sounds like a film star."

Bea took it and frowned. "Not much inside; just a letter from a priest saying he knew Greg to be a good worker and another from our own gardener saying that Greg is his second cousin and a good worker."

"No history of education or former employers unless he worked for the priest ever since he left school. Comparing this with other folders, they are far more detailed and the applicants obviously were interviewed before being accepted."

"This one was employed at roughly the same time and we have much more detail about him."

"We can put the rest back in the office but I think I'll check with the priest. Too late now, but I'll telephone in the morning. I think I'll do this. Dwight wouldn't want the staff to think he was checking them out as if he thought they were not all they professed to be."

She made a note of St Saviour's seminary, New York City, and just after nine the next day, she contacted the right number.

"Nolan? I do recall a Nolan here." The voice was brisk and Bea knew that this was a man who had no time to waste on idle talk. "What's he doing now? No trouble?"

"I am making sure that all our employees are as their references state and his name was in our files with very little detail apart from two letters, one of which is yours."

"Mine? Now let me think. I wrote a note to the owner of a café after he left here and when they rang for more details as they noted my address, I said what was true, that he was a good worker. No need to say more as I thought he'd have gotten over his earlier troubles. I hoped he was completely rehabilitated and I heard no more of him. Is he still washing dishes and slinging hash?"

"No."

"He knows he must get in touch with the authorities if he changes employment. Are you about to employ him?"

"He has been an undergardener at the home and offices of an important Air Force family for six months."

"Is he in trouble?"

"I'm not sure. We have no proof of any misdemeanour but a few small items are missing from the residence. You seemed to think I would know about you and your seminary."

"I run a unit to train juvenile delinquents and show them the right path. Nolan did time in a centre for petty crime and before that was in a home for young offenders."

"Oh!"

"It would seem that he slipped through the net, Madam. I hoped he would make out and maybe he can if he knows he is being watched." It was almost a plea. "I could talk to him and warn him if that would help, but he must be stopped if he is pilfering again."

"He works hard in the gardens and is well liked. May I leave this with you, Father, at least for a few weeks and we can talk again." Bea gave him details of Dwight's rank and address and telephone number so that Nolan could be contacted. "If possible I'd like to keep him in our employ but he must be told the alternative to complete honesty on our property."

"I think that you have handled people like this, Madam. I sense experience and caring. Many would dismiss him as worthless when he might respond to encouragement."

"A ward of soldiers is a great education, Father."

He laughed. "I see I need tell you nothing. I am pleased to talk to you. Maybe we can save the lad, as I think he has no real vice."

Emma nodded when she heard about the conversation. "We met a few like him at Heath Cross, a bit weak but not really bad."

"All I have to do is to sell the idea of keeping him to Dwight, reminding him that we have no proof that he stole anything."

"It's a lesson to take nothing for granted and to lock up all treasures. It must be tempting to see something pretty and never have a hope of owning anything as good."

A few days later, a large brown envelope with no note inside arrived for Mrs Miller, hand delivered, containing every small trinket that Bea had missed over the past few weeks and she told Dwight that she had found what she thought she had lost.

Nolan and the gardener seemed embarrassed when she made a point of going into the garden to talk to them. Bea made no mention of having spoken to the priest but suggested that they might like to enter a flower show and maybe earn a prize and a lot of local fame. "You really like your job, don't you, Nolan?"

"Yes, Ma'am."

"Then make sure you keep it. We'll help you if you get into difficulties, and Mr Miller would like you to enter shows and be able to take people round the gardens."

"Greg works hard, Mrs Miller, and in many ways he's better than I am."

Bea saw the sweat on the gardener's brow and the anxiety as Nolan shifted uneasily, half expecting to be sent away, and she thought of many boys who became drifters after being demobbed, because they were not given a chance.

"I trust you to do a good job here and to keep your record clean," she said solemnly. "That's all, and I look forward to seeing you hold a challenge cup one day. Did

191

you know that a winner has to return the cup each year but is given a small real silver copy to keep for ever? Something good of your own, that you could earn, if these roses are anything to go by."

Nolan flushed and to hide his relief and emotion bent to cut a rose which he handed to her. "This is a new hybrid and I could show this next month if that's okay."

Bea turned away. She smelled the open rose and admired the closed bud with it. "Keep me informed, but do that through Chris, as you are not indoor staff and must never come into the main building." She strode over the terrace and into the house aware that they knew how close Nolan had been to dismissal and that it was up to him to remain in the garden he had grown to love.

"Sorted?" Dwight asked.

Bea kissed him. "Nolan had a little trouble as a boy but now he wants to concentrate on making the Miller garden famous.

"You'd better be right," he replied ominously.

"Don't worry, Chris will keep him in line and he does grow wonderful roses." She laughed. "I haven't lost the touch, Dwight. I mentally wore a starched apron and I think he's scared of me."

"Aren't we all?"

Fifteen

"So this is where they had the Boston Tea Party. It all looks very peaceful and civilised now," Paul commented.

"Why does it remind me of home?"

"The trams. We are getting rid of ours but they are wise enough to leave them and make a tourist attraction of them. It really is a lovely city."

"I wish that Rose was here."

Paul regarded her with an indulgent smile. "We did agree not to say that more than five times a day. She's perfectly happy with the other children and most of the time here she'd be bored." He sighed with contentment. "Make the most of this time together. When did we sit outside a café in the sun, drinking really good coffee and having the leisure to explore on our own?"

"In that case, Mr Energetic, finish that coffee and follow me. I have a leaflet that shows a route through the city, taking in all the old buildings here."

"Really ancient monuments? Those I must see."

"Stop being superior. I know they have nothing to touch our cathedrals and castles but to the Americans anything over two hundred years old is historic. The native Indians have a long history but not in elaborate buildings. Nothing here is older than a couple of hundred years, but old by American standards and most dating from the time of the Pilgrim Fathers."

"She'd love the squirrels," Paul remarked as a scurry of grey squirrels swung along the branches overhead. "But not this." They went into the old courthouse and Emma shivered. Inside it was dark and forbidding and the portraits of long-dead dignitaries, dour-faced and dressed in the plain sombre clothes of the Puritans seemed to accuse anyone who entered the solemn place.

"They look very . . . hard."

"It was a hard life. It took courage to leave their homes for a foreign country, in spite of the fact that they suffered persecution in England and the Netherlands. Many died during the first year after the pilgrims landed in America and these pictures date from that period. The harshness of their own laws came with them and their religion was based on self-sacrifice and discipline and frugality, so they reflect the harshness of the times. Later we may see relics of the Civil War and everywhere there will be signs of the struggles of a new nation."

"It's good to be out in the sunshine. How do we cross the river to Cambridge again? Cambridge, America, on the River Charles, and not Cambridge, England on the River Cam."

"There's a bridge or ferry. It's easy. You could come back here while I'm lecturing," Paul suggested. "I don't want you to be bored."

"That's all settled," Emma said firmly. "I shall, as they say here, have a ball. They think of everything. I am to be shown over Harvard University tomorrow and then I have lunch with one of the women professors. I *might* spare you time tomorrow afternoon, and we have the big reception with the members of the faculty in the evening." Her eyes sparkled. "I'm enjoying this, and someone promised me that he'd take me on the river the next day."

"You certainly made a few friends last night at the party. Who is your ferry man? Does he know you are married, and is he bigger than me? Do I have to worry?"

Emma giggled. "He's enormous but very muscle-bound and he got the idea that I like boat racing as I know Cowes and I have been to Henley."

"He'll make you cox for an eight."

"Heaven forbid. You don't think that he meant that kind of boat ride? I thought more like a punt and a gentle drifting down by the banks with a nice cup of tea after it."

"As you said, this isn't Cambridge, England. No lazy punts and picnic baskets under the willows. Did you bring any slacks with you, and a waterproof? Play your cards right and he may take you tenpin bowling for afters."

"I knew I should have stayed with Bea."

"We have time to sit and watch the squirrels for half an hour. This break is good for everyone. Bea was delighted to have Rose to stay with the children and you needed to be with me. We do need an oasis of calm and being together alone," Paul said gently.

"It's wonderful, and I feel guilty because I don't feel guilty about leaving Rose. You're right. It's wise to make her more independent and that goes for Bea, too. We know we can go back home after the tours, but she can never do that. This is her home now and England will be her place for holidays and visiting friends."

"She has been a bit clingy which isn't like Bea." Paul grinned. "Dwight and I agree that memory lane has a lot to answer for. Bea's good memories began when she was at the Home in Bristol and you all had an effect on her."

"That place had an effect on all of us and a little suffering is a great means of making bonds! Beatties and Heath Cross were important in many ways."

"People were important too." His eyes were dark and the flecks of gold were dormant.

Emma tucked her hand into the angle of his arm and looked up at his face. "Guy was important. I would never have met you unless I knew him, and for that alone, I owe him thanks. He helped me to grow up, but the grown-up Emma needed *you*."

"Thank you for that." His voice was husky. "I had been waiting for you all my life and I still can't believe my luck in finding you." He kissed her tenderly, then laughed. "Did you see the disapproving look that statue gave us? We'd better be on our way before he condemns us to an afternoon in the stocks for kissing in the park."

A small ferry took them over the River Charles and they walked along the river bank beneath the trees in the waterside park until they reached the pleasant apartment put at their disposal by the University authorities. Young men swooped along the riverside paths on roller skates or rowed small, elegant skiffs on the river.

Paul showed their identity cards to the janitor of the block of apartments and Emma realised why they had been asked for passport photographs before they reached

Harvard. "Better than our wartime identity cards," Paul decided. "I never thought they were 100 per cent safe as they had no picture. Anyone could use them."

"Bea said that ID cards are used to check on undesirable visitors to important places and to make sure that anyone under twenty-one can't buy alcohol. They are strict about that here and if a boy who is well built and looks as if he is old enough to buy spirits tries to buy some without showing that he is old enough, the licensee will demand to see his ID if he is suspicious. Looking at all those huge lads rowing, I can see that a real check is essential, as many of them look older but may be only seventeen or younger."

"It's all those steaks and chickens they ate while we were strictly rationed but I wonder if they are any healthier than we were?"

"The boffins now say that we were healtheir during rationing than we had been for decades. Even though supplies were scarce, everything was divided evenly and everyone took their complete rations in case they missed something to which they were entitled. The free orange juice and cod liver oil did wonders for children."

"Some people managed to get extras."

"The black market added something at a price, but not many people could afford to buy illegal supplies at inflated prices. Hard work and hunger made most food palatable, except for the fish cakes we had at Heath Cross, mostly potato with a fish bone to show that fish was mentioned in the recipe!"

"I doubt if Aunt Emily ever went short but if she did, at least she could make her food edible."

"She was lucky to have her doctor friend handing over farm produce from grateful patients, but I know that even when she was tired after running the British Restaurant she often cooked and gave away pies and good soup to a lot of needy families. My mother would fry sausages until they lost their flavour and serve them with boiled potatoes but Aunt Emily would make really good toad-in-the-hole with onion sauce. I learned a lot from her. She taught me to make omelettes from dried eggs and they weren't at all bad if they were cooked quickly and served at once." Emma laughed. "We probably were more healthy, as we had no chance to put on weight and that awful National loaf was full of calcium and added vitamins, but I remember the first time I tasted really good white bread after years without it. It was wonderful."

"And now we have anything we like over here. It seems ridiculous that meat is still rationed in England after all this time." Paul grinned. "All this and yet I don't really want a steak. Do you know what I want for lunch? The unattainable!"

"Is there such a thing?"

"British fish and chips, with salt and vinegar and crisp batter."

"We had very good fish with Bea and Dwight," Emma smiled. "Very elegantly served but I know what you mean and Bea pines for it too." She looked dreamy. "Fresh, and very hot, with chips fried in dripping and wrapped in greaseproof paper and newspaper."

"You are in America now," Paul pointed out sternly. "When offered it, you'll eat a hamburger and like it." He sighed. "Time to collect my notes and try to look like a very important English psychiatrist, but this lecture is a short one and will be an introduction to the main one tomorrow. Why not sit in this time? It will be no different from the times when you sit in and guard me from my nymphos."

She raised her eyebrows. "Like that is it? Maybe I'd better come along."

"I'm not sure. Maybe I'm getting paranoiac but there's a group of first-year girl students who followed me around after I'd been over to see the head of studies."

"Freshers," she corrected him, "or bobby soxers if you prefer." Emma tried to see her husband through the eyes of vulnerable students and laughed. "I think they see you as a film star, or it's the same image. They adore male British voices and you do look good in that suit. They see very few men dressed as smartly here. Few of the staff wear neckties, and as for jackets, well! Maybe the local baseball team will come back from their tour and the girls will wave streamers and pom poms at them. You'll have your nose out of joint."

"The sooner the better," he replied with feeling.

"I'll protect you and be the perfect possessive house-wife. I can let them know that however much they feel the need, you do not take private patients to examine their fragile libidos."

The lecture hall was vast and the many-tiered audi-torium was almost full when Emma sat in the front row and Paul left her to find his way onto the platform.

"Isn't he cute?" Emma realised that the slightly over-blown wife of the head of the language school who she had met briefly the evening before was referring to Paul.

"I wish he was here forever. I could eat him." She stared at Emma and seemed envious. "You are his wife?"

"That's right and I agree. He's sweet enough to eat." Emma smiled in a friendly way to avoid embarrassing the woman who now regarded her with speculation.

"You're very wise, Honey. If he was mine I'd not let him out of my sight. I shall attend all his lectures."

"You are studying psychiatry?"

"Not me. I just love to watch good-looking guys, hear wonderful voices and dream," she admitted cheerfully and Emma decided that she must tell Paul that it wasn't only the teens who lusted after his body!

It soon became apparent that most of the audience was hooked on the subject and the introductory talk about early signs of mental instability in children made a great impression. The time allotted for the talk was overtaken by questions and more questions and the applause, when at last Paul sat down, was prolonged and spontaneous. Emma smiled. He had never expected such a welcome, but then he was always surprised how interested people were when he talked to them.

"Well done," she whispered, when he came from the platform and sat beside her while the chairman read out the programme for the next day. "Oh dear!"

The woman's voice was saccharine sweet as she reached across to speak to Paul. "Doctor, I did enjoy your talk and I want you and your lovely wife to come to dinner with us tomorrow. Just a few friends who are dying to meet you."

Emma assumed a formal expression and took her diary from her purse. "What a pity," she said, as if she meant it. "Not a single gap, I'm afraid. Dr Sykes has to attend a formal dinner tomorrow and he has a very full schedule until we leave in a few days' time." She looked sad. "I feel they are working him far too hard and that leaves little time for enjoying the company of people he meets during the lecture tour."

Paul just smiled and nodded.

"If you are free now, Paul," Emma continued, "we ought to be on our way. The Professor is expecting us and then we have to dress for the reception." She extended a hand to the woman who now looked very disappointed. "It's been so nice talking to you."

Paul shrugged as if he was making a sacrifice, murmured a goodbye, then shook the woman's hand and followed Emma from the hall. "You are indispensable! You even remembered to say 'skedule' and who is this professor I am meeting now?"

"I lied," Emma said complacently. "Did you see the others who were homing in on us to lionise the best-looking man they've seen this side of Christmas?"

"Doctors don't get this treatment in England."

"You do but Mick and I protect you, you poor innocent, but the women here are far more liberated and pushy. I think we have to abandon the walk we promised ourselves and settle for tea in the apartment before we dress for dinner."

"We've plenty of time. Don't walk so fast!"

"Three girls with a lot of determination are heading our way." Emma saw that one pretended to fall over and sat on the tarmac. "Whoops! Don't look back, Paul. Keep going and I'll meet you in the lodge."

Emma turned as one of the girls ran towards her. "My friend fell down and I think she needs a doctor. She's hurt her ankle," she said breathlessly, her face flushed, but not with anxiety as she gazed towards the doorway through which Paul had taken sanctuary.

"Maybe I can help. I am a registered nursing sister and far more likely to know what to do than Dr Sykes, as he isn't an accident doctor. He treats the mind and the nervous system."

"She wants to see the doctor."

"I'll ask the janitor to ring for a University medic," Emma offered, but the girl looked sulky and her glance could have curdled milk.

"It's no good, he's gone," she called and her friend made a miraculous recovery and walked away.

"I knew you had a healing touch," Paul said, when she joined him in the lodge, "but this is wonderful. You just speak to them and they walk away completely cured! Even Aunt Emily isn't that clever."

"If you tease me I'll let you loose with the lions in future," she warned. "Film stars and other celebrities must suffer all the time."

"That's why so many of them need shrinks," Paul said wryly.

"Dwight says that you could make a fortune here."

"If I set up here I'd need my own head examined."

"Being here hasn't changed your mind?"

"Don't look so anxious. I love my home and my country and although I find America fascinating, it could never be home to me."

"Poor Bea."

"Not at all. They are rich enough to have a *pied-à-terre* back home and another on the French Riviera if they wanted that and now Bea knows that transatlantic travel is easier she will come back more often."

Emma smiled happily. "We can come over again, too."

"I want to talk about that. I have been offered a series of talks next year, based on Harvard, with a house and all the trimmings." He watched her face. "We would be independent and the house would be big enough to have guests of our own choosing, but we would be here for three months. They tried to make it six months but I reminded them that I have my own work in London and we agreed on three months."

"They are trying to make you stay here," Emma remarked shrewdly.

"I did gather that they had considered it, but we could never give up what we have built and the people who mean a lot to us."

"Three months is possible," Emma said slowly. "If we told Bea that we'd be back soon, it might make a difference to her. What do you think, Doctor?"

"When we arrived, I was worried about her, and when Mark was lost I thought she'd need my help. Underneath her usual bright aplomb, she still has patches of insecurity, but if she knows that we shall not lose touch it will help a lot."

"Her father and Miranda are there now and she has built up a good relationship with him at last."

"Not the same. She has only to feel miserable about something trivial and the past could hit her again. She

203

was very insecure when her parents virtually rejected her during the war. She needed them until she made new friends, like you. Now she is fine with Dwight and the children but she still needs good friends." Paul regarded her seriously. "It's a two-way thing. You need her, and if we have only one child, Rose will need companions. Eileen's little girl is fine for a playmate but Rose does seem to prefer boys."

"Mark in particular. He is good for her. He makes her share and doesn't let her have her own way all the time."

"So, shall I accept? The practice will stand it as we seem to have aquired someone who might become a full partner on our return. I spoke to Mick yesterday. He sounded very cheerful and he really likes Robert Forsyth."

"You didn't let me speak to him!"

"There wasn't time. The office here said there was a gap for a transatlantic business call and would I like it, so of course I took the opportunity of getting in touch with Mick, on official business." He grinned. "Hardly office hours. It was midnight over there."

"Accept the offer. It sounds exciting and we shall be able to see a lot more of America." Emma bit her lip. "When would we see Aunt Emily?"

"If you consider that we see her only two or three times a year, it will make no difference and it's becoming easier to get in touch by phone. Why are you smiling?"

"I like the idea of being able to make my own tea in a proper pot with real tea and not have to use these bags on the end of string. It didn't seem worth buying loose tea as we are here for such a short time, but if we had a house . . ."

"Maybe a service flat would be better if only to stop you baking and cooking for an army!"

"I shall remember that when you grumble about American sponge cake and sigh for good rich fruit cake."

"Ah! that's different. You may cook that if only for Dwight." He sounded generous and she gave him a dirty look. "Get changed and meet the intellectuals. We are invited to a film show after dinner."

"A strange foreign film with subtitles and lots of deep meaning?" Emma asked apprehensively. "I saw the poster advertising it."

"Of course not! That's for the young and earnest and those who haven't acquired a bit of taste."

"So what have we to suffer?"

"You remember during the war when dubious characters came a lot too close and whispered that they had something off-ration to sell? One of the professors made a suggestion like that to me."

She giggled. "That sounds compromising. What was it? A visit to a brothel or a blue film?"

"Nothing that would have me drummed out of the Boy Scouts. A genuine 'Saint' film starring Tom Conway with the mellifluous voice and the smoothy manner."

"Don't look so disgusted. I think he's lovely and so does Mrs Bristow. I shall tell her when I get back."

"I shall buy you popcorn and promptly fall asleep."

"That's America, God's own country! I love it."

Sixteen

It was good to be sleeping in the wide comfortable bed again and to hear the early morning giggles of the children as they tapped on the bedroom door to see if they were awake.

"Hush! You can see them after you've washed and dressed. No, Mark, they don't want to see you in your cowboy gear." Jan sounded anxious and her voice receded along the corridor as she persuaded the children to go with her.

"What luxury," Paul said, and yawned. "Do you think Jan would come back with us?"

"Bea would go mad," Emma said equably, "but I could get used to having a really good nanny for Rose."

"Seems a waste just for an only child." He drew her closer and Emma snuggled against his bare chest. "It was quite a 'homecoming'," he added. "They did everything but put the flags out and fire a twenty-one gun salute; and we made love."

"Looking back it seems that we were away for ages, but now I feel that we can pick up the threads as if it was only yesterday that we went to Boston."

"Before the children burst with energy and the desire to

show us all their new toys, thanks to Miranda and Bea's father, we'd better get moving."

"It was a good time," Emma said quietly. "A time to meet new faces and a time to think clearly, away from everyday events."

"Rose seems happy and didn't really miss us." Paul touched her cheek gently. "She'll miss the others when we go home."

A soft glow made Emma's cheeks bright and her voice was tender. "I had time to think of the future. We met a lot of people of our own age group and enjoyed it, and Rose did the same. We needed that and I knew that she must have a companion."

"And so?" His eyes seemed to grow bigger and the flecks of gold were there again.

Emma took a deep breath. "Last night I took no precautions and it will stay that way. Maybe we shall have no more children but I think we could now. Stella said that Rose's birth made another baby possible and warned me against leaving too big an age gap." She laughed. "At least I can face her and say I am trying." She examined her reflection in the long cheval mirror. "Can you bear to see me fat and ugly again?"

"You were never that," he replied with feeling. "I'm not surprised, as I know we saw our future more objectively when we were away and this is the natural outcome."

"*Mummy!*"

"Ouch! Next time do try to have one with a softer voice." Paul opened the door and picked up the laughing child. "I want my breakfast," he said and kissed the warm cheek before he put her down.

"Mark says he wants to come home with us when we go to England."

"His mummy couldn't spare him," Emma said firmly. "But we'll think of something."

"I can make time for coffee before I do some work," Dwight said. "My, you two look really good. Kinda smug. I know the feeling." He leaned back in the patio chair and grinned. "We had a good night, too. Nothing like hitting the sack early and having a good night."

"Shut up," Bea said firmly, but she had the same glow that Emma knew surrounded her too. "Must be the weather."

Jan walked past with the children dressed in swimming things and huge inflatable armbands, heading for the pool. Bea took another muffin and piled English marmalade on it. "They'll be in there for hours," she said comfortably. "Jan loves it, too, so that lets me out."

"I can't sit here forever. I must sort out my clothes if you say we leave for the mountains tomorrow."

"Relax. I've told the new girl to do your laundry and she'll pack your bags ready for the next lot. She acted as Miranda's maid and enjoyed it so she might as well do the same for you. There's no need for you to feel guilty." Bea shrugged. "There are lots of very nice people without jobs and if we can help out it's good from both sides."

Paul and Dwight left to sort out their individual appointments. Paul said he'd see them later as he had a lecture to give after lunch.

"Johnny and Avril missed you more than Rose did," Bea said.

"That's because Rose and Mark are so close," Emma

replied. "You'll be relieved to hear that I have already refused his offer to come back with us!"

"If he gets too bad, I may put him in a parcel and send him over to you."

"Bea! You have that Siamese cat with the cream expression. That usually means you are plotting, or you have a secret that you are dying to tell me but want to make me edgy first. What do you know that I don't? Are you coming over to visit us soon?"

"In a month or so. That's a promise."

"And what else?"

"Nothing." Bea was all wide-eyed innocence but her smile was affectionate and malicious at the same time, and Emma was suspicious.

"There is something."

"Have some more coffee."

"I've finished, thank you. Is it something that Paul knows but I don't?"

"I doubt it. Come on, I want to see the cup that Nolan won for his roses. I promised to take pictures and when we come to the island again, I've begged cuttings from Aunt Emily's old moss rose tree. Nolan has never seen a moss rose and it would be a sensation if he grew it here."

"Moss roses? When did you talk to Aunt Emily about roses?"

"Don't be jealous. She's my honorary aunt and she likes to have a chat without you listening in."

"That's the second time you've hogged the phone and given me no chance to talk to her. When did you phone?"

"Dwight arranged another link and just because you were living it up in Boston was no reason for me to miss out on the call!"

"How was she?" Emma sighed. "She's one of the reasons I could never move to another country. She's my rock."

"And mine," Bea said quietly. She's the aunt and mother I never had and I owe her a great deal."

"How was she?" Emma repeated.

"Fine, but busy helping to prepare for George's wedding. She hopes that little Clive will stay with her when you go there. She said he would be company for Rose . . . that is until he has his own brother."

"Rose loves Clive."

"Aunt Emily knows that but has a feeling that Rose needs her own brother." She looked at Emma with the sideways glance that Emma called shifty.

"So what did she say?" Emma's pulse began to race but she remained calm, unable to tell if she felt elated or full of a strange dread.

"She wore her witch's hat," Bea said.

"Too much whisky in her tea."

"No, she wanted to talk to me about you. By the way I've saved a lot of Mark's clothes that are hardly worn and some are things you can't buy in London."

"You may need them."

"No, *you* may need them."

Emma's voice was a whisper. "She said that?"

"Among other things, she said that Rose is like you and getting more so but the boy will be Paul all over again. Come on, the sun is just right for photos. We have time

210

to see the garden properly without the children larking about and trying to be in each shot."

Bea gave her a hug and Emma smiled tremulously. After their love-making last night, she knew that anything was possible. "A hundred or so years ago they'd have burned my sainted aunt at the stake," she murmured.

"What a waste! I bet the inquisitors would have demanded that she tell them the future first."

"Mountains are impressive but cold," Emma said, after the first day in the hills.

"Only the top crags," Bea protested. "The lower slopes are green and very pretty and heavenly cool just now after Washington. It almost makes up for being a couple of grass widows but Dwight had to go away to Ontario and Paul has lectures to give in so many places that it would have been very uncomfortable and lonely for you. Men travel faster alone with just a suitcase, and his hosts will take pity on him and swamp him with hospitality as he has no wife to spoil him." Bea laughed. "He could have everything, but *everything*, offered to him for his comfort and entertainment."

Emma looked shocked. "Women?"

"Of course! Men from some countries expect it and the female company is . . . laid on . . . if you'll excuse the expression, ready and waiting for it."

"Has Dwight been offered perks like that?"

"Often very young and nubile but he wouldn't dare." Bea grinned. "My comprehensive lectures on the dangers of illicit sex made him squirm with horror. He is a sensitive man under that macho boldness. I also said

211

I'd castrate him if he ever as much as put a hand where it didn't belong and he knows that I would sense it if he ever strayed."

"After you, how could he think of another woman?"

"Paul must be the same."

"Paul often has to retreat from women with sex problems. He has a lot of experience of recognising the signs. They aren't mad, and others are so unstable that they long to latch on to a strong and good-looking man. I feel like a Victorian chaperone at times but Mick and I deal with the situation."

"Mick?"

"He deals with the deviant males. Paul could have a very colourful life if he was that way inclined!"

"Poor darlings. How their ears must be burning. At least we are thinking of them and missing them," Bea said virtuously.

The children ran down to the chalet and demanded lemonade. Mark wore denim jeans and a bright check shirt and Rose followed close behind, carrying a bunch of wilting wild flowers. Paul would love a son. Mark's cheeks were beginning to freckle and Bea brushed his hair out of his eyes.

"You don't freckle and neither does Dwight."

Bea smiled. "Dwight's mother will be pleased. She has freckles, and was complaining that none of our children have family resemblances to her or her husband. Mark, ask Jan to cut your hair. You look like a shaggy sheepdog. Oh, now what have I said? He'll bark all through lunch and make his hair fall over his eyes even more."

"Girls are easier."

"Just you wait. What are you going to call him?"

"We aren't about to buy a sheepdog."

"Funny girl! Aunt Emily needs to talk to you."

The time passed quickly and Dwight and Paul joined the party for a few days, riding and walking and eating in the open with food cooked over wood fires.

If only the sea was there beyond the trees this would be perfect, Emma thought, but kept her opinions to herself as Bea was in her element.

It was wonderful to be with the family that had meant so much in the past and now seemed even closer, but with this journey Emma's dream had been realised and she felt a quiet calm in the conviction that this dream could go on even when the two families were parted. There would be other times, other meetings, and the children cemented the bonds of friendships.

"When we come to England, I want to take the children to Somerset as well as down to the island. Johnny and Avril need to ride over open country and to learn to use our saddles instead of these armchairs."

"You are looking forward rather soon."

"I want them to get used to both countries and to love the English countryside," Bea told her. "You may not know this but when I came to America I cried for a week when Dwight wasn't around and I dreaded going back to London in case I refused to come away again."

"I guessed, and Emily warned me to say nothing to make you homesick," Emma said dryly. "It was strange that you should feel homesick. You took enough stuff with you to remind you of London. Our house seemed half empty after you left and Dwight must have been tearing his hair when he saw just how much old furniture you sent over."

Bea giggled. "I still sit in that tatty old chair when I feel blue but I found Avril in it one day sucking her thumb and feeling unwanted. There must be more than horsehair in the stuffing."

"I think that Paul talked to London yesterday and contacted the airport. That means we shall be leaving."

"It's sad but not all that sad. I can reach out and almost touch you across the ocean in future, and think of the wonderful things we can store up to tell each other."

"Don't come to the airport. I hate goodbyes, and Mark and Rose could be difficult."

"He can ride that morning and Rose can take a few small wrapped gifts to undo on the plane."

"I'll give your love to Aunt Emily and Janey. George is safely married and I can feel free from him completely."

"When do you see Clive?"

"He will be with Aunt Janey on the island for a while, so I must make time to take Rose there for a day or so and I hope he'll visit us with Aunt Janey and help to fill the gap that Mark will leave."

Everything was suddenly rushing into the future and Emma hardly drew breath before they landed at London Airport. America faded away, but not the dreams she'd discovered and stored in her memory. She was happy.

A familiar figure waited by their car and Mick waved. "Welcome back," he said.

Emma and the Leprechauns

One

"You don't even look tired, sister." Eileen regarded Emma Sykes with an almost disappointed expression.

"We've been spoiled for so long that we were quite fit enough to face the plane journey home, and it was very comfortable." Emma laughed. "Having such a good housekeeper and seeing everything so immaculate helped, and I think I am quite unnecessary here and might go back to the States."

"Don't you dare! We've missed you something awful and Jean has been so excited that she will be playing with Rose again, you wouldn't believe."

Paul Sykes grinned and followed Mick into the office, noticing the air of confidence that showed how well Mick had reacted to the added responsibility of being in complete charge of the psychiatric clinic accounts and the general running of the establishment for so long while his employer lectured in America.

"I think you'll find everything OK, doc," Mick Grade said. "There were a few grumbles from some of your patients who wanted you and not a stranger to treat them, but most of them soon got used to Dr Forsyth and nobody really threw a wobbly. I promised the others

1

I'd book them in for appointments with you as soon as you felt like taking over, but most of the old lot needed help before you came back and you were away for so long that they finished their sessions with Dr Forsyth and liked him. The new ones have never met you. I've left a list of old patients who definitely want to see you, but I think it's more the fact that they like you as a person that makes them feel you're a friend. I've left the list on your desk and I'll get in touch with them when you're ready."

"Good thinking," Dr Sykes said approvingly. "I have to see some people today, but I can start a few sessions again in a day or so." He glanced in the desk diary. "Has it been as busy as this all the time we've been away?"

"No." Mick laughed. "Word got about among the medics that you were away and they hung back. There are a few fresh referrals now. They don't all know Dr Forsyth yet and they prefer you, but he's been a good locum and has been quite busy. Always cheerful and seems to enjoy it." Mick grinned. "Doesn't work as hard as you did because he didn't have the private patients to treat."

"He isn't here today?"

"Thought you'd like to nose around on your own first."

"Very tactful, but I shall be out for most of the afternoon."

"He said he'd be in for dinner tonight and, as my dear wife is besotted with him, that's no problem."

Paul laughed. "I gather that Eileen enjoyed being in charge as much as you did."

"Seventh heaven! Mind you, we missed you both. We all did. Mrs Coster was convinced that you would be killed by gangsters or little Rose would be kidnapped – but she's got a heart of gold really . . . sometimes." Mick shuffled some papers and looked cautious.

"Something wrong?" asked Paul.

"Not really. It's just Mrs Coster's daughter, Maureen. She really is good with kiddies and liked it when we said she could babysit and help out when Eileen was busy, but she wants to be a regular nanny and keeps on about it. Mrs Coster isn't much help as that's what she wants her to do. We can't afford a nanny for Jean and it wouldn't be fair to you and Emma to have you pay for one for both Jean and Rose."

"I'll leave that to my wife to settle, but Maureen might as well stay on to babysit and make herself generally useful on a part-time basis."

Mick looked relieved. "If we had another baby . . . or you and Emma had another, there's no doubt she'd be very useful."

Paul raised an enquiring eyebrow but Mick shook his head. "Nothing to report on that angle. Eileen made the excuse that she couldn't be pregnant while you were away, but you are back now and I'll have a few words with her. Jean needs a brother or sister."

The two men exchanged serious glances. "You'd love Bea's three youngsters now that they're growing up," said Paul. "I hoped it might make Emma broody, but we mere men have to wait and see."

"Tea and scones for now," Eileen said, coming in and putting a tray on the desk. "There's a nice shoulder of lamb for tonight. Dr Forsyth used to give me all his meat coupons and hardly ever ate his share here, so I saved them for a real joint when he brought Sister Bright over for an evening, and I still think in that way." She laughed. "I can't get used to rationing being over at last and meat being the last to come off coupons, but I've kept my ration books, to show Jean when she grows up just what we had to put up with for all these years. But there are still shortages, and I buy what I see when I can and put it in the fridge. It's got to be such a habit that I carry a newspaper in my bag in case I see something I can buy that needs wrapping up!"

Emma poured tea and sighed. "There's a lot that we shall miss that we had in America. It's wicked what there is so freely available over there; people waste a lot of good food. Who would believe that we still queued for the basic provisions so long after the end of the war? Maybe next year, in 1957, we shall be able to forget the hard times."

"We were better off than most," Eileen said.

"Is Sister Bright coming tonight?" Emma asked, and Eileen giggled.

"They hit it off right from that night you had them to dinner to see if Dr Forsyth was suitable as a locum. They see a lot of each other now and I thought you'd like to see her."

"No ring?"

"Not yet, but they are very keen." Eileen nodded wisely. "You can tell at a glance."

Emma stretched. "I ought to drag the girls away from Mrs Coster and unpack Rose's case. I gave Rose the presents for Mrs Coster and one for Maureen and I left them oohing and aahing over them. It seemed a good idea at the time when we bought them, but now I wonder if six pairs of coloured stockings will suit Maureen. She does have rather fat legs." She wrinkled her nose. "My mind went blank when I tried to choose something for Mrs Coster but Bea said she'd want something useful. We bought a pile of very nice bright pinafores and one really frilly one for fun."

Mick laughed. "She'll be wearing one as soon as she sees them. Don't be surprised if she spends tomorrow brushing the front steps so that the cleaner next door will see and admire."

Emma glanced back from the doorway to the warm and comfortable room and decided how good it was to be back home again. What now? she thought as she ran down the broad stairway. The idea of hard work was oddly satisfying, and she looked forward to meeting Robert Forsyth again; but she had decided while she was away that she must make sure she did less on the housekeeping side as Eileen was now officially the housekeeper and thriving on the responsibility.

There would be time to take Rose to visit friends, and she'd have free time for herself, unless . . . Unless she had another child. Her pulse quickened. It was possible. She felt a mixture of hope and dread and turned her thoughts away to the two little girls "helping" Mrs Coster to dust the banister rails.

Two floral blouses and a folding silk umbrella for

Eileen were in the main suitcase, and Emma partly unpacked enough of Paul's cases to find the leather jacket that they'd bought for Mick.

"It's better than Christmas," Eileen said as she held one of the blouses up in front of her dark dress. "No, Jean, you mustn't open the umbrella indoors. It's bad luck!"

"I bought one for Jean, too." Emma handed over the small umbrella and a matching rain cape and hood. "Rose loves hers and we used them twice in the States." She went back to the bedroom, suddenly unsure of what to do. Ridiculous! she thought. I'm home again and should be in charge, but I feel like a visitor. Paul was meeting colleagues in St Thomas's and Eileen was preparing dinner and obviously needed no help in the kitchen. Rose came into the bedroom and sat on the stool by the dressing table, dangling her short legs and looking into the mirror with an expression that showed she was not happy. "What is it, darling?"

"I want Mark," she said, and a tear escaped and rolled down her cheek.

"I know." Emma hugged her and the two faces reflected in the glass had the same expression. "Tomorrow we'll go and see Peter Pan in the park and buy ice cream."

"Pistachio? That's my favourite."

"I doubt if they sell it here. I remember vanilla and strawberry and sometimes chocolate, but I've not tasted pistachio in London."

"Mark likes strawberry," Rose said. "Why didn't he come back with us?"

Emma sighed and for the third time explained that Auntie Bea couldn't spare any of her three children and Mark, the youngest, wouldn't want to leave his family. "When I ring Bea, you shall speak to him."

"I'll be in bed," grumbled Rose.

"If you're awake I'll bring you down to the phone," Emma promised, and saw that the long journey was catching up on the little girl. "Bath and bed early, and maybe you'll wake up in time to talk to Mark."

The house was peaceful. Rose and Jean were asleep, worn out by the excitement, and Emma set up a drinks tray in the drawing room ready to receive Dr Forsyth and Sister Joan Bright.

Mick stood in the doorway and smiled. "It's great to have you back, and everything must be as it was. Don't think you have to ask us to your dinner parties and social things. We don't have them and we have our own flat and a life of our own downstairs. I believe in a bit of space out of working hours," he said bluntly.

"What a wise creature you are, Mick, but you'll have a welcome-home drink with us, won't you?"

"Sure. Business as usual tomorrow?"

"Yes, business as usual, but Paul and I were talking about you on the plane and decided that you and Eileen will need a holiday after all the responsibility we left for you. Any ideas? My Aunt Emily on the Island has said often enough that you're welcome to use my cottage there at any time, but perhaps there are other places that might appeal more?"

Mick sighed. "Eileen wants to go there, but if I can twist her arm I'd like to go to Ireland."

7

"Of course, you are half Irish and must have family there."

"Not really. Maybe an old aunt or two, but we've never kept in touch and I shan't visit them. I haven't been there for years but I like the people and I think Jean would have a good time. They like kiddies over there."

Emma heard the front doorbell and hurried to meet her guests, but said to Mick as she left the room, "Make any arrangements you like and we'll fit them in. Do it soon – you both deserve a rest and a change."

Joan Bright looked pretty and had the kind of expression that hinted at a deep contentment. She hugged Emma and Robert Forsyth grinned and kissed Emma's cheek. "It's good to see you again," he said.

"Paul and I have so much to thank you for, Robert. I doubt if he would have been able to concentrate on his work in the States without knowing that you were here in charge of his patients." Emma's eyes twinkled. "Not that you look worn out. I think this place suits you . . . or something does. And nobody would think that Joan was a hard-working casualty sister."

Joan blushed and removed her left glove. The ring sparkled under the hall light and Emma caught her breath. "We decided yesterday before you came back, as we have to plan our future, together if possible."

Robert looked serious. "When this job ends I could go anywhere, and I can't leave Joan at Beattie's and risk losing her."

"Let's have a drink to celebrate your engagement," Paul said, and Emma realised that he had been listening from the stairs. "Wonderful news," he added warmly and led the way to the drawing room. "Drinks now and dinner while we bore you with talk of America, and shop-talk about work here can wait until coffee-time."

"I should have rung Aunt Emily," Emma said.

"As you'll need at least an hour, leave it until tomorrow," Paul said drily. "Better still, pack a bag and visit her for a few days. Rose is upset at leaving her friends and Aunt Emily is good for her."

"I can't go now," Emma began.

"Why not? Cheers," Paul said dismissively. "Have some of these Yankee crisps. Not as good as ours but not bad."

"Do they come with a twist of blue paper of salt in each packet, like ours?" asked Robert.

"Nothing so sophisticated. All neat and tidy in a box, but almost too salty. However, can't look a gift horse as they say, and we can go back to Smith's crisps next week."

Emma felt nostalgic as the meal progressed and the picture of life with Bea, Dwight and the children unfolded. Paul said little about the work there until coffee was being poured, then eyed Robert speculatively. "Have you decided what you'd like to do?" he asked.

Robert shrugged. "I've had two offers, one from Wales and one from Canada, which would mean a fairly traumatic break for a number of years." He glanced at Joan, who sat very still but looked pale. "It's a good offer but we both prefer to stay in England and Joan wants to go on working."

"Tell me, did you really enjoy working here?"

"It was marvellous, and I had the feeling that I was doing some good with at least five patients who really need long-term therapy."

"And you hate the idea of handing them over to me?"

Robert looked embarrassed. "It's not that." He grinned. "I don't think so. But in a way you're right. They trust me."

"Then why not continue with the treatment?" Paul said casually.

"What do you mean? If I take another job that will be impossible."

"Not if you stay here and work with me."

"But I can't do that . . . can I?"

"I asked Mick to give me a run-down about expenses and bookings and a lot that I had no idea we'd need to study about the private patients. I asked Dr Shilton to take over while I was away, as I wanted a salaried locum here to deal with just the National Health patients. I couldn't expect my private patients to accept a new man who wasn't a recognised consultant. In any case, it would have overloaded you, as it has me at times."

"I had noticed," Emma said with feeling.

"Mick is wonderful. He works hard and has a fund of common sense that outweighs any lack of formal education. He says very firmly that I need and can afford a partner. One man can't be on call all the time and everyone needs regular breaks covered by someone who really knows about the clinics." Paul smiled. "I heard quite a lot about you today, Robert.

Shilton handed me back my patients and suggested you were ready to take some of them, as he'd heard how well you managed the National Health list."

Robert's voice was unsteady. "Do you mean you want me to stay on a permanent basis?"

"I'm offering you a junior partnership unless you have other plans."

Joan Bright sank her head on to her hands and gave a strangled sob. When she looked up her eyes were full of tears. "What a wonderful engagement present," she said.

"That's a relief," Paul said lightly to break the tension. "I couldn't go through all that fuss, interviewing suitable and unsuitable candidates again."

"I'll keep the flat in Covent Garden and use the rooms I've had here while you were away, if that's OK?"

"We'll discuss what alterations we'll need to make another spare room into a second consulting room tomorrow. It will be a relief to get you settled: I may have more lectures to give and that will leave the bulk of the work with you for a while," Paul said apologetically.

"Fine. I want to earn my keep!"

"More lectures?" Emma asked.

"Some I can do alone if they take only a weekend, but others might be longer and you'll have to hold my hand. You know how I loathe lonely hotel rooms," Paul said.

"Not yet I hope," Emma said with feeling. "We've just arrived back and I have a hundred things to do and people to visit."

11

"Times change," said Robert. "Paul has so many contacts now and is important in the profession."

"It cuts both ways," Paul replied. "I have prestige and work I enjoy, but increasingly there will be times when I don't treat patients, but just talk about how it should be done."

"The price of fame," Robert said drily. "Maybe some day I should be so lucky! But lectures are important and the next generation of psychiatrists will need you, Paul."

"I do seem to have achieved a reputation for the treatment of battle fatigue and the functional disorders caused by trauma," Paul admitted. "But I enjoy the hands-on, one-to-one situation between doctor and patient and would hate to miss that. I think one's sensitivity could become blunted by all the theory and no human contact."

Joan sighed. "I know what you mean, Paul. We find the same thing happening in nursing. If a nurse is good, she has promotion to ward-sister status or in one of the departments such as theatre or my department, casualty, but we either find that we are indispensable in that category and stay on that salary or we are shunted up to an admin post where we lose touch with the everyday life of a department." Her laugh was without humour. "Often the ones who are not very efficient as working sisters are given admin jobs with increased salaries just to get them out of the way of doing something harmful on the practical side. I can think of at least two who should not be in charge of a busy ward, so they have been promoted out of harm's way, and now they swan about looking very important."

"You know you'd hate that," Robert said firmly. "I heard on the grapevine that you'd refused to be home sister."

"Who told you that?" Joan looked indignant and then smiled. "Can you imagine me checking rooms for new nurses, making sure they come in before midnight and all the silly things to do with linen and laundry?"

"I believe you'd soon be out of a job if you were home sister," Emma said. "I hear that soon such jobs will be done by what amount to civil servants with no hospital background at all."

"As it hardly affects the patients, I can see why it would free real nurses for more important work; and if they allow nurses to live outside the nurses' home and have private lives of their own it will be impossible to impose all the silly rules that have tied nurses in training for so long." Joan laughed. "Until they open that door, I'd better get back to my chaste room in hospital! I'm on duty tomorrow morning, so we'd better go now, if Robert is ready."

Two

Emma sounded the motor horn and Rose tried to open the car door as Emily Dewar walked down the garden path to the gate. "Are you sure you want us in the house? We can go to the cottage," Emma suggested.

"I'll see more of you here. If Rose is in bed, you'll be tied, so park that thing over there and bring in your bags. I've got the kettle on the boil."

"When wasn't a kettle ready for tea in this house?" Emma released the door latch and Rose flung herself towards her great-aunt Emily.

"Steady! You've grown so much you'll have me over," Emily said with barely hidden delight. "Come in and get your coat off and tell me all about America." Emily accepted Rose's hugs but made no attempt to embrace her niece. Emma smiled, knowing how much this visit meant to the elderly spinster aunt who had been more than a mother to her all her life. Outward signs of affection had never been Emily's way, but the love she felt for Emma and now Rose was there as she said, "You look well, I must say."

Rose carried her own small case and put it in the large cot that Emily kept for her use and had used for Clive, Rose's cousin, when he was small enough to fit into it.

Emily looked amused. "You're staying then?"

"Yes, and I want to see the chickens next door."

"Play with your Noah's Ark while Aunt Emily and I have a cup of tea and then we'll walk to the farm and buy some eggs, if we need any."

Emily added a generous tot of whiskey to her own cup and handed Emma a less lethal brew of weaker tea and milk. "Now tell me how Bea is, and the children." Emily's dark brown eyes glowed both anticipation and for the next half an hour Emma recounted details that she knew she'd want to hear, the amusing episodes and the less pleasant details of the time when they'd thought that Mark had been lost or stolen – but he'd been found hiding in the trunk of Dwight's car.

"And little Rose sat on a pony?"

"She loved it."

"My father would have liked that. He was a fine horseman and tried to make us all take to the saddle, but we were no good at it."

"Bea sent her love and hopes to see you soon if Dwight can spare the time. He may have to come over on official duty so keep your fingers crossed."

"They can't come for another month or so but I shall see them again when they come to London."

Emma laughed. "I might have known that *you* could tell *me* that. You were also right when you said we must watch Mark, and to warn Bea that someone was stealing her trinkets. Dwight now regards you as his personal

15

oracle and he wants to know when you're going over to sort out the White House!"

"Silly monkey!" Emily said but blushed slightly.

"Now for *your* news."

"Not a lot to tell. You know that George and Margaret were married soon after you left for the States." Emma nodded. "Nice wedding. His mother was shedding a few tears of happiness. Janey always was a bit like that, but it was a relief to her that George seemed to have got over his crush on you."

"It could never have been possible," Emma said firmly. "First cousins, and other things like the fact that I love Paul. Now that I have Rose and George has Clive from his first marriage, any closer relationship between us gets ever more remote. He does love Margaret. He said so. They have a lot in common and they're good together. The fact that they have both suffered helps to give them mutual sympathy."

Emily gave her an old-fashioned look. "Just as well you were in America and stayed away long enough for them to get their bearings."

"That's ridiculous. He's . . . cured, and they'll be very happy." Defiantly, Emma looked at her aunt. "When we're settled I intend inviting them to stay. Paul thinks it's a good idea and I want to get to know Margaret. I've met her only once or twice and I like what I saw."

"Give it a few weeks." Emily's gaze on the glowing fire that she kept alight winter and summer was steady and absorbed, as if she saw visions in the caverns of red coals. "George is happy, but she needs time."

"What do you mean?"

"She lost her first love at sea and she needs George to be completely hers. Inside, she's frightened of losing him, not by death this time, but to another woman."

"But she knows he meets many attractive women in the Admiralty and onshore bases, and they mean nothing to him. They chose each other, Aunt Emily, and they had enough faith to be married!"

"Not just any other woman, Emma. You."

"I can't listen to this. When I saw George here before we went to the States, he was calm and friendly but that's all. He will remember me with affection, family affection, but that's all."

Emily looked at Emma's flushed face. "I agree that you have nothing to fear from George, but you can't avoid the fact that he was in love with you and there will always be a trace of that left whatever happens. In her mind, Margaret might believe he still hankers after what she imagines might have been."

"Sometimes you talk rubbish, Emily Dewar," Emma said. "It's time I fetched the eggs with Rose, before she goes to bed. Anything else you need from the farm?"

"Take the small basket for Rose and let her find the eggs. Take your time: the casserole will be fine in the oven for another hour. Rose can have a fresh boiled egg with toast when you come back."

"It really will be all right," Emma said, as if to convince herself, but she needed reassurance.

"It will be when she is expecting, but she may need help."

"Soon?"

17

"Soon enough. Now put Rose's coat on. It's turning chilly."

Rose ran on ahead, waving her small willow basket, and looked under the hedge where she knew some hens laid eggs away from their pens. She shouted and an irate hen clucked and flew out from the hedge, leaving an egg that Rose pounced on with glee.

Emma left her to search again and walked slowly up to the farmhouse. She was troubled. George was a friend and nothing more. Well . . . maybe a little more than that – a cousin for whom she had great affection – and she was proud of his achievements in the Navy. He was a good son to Aunt Janey, Emily's sister, and a loving father to Clive, the boy born to Sadie, George's American wife, not long before she died of meningitis.

She pulled at a long grass and plucked off the feathery top, sending a cloud of small seeds into the breeze. The green stem was crisp between her teeth and reminded her of picnics on the Downs near Tennyson's monument, and Philip, the boy who had wanted her from their schooldays.

Don't be stupid, she told herself. Aunt Emily is too fey at times and she sees what she thinks she wants to see. George and Margaret have been married for such a short time that any undercurrent of doubt has not had time to show, if indeed it exists, and yet . . . Thinking of Philip, she knew that she had never felt anything more than a sibling affection for him, and the pleasant *frisson* of sexuality between two young people thrown together by school contacts and sport.

She had been relieved when the handsome Air Force officer he became had gone to live and be married in South Africa.

George was different, she admitted. He was family and as such had a warmer place in her heart, and they shared a similar sense of humour, but he was no longer in love with her and she couldn't imagine him giving his new bride cause for concern.

"Emma! Your aunt told me you'd be here today." Meg Caws smiled and took the basket that Rose held up. "Four eggs? You have been busy," she said. "Come in while I make it the dozen and take some butter, too."

The old dairy was light and cool. Eggs were stacked ready for sale in cardboard trays while damp butter-muslin was draped over pats of butter carefully weighed into half-pound slabs so recently that beads of whey still clung to the pats. "Can you spare the butter?" Emma asked.

"We've more than enough for the shop, and rationing never was more than a joke with us. I used to make pats like this to a given weight in case the inspectors came nosing around, but I made some the old way to please the people up at the manor and did some in moulds like my granny used to do." She smiled down at Rose. "I've made one for you. Do you want the sheaf of corn or the cow's face, my love?"

"The cow." Rose gazed at the round slab of butter with the face of a smiling cow moulded on the surface. "May I keep it?"

"Only until you get home, then Auntie will put it in

19

her fridge and you can have some bread and butter with your boiled egg."

"It's too nice to cut up!"

"The weather's too warm to keep it out of a fridge and it would melt if you tried to play with it." Meg saw that Rose was about to rebel and changed the subject. "What was your favourite thing that you did in America? You are a very lucky little girl. I've never been in a great big ship like the *Queen Mary*."

Rose prattled on about Mark and the ponies, and Mark, and Mark, until Emma tried to keep him out of the conversation. "We must go back. Aunt Emily will think we're lost. Thank you, Meg. Aunt Emily said to put the eggs and butter on her bill, and she'd like another dozen eggs the day after tomorrow as she wants to make cakes."

Emma walked along the lane by the farm and stopped to unlock the door of her cottage. She glanced in each room to make sure there was nothing urgent needed there. Wilf, the handyman, had left fires laid, and the stove and windows shone. If Mick and Eileen chose the island for their break, the cottage would be neat and tidy and welcoming, but when she took Rose back to Aunt Emily, boiled eggs and fresh bread and butter she wondered if they would use the cottage or go to Ireland instead.

"Have you ever been to Ireland?" she asked when Rose was in bed and Emily was serving the rabbit and dumpling casserole.

Emily paused with the serving spoon over the dish.

She gave the rabbit a prod and ladled joints out on to plates. "What brought that on? You aren't thinking of going, are you?"

"No," Emma said slowly. "At least I had never really considered it, but Mick has his heart set on going there and it did remind me that you are half Irish; and from what I hear the country is very beautiful."

Emily frowned. "None of us went there. My mother left her family when she married my father and pride made her stay away as they didn't approve of her marrying an English soldier and she was a lapsed Catholic." Emily thought for a moment. "She talked enough about the green fields and the goats and donkeys on the hills, the wonderful fishing and the lilting music played in pubs and at family gatherings, but she never would tell us about her parents and friends. Your grandfather didn't encourage talk of Ireland, and she was a peace keeper, so she kept her thoughts to herself."

"It must have been hard to leave all that behind and come to live in a strange land."

"There were times when I thought she needed to cry, but for all her sweetness she was a strong woman. You have her picture, Emma, and in many ways I see her in you."

"I'm glad. Maybe one day I'll go there and try to find something or someone with memories of people close to her."

"Eat up before it gets cold," Emily said briskly. "You wouldn't know where to start looking, and she was there so long ago that nobody will be alive who knew her. I never asked the name of her village or town.

21

They all seem to be called Ballysomething and meant nothing to us. We were heedless children and it never seemed important. She belonged with us and that's all we needed to know. Ireland was a foreign country and none of us wanted to kiss the Blarney Stone." She chuckled. "Mother did say that my brother Jack must have kissed it as he was so full of himself and never at a loss for words."

"Isn't it strange that when someone or a place is mentioned by a friend or in the newspaper, the same name crops up again and again? Since Mick mentioned Ireland, I've read two articles about it; one on the Ring of Kerry and one on the Mountains of Mourne. They sound so romantic, and a patient of Paul's who is Irish talked about his boyhood there, when he was under hypnosis."

"Did he give Mick the idea of going there?"

Emma's eyes widened. "I think you may be right. It wasn't a visit to Ireland that he wanted to describe to Robert when Mick was in the consulting room, but affectionate references to what must have been a very relaxed and happy childhood. His psychiatric trouble began later, in the war." She laughed. "He's very well off and tried to persuade Mick to leave us and go with him to his stately home over there to act as chauffeur, valet and general dogsbody, but Mick laughed it off. He said he liked the old smoke, and had a wife and child to keep him here, and his work with us was more important than being a general skivvy in Ireland, however well paid it would be!"

"But what he said must have made an impression on Mick."

"Enough to make him want to see where he had his roots. I know from experience of patients that Irishmen have a lot of charm and the ability to describe places and people very well."

"Mother used to say that some of them could charm the birds from the trees if they had a mind to do so." Emily shook her head. "She chose your grandfather. He had charm when he wanted something, and he was a hard man who knew what he wanted."

Emma helped herself to more mashed potato. "Some of the things you cook are Irish. There's plenty of potato left, so can we have colcannon tomorrow? It's one way to make Rose eat cabbage when it's mixed with mash and butter."

Emily lit an oil lamp as day merged with twilight and set it on the faded chenille tablecloth. Emma felt cosseted as they sat and drank more tea, and talked or were silent, in perfect contentment.

Emma glanced at her aunt's face, thinner than she recalled it from childhood but still strong and kind. The soft lamplight and the dying fire made shadows and wove dreams, and Emily seemed more Irish than usual as she sat with a small piece of crochetwork turning between her fingers. Emma suppressed a yawn. "It's been a full day," she said. "I'll get the present I brought from America and the parcel that Bea wanted you to have. Her father packed what she ordered, so it's really from Switzerland and not from the States. Bea knew you'd prefer the real thing as you don't care for American biscuits."

Emily gloated over the sealed tin of Swiss chocolate

biscuits and the slabs of milk chocolate. "Bea knows I like a nice biscuit," she said with satisfaction. "I shall keep these for when I'm alone or when Janey comes to stay. I'm not wasting them on Rose or you!"

"Very wise. I wondered if your feet were still troubling you? These might help in the house."

Emily slipped into the soft leather moccasins and regarded her feet with amusement. "As Mother would say, 'They're grand, just grand.'" She smoothed the line of coloured beads that decorated the fronts and the slender thong that adjusted the fit.

"They're real Indian moccasins; you can wear them out of doors as well as in the house. They're strongly made, of real deerskin."

"I shall wear them in the house. I may have dark hair and eyes but I'm not a squaw."

Emma heard her chuckling as she climbed the stairs to bed, and was soon asleep, hardly hearing the country sounds of the night.

Three

"We took you at your word, sister, but I wonder if it isn't a bit too soon."

"You both need a holiday, and I'm glad you chose Ireland. The North sounds a bit risky just now but you should be fine in the countryside of southern Ireland." Emma regarded Mick with interest. "You look Irish enough to pass for a local and Jean has the creamy skin and slightly auburn hair that shows her heritage."

"Don't worry about us, sister. There've been troubles in Ireland since Cromwell's time and I shall agree with every political opinion I hear over there. I managed to get on with Jocks and Pats in the Army and never had any trouble." He grinned. "You know me, a born coward."

"That isn't true! Sometimes I wish he was a bit more placid," Eileen said. "But he does get on with most people and gets his own way most of the time." She sighed. "I'm looking forward to it, but I hope it doesn't leave too much for you to do, sister, now that Dr Paul's clinic will be busy and he'll need you in there for most of the time." Eileen poured coffee and handed round the home-made cakes, making sure that the two little girls had plates to gather their crumbs.

"Maureen can take Rose out for walks while I'm in the clinic, and Sister Bright has some unused holiday that she's taking to settle their rooms here to her satisfaction, and she'll help in Robert's clinic too."

"Everything seems to be organised," Eileen admitted. "I wish it was like that everywhere. I hate to read the papers, and Mrs Coster gets very upset at some of the things she reads and takes as gospel truth. She was almost in tears about Princess Margaret."

"Something I missed?"

"They said she was being forced to give up that nice Group Captain Townsend. If ever there was a love story, that's it, and yet they aren't going to be allowed to marry as he's divorced!" Eileen sniffed. "The Archbishop and the Prime Minister both had a go at the poor girl and I think they'll send him off to a faraway place so they can't meet again."

"Nice-looking couple," Mick said. "But there's plenty of unmarried men she can have, and some have wealth and a title into the bargain."

"Are you suggesting she would want anyone else, Mick Grade? What if I'd been told not to marry you, would just any man have done for me? She ought to fight for him, or so Mrs Coster says."

"Surely she wasn't crying over *them*? That's old news. I found her in tears but then I had to answer the phone and couldn't find out why she was upset." Emma looked worried. "It must have been something more."

"She went to the market and saw her son who runs a stall there."

"One of her grandchildren isn't ill? They seem to

have charmed lives, in spite of their surroundings and living conditions. It must be impossible to keep rooms clean with all that smoke from the laundry chimneys next door."

"Sid was telling her that since Ruth Ellis was hung for murder, there have been rows in Parliament and the lawyers are having a fine old time as usual."

"When I heard that she was condemned I never thought they'd hang a woman. That went out years ago and most cases of murder have life imprisonment." Emma felt cold. She had seen photographs of the pretty young woman and suddenly the thought of that slender neck being subjected to the hangman's rope was frightening. What must the hangman have thought? she wondered. Could he forget his day's work and go home satisfied? "Mrs Coster reads all the newspapers that carry lurid articles and horrible pictures and seems to enjoy them, so why did this affect her so much? I know it's been in the papers for months and everyone seems to have his or her own ideas about capital punishment, but it's hardly news any more."

"Sid said that all tarts should be shot, not hanged like Ruth Ellis. He said she killed her lover in cold blood and hanging was too good for her! I think Mrs Coster is more upset about her son than about the hanging of a murderess. It's more personal than that." Mick put his empty coffee cup on the tray.

"Why?"

"Sid's girl jilted him and he's seen her about with another man, so he's very bitter. Mrs Coster thinks there'll be a punch-up," Mick said calmly. "If there is it's best to get it over somewhere quiet, but she thinks he'll do Maisie's new boyfriend a real injury. Sid's a big lad and he's been in trouble before, for a fight in the Mason's Arms last year."

"Mrs Coster talked to me about Maisie and said how much she liked her. She hoped it would make Sid more reasonable as she had a good influence over him. If they have parted, I know that Mrs Coster will be very upset," Emma said. "She might worry in case Sid hurts Maisie as well as her new boyfriend."

"Sid's a wide-boy with too much to say for himself," Mick said. "He means no harm until he drinks, then his fists talk louder than words. He dresses like a teddy boy and mixes with some very odd people. Most of the teds are OK but some carry bicycle chains and flick-knives, and I wonder if Sid is one of them."

"No wonder his mother is frightened," Emma said. "I must have a chat with her."

"I think he imagines strange things, like a man has DTs when he drinks too much. He swore he saw a flying saucer last week and started a fight with a man who said they were a hoax and didn't exist, but Sid swore that he's seen one like the ones they're seeing over Warminster."

Eileen sniffed. "He saw it in the bottom of a beer glass, I expect."

"A lot of people say they've seen them, and a man told the papers that he saw strange men peering at him from one that came down low."

Paul grinned. "I can't wait for someone to tell me all

28

about how he met little green men. That will happen one day, under hypnosis. It's bound to happen!"

"What if there *are* people living on another planet in outer space? It isn't impossible, is it?" Emma asked.

"Best ask your Aunt Emily. She's the one who knows what goes on everywhere!"

"No, Mick. I can't think of her talking to aliens from another world. She's far too busy sorting out her own friends and relatives."

"Any news that we should hear?" asked Paul with amusement.

"Nothing that isn't private," Emma replied with dignity.

Eileen looked anxious. "Nothing bad, I hope."

"Nothing that can't be put right for us, and she thinks you'll enjoy Ireland."

"I told you it would be all right," Mick said triumphantly. "If Miss Dewar says we'll be OK that's enough for me." He glanced at the clock on the wall and hurried out of the office and Eileen took the two girls along to the nursery. Paul turned to Emma.

"We haven't had time to talk since you came back. Did Emily say something that wasn't what you wanted to hear?"

Emma moved restlessly and fiddled with a pen that lay on the desk. "Nothing specific, but she is concerned about Margaret, George's new wife."

He nodded. "Go on."

"You aren't surprised?"

"Not really. George will never be free of you, Emma. Can't say I blame him," he added and smoothed her hair away from her troubled face. "Let's invite them to stay and make sure she's convinced she's the only important lady in his life."

"You've planned something?"

"I've told Robert about them and he agrees that she may need help."

"Aunt Emily said she'd need help but I thought it might be when she's pregnant, not that she'd need a psychiatrist."

"When she's here Robert will speak to her if she needs someone. I'm too close and he can be objective. I think he could be very helpful."

"It might be tricky. If she thinks we want to help in that way she may jump to the conclusion that we think she's crazy, or that I'm trying to hide something."

"If she talks to Robert, who she's never met, it will be in order for him to ask casual questions about her past and what she wants to do in the future. We keep quiet and just make sure she has a good time in London. What does she like? Concerts, rock and roll, shopping?"

Emma giggled. "We can try all three, but I don't think she's the type for 'Rock around the Clock'."

"You never know. Even cool-looking blondes like Bea have been known to do it."

"Bea has to be half American now, at least on the surface, and she always did enjoy dancing."

"Do you think we should lend Mick a car for Ireland? I mentioned it, but he seemed a bit unwilling to take it."

"Some people have had damage done to cars with English numberplates, so it might be wiser if they hire a car when they reach Dublin."

"At least we can drive them to the station and see them off. Why the pensive face?" He kissed her. "They'll be fine, and you'll be too busy to miss them."

"It's not that. In a way I envy them. I talked with Aunt Emily about Ireland and I believe I'd like to go there one day."

"We might have to do that anyway. I have invitations to lecture in Dublin and Belfast, and they would like me to go there soon."

"Why the urgency?"

Paul shrugged. "I seem to be the one they want as they have so many soldiers and civilians caught up in the troubles. There's a lot of battle fatigue." Paul looked thoughtful. "I met a doctor who was on leave from the Army after being stationed in Belfast. He hates his work there after seeing more torn limbs and wasted lives than he knew existed. I think he needs help as much as some of his patients, but as he's a surgeon and not a shrink he fails to recognise his own need."

"If Mick and Eileen leave in five days' time, we could be ready for visitors the next weekend, if George can get leave."

"Try your Aunt Janey. She knows what they do and when they're free as they go to her often to see Clive."

"Did you get through?" asked Paul later.

"She's going to hear from George tonight, so I left it with her to arrange something. That may be her now, but you'd better answer it as it might be for you."

Emma sat on the edge of the desk and eyed her

husband with curiosity. The Paul she knew sounded quite different from the Dr Sykes who spoke about patients and his work on the phone, but he was smiling as he handed the receiver to Emma.

"Aunt Janey? Yes, we had a wonderful time." At least five minutes passed before Janey was convinced that her niece had returned from the terrors of Washington in one piece, but at last Emma asked if she thought that George and his wife would be able to visit them.

"They're both at the Admiralty place in Bath," Janey said. "It's been wonderful for them, as George could easily have been in Scotland and Margaret in Portsmouth."

"So you think they'll come to stay for a few days when they have leave?"

"It would fit in very well. I want to go over to see Emily, and if they can bring Clive to you it would be a change all round." She hesitated.

"Something wrong, Aunt Janey?"

"No. George is having leave almost at once, as if he might be sent away, and as this awful business about the Suez Canal is getting out of hand, a warship might be sent there to look after British interests. George says that Colonel Nasser intends to nationalise the canal and throw out all foreign pilots and personnel."

"I thought the pilots taking liners through the canal had to be very skilled. Surely they can't let untrained men take over?"

"George says that we underestimate the Egyptians. After all, they have sailed the world for hundreds of years, just as we have, and a lot of Egyptian sailors and soldiers have trained at Dartmouth and Sandhurst and done well."

"Margaret must be worried in case there's a conflict when George is there. I hope they agree to come to us. I want to get to know her well, and if Clive comes too Rose will be very excited."

"Clive might help a lot," Janey said drily. "Nothing like a couple of noisy children to take Margaret's mind off her own doubts."

"You've been talking to Aunt Emily," Emma accused her.

"I have eyes too! Margaret is happy in many ways but George is as attractive as his father was and she's afraid of losing him." She sounded wistful. "I see my first husband every time George is here."

"George doesn't want other women, just as your husband wanted only you. When you were widowed and then married his best friend, Alex, it may have been second best but you are very happy. It's quite obvious that you have a good marriage, and a bond because of Clive."

"Yes, I'm happy, and I worry too much. I hope you're right, Emma. I know George doesn't run after other women but you were the first love of his life, before Sadie and before Margaret, and this meeting will be important to both George and Margaret."

"George and I are cousins and could never be more than that," Emma reminded her firmly. "If you can arrange to have Clive brought here or to George, and let us know when they'll arrive, we can do the rest."

"Do you think they'll come?" asked Paul after Emma had replaced the receiver.

"Aunt Janey seemed almost certain, and once they mention it to Clive I know they'll have no peace until he comes to London. He missed the Changing of the Guard at Buckingham Palace when he came here last and we must make sure he sees it this time."

"You seem pleased."

"There's no reason why I shouldn't be," Emma said shortly. "They are family, and Rose adores Clive." She smiled. "You do like George, don't you?"

"Very much, but I feel for him if he has two lovely ladies to tug at his heartstrings! Maybe I shall flirt with Margaret."

"You aren't the flirty type," Emma said with satisfaction. "And you wouldn't dare!" She looked at the rolled-up map on the desk. "Have you lost Europe?" she asked.

"Mick was looking at the map of the world and trying to seem unconcerned, and I doubt if geography is his favourite subject, but I think he's worried about the international situation. If our troops become involved with another country, he's still young enough to be called up, even if he was given a complete discharge and isn't even in the reserve."

"Why is he worried?"

"Suez is important, as George knows. Nasser was furious when Britain and America refused to pay for the new Aswan Dam in Egypt and has turned to Russia for help. To show his independence he's threatening to sink several ships to block the canal and says that we now have no claim on the canal and its future revenues. If ships can't use it, they will have to sail an extra six thousand miles round Africa to get to the Red Sea from the Mediterranean, which could involve our navy."

"That shouldn't affect Mick. He isn't a sailor."

"That's not the only trouble spot. He's been a soldier and he thinks that the situation in Hungary is dangerous too. From Mick's point of view the Hungarian uprising could bring our army into their conflict with Russia."

Emma looked worried. "So George might be sent to Suez, and United Nations forces could be sent to Hungary to try to make peace there. They say a huge statue of Stalin has been destroyed by demonstrators in Budapest and important prisoners have been freed by rioters."

"All we can do is to make sure that we do what we can in our own circle, and that means making Margaret welcome and reassured, and sending Mick and Eileen off on a well-earned holiday," said Paul.

"Our circle expands all the time. This time last year we had no idea you would have a partner and that Joan Bright would marry Robert. What a good thing it is to have a really big house that swallows up a lot of people."

"And that makes you happy?"

"Yes. We have each other and a very thriving clinic and there are a lot of people who really do like us. I am happier than I've been all my life."

"Me too, but I think this big house is going to need your full attention if you want to make your visitors comfortable. Eileen can help before she leaves for

Ireland and then, if you continue to daydream about us, I shall have to put Mrs Coster in charge!"

"At least she'll be smart in her new pinnies! . . . I must sweet-talk the butcher. We may have finished with rationing but some things are hard to get, so I must make sure of a couple of good joints of beef and lamb to feed the five thousand. I'll remind him that he has a piece of silverside in pickle for us. I hope they all like boiled beef and carrots and cold beef sandwiches."

Paul watched his wife hurry from the office, and thought how lucky he was in his married life and his work. He chewed the end of a pencil and looked sad. He hoped that Emma would not look as attractive as she did now when she talked to George, and that George really did love his new wife.

Four

Emma checked the freshly cleaned bedroom for the third time while Mrs Coster eyed her with deep suspicion. "Did I miss something, sister?"

"Everything is fine," Emma said hastily. "I was wondering if *I* had missed something, not you. Not everyone likes flowers in their bedroom, but that is only a pot plant and it does look nice there."

"They'll be in clover," Mrs Coster asserted. "You've made more fuss about this room than you did when Mrs Miller and her American husband came to stay."

"Bea is almost family – we've known each other for years – but I have to make friends with my cousin's wife."

"Don't try too hard," was Mrs Coster's advice. "Treat her like the furniture and let her help. She must be as nervous as you are as her hubby was sweet on you and probably is still a bit keen."

"Mrs Coster! That isn't true. George is happily married and has forgotten that he fancied me a little."

"If you say so." Mrs Coster sniffed eloquently.

"Any news of Sid?" Emma said to change the subject.

"He went off to his pal in Kent and said he'll stay until the harvest is over. They used to go hopping when

37

they were boys and Sid always said he might go on the land one day. Good riddance! They used to come home from the hop fields covered in dust and bits of straw and smelling like a brewery even then, as the adults had a ration of ale as part of their pay and the boys often stole some. He was getting really bad after Maisie left, but his pal knows him and won't let him drink too much. My other son is looking after the stall so he won't lose anything by not being there. Speak as you find, I say. My family stick together and help each other out and Sid has always been generous to the young 'uns so they like him."

"If Maureen could look after Rose and Clive tomorrow morning, I want to show Margaret some parts of London that she hasn't seen."

Mrs Coster shook her head. "Beg your pardon but I wouldn't. If I was you, I'd take the children to see the Guards and be a family. Kids make people laugh and be themselves, and she might enjoy it. Maureen can take over in the afternoon when they have a play and then go in the park."

"You're as wise as my Aunt Emily."

"I take that as a real compliment. I have a lot of time for your aunt, and it's time she came to stay here again."

"Mick and Eileen must be having a good time. The weather over there is warm just now. I'm anxious to know what they think of Ireland since my husband might have to give lectures over there and I shall go with him."

"Dangerous place, Ireland," Mrs Coster said with the air of a permanent resident who knew all the bad places and life-threatening incidents of the country. "You wouldn't take little Rose there, would you?"

"Of course. Eileen and Mick took Jean and had no doubts that she'd be safe and enjoy herself. When we were in America, I had a few bad moments and wondered if we were safe, but Ireland is close to home and I like Irish people."

"I can wear my best apron when they come," Mrs Coster said. "I do like the one with the frills. Rather saucy but very nice and too good to wear doing the hall."

Emma laughed. "Now who's making far too much effort for the visitors?" She looked at her watch. "Is that the time? I must get on in the kitchen if I'm not to be covered in flour when they arrive. I want to make some pasties and a lemon meringue pie."

"You've got a fridge full of nice things already, and they will be here for only four days."

"You forget that I shall be alone as far as catering is concerned. I think I depend on Eileen more than I realised."

"That's her job, and you have enough to do with the clinic and entertaining Dr Paul's doctor friends, but I must say Eileen has come on well from the poor little thing she was when Mick brought her here. She couldn't say boo to a goose and had no idea about cooking."

Emma made pastry and left it ready to use while she cut up steak, potato, onion and a little turnip for the pasties, and soon the smell of baking leaked out of the kitchen.

"Close the door or you'll have all my patients wanting to stay for lunch," Paul said as he sat on the edge of the kitchen table and munched a piece of pie that had fallen off as it was lifted from the baking sheet.

"Busy?" she asked with a disbelieving smile. "No! That pasty isn't a misshape and you'll have to wait an hour for lunch, unless George and Margaret arrive early and hungry."

"You've got flour on your eyebrow," he said tenderly and kissed her. "I've never seen you make pastry without getting paler and paler with white streaks in your hair."

She dashed to the mirror over the kitchen sink and turned to deny it, but Paul had escaped back to his consulting room where Robert was waiting to talk to him.

The last of the baking was finished and Emma smoothed her hair and hoped she didn't look too hot. She moved restlessly about the house, twitching a curtain into position, rearranging flowers and making sure the table was set for lunch.

Why am I on edge? she wondered. We have a lot of visitors and these are family so it should be easy; but she remembered the expression in George's eyes when they had last met. He had regarded her sadly, with a lingering memory of his earlier love for her.

That was before he married Margaret, she told herself crossly. He told me that he loved her, and they've had time to settle into married life and forget any hitches in their separate pasts.

Rose wandered into the kitchen, sleepy from her nap. "Has Mark come yet?" she asked.

Emma hugged her, revelling in her softness and the smell of flower-scented talcum powder. "Not Mark, darling. It's Clive who's coming to stay, and they should

40

be here very soon, so why not go down to Mrs Coster and wait for them?"

Rose held up a sandal. Emma adjusted the buckle on the one that Rose had managed for herself and made sure that both were secure. "I'll be careful on the stairs," Rose said, anticipating her mother's concern, and Emma shrugged: one more sign that Rose was growing up into independence. And when, five minutes later, Clive burst into the hall and Rose gave squeals of delight, she knew that Rose was badly in need of a brother or sister.

"Margaret! This is a real pleasure," Emma said warmly and hugged the rather pale woman who came into the hall with George behind her. "It's good to see you, George." She raised her face to brush his cheek in a formal kiss then turned back to his wife. "Come in and leave your cases for us to take to your bedroom."

"I'll help you up with it," Mrs Coster said, and Emma saw that the frilly apron was being flaunted in all its full glory.

"Let her do it," Emma whispered, "and please say that her apron is pretty!"

Margaret relaxed. "How kind of you, Mrs Coster, but isn't that lovely apron too smart for heavy work?"

"All the way from America," Mrs Coster said proudly, and stomped up the stairs with two cases, obviously delighted that Margaret knew her name and had noticed how smart she looked.

"You have a slave for life," Emma remarked with a smile. "All our guests have to be approved by Mrs Coster, and those who don't pass get very funny looks at times."

"I didn't realise *she* was in charge!"

Paul laughed. "That's the least of it. If she takes a dislike to certain patients she tells me what she thinks should be their diagnosis – and sometimes she's right!"

"Clive seems to have disappeared with Rose, so we have time for a drink before lunch, if Paul has finished?"

"All done, and Robert can join us for five minutes before he goes to lunch at Guy's."

"Can I help?" asked George.

"If you would. It's all there, I think. Lots of gin and mixers but a bit short on whiskey."

"I'll show you your rooms, Margaret," Emma said. "When we bought this house it seemed far too big for just two people and a consulting room, but now we fill it all and it's good to have visitors who know that they can do as they want without falling over us."

"It's lovely and has a very home-like atmosphere," Margaret said rather sadly. "I do love my work, but sometimes I wish that George and I had started with a home of our own."

"Is the house in Hampshire nearly ready? Aunt Janey said the two apartments were nearly finished and then you'll have your own place to furnish and arrange to your liking." Emma glanced at her guest. "I know Janey and Alex are looking forward to having you close to them when you're on leave, and I shall be relieved that Janey has a real friend to keep an eye on her as her arthritis is bad now."

"She's very independent and I wonder if she really does want me there."

"She needs you, Margaret," Emma said gently. "She

has reservations about the arrangement too, but it's hard for anyone as active as Janey to admit she needs help. She has enough domestic help to limit what anyone else has to do for her and Alex is wonderful, helping out with anything heavy. He has learned to cook when Janey's hands are swollen. Don't feel that she doesn't want you there. She hates the thought that you might feel obligated to them in any way and so holds back a little."

"They have done so much for us, giving us half their house and making it so comfortable."

"You have a flat in their house for when you need it but you forget that Janey will be for ever in *your* debt for lending her Clive to look after," Emma said firmly. "She thinks that it is wonderful as she found that with Alex as her husband she could never have more children. George is her only child and she'd wanted a big family. Clive makes up for a lot, especially as he reminds her of her first husband."

"I think she wants us there because of George, not me."

Emma saw the tense line of Margaret's mouth and sighed inwardly, but managed to smile. "My aunts are similar in many ways. They were brought up in a large family that generated its own happiness, but my grandfather was a hard man and discouraged any outward show of real affection. It wasn't difficult for some of the family to be like him. I know, as my own mother was a selfish and unloving woman, but Emily and Janey are different. They have a lot of love that they seldom show, except towards the children. Even now I'm allowed to hug Aunt Emily about once a year," she added lightly. "But she lets

Rose sit on her lap and hug her and I know that she really does love me very much."

Margaret looked surprised. "I can hardly believe that. She talks of you with great pride and affection each time we're there, and George's mother does too."

"That I can believe, but although they're devoted sisters they never kiss or hug each other and are not well disposed to strangers who try to be over-affectionate."

Paul called that their drinks were getting warm, and Margaret followed Emma, looking pensive.

Joan Bright handed out the drinks and Margaret was introduced to her and Robert. Clive and Rose were giggling over tumblers half full of orange squash which they were drinking noisily through straws; Paul watched them with a wry smile.

"They look good together," Margaret said with sudden warmth.

"Children do make a difference," Paul said, and glanced at his wife. Emma looked away: she knew he wanted another child, but there was no sign of one on the way even though she'd given up birth control since returning from America.

George stirred the ice bucket and took another ice cube for his drink. He smiled at his wife. "Margaret is wonderful with Clive and he loves her, so we have a family ready made."

Robert moved closer to Margaret and offered to freshen her drink but she shook her head. "That's something we both face in the future," he said quietly. "Joan and I have just become engaged, and I am anxious to know how it feels for a woman with a good career to give it up when she has a child. You may have to do that, I suppose, as Joan certainly will, unless you don't want your own children?"

"I want my own baby," she said with sudden passion. "I want a baby made by George and me." She blushed. "I am very fond of Clive, but I want our own baby and until we have that I shall not be safe."

"Not safe?" he asked gently, and she found that somehow they were sitting on a settee slightly away from the rest.

Margaret held her empty glass so tightly that Robert thought it must snap, so he took it from her hand. "I am in love with my husband and I want a family of our own but I can't be certain of anything." She looked at him questioningly. "Why did I tell you that?"

"Because we have much in common over this matter, and because people do talk to me."

"Why you, when I can't talk about this to George?"

"He's too close; I am not involved, but I have ears and sympathy."

She smiled weakly. "You're a doctor, so you know about people and their thoughts. Don't you find that a terrible burden?"

"Not often, and sometimes a doctor gains help for himself from talking to patients, in unexpected ways."

"I don't see that we have similar problems."

"Not the same problems, but there are some that concern the physical and mental welfare of two women faced with the loss of their careers when they bow to the needs of marriage and parenthood." He eyed her with interest. "Joan is luckier than you in that respect. She can carry on working in some capacity even after we have children. My clinic will need her and she will always meet people in her own profession through our mutual contacts, but you will leave the Navy and be . . . no, not 'just a housewife', but a much loved wife and mother, a homemaker."

"A housewife would be more correct!" She turned her face towards Robert, her eyes wet and her mouth contorted with anguish.

"You have a loving husband and you are in love with him, Margaret. The rest will follow."

"You don't understand! He says he loves me but he isn't mine completely."

"I believe he was a widower when he married you, and Clive is the child of that marriage?" Robert sounded as if he had heard only sketchy details of her past.

"I love Clive; there will never be the wicked stepmother syndrome between us."

"I suppose it's natural to wonder what Sadie was like," he suggested.

"Sadie?" Margaret looked blank. "Sadie wasn't important, except for the fact that she gave George a son. Janey doesn't talk about her with any affection: she thought she was shallow and selfish behind that glamorous façade and she was sure the marriage wouldn't last."

Robert smiled his understanding. "So you came along and made George really happy, being not only the wife he wanted but a WREN officer, a companion from the same naval background."

"You can forget Sadie. I think George did that very quickly. She was pretty enough to make any man want

46

her, but so are hundreds of sexy girls he meets in the services."

"What then?" Robert asked gently. "What more have you to face?"

"Nothing." She stood up and walked over to George.

He put an arm round her shoulders and smiled down at her. "How's my girl?" he said.

"Fine," she replied. "Did I hear someone call us for lunch?"

"I have to go to the hospital, or they'll have eaten all the food," Robert said. "It's an informal buffet and shop-talk, but the average medico is a starving gannet and it's survival of the fittest there." He grinned. "I'll be in tomorrow morning." He glanced at Margaret. "We must talk again," he said. "I enjoyed meeting you, and I think George is a very lucky man."

"I second that," George said, and when he smiled at his wife it was plain to see his sincerity, but Margaret blushed in sudden confusion, as if he'd made a remark that she welcomed but couldn't quite believe.

Lunch was lightened by the presence of the two children who were excited at the prospect of seeing the Changing of the Guard at Buckingham Palace and the waxworks at Madame Tussaud's.

"Not all on one day," Emma warned them. "We'll be worn out, and Margaret and I want to see the shops."

"Oh, *no*," they groaned. Clive was sitting next to Margaret and looked at her with pleading eyes. "We *are* going to see the Maritime Museum, aren't we?"

She smiled. "I wouldn't miss it for the world."

"Thanks, Maggie Mum," he said and hugged her, to the detriment of the forkful of salad she held in her hand.

"Maggie Mum?" George looked amused and puzzled. "When did you decide on that name?"

"She told me she wasn't my real mother so I can't call her Mummy or Mother, and she's not just a relative like Auntie Emma. We had to think of something nice as she's my friend."

"I see." George lifted an eyebrow and laughed. "I wondered how long it would be before you both came to some kind of decision and that does do as well as any, if you like the name Maggie. Why Maggie?"

"She said she was called Maggie at school and I like it," Clive said with satisfaction. "I like having a Maggie Mum who is a kind of sailor and likes boats."

Emma smiled. So I'm just a relative, she thought. It put distance between her and her cousin George in a natural way. "When you see the scarlet uniforms and huge bearskin hats tomorrow you may want to be a soldier instead of a sailor," she said.

Clive looked at her as if trying to convince a baby of limited intelligence that he knew best. "You don't understand. We're sailors in our family, aren't we, Daddy?"

"Yes, sailors are different," George agreed.

Five

Emma parked the car in St James's and Margaret handed the bulging brown paper bags to the children. "We can't see the Guards for another half an hour, so we'll feed the ducks in the park first."

Rose skipped down the broad steps into the park and ran over to the lake, followed by Clive who, being older, tried to appear unmoved by the excitement of the morning. The leaves were dark and the grass had yellow patches where many feet had trodden. The area round the bandstand was almost bare after the dry spell, and Emma felt as if autumn was not far away, but knew that it was in her mind rather than a reality as there were likely to be several weeks of hot weather to come before the chill started.

Ducks of every description fought and chivvied each other as they saw the crusts being thrown from the bridge. The water was turbulent with bright feathers and quacking beaks.

"I want that one with the green feathers to have my bread," Rose stated, and was delighted when he roughly thrust away a couple of dowdier birds. She looked at Emma with sparkling eyes. "Why don't we come here sometimes, Mummy?"

"I thought this park was very popular, especially with children," Margaret said.

"We use the park nearer home, and they like to look at Peter Pan," Emma said. "I came here a lot when I was training. It was a place where friends arranged to meet, just as the National Gallery was a good place if it was raining."

"Had you forgotten how much you enjoyed it?" Margaret eyed her with curiosity. "Or is it a place that you want to forget, because it holds memories . . . as it does for me?"

Emma glanced at her sharply. "Times change, people come and go and some meetings all over the West End were good and some bad. You're right. There are memories here that are firmly in the past, mostly to do with my fiancé, who died in Belsen, trying to help in terrible conditions when the camp was liberated. I don't often actively remember him and other friends I made during the war but sometimes, in old haunts, I feel sad, as if remnants of happy and miserable times are there beyond a veil."

"I know exactly what you mean. I came here on leave with my fiancé and we had so little time to discover each other." She laughed. "I swear the ducks are the same ones we fed all that time ago, but I haven't been here since then."

"How strange," Emma said slowly. "You and I have both been engaged to men who died, but now have husbands who are right for us." She smiled. "We're the lucky ones, and when I look at Rose and think that she might never have been born I am deeply grateful to whoever arranges such things."

"Did you miss him very much?"

"Paul was there in the background, ready to help and hoping I would fall in love with him, which I did, and realised that he was a better, kinder man and would make a better father than Guy would have done."

Margaret looked across the lake as if she wanted to keep her mind detached from the woman at her side. "Were there other men?"

Emma made herself answer calmly. "A childhood sweetheart who was just a warm friend and not really for me; one or two patients who swore undying love; and I was asked to marry a wealthy man who had a manor house, horses and all the trimmings of rich country and county life. But I think that one's own heart dictates what is suitable and I turned him down, much to his mother's chagrin, as she thought he should have turned *me* down."

"That must have been fun." Margaret smiled more normally. "I've met women like that, high-ranking service wives who can be very arrogant."

Will she mention George? Emma wondered. "And you? As an attractive woman you must have had other boyfriends?"

"A few, before I was engaged, but I confess that when I met George, which was before my fiancé died, I fell in love with him and in my heart I knew I couldn't marry the man who thought I was in love with, even if I never saw George again." She took a deep breath. "George ruined any other man for me, and I couldn't believe it when he seemed to like me a lot and was sympathetic

51

when my fiancé died, but I never thought fate would let me marry him."

"George was your fate, as Paul is mine," Emma said. "We have the future settled as far as love and contentment go."

Margaret screwed up the paper bags that were now empty and gave them to Clive to put in the rubbish bin. "If only it was that simple," she murmured. "Come along, children. Time to watch the smart soldiers. We'll walk along the Mall and soon we'll hear the band."

Emma paused to button the jacket that Rose had undone earlier.

What had Margaret meant? Life was now much simpler for her. She was married to a man she adored and who obviously loved her, she had health and a career that she could follow or give up at any time she wanted to leave it, and she had a future with no obvious clouds to make her depressed, and yet her insecurity was palpable.

"Look, Mummy!" Rose put her face to the palace railings while Clive tried to appear nonchalant, as if he saw the tall, bearskin-hatted men every day. "It's just like Christopher Robin in the song," Rose said, enchanted with the scene. "I wonder which Guard is the one Alice is going to marry?"

"He might be off duty," Emma reasoned.

"Or pensioned off, if he's that old," Margaret whispered and the two women giggled, finding a rapport that had not been there when they fed the ducks.

The spark of humour and the spontaneous giggle transformed Margaret's face, and Emma saw the pretty girl whom George now loved. "We can have something to eat in a Lyon's Corner House, unless you know a better place," Emma suggested. "It's ages since I came here, but it used to be a convenient place where girls could eat unmolested by men trying to pick up young nurses and servicewomen. The crimson plush and neat tables in the Vienna Café, with the waitresses who were nicknamed 'nippies', dressed in black and white, were a sanctuary for a girl alone or with another off-duty nurse."

"It was cheap, too," Margaret added. "And filling! Did you have Danish pastries as big as cartwheels with lots of lovely marzipan goo leaking from the coils?"

"I want a cartwheel," Clive said. He slipped a hand into hers and looked up at Margaret with an ingratiating smile. "Can I, Maggie Mum?"

"Oh dear, George says I exaggerate. Maybe they're only as big as ordinary buns, but we'll see what they have."

"We'll have to walk along to the one in the Strand; I heard the old Coventry Street restaurant might not be there any more. They've made the new one as much like the old as far as possible, with the old-style uniforms and green and cream tablecloths and trimmings."

"If they are going back to old times, they may have the kind of pre-war sweets they sold then. If they have any, we'll take a box of Nippy Chocolates back to Daddy," Margaret promised.

"I'll take some for *my* daddy," Rose said. "Then he'll give me some."

Margaret laughed and Emma inwardly blessed Mrs

Coster for suggesting that this kind of outing was better than having Margaret to herself in an adult situation, just looking round shops and perhaps a museum.

"Do we have to go back for lunch?" Margaret asked.

"No, I told Paul not to wait for us. The three men are capable of finding food and there's plenty of cold meat and salad and fresh bread, so let's have something here."

"Clive seldom has a meal in a café, as Janey insists that she can provide better and more suitable food at home, and most of his outings are close to home, with no real excuse for cafés, so this will be a treat."

"I do like you, Maggie Mum," Clive said, and forgot that he was much too old to hold an adult's hand. As they crossed Trafalgar Square he held on to Margaret with an unusual show of affection.

Rose stared up at the Landseer lions and stayed close to Emma. Pigeons gathered as each new party of people crossed the square, and Clive wished he'd saved some bread for them, but Rose thought they were too big and bossy and hurried to get past the fat, strutting birds.

Emma glanced up at the façade of the National Gallery where she had met so many people during the war.

"There must be thousands of ghosts milling around those steps," Margaret said. "Some of people in love, some tragic, and all a part of London in wartime."

"I remember," Emma agreed and thought of Philip, the RAF officer who'd come down in the sea off the coast of India and nearly died. It had wrung her heart when he appeared on those steps, gaunt, uniform hung on him, but recovering as far as his physical condition was concerned. He'd still wanted to marry her, even though she'd refused him long before his accident, but she knew she couldn't do so, however much she pitied him. "Come on, before we get maudlin!"

The open-slatted stairs curved up to a second floor and the whole restaurant was bathed in light. Rose unfolded the pale green table napkin and then tried to make another shape of it but finally placed it across her lap as she saw Emma do and picked up the menu. "What does this say, Mummy?"

"It tells us what there is to eat," Clive said in a superior voice. "I can read it."

Margaret read from another menu. "Not a lot of choice, but the children will like it," she said. "What's it to be? Sardines on toast, beans on toast, spaghetti on toast, egg and chips or fish and chips? I don't think we'll risk lamb chop and peas or pork pie and chips. I like to know what goes into pies and how long the lamb has been running on the hills!"

"Not fish either," Emma said. "We can get some tomorrow from our local fish and chip shop and it's very good."

"I can't see cartwheels." Clive was disappointed.

"Try Danish pastries," Emma suggested. "We can have them for pudding."

The Danish pastries were as Emma remembered them: fresh and delicious with thin white icing and lots of sultanas. They bought some to take home, even though Emma knew that by evening they wouldn't be as fresh.

"I must be getting old. That bun gave me heartburn," Margaret said.

"They *are* very filling," Emma admitted, but the children had eaten one each and couldn't wait to take the others home to eat later.

They bought small boxes of chocolates and candies, each with the picture of a "nippy" waitress on the cover, and went back to the car as Rose showed signs of needing a nap. Emma drove back to Kensington and Margaret yawned as if she too was tired. George came to meet them and kissed his wife. "I missed you," he said.

"We saw the Guards," Clive told him, "and I had beans for lunch."

"We fed the ducks and I had sardines and a big, big bun," Rose added, not to be outdone.

George laughed. "You make me envious."

"Let's give Daddy his sweets," Emma said and followed Rose up to the office. Robert left Paul and Rose to open the chocolates and eyed Emma with interest. "How did it go?" he asked.

Emma frowned. "We had a very good morning and the children were very excited. They're tourists in the making, and even Clive was impressed by the marching and the uniforms."

"And Margaret?"

Emma met Robert's steady gaze and shrugged. "Fine, I think, but she's not entirely happy. She said a curious thing when I said that George was her fate and Paul was mine and we were lucky. She muttered something but I did catch one sentence. She said, 'If only it was that simple,' and sounded bitter."

"George went down to meet you and seemed eager to see Margaret again."

"He loves her, Robert. It's quite obvious, but I don't think she believes him."

"He didn't pay a lot of attention to you while Margaret was there yesterday and I had a long chat with her. I agree that she's insecure, and maybe I should talk with her again." He grinned. "If you're anything like most nurses I've met, you're now dying for a cup of tea. Joan would rather have tea than the best champagne, which is good as I don't think we can afford champagne on a regular basis," he said lightly. "She accepts that I make a good cuppa so I'll do just that and you can make sure that Margaret stays to join us. See you in five minutes in the sitting room."

"No thanks, Clive. I won't have another sweet. That bun was very big and I doubt if I'll want anything more to eat today." Margaret accepted the cup offered and Robert sat companionably by her side, sipping his tea. "Tell me about this morning," he suggested. "How do the children fit in together? I once had a cousin who everyone told me that I would like to have as a friend and we hated each other on sight," he said cheerfully.

"Nothing like that with Clive and Rose," Margaret said warmly. "They have a nice easy relationship and find the same things funny. Emma is very good with both of them and is careful not to favour Rose too much when Clive is with her."

"That's important. Clive could have had a very rough time after his mother died and his father had to go back on duty. I know he doesn't remember his mother but she must have left a gap that a father alone couldn't fill. Relatives are so important, and now Clive is a very normal little boy with no petty jealousies or chips on his shoulder thanks to his great-aunts and now you."

"And Emma?"

"I doubt if she had much contact with Clive, as she saw very little of George except when she visited her aunt on the Isle of Wight." He refilled Margaret's cup and sat down again. "Emma has had her own problems that were no concern of George's and she didn't have the time or inclination to take on a cousin's child."

"What problems?" Margaret showed her disbelief. "She always seems so happy and settled, as if nothing could stir her calm. I think she could have anything or anyone she wanted."

"She has a vast experience of people through her work and the war and she has suffered from Guy's death and her own arid family life with parents who were cold. She recognises true values and would never take what wasn't hers to take or encourage anyone to come closer than was advisable or necessary. She's seen enough suffering to make her cautious about people and has no intention of adding to any other person's heartache." He watched her face. "Did you know that Rose was a miracle to her, as she thought she could never have children?"

"George has never mentioned it."

"Why should he? If he did know, then it was still none of his business, except for his interest in Emma as a cousin. He had his own life to find after Sadie. He

58

found you, and thank God you love each other – it's so clear that you do."

"I do love him."

"And he loves you," Robert said simply. "He loves his wife and has no place in his life for any other woman. You also love Clive, and that binds you even closer to George."

She gave a shuddering sigh. "You must think I'm a suspicious fool, or depressed and incapable of believing in the good things," she said. "I know he loves me and yet I don't know how deep it is with him."

"I think you have been hurt in the past and so has George." Robert laughed. "You may have had good friends who comforted you, but George had only his relatives, and older women can be a little maudlin and not what a suffering, active man requires."

Her eyes held an accusation. "He had Emma."

"Emma? No. Emma has had no part in his life except as a warm friend. She was an only child, like George, and missed having siblings. George is a good friend, although they have met so seldom. And there is a family link that helps take away any atmosphere between a man and a woman, making a relationship safe: there could never be a sexual link."

"You think that blood relations are different?"

"Truly, if they have integrity. The ancient laws have it right, and most people know instinctively that it is so." He stood and looked down at her with a stern expression. "Love and care for him, and you will find out how much he loves you, but never insult him by hinting he has any unworthy thoughts about another woman."

Margaret began to sob quietly. "I think I hate you," she said, then dried her eyes. "A part of me wanted to blame Emma for any imagined neglect that George might show me, but I can't blame her, and I don't want to. I like her."

"Are you all right?" Robert asked her.

"I'm feeling rather emotional today, that's all."

"Because you went out with Emma?"

"No. Strangely enough I did enjoy that, and I was relaxed with her and the children, but now I'm tired; I'll go to bed early."

"Margaret doesn't want any dinner," George said later. "She's in bed reading, and I'll take some hot milk in later. What did you have for lunch that was such a huge meal? Usually my wife can eat more than I can!"

"She said the Danish pastry was too big and gave her heartburn," Emma said, and regarded the now limp and unappetising buns with distaste. "Do you think anyone will eat them, or shall I throw them away?"

"I'm starving! They look OK to me," George said and selected the one with the most marzipan. He grinned. "I know! Granny would have said I'm greedy and a bun now will spoil my dinner, but I didn't have much lunch as I had to make a few emergency phone calls and could only grab a sandwich."

"Duty?" Emma asked.

"I have to see a couple of brass hats tomorrow morning at the Admiralty and needed to get some information. It may not be a crisis but I could have to go away." He looked serious. "Is it all right if Margaret stays on for a while until her leave is up? She's due back in four days and we would have travelled together but I may not be going back to Bath."

"She can stay as long as necessary," Emma said, smiling. "I hope Clive can stay on too. Rose adores him and it's helped to take her mind off Bea's family in America."

"You are a gem . . . but I always knew that." His smile was wicked and Emma shook her head slightly. George must never look at her like that again, even in fun.

"Eat up your bun and don't blame me if you have hiccups all evening," she said severely.

"Yes, Aunt Emily," he said. "You frighten me when you sound like her!"

"Good."

"Buns?" Robert pulled a piece of soggy pastry away from the rest of the bun and ate it with every sign of enjoyment.

"Not you too? I think they look revolting after being sat on by Rose in the car."

"Just what I need. I'm meeting Joan for a late supper when she comes off duty and, as one of my patients said when he had everything by mouth withheld before a test, 'Come on, Doc, let me have a bit of something. My stomach thinks me throat's been cut.' I shall feel the same by nine o'clock."

Paul left the office and joined them. "Where's Margaret?"

"She's gone to bed. Nothing terrible, just tired,"

George said with more vehemence than seemed necessary. "No headache and no temperature, just catching up after a busy day."

"I'll go in and ask her if she wants anything before we have dinner," Emma said casually. "George, make yourself useful and mash the potatoes in that saucepan, and then we'll be ready."

Paul eyed her with speculation and followed her from the kitchen. "Anything wrong?"

"I'm sure there is nothing but George hates illness and when Sadie died you remember how she was . . . Tired and listless before the temperature soared and she died of meningitis. George must dread anything that could harm his second wife, a woman who is usually fairly tough."

"So you made him mash potatoes while you cast an expert eye over her?"

She tapped on the bedroom door and opened it. "Have you changed your mind and could eat some beef?" Emma asked. "George and Robert have both eaten some squashed buns so there will be plenty of beef left over if they have indigestion."

"I feel a fraud. I had a nap and now I do feel hungry. I'll be dressed in five minutes."

Emma breathed an inaudible sigh of relief and the ghost of Sadie fled. "No headache?"

"Not now," Margaret said and reached for her clothes. "Just a kind of lethargy. I think I must be overtired." She rubbed her cheeks to take away the pallor and applied a bright lipstick before emerging for dinner.

Six

"Up so early?" Paul yawned. "And tea? It isn't my birthday or a national holiday is it?"

"I slept well and we were all in bed earlier than usual as Margaret was tired and George has to go to the Admiralty, so I thought an early breakfast would be welcome, unless you want stale Danish pastries?"

"I think I've eaten my ration of them for at least five years," Paul said with feeling. "If you have any more relics of nostalgic wartime food, do you mind trying them on Mrs Coster or someone else with a cast-iron stomach first?"

"You feel all right?"

Paul swung his legs out of the bed and stretched. "Only teasing. I never felt better. Come here."

"Paul!" Emma protested when at last he released her. "I didn't know Danish pastries had *that* effect."

"Buy some more and we'll set up a serious experiment."

Emma kissed him and rumpled his hair. "Breakfast in half an hour when I'm more suitably dressed." She belted her dressing-gown firmly and made for the shower.

Emma heard muted sounds from the bathroom on

63

the other side of the partition wall that separated the original bathroom into two shower rooms, one for her use and one for the guest room. She turned on the taps and hurried over her shower, thinking that George might want breakfast really early.

She dressed and was busy in the kitchen when George appeared. She laughed at his sleepy expression. "Bacon and eggs and toast, or are you another who ate too many buns yesterday?"

He looked blank for a moment and then smiled as if relieved. "That's what it was. Bacon and eggs sounds fine, as I have no idea if the top brass will give me lunch, but Margaret wants to stay in bed for a while and doesn't want breakfast. Now I know why."

"Those buns have a lot to answer for," Emma said. "Margaret said she had heartburn after she'd eaten one but I enjoyed mine. Obviously Clive and Rose haven't been affected. It's good that they will eat anything and aren't faddy over food."

Paul joined them, looking pensive.

"Anything wrong?" asked Emma.

"No, I was just thinking," he replied blandly. She gave him a sharp look, but he didn't share his thoughts with them. He asked what time George was due for his appointment and offered to drive him as he had no patient booked until ten o'clock. "We'll leave soon, as I think you need to be there."

George nodded and went to fetch his briefcase. He came back putting on the cap that completed his smart naval uniform. "Margaret's asleep, so tell her I said goodbye."

Emma watched them leave and slowly climbed the stairs out of the kitchen, then hurried to the nursery where Clive had a bed and Rose still had her divan with the cot sides. She helped Rose to dress and sent Clive to wash but warned him that he mustn't disturb Margaret as she was still asleep.

Rose and Clive were settled with cereal and toast and Emma was drinking a second cup of tea when she heard Margaret moving about outside the kitchen. She opened the door and gasped. Margaret was in her nightie, looking pale and trembling. "Back to bed; I'll get a hot-water bottle," Emma said briskly. "You look frozen."

"I'll be fine," Margaret said. "I'm better now, but I think I will have another nap."

Once in bed her colour returned to normal. When Emma made her suck a thermometer all was as it should be.

"I must have had a tummy upset," Margaret said. "I woke up feeling terrible and while George was having breakfast I was sick."

"Do you still feel like that?" Emma asked casually.

"No, and can I be very awkward and have some toast or something? I'm warm now and don't want to stay here."

"I'll put the kettle on again and make toast, unless you'd like an egg and bacon?"

"Just toast and marmalade and tea would be wonderful. Whatever it was that made me sick must have gone; I feel hungry now."

When Paul ran up the stairs fifteen minutes later Margaret was still eating and talking to Emma. "Good.

You haven't cleared away. I think I'll have some more toast," he said and laughed when Emma tried to slice another reasonable piece of bread from the end of a loaf that had been badly plundered. "I'll have the crust," he offered and piled it high with marmalade. "George is safely settled at the Admiralty and, from the look of several gleaming motors setting down a lot of caps with scrambled eggs and gold bands on uniforms, there's a lot of activity there today."

"It's almost certain that we'll move big ships into the Suez area," Margaret said calmly. "I packed a bag for George last week and brought it here as it could happen without more warning. We wondered if it would be today."

"George is very fortunate to have you to understand what naval personnel have to do," Paul said. "If you need someone to take you to him to say goodbye, Robert is free this morning and has no cases so he's at your disposal as soon as he arrives here."

"I'd like that," Margaret said, with a slight smile. "Robert is a very nice person. I'm sure his patients must respond to him very quickly and feel they can trust him."

The telephone seemed extra loud and insistent; Paul went to answer it. He closed the door to the office and listened. At last he said, "I advise you to stay there, George. You haven't a lot of time and Margaret will want to see you alone, not with a crowd of your relatives." He listened again. "I'm sure Robert will find the club, and you and Margaret can have a few hours together in private. She has your case and we all wish you the best of luck. We'll look after her for as long as she wants to stay with us." He put down the receiver and returned to the kitchen. "Action stations," he said cheerfully. "I heard Robert downstairs so I'll brief him if you want to get ready for him to take you."

"George isn't coming back here?"

Paul grinned. "I know I'd feel the same. He wants his wife alone for the few hours before he has to report on duty and he suggested his club in St James's. A private room with lunch there was what he had in mind, so don't hang about!"

"You almost *pushed* her out," Emma complained. "And don't we have a chance to say goodbye to George?"

"I think Aunt Emily would approve," Paul said complacently.

"Do you really believe I'd hug him with tears in my eyes and say how much I'll miss him?" she retorted.

"No, but he might have done something to make Margaret think things!"

"That's ridiculous."

"There's something more. You noticed that he was on edge when he thought that his wife was not well and had a headache and lethargy last night?"

"I confess I was anxious too. It was so like Sadie and the onset of her fatal attack, but I took her temperature and pulse and after that brief nap this morning she was fine." Emma looked anxious. "George must go away as happy about her as possible."

"He will be after this last private meeting. She looks blooming, and so in love."

67

"And pleased that she'll have him all to herself? Who suggested the club for their farewells?"

"I did mention that they'd have more privacy there, and he took the hint and told me to say goodbye to you."

"Thanks. I enjoy offhand, long-distance goodbyes," she said drily.

Paul looked into her eyes. "They'll be fine, but I wanted him out of the way this morning before he got worried again."

"You heard her being sick?"

He nodded.

"Sick first thing in the morning, doctor?"

"You think so, too."

"Yes, but Margaret has no idea and we must keep quiet until she's convinced she's pregnant. If George is away for a month or so, he can come back to a loving wife who has forgotten the morning sickness and is healthy and active."

"A little bit sad?" Paul kissed her tenderly. "We have Rose, and she's more than we thought possible so don't worry. If we are to have another child, it will happen, but if it makes you more settled, why not see Stella again and have an examination?"

"I thought about it, but wanted to leave it until we'd been back in England for a while. I tried to convince myself that my body wasn't ready for change after all the travelling." She smiled. "I know that's not true. I can't put it off and I think a visit to Beattie's might be in order now."

"Don't ring her yet. Maybe, if we're right, Margaret

might want a consultation to confirm her condition, unless she would rather have a naval doctor to see her."

"We're jumping to conclusions," Emma said. "It might have been a tummy upset."

"Mind where you're walking," Mrs Coster said in the hall. "Oh, it's you, Dr Forsyth. That's all right then."

She wrung out the floor cloth and stood up. "Gone to war, has he? My Maureen said that a sailor she knows had to report back to his ship and I told her not to get too sorry for him. You know what sailors are," she added darkly.

Robert grinned. "I'm sure that Maureen wouldn't fall for that sort of chat-up line, and it may be a false alarm and George will be back again later."

"His missus won't like it if he goes away just now."

"Why now in particular? She's in the Navy too, and knows that he might be sent away at any time."

Emma paused on the stairs and laughed. "Mrs Coster, you're as bad as my Aunt Emily, but this time you could be wrong."

Mrs Coster wiped her nose with the back of her hand and picked up her bucket. "You mark my words, Sister."

"What's all this? Am I missing something?" Robert asked plaintively.

The two women looked at him with superior pity. "And he's a doctor," Emma said.

Robert still looked blank, and Mrs Coster began to sing in a reedy, out-of-tune voice, "Rock-a-bye baby in the tree tops."

"How do you know?" he asked.

"Sick this morning, and, as my Aunt Emily would say, it shows in her face."

"What I like is a purely scientific diagnosis," Robert said.

"Come and have some coffee and leave the two witches to their spells," Paul called. "All safely delivered?" he asked.

"I can't wait to be married," Robert said. "It must let you lose all your inhibitions and life must be wonderful."

"It is," Paul said. "Margaret has a little way to go before she can really relax and believe that George loves her alone, but it's coming, and if they are expecting a baby as we suspect, that will make them really close."

"They were very happy when I left them. George said he'd put Margaret into a service car to bring her back here when he leaves, and that might be early this evening."

"Meanwhile I have work to do," Emma said.

"Can you spare half an hour first?" Paul glanced at the papers on the office desk.

"You need a chaperone?"

"Normally Mick would be here, but I need someone, and you especially, to gather your own opinions of the patient."

"Is he new?"

"I saw him before we went away and he wanted to see me again."

"Not Robert?"

"He wouldn't come to the clinic while I was away but now says he needs me urgently."

Emma's lips twitched. "I'll be there right beside you, doctor," she said. "Now what do I need to put in the consulting room so that I have no need to leave you alone with him? A carafe of water, a few fruit pastilles, a small cushion, a spare larger cushion and a warm rug in case he has hypnosis. I can't think of anything else, can you?"

"Let's hope that's enough," Paul said drily.

"You shouldn't be so devastatingly handsome," Emma teased him.

"I've asked Mrs Coster to bring him up here as soon as he arrives. The last time he came he wandered about the place into rooms where he knew he had no right to be and was late for his appointment. I think I hear Mrs Coster now."

"It's all part of the service," they heard and Paul grinned.

"She's using her West End voice, and I bet she's wearing the frilly apron."

"Ah, Mr Symonds. What can I do for you? It's so long since you came here that I'd come to the conclusion you needed no further treatment. I think I would like to make a few more notes." Paul had his hands full of papers and seemed not to notice the eager hand held out in an effort to grasp his. "Would you mind, sister?"

Emma nodded and helped Mr Symonds off with his jacket, untied his shoelaces and settled him on the couch.

"I haven't been well," the patient began.

"You could have seen Dr Forsyth while I was away."

"Not the same. I wanted the personal touch. I'm a very sensitive man, doctor, and I took to you as soon as I saw you." He smiled. "I like to think you felt the same, and so I waited."

"If you felt ill it was unwise to postpone an appointment," Paul said calmly. He took a pad and pen and Emma sat on the chair beside the couch while Paul sat further away. "I have your previous medical history from the hospital, but it helps to fill in a little of your background. What hobbies have you?"

"I don't bother with hobbies."

"How do you fill your spare time?"

"I go to a club after work and chat to friends, and some of them come round to my place for drinks."

"Do you have many friends?"

"They come and go, and some just don't understand me, doctor. I need people who really care about me but it's hard at times."

"Have you a girlfriend? Girls are often better at caring for people. Sometimes that's true of sisters too. Did you have sisters?"

"I have two sisters who are horrible to me. They laugh at me and call me names and they don't let their children play with me. I like children," he added as if that was a real plus in his favour. "I won't have my sisters in my flat, and when I had to go to court they didn't want to know."

He stopped, as if he'd said too much. Paul made a note and referred to a case history on the desk, then looked at the man on the couch with no change of expression. "I want to ask you about that. You were referred to this clinic by the court and I made an assessment at the time, but you didn't accept treatment and later, when I was away, you refused analysis."

"Could you go and get me a glass of water, nurse?"

Emma walked over to the table and poured a glass of water from the carafe. She handed it to the man, who looked very cross. "I want to talk to the doctor alone, nurse," he said.

"You may speak freely while the sister is here, Mr Symonds. What is your story about the court appearance? I have notes from the police psychiatrist but I want to hear what you have to say."

"That man wrote a lot of lies! I was up for shoplifting and he wrote that rubbish instead."

"Shoplifting at night in a public lavatory?" Paul raised his eyebrows.

"They had no right to show you that rubbish. It was all lies. I nicked some things from the shop and got taken short and had to go to the lavatory, that's all. That's why I was there, and a nosy copper nicked me."

"They arrested another man, too. He confessed."

"Copper's nark."

"That's over now, and you have had a clean record since then. We want to help you control your urges, not to condemn what you did."

Mr Symonds looked artful. "There's nothing wrong with my mind, doctor. It's physical. I have pains and I need a doctor to examine me thoroughly." He began to undo his shirt buttons, baring his chest.

"I'll make an appointment at the hospital for you to see a physician. I can't examine you here. I am a psychiatrist and don't do physical examinations."

"I'd rather have you, doctor."

I bet you would, thought Emma grimly, but remained silent.

"Sister, I'd like you to take a sample of blood for examination. That much I can do, to eliminate certain conditions that you might have caught due to your lifestyle." Paul immersed himself in the notes while Emma swabbed the patient's arm and found a vein. She drew up blood quickly as she had a feeling that he could refuse to co-operate even when the needle was in position. She swabbed the arm again after the syringe was full.

"That was a bit quick. I wasn't ready," he said resentfully. Emma smiled. She had a memory of a man who didn't want blood taken from him and pulled the needle out when it was half in place; he'd called her a careless bitch before the very butch casualty sister took over and would have no nonsense from him.

Carefully she labelled the phial of blood and put it in a thick envelope.

"I think that's all I can do at present," Paul said. "You asked for a physical examination and we must wait until that has been done and the blood has been analysed before we think of psychiatric treatment. I must impress on you that if they prescribe drugs you must take them every day, or you could end up in real trouble."

Paul turned away, leaving Emma to make sure that

the patient had everything of his own ready to take with him. She opened the door and followed him down the stairs.

"The doctor will be here all the time now he's back from America?" he asked hopefully.

"Not all the time, but Dr Forsyth will be here and Mr Grade is due back from holiday soon. He will be in the consulting room." She thought of Paul's repugnance for the man, even though he showed no sign of it. "Dr Sykes, may be away a lot quite soon," she said. "He has to lecture in Ireland and London and maybe the States again. That's why he needed a reliable locum to take over."

Mrs Coster watched the man leave and closed the door firmly after him. "Glad none of mine turned out like him. Some can't help it, poor souls, and that's sad, but worms like him are wicked. I saw him looking at that nice picture of Rose and Mrs Miller's three that you have on the wall over there and I could have hit him."

"He thinks Paul is going away, so he might decide he doesn't want to come here again."

"What a sauce!" said Mrs Coster.

"I think he should be admitted to a psychiatric hospital for treatment, but there are tests to be checked first," Emma said. "If he turns up here on some vague excuse, I rely on you to tell him that the doctor cannot see him and if necessary ask Mick to see him in the hall."

"He needs to have his flies sewn up and a dose of bromide," Mrs Coster said cheerfully. "I'll deal with him if he shows his face here and walks over my nice clean hall tiles."

Seven

"You don't need me to tell you, but of course the powers that be will want the relevant forms filled in." The obstetrician smiled. "I don't know what happens in the Navy, but I shall recommend leave for the next six weeks until all sickness has subsided, then duty as usual until the lump becomes too uncomfortable and you have no uniform to fit you!"

Margaret picked up her clothes and went behind the screen to dress. "I wish it was me, Stella," Emma said.

"I know, but it will happen, and they say that pregnancy is catching. I'll sign a form and then Margaret can wait outside with some coffee while I take a look at you. Any trouble?"

"None as far as I know. I left off the diaphragm in America and everything is regular. Not even a bad period pain."

"Does George know his good news?"

"He's out at sea, standing by Suez, and Margaret doesn't want to worry him, but now it's definite she might tell him. She's talking of leaving the Navy and settling down in Hampshire, and I think he will urge her to do that."

"George has one child, I believe?"

"A boy, and Margaret is very fond of him. He will also have an adoring grandmother in the same house but in a separate flat, so he will never lack for affection and care," Emma said.

Stella gently probed Emma's flat abdomen and then washed her hands and examined her internally. "Nothing abnormal here," she said at last. "I'll write you up for some vitamins and a boost to your hormones, but only a marginal amount as you are so healthy. I have no doubt that having had one child successfully you can have another. If we stimulate your thyroid, that will urge your other hormonal glands to do their stuff."

"Thank you, Stella. I'll do what I'm told and risk being in the sick stage when we have to go to Ireland."

"North or south?"

"Both Belfast and Dublin. Paul is in great demand now and we have a new partner who can cope while he is away."

"You go with him?"

Emma nodded.

"Very wise, if you have to stay in unfamiliar hotels that have no character. I hate those places, but my husband is very good and comes with me to what must be boring congresses. Not being a medic, he likes to skive off and look at old churches, and we meet up for meals and bed."

"He's a writer, isn't he?"

"Yes, and it means he can work anywhere. As he prefers to do the first draft of a book in longhand, that's easy."

Emma sighed. "I hope to see you again soon. Rose

77

is getting a bit spoiled with no competition and Clive isn't a lot of help as he does what she wants most of the time – unlike Mark, Bea's youngest, who has a will of his own and was definitely boss when we were in the States."

"Go home and forget about babies. If you worry about it then it will never happen and, as one old midwife used to say, 'The fruit will grow without you shaking the tree.' I've known women who adopted and gave up all idea of having their own babies as they thought it was impossible, becoming pregnant when they were up to their eyes in adopted babies and nappies and mumps! So enjoy Ireland with Paul and bring me back some shamrocks."

Margaret already had the bloom that clings to newly pregnant women and her expression was soft. "I still can't believe it," she said as they walked from the hospital and out to Emma's car.

"Have you written to George?"

"I shall write this evening and tell him that I'm fit and well and have seen an obstetrician."

"Good. Did Stella advise antenatal exercise classes?" asked Emma. "They're becoming popular and when I had Rose I was glad to have some sort of a pattern to follow with breathing and so on." She giggled. "We were all shapes and sizes and when we were on our backs on mattresses the lumps varied from four months showing very little to positive mountains that looked ready to be delivered at any moment. Quite relaxing and it was good to know that I wasn't the only one with frequency and backache!"

"Thanks very much! I'm looking forward to the back-ache!" Margaret said with dry humour. "Where shall we have lunch? I'm starving."

"Do you want a snack or a stodgy meal?"

"At the moment I could eat a horse."

"That isn't on any menu I know about, unless you want to pop over to France! As we're nearly there we can go to the restaurant in Dickins & Jones. I hear the food is fairly good but very filling. Restaurants have a tendency to major on pies, potatoes and gooey puddings."

"Just what I need." Margaret got into the car and turned to Emma. "Thank you for taking me to see Stella. She's exactly right for her job and gave me a lot of confidence." She blushed. "In fact, I have a lot to thank you for."

"Not really," Emma said casually. "Paul and I are enjoying your visit and you're welcome at any time. Why not stay for a while until the morning sickness is over? I believe Stella suggested sick leave from the Navy, so you either stay with us where I can keep an eye on you or go back to Hampshire and have to cope alone until George comes back."

"I hate to impose on you," Margaret said.

"I haven't heard that you have close family who would help at this time. Is that right?"

"I have a stepmother who is pleasant but who wouldn't be interested in me now. She works as a secretary and I think may marry again. It's three years since my father died and she's attractive."

"No doting aunts like mine?"

"None. You're very lucky."

"It's only in the last few years that I've been aware

how much we mean to each other. When George lost Sadie, they were wonderful and we all came closer as a family. George is so fortunate to have you, Margaret. You are the rock he needs. If you hadn't come into his life he might have drifted and been very lonely." She smiled. "Aunts and cousins are useful but he needed a wife to surround him with love . . . and a family to keep Clive company."

"You might have been better at it than I shall be," Margaret said, but refused to meet Emma's eyes.

"Me and George?" Emma hoped she sounded very incredulous. "We're cousins! I fell in love with Paul and George married Sadie. George is a very nice person but not for me and I was not for him," she added firmly. "You've met my Aunt Emily?"

Margaret nodded.

"You should hear her opinion on badly matched pairs. She's usually right. She said that George and Sadie wouldn't last even if Sadie had lived, and there's never been any question of George and I coming together."

"I really thought . . ." Margaret began, but Emma interrupted her.

"I envy you, Margaret," she said. "You became pregnant soon after you were married, but I had to work at it, with Stella's help, to have Rose and now I want another baby and I have no idea if it's possible."

"Has your Aunt Emily said anything about me?" Margaret asked almost humbly.

"She approves of you, and so does Janey, and when they hear your news they'll be over the moon."

"Do you want the rest of the potatoes?" Margaret

laughed. "Do you know, I feel wonderful but still hungry. I feel I'm being accepted into a very nice family and it's a good feeling."

"I'm glad," Emma replied simply, but inwardly she was relieved to think that Margaret had lost her suspicions that George might be in love with his cousin. "Are you going to leave the Navy as soon as possible?"

Margaret took a deep breath. "The Navy has been my life ever since I left school and I shall miss it, but I want to settle down to being a wife and mother. I know George would want that too, so yes, I'll write to the Admiralty tomorrow and be free to buy civilian clothes and put my feet up when I feel tired! Such self-indulgence."

"You look different already," Emma said, laughing. "Don't go mad and buy too many dresses to fit you now, as you'll be surprised how much weight you'll put on and need to have fresh clothes all the time."

"How did you manage with clothes rationing? In uniform it was easy, as we had only to buy for holidays and off-duty, and I had friends stationed abroad who brought me gifts of dress materials from the Far East; but you had to have maternity wear as well as normal clothes that would fit you afterwards."

"Bea's father travelled to Switzerland in the diplomatic service and brought a lot of goodies back for Bea. He was very generous to me too, and Aunt Emily had material stowed away from pre-war. We made a lot of our own clothes when we were hard-up nurses in training; looking back, I'm amazed how well we looked in topcoats made from unrationed bed blankets. Lace blouses were pretty and lace with butter muslin to use as linings was off ration too. Bea had a wonderful maternity suit made from crushed velvet. Sadie saw it and wanted one like it, but she wanted everything that anyone else had and sulked if she couldn't have it."

"I'll spare George that! I don't think I'm the sulking kind, and I'm so happy, I can't wait to tell him the good news."

"Ask him to bring you a couple of kaftans from Egypt. They're fashionable now, and so much more attractive than the 'sack' dress and the other odd designs that appear in Mary Quant's Bazaar in the King's Road. You'll find them practical when you lose your waistline."

They drove back to the line of shops close to the clinic in Kensington and took their prescriptions for vitamins and Emma's mild thyroid tablets into the chemist there.

"Mick and Eileen are due back tomorrow," Emma said. "I'm curious to hear what they thought of Ireland."

Margaret went to her room to rest and Emma sorted out clothes suitable for formal dinners Paul might have to go to in Ireland and tweeds that would be useful if autumn came early, although the weather was still very warm and a prolonged summer looked likely. Rose wanted to help and was convinced that any packing meant another visit to Mark in America.

"Not this time," Emma said sadly. "I miss them as much as you do, darling, but Daddy needs us to look after him when he has to go to Ireland."

"I can go to America on the plane on my own. Mark said he went on a plane without his mummy and daddy and so could I."

"Mark sat with the pilot when Dwight took him to an air show, but they didn't fly," Emma said gently. "Mark has a great imagination. We're going to Ireland to help Daddy. If we find a leprechaun we'll bring him back with us."

"What's that?"

"A tiny little magic man with green clothes and a floppy hat. He grants wishes to good people, and plays tricks on bad ones," Emma said, smiling.

"I'm good," Rose said seriously. "I'll wish for lots of things."

"It's no good unless you ask the leprechaun, and there aren't a lot of them," Emma added hastily.

"I'll find one," Rose said firmly and Emma wished she'd never mentioned the Irish folk myth.

"Daddy, when can we go to find a leppercorn?" Rose asked as soon as she saw her father. "I want to go to Ireland *now*!"

Paul grinned. "That's one way to make her want to come with us. I thought she was hankering after Mark and the States."

"That too, but she's intrigued by little men in green who grant wishes."

"I leave you to sort this one out," he said hastily. He picked Rose up and hugged her. "We're going to Ireland next week." Paul glanced at Emma. "Everything OK?"

"Margaret will leave the Navy and get broody, and I have to tickle up my hormones."

"Good girl."

"I *am* a good girl and I want to have lots of wishes,"

Rose said complacently. She ran off to fetch her own small case and Paul kissed Emma.

"At least I don't have to go into Beattie's for another insufflation of tubes. Stella was definite about that and thinks it's only a matter of time before, as Mrs Coster would say, I 'get caught'. What an expression!"

"I'm glad you aren't as fruitful as her. What would we do with six children?"

Emma hid her face in his jacket and her voice was muffled. "We'd love them, every one."

Mick and Eileen brought Jean to see Rose as soon as they arrived home and the two girls played happily with the dolls that Eileen had bought for them until suddenly Jean rushed out and clung to Mick in tears.

"Hey, what's up?" he said, thinking the girls had quarrelled.

"It's not fair. Rose is going to Ireland and bringing back a leppercorn and she'll have lots of wishes."

"*You*'ve just come back and you have a lot of toys we bought for you over there."

"It's not a toy. He's a tiny man in a green suit and he's magic."

"Oh dear! My fault, I'm afraid. It's a joke, Jean," Emma said but knew that once Rose had an idea it would take more than magic of any kind to shift it.

"We didn't see one, but if Rose sees two she'll bring one back for you," Mick said and laughed. "There's magic enough there, sister. You'll love Ireland. Eileen's unpacking but she said she'll be ready to cook dinner as soon as you want her."

"Not this evening, Mick," Emma said firmly. "We want to hear all about your holiday. I've made pasties, and there's jelly and custard and cheese for everyone in the kitchen tonight."

"That's a relief. Eileen was knackered after the boat crossing and Jean wasn't much help as she wanted to go back to Ireland." He stared at Margaret as she came into the office, yawning. "You look like Eileen did when . . . sorry, nothing," he mumbled.

Margaret laughed. "Do all women expecting a baby have that look?" she said. "I can't keep anything private any more!"

"You really are?" Mick went pink. "Wish it was Eileen. Jean did me out of my train set so we need a boy."

"I heard that, Mick!" Eileen came into the office and smiled at Margaret. "Did I miss something?" she asked.

"Only that you're let off dinner duty as Sister wants to hear about Ireland," Mick said quickly.

"It was much nicer than I thought possible," Eileen said. "We stayed with very nice people and Jean had a good time as they love children and have a lot of their own."

"I paddled in the lake with Curran and Maeve, and picked lots of flowers," Jean said.

"I shall do that too," Rose asserted firmly, "and when I find my leppercorn he can help me."

The two girls tried to outstare each other. Eileen and Emma exchanged glances: it was becoming clear that they needed something more than each other's company, and Rose's holiday in America and Jean's visit to Ireland had brought other dimensions into their lives.

"Help me to unpack the other case," Eileen suggested to Jean after they'd eaten, and she took her down to their own apartment.

"It was so easy over there," Mick said. "They take children for granted and let them have a lot of freedom but they don't seem to come to much harm as there are eyes everywhere in the villages and no real danger." He laughed. "They want to know everything about you and after the first evening they knew our names, where we came from and what we did for a living." He grinned. "They didn't ask the colour of my granny's eyes but they had everything else off pat! Complete strangers addressed us by name and asked after Jean if she wasn't with us." He shrugged. "Eileen got a bit fed up with them as they all wanted to know why she had no more children. I shut them up by saying there were medical reasons and they looked sympathetic, as if they took it for granted that Eileen wanted a big family."

"I shall say that we left the other seven at home with a nanny," Paul said.

"You'd better make that an unmarried aunt, not a nanny. They still have such angels, who stay at home and look after elderly parents and are on hand for the children."

"What if the angel wants a career?" Emma said.

"Nursing is OK, as they look to the future care of their old people, but they aren't keen on them escaping into the big city or being free to choose what they want to do."

"They could get married if they went away and met

more men," Emma said. "Most Irish girls are good-looking."

"The men tend to marry late over there. They have to find work and earn enough to support a family and there aren't that many jobs going. As soon as they have a good job they may marry but they are afraid of too many babies arriving, and with no birth control allowed that is a problem."

"It isn't just the Irish who use unmarried aunts and sisters." Emma frowned. "I know that Aunt Emily is only half Irish but her Victorian parents had the same conviction, that the youngest unmarried girl stayed at home and looked after the parents and the home. In Emily's case they had a shop that kept her busy, but she did have a sweetheart. She dared not break away and marry him." She shrugged. "He died in the First World War but she was almost content as she was close to her mother and her brothers and sisters."

"She never shows any sign of being embittered by that," Paul said. "If all my patients who grumble about the 'might have been' could see her, they might be ashamed."

"Life *was* hard, even in families who had enough to live on," Emma added. "It taught them to cut their losses and count their blessings."

Paul began to clear away the dishes. "You can count your blessings that I don't ask you to help wash up, Mick. Go on, off to bed and get some sleep. You are all panda-eyed."

Eight

"I think Eileen was glad to see us leave," Emma remarked. "She loves her job as housekeeper and coped so well while we were in America that I feel an intruder in my own kitchen."

"It's not really a problem, is it?" Paul asked rather anxiously.

"No." Emma tried to sound convincing. The last few days had been so full of packing, and seeing even more friends who wanted to meet and hear about Bea and America, that there had been no time for friendly chats over cups of tea. And Eileen was having trouble with Jean, who had been so enchanted with Ireland and the many friends she made there that she was now slightly sulky. She annoyed everyone, including Rose, with her boasting.

"Nearly there," Paul said, and Emma saw masts appearing over the tops of the buildings by the quay and heard a ship's siren through the morning mist. It was so familiar, and the sea was as blue as it was in Cowes Roads. Rose stirred and sat up after sleeping through the train journey from Swansea to the docks. "It was a bit of an early start for you, Rose, but at least you'll be wide awake when we're on the ferry."

"The boats aren't as big as the one we went on to go to America," Rose said in a self-satisfied tone. "Jean said she went to Ireland in a big, big boat but these are little."

"We went on a liner. That's different. These are very big as far as ferries go and you mustn't compare the two." Paul spoke sharply, as he had noticed a growing-apart of the two little girls and hated the thought of dissension between the two families who depended so much on each other.

"Jean said she put money into a machine and chocolate came out," Rose said and looked hopeful.

"We'll see if there is one as soon as we're on board," Emma said. "What else have we to do to keep up with Miss Jean?"

"She showed me her name on a piece of metal. The machine stamped the letters that her daddy picked out and it said 'Jean Grade' but there weren't enough letters for the money they put in to spell out where she lives."

"I remember that from when I was at school. I thought they'd all gone," Emma said. "Unless I held on to the letter I wanted the arm jumped, and I had some very strange messages from the ones on the Portsmouth ferry. I kept one for ages that spelled out 'Emma Jexa' and I never did get one right."

"The wonders of modern science," Paul said solemnly. "Here we are and I'm glad that we sent the main luggage in advance as I see no porters who look strong enough to carry it! No, Rose, we carry our own hand luggage and yours isn't very heavy, so come on and don't hold up the people behind us."

Emma raised her eyebrows. It wasn't often that Paul spoke so sternly to his daughter, but she saw that it might be necessary if Rose was not to rule the family as Jean seemed to do with Eileen and Mick.

The crossing was calm and the sun broke through early cloud to shine on the water and bring warmth to the passengers reclining on the steamer loungers. Rose found the machine that gave out small thin bars of Nestlé milk chocolate for a penny a time and was allowed to eat one as there was so little in the packet.

The name-printing machine had a line of children waiting to use it and Rose was impatient. "When is it my turn?" she asked, and Emma recognised the whining element that Jean now used to great effect with her mother Eileen.

"There isn't going to be a turn if you speak to me like that," Emma said. "If there are people before you then wait your turn politely and be quiet." Rose lapsed into moody silence and went to look over the rail at the creamy wake from the stern of the ferry.

"It's nearly lunchtime," Paul said tactfully, and Rose had to abandon the printing and follow him.

"Cheer up," Emma said softly. "We'll be on this boat for hours and when we have finished lunch I expect there will be very few children round that machine."

"Promise?"

"No, I can't promise that, as what happens on the boat has nothing to do with me," Emma replied. "There are lots of children on the boat who want to be first in everything just like you, but we must wait our turn."

"But I want . . ."

"I remember someone saying to me when I was a little girl, 'You want and make a fuss, then you must go on wanting. Wait or go without!' I learned that I wasn't the only important person in the world," she added, but smiled as she recalled the agony of a four-year-old's frustrated wishes. "I know it's hard to wait but there will be lots of lovely things to do when we get to Dublin and you'll make friends just as Jean did."

"I want to see my leppercorn," Rose said. "Jean didn't see one."

"Mark has never seen one, nor have Avril and Johnnie, so does it really matter if you don't see one either?" asked Paul.

"They didn't have leppercorns in America," Rose said in a superior voice.

"No, but they had a lot of other things and you were very happy with what you had," Paul told her.

"I miss Mark," Rose began and the corners of her mouth turned down.

"So do we. We miss America and Bea and Dwight and the children and I miss American pizzas," Paul said.

"Come on, Rose, don't just stand there looking at that poster," Emma said. "I'm hungry. I hope there are some good things on the menu."

Paul grinned. "Talk your way out of this one," he said to Emma.

"Oh, *no*!" Emma burst out laughing and Rose looked

triumphant. The poster showed an Irish beauty spot with a signpost in the foreground. Rose couldn't read the sign that said LEPRECHAUN CROSSING but she could see the picture of a little man in green, wearing a floppy hat and a wicked smile.

"That's where he lives," Rose asserted. "I want . . . please may I go there?" she asked more politely as if to make sure her parents would agree with her.

"That place is in Kerry, a lot further on from Dublin," Paul explained. "However, we shall be going to a lot of villages where they may have signposts like that, so we might find another later."

Rose giggled. "It shows there are lots of leppercorns and we can find them and take some home."

"That signpost only means that you must wait and look both ways before you cross the road," Paul said. "It doesn't mean there are real leprechauns there. I'm afraid you'll be disappointed; they're only like fairies in books, and don't really exist."

"I shall find them," Rose asserted rather grandly, as if her father was not quite as clever as he thought.

"Good! You can look for them and let us know when you find one," Paul answered. "It will give you something to do when we're in the car on long journeys. Better than I Spy."

Rose unpeeled the foil from the tiny portion of butter and put butter on her roll. "How did you know that was butter?" Emma asked.

"Jean told me."

Emma sighed. Was the whole journey to and stay

in Ireland to be an echo of what Jean Grade had seen and done?

"Can I have another penny for chocolate? Will there be many children waiting to print their names?" Rose asked hopefully as soon as she finished eating.

To Emma's relief, the printing machine was old and cumbersome and out of true and Rose found it boring after the first two efforts. Her chocolate bar was broken in half and gradually Jean was mentioned less as the expected results of everything she had boasted about were cut down to size and no longer impressed Rose. Soon she was more like her usual cheerful self.

A taxi took them to a pretty hotel where they were to stay the night. It was by the shore, with a path that led down to a small beach, and Emma wished they could stay for a few days before going on in a hired car to Dublin. But Rose made the most of what time they had there as she found a swing hanging from a tree in the garden; while Emma and Paul sat on a rustic bench and drank in the view over the harbour, Rose was completely absorbed.

"I didn't realise that Mick looked so Irish until we came here. The hotel manager looks very like him but Mick's cockney voice isn't like his."

"The elderly lady over there has a bit of Emily about her, and I'm sure we shall see faces that are half familiar all the time we're here."

"I haven't seen anyone as lovely as you," Paul said, "but after seeing the picture of your grandmother, I do see traces of her in certain faces here, and Emily swears you are like her."

"Somehow it seems familiar. I know it's only because I'm expecting to feel a kind of kinship, but I love the deep green of the meadows and the fact that the sea is over there."

Rose swung slowly and hummed to herself as she'd done when she was a baby and was tired. "Bed for you, Rose," Emma said firmly. "The bath is huge and there are a lot of packets of soap and shampoo that we can use."

"Are they ours?"

"Yes; most hotels have them now."

"Can I take them home if we don't use them?"

"I suppose you can, but there will be packets of soap in the other hotels," Emma said. "I have soap and shampoo in my bag if there's none in the other bathrooms so you needn't collect these."

"Please. I want to take some back for Jean," Rose said self-righteously, then added maliciously, "She didn't stay in proper hotels. They stayed in ordinary houses with other people."

"I was very impressed when Mick told me about the lovely people they met," Paul said. "I almost changed our plans as it sounded far more warm and homely to stay on farms and in private houses with families."

Rose set her jaw, annoyed at having her one-upmanship spoiled. "I shall take the soap home," she said firmly. "Jean didn't have free soap."

"We'll collect all we can," Paul said. "It will be useful in the handbasins of the patients' lavatories. Personally, I shall use our own while we're here as I don't think the hotel soap is very good."

Emma tried not to laugh and took Rose to have her bath. She tucked her into the small bed in the alcove at the side of the main bedroom after giving her fresh milk, biscuits and a banana.

Paul was waiting by the dining-room door. "I asked the girl in reception if someone could listen outside our room at intervals in case Rose was awake, but I think she's so tired that she'll sleep the clock round. I'm hungry and we deserve some wine with our meal."

Emma smiled. "I really do miss Mark," she said. "It takes one bossy child to manage another. Rose needs him."

"Rose needs a brother or sister of her own, but she'll have to be patient, as we are. It will happen. I have faith in nature and Stella, in that order."

"We'll have coffee in the bar," Paul said after the meal. "I have some notes I should glance at and I can do that there." He sighed. "A flask of wine, good food and you is paradise," he misquoted, "but Dublin looms up and I must be ready tomorrow. I'm being very selfish, bringing you over here while I work, but it does make all the difference to see you, touch you and share the good and bad bits with you."

"I wouldn't miss it. I was ready to come away again. Rose and I can sightsee while you give lectures and we can meet different people in the evenings."

Paul laughed. "You have a very important task. You're responsible for leprechauns."

"Don't remind me. I want to forget little green men this evening." They walked out through the main entrance to breathe the warm evening air and the smell of night-scented stocks came to them, sweet and nostalgic. "Aunt Emily grows them," Emma remembered, and suddenly her aunt felt close. A dampness in the air made them go back into the bar and a man smiled as he entered the hotel, droplets of fine dew on his jacket. "Sure it's going to be a soft night, God be praised," he said in a low voice, and Emma knew that she was in Ireland, among the people from whom her grandmother came.

Breakfast was a big meal with bacon and eggs and fruit. The waitress put a small breadboard on the table with a warm loaf on it.

Rose eyed the bread with concern. "It's a funny shape, Mummy."

"It's Irish soda bread. Aunt Emily makes it sometimes for Aunt Janey. I've tasted it and it's very good." Emma cut a thick slice that included one of the points of crust rising from the cross-cut loaf, and then cut it in half. Rose piled butter on her piece and added strawberry jam. "Why don't we have this at home?" she said through a mouthful of warm crumbs.

"I'll make some when we go back, but it doesn't keep well. It has to be freshly made and I haven't time to make it often." She laughed. "That's one very nice thing that Jean had when they were here. The farmer's wife gave Eileen a good recipe, so we'll all have some."

"I wish we were staying on a farm," Rose said.

"And not have free soap?" Paul asked. "Eat up, we're

ready to leave in half an hour and it's a long drive to Dublin."

"Are there any leppercorns in Dublin?"

"I have no idea, but before we leave here you could buy a postcard with a picture of a leprechaun on it."

"I want . . ." Rose began, but her parents ignored her until she smiled, put her hand in Paul's and asked sweetly, "Please Daddy may I buy one for Jean as well?"

Emma looked pleased and Paul hurried with Rose to the stand full of lurid picture postcards. "Hurry up," he said. "Those are the ones you need." He paid for the cards and managed to move Rose away from the pictures of Irish dancing and some vulgar cards with even more vulgar captions.

"But Daddy, can't I have that one? He looks just like Mario down the road from us and I'm sure he'd like that card."

"I don't think so," Paul said hastily and wondered what Mario would think of the awful picture and unflattering words. "Mario is Italian, not Irish, and he wouldn't understand."

They put the luggage into the car boot. "It's good not to have to depend on taxis and buses," Emma said. She gave Rose a picture book and told her that she would have to amuse herself for a while. "When you've looked at your book you can watch for leprechauns and girls in green and red cloaks like the dancers on the cards."

Cows stood in deep pastures, cottage gardens were bright with late-summer flowers, and a lad with red hair on a rough-coated pony gave way to the car in a

97

country lane. "He isn't riding on a saddle," Rose said. She turned round to stare at him as the car accelerated and the boy grinned. "Why doesn't he fall off?"

"He probably rides like that every day and is used to it," Paul said.

"Mark fell off when he did that," Rose told him, "and Auntie Bea said it served him right if he was hurt. Does that boy live on a farm? I like that horse. Can I have a ride?"

"Not without a saddle, and you'd find an English saddle very different from the ones you had in America."

"Do all the boys in Ireland ride like he does? Perhaps there aren't any saddles in Ireland."

"Only farm boys and gypsies who have been with horses all their lives ride like that," Emma said.

Paul slowed the car and wound a window open. The smell of horses came in on a whiff of cooking and Rose gazed entranced at a group of gypsy wagons on the wide verge, with the haltered horses cropping the grass. "We'll see a lot of those," Paul said and drove on in spite of Rose's plaintive cries to him to let her smooth the horses.

"Auntie Bea told me that the Irish love horses and have a lot of beautiful racing stables. Maybe we can see one when Daddy is busy, or there might be a riding school that you can go to later. Her father knows a lot about racehorses and he said he's going to buy one."

"Will he let me ride it?" Rose asked.

"He'll have a real jockey to ride it. He doesn't ride and I doubt if he could manage an energetic horse," Emma pointed out. She was amused at the idea of Bea's rather solid and sophisticated-looking father riding anything less comfortable than a smooth limousine.

"Why does he want a horse if someone else is going to ride it? When I have a horse of my very own, I shall ride it," Rose said.

"I don't think Jean went riding over here, so it isn't certain that you can find somewhere to hire a horse," Paul pointed out.

Rose looked surprised. "Jean doesn't like horses. She said there were two on the farm where they stayed and one tried to lick her and she cried."

"I thought she liked animals," Emma said. "She has lots of cuddly toys like rabbits and kittens."

"She doesn't like real ones. Her mummy makes the toys but said she is glad that Jean doesn't like pets."

"I remember that Eileen wouldn't take Jean to the zoo," Emma recalled. "Mick took her but they came back after only half an hour because Jean was frightened of the monkeys."

"Two little girls being brought up under the same roof, even if they are in separate apartments, are becoming so different," Paul said quietly while Rose became engrossed in her picture book.

"I think that Bea's family influenced Rose in America but I noticed even before we went there that the two girls often played with very different toys. When they go to school next year they'll make other friends and we shall see further changes." Emma frowned. "I am very fond of Jean, but when she comes back from playing with Betty, she says spiteful things, and last week she had a nasty bruise on her arm where she'd been slapped."

"I know that Eileen has a friend and goes to her house once a week," Paul said. "Mick isn't all that keen and refuses to invite her to the flat, but Eileen says she makes her laugh. I know very little about her."

"Eileen's friend has three small children including Betty and they are a bit wild. Betty is the same age as Jean and younger than her brother and sister who I think bully her. Eileen was cross about the bruise but couldn't find out who'd done it. She decided that it was an accident, but when Mick insisted on knowing what had happened and asked Jean, she said that it was Jack who hit her and told her she mustn't tell anyone, or, to use his own words, she'd get another one."

"Nice child," Paul said drily. "Which one of that family do I see first in the clinic? Was that why Mick was laying down the law to Eileen?"

"She wouldn't tell me, but I'm sure that was what caused the tension. I expect it will be sorted out by the time we get back," Emma said. "I'm going to forget about them all now, and enjoy Ireland."

Nine

"This is more convenient, as we are close to the university, but I enjoyed the Meadow Lane Hotel," Paul said.

"Endless corridors where I shall get lost and a more impersonal staff," Emma decided, and sounded uncertain. "I suppose there's a lot more to do here and Dublin *is* a beautiful city, but Rose was happy with the swing and trying to find crabs under the seaweed on the beach."

"And you? I feel guilty when I think you're bored."

"Paul darling, I am not bored," Emma said firmly. "I want us all to find what we need to do and to enjoy it. You have a lecture to give, but we can explore Dublin and every time you're busy, Rose and I will be happy going on one of the many trips that seem to be available. I never thought I'd look forward to being a real tourist, as on the island we rather stood back and looked at visitors as strange creatures who had no part in our lives, but here I shall become a culture vulture like the average American matron and see everything."

"You'll be looking for leprechauns, and I doubt if Dublin is true leprechaun country."

"Don't remind me. I think we are over that hurdle

as Rose saw some dolls in the showcase in the foyer and among the dancing girls there were two small dolls dressed as you know what! We spent ten minutes wondering if they were really dolls or just sleeping."

"I hope this isn't developing into an obsession," Paul said seriously.

"I don't think she needs a shrink just yet, and I believe she's convinced now that leprechauns are only in the imagination. It was a bit sad when she decided that the ones in the showcase were dolls."

"It isn't just the leprechauns. Her general attitude with Jean isn't as good as it was and each one wishes to do everything better than the other and to crow about it. They're definitely not as close as they were."

"Rose was determined to find a leprechaun, and believed that they are real and are here in Ireland for her to find," Emma said. "It's hard to have your dreams shattered, but as yet she hasn't cried over them as she still hopes that I'm wrong. Do you recall the floods of tears when someone told Jean there was no Santa Claus, and Jean told Rose and they both had a good cry?"

"I think I'll buy a couple of the dolls and hide them in the luggage. One each when we get back will smooth the way for Jean to be a part of Rose's fantasy," Paul said.

Emma reached up to kiss him. "You look terribly formal," she said, laughing. "Your audience will be very impressed."

"I wish I was coming with you. They want me there for lunch so it will be almost dinnertime when I get back."

"You'll love it, and we shall have a ball looking in every souvenir shop that Rose sees. I have a built-in nostalgia for trashy memorabilia, so it isn't all for Rose!"

"Rather you than me – and I don't want a joke glass that spills Guinness over me when I try to drink it."

"I promise. What about boxer shorts with shamrocks all over them?"

"That will do for Mick."

She watched him stride away and knew that he was already concentrating on the work ahead, but when Rose insisted on going down to the foyer to see her "leppercorn" dolls, the girl serving in the kiosk shook her head and told Rose that a gentleman had already bought both of them and she had parcelled them up to be collected later. Emma smiled tenderly. He'd remembered, even though his mind was full of his lecture about battle fatigue.

"We'll see if there are any more in the shops," Emma promised, but added gently when she saw that Rose was upset, "They really are only dolls, Rose. They aren't real and you will see a lot of them, I'm sure."

The tourist map of Dublin suggested many interesting places to visit, but it was enough to wander from the hotel into the main part of the city and just look at the lovely streets and the inviting shops. Emma was reminded that the historic buildings in Dublin hadn't suffered during the war, since southern Ireland was neutral. The soft sunlight cast a warm glow over the old, untouched stones. The late-night shower had washed the leaves of the trees lining the main thoroughfare, leaving them glistening and turning in the morning breeze. She wanted to turn to Paul or Bea to share everything and felt a tinge of sadness, but Rose dragged at her hand to show her a shop that sold Irish linen embroidered with shamrocks and tiny figures of dancing girls in red and green.

"There aren't any leppercorns," she said disconsolately.

"I want to buy something for Aunt Emily, Aunt Janey and Eileen, so you must help me choose," Emma said.

Rose relaxed and suggested a lot of unsuitable gifts.

"We can't buy them now as we might see something we like better," Emma pointed out, and put back a luridly decorated crinoline lady destined to cover some unlucky person's telephone.

"Eileen would like that," Rose said, and Emma was inclined to agree, but they moved on and by lunchtime were tired and hungry.

Music from a pub almost convinced Emma that they could eat there but she was shy of going anywhere unfamiliar like that without a male escort. It's not unlike London, she thought. There must be areas such as the ones she knew where unaccompanied women could or could not eat in safety. They settled for a department-store restaurant and ate fish and chips and ice cream, which suited Rose but was uninteresting. The steady buzz of Irish voices was everywhere and Emma doubted if the Irish really needed to kiss the Blarney Stone to give them the gift of eloquence, as they seemed to talk even when they were eating.

A feeling that she was missing something was unsettling. She watched and listened but was on the fringe, apart from what was being discussed, and the intimate laughter was beguiling but not for her. It was full of English-speaking Irish voices and yet was foreign. I'm expecting too much, she decided. I came here wanting to feel at home because of Aunt Emily and the family but I am an alien.

Rose was tired; they returned to the hotel so that she could have a nap, and Emma was free to explore the hotel and the garden. The boutique was similar to the ones in American hotels, full of extravagant clothes and costume jewellery, and the music from muted speakers was featureless and bland. Emma bought a magazine and a paperback novel and wished they had been able to stay in a smaller hotel or on a farm as Mick and his family had done.

The tailored gardens were like a public park and the sound of traffic came through the high hedges, loud enough to make sitting on a bench impossible. A hint of panic threatened to overcome her usual good humour. Was every day here going to be as boring? She sat in the lounge and firmly opened her paperback, then ordered tea to be served in half an hour after she had brought Rose down from her sleep.

"Where are we going now, Mummy?"

"We're going to have tea and wait for Daddy."

"I want something to do."

"So do I!" Emma laughed. It was a relief to know

that they were both bored in a wonderful city where life throbbed and there was so much to see. "We'll go down to the shop on the corner again and buy a jigsaw puzzle."

To Emma's relief there was no sign of leprechauns on the pictures showing the finished puzzles and they bought one with fairies, toads and rabbits.

"My my, you do look busy," Paul said when he arrived far earlier than expected. He grinned. "Is that the best entertainment that Dublin's fair city can offer?"

"All the trips were too long for Rose, and we've explored so many shops that I have shopper's indigestion! We bought nothing but one jigsaw and we had lunch in a very dull store and tea here."

"Great! I did rather better. We had a light lunch and I sampled real Irish Guinness, which was good."

"Lucky you," Emma replied without enthusiasm.

"We also have an invitation to dinner tonight in a real Irish home."

"But surely we can't leave the hotel?" Emma said with a glance at Rose, who was trying to force a piece of jigsaw into the wrong place.

"I hope you don't object to leaving this wonderful palace?"

Emma looked surprised but rather pleased. "We aren't going *home*? Didn't they enjoy your lecture?"

"As Dwight would say, I wowed them and they begged for more. I met a professor who was in Harvard when I was there and he was keen for us to visit them when we came to Ireland, but I dismissed it as one of those invitations that says politely that we'd be welcome if we were passing but they might be at a loss if we turned up unexpectedly."

"Does he know of a better hotel? Is that where we're going to dinner tonight – once we've solved one small problem?"

"Rose? No problem. She comes too, and we all stay with them just outside Dublin."

"Stay with them?"

"Close your mouth, dear. Is that expression one of amazement or dread?"

"Spell it out in words of one syllable for my poor little brain," she suggested caustically, but her eyes glinted and she felt happier than she had done all day.

Paul hugged her. "You must have been bored! You haven't asked me if they're pleasant or house-trained or if they live in a tent."

"So long as it's a big tent, I'll change for that," she said with feeling. "This is a sad place, Paul, the kind of hotel that takes only people passing through, and I saw nobody I wanted to chat to as most of the guests are men alone or older couples without children who are booked every day on tours."

"Poor darling. I know exactly what you mean, and I felt guilty leaving you. Think what it's like to be a man alone here, and even worse for a woman who can't go out to the pubs on her own."

"You are serious? We *are* moving to stay with them? Tell me a bit about them."

"Michael O'Dwyer is a professor of anthropology who was in the States studying ethnic tribes of Indians. He's attached to the University of Dublin where his main work is with Romany gypsies. Remember, we saw a camp on our way here. He is fascinated by their old customs and ways of life."

"We have a few genuine Romany families at home – Aunt Emily knew a family when she was a child. She says they are not like the tinkers who say they are gypsies. The ones she met were honest, very wise and proud of their heritage."

Paul laughed. "I can see that you'll have a lot in common with Michael, as you have a witch for an aunt who tells the future. Are you sure Emily isn't a foundling left by the gypsies?"

"Is there a Mrs O'Dwyer?"

"Nuala, a real Irish name. I met her once at Harvard, and she's very nice."

"Nice? Does that mean a homely body who knits, or is she too glamorous for you to admit that she's pretty?" Emma teased.

"Very pretty and a busy lady like you."

"Children?" Emma glanced at Rose, who seemed to be oblivious to their conversation.

"Three, including the youngest, a boy of six."

Rose looked up. "Is his name Mark?"

"No, it's Liam."

"Isn't this an imposition? Do we stay for a day or so and then have to find another hotel?"

"No, they insist on our becoming part of the family for as long as we're here."

"Do you think they'll like us?"

"We'll soon find out. Pack everything and I'll check out of the hotel and collect some things from the foyer."

Paul grinned. "You'll have to ask Liam if he's ever met a leprechaun, Rose."

"Mummy says they're not real and I shall never find one but you never know," she whispered in a conspiratorial voice. "Where are we going?" Rose crammed her book in with her clothes and picked up the pieces of jigsaw to put in the box. "I might let Liam do some of this," she said in a lofty tone.

"You're going to stay with a family who have been kind enough to invite us. We don't know them and you must be on your best behaviour. Liam might feel too old to play with you, so be careful what you say to him."

Rose saw that her mother was serious and nodded. "I want to go there. I don't like this hotel."

"Everything ready?" said Paul half an hour later.

"Everything, including the soap that Rose insisted on taking for Jean."

"I'll ask the porter to bring the bags down to the car," Paul said.

"I still have no idea where we're going," Emma said. "I feel that we're being kidnapped." She hugged Rose and they giggled.

"That's better. I thought you'd given up laughing," Paul said. "If this invitation hadn't come we'd have had to rent an apartment to feel more at home. I'm always amazed how a house or a hotel affects me and I know it does for you. I walk into Aunt Emily's house and feel warm and wanted but that place," he added with an exaggerated shudder, "makes me feel there are skeletons in the cupboard."

"Watch it! This little jug has big ears," Emma pointed out as she saw Rose becoming interested in the conversation. "Look, Rose! What a big dog."

"I didn't see it."

"We'll see another soon. We seem to be heading away from the city."

Industrial buildings gave way to sparse groups of suburban villas and then a patch of open country. Paul stopped the car to consult a map and Emma suggested that he ask someone the way.

"Michael said a map would be better. If you ask an Irishman for directions he'll tell you in detail. Even if he has no idea where a place is he'll want to be obliging, even if he sends you in the wrong direction! I'll follow this side road and we should see the house in five minutes."

A high fence ran along the side of the lane and a thatch-roofed lich-gate opened on to a driveway leading to a large house of ochre stone. The porch door was open and a woman sat on the side seat sorting eggs into two baskets. "She's like Mrs Caws who has the hens on the island," whispered Rose.

Carefully the baskets were set on the ground and Emma smiled at the dark-haired girl who stood up to greet them.

"I'm Mary, the nanny, but you'd never guess it. I fetch eggs and go to market and make bread and sometimes even look after the children! Come in while I find Herself."

Paul smiled. "How's this for atmosphere?"

Rose ran ahead into the dim hall and stared at

the embroidered hangings on the stone walls. A long refectory table was covered with a dark woven cloth and on it were ceramic dishes that Paul thought must be very old. "It's like a film set," Emma murmured. "Look up there! It's a minstrels' gallery."

A pretty woman in blue trousers and a man's shirt of bright green came into the room. "It's good to see you," she assured them. "I've been anxious to meet Emma and Rose, and I remember Paul with pleasure from Harvard."

Her voice was warm and lilting and her laugh welcoming. "I won't shake hands as I've just mucked out the animals. I'll tidy up and leave you with Mary to find your rooms." She glanced at the wall clock. "Drinks in half an hour and dinner to follow, but don't bother to change."

"Where are the children?" asked Rose.

"They're doing their chores," Mary said. "Sure you'll see enough of the rascals, but if they want to keep rabbits then they have to clean the hutches and feed them. If they don't put them in the hutches at night the fox might get them."

Rose smiled. "I like it here."

Emma picked up a case and followed Paul and Mary up the sweeping stairs. She noticed that Rose carried her own case and her jacket without being told to, and that her face was wreathed in smiles.

A slackening of tension in the comfortable bedroom and the fact that Rose accepted that she would sleep in a small adjoining room alone was reassuring, and the view from the windows of farmland and horses was a far cry from Dublin's streets. A box of shabby toys and a pile of well-thumbed books in the small bedroom took Rose's attention and she was reluctant to go down to dinner.

"Come on, Rose. You haven't met the children," Emma said, and wondered if the family all ate together or if the children ate with the nanny as they did in the evenings in America when the Sykeses had stayed with Bea and Dwight.

Mary was waiting at the foot of the stairs. "Ah, there you are! Aren't you the punctual ones!" She led the way into a large living room where drinks were set out on a low table with crystal glasses and fine bone-china dishes full of crisps and nuts. More solid glasses were full of orange juice for the children and Rose was suddenly shy as a bigger girl offered her a crisp.

"I'm Tara and this is Patrick. He's the oldest and the bossiest," she said. "Liam is having to change his shirt as he smells of horses," she added cheerfully.

"I'm Rose and I don't have any brothers or sisters."

"I wish I was called Rose," Tara said. "It's so pretty."

Patrick gave a derisive snort. "You couldn't be called Rose. You should see her after she's cleaned the rabbits. Pooh!"

"Patrick!" Nuala sounded firm but didn't raise her voice and she was smiling. "Make yourself useful and fetch Liam if his fingernails are clean. Myra will be wanting us sitting down in five minutes. Michael, you're on time for once," she said cheerfully as a tall man with light brown hair and freckles greeted

Paul with enthusiasm and turned to smile at Emma and Rose.

"I don't know how to thank you," Emma began.

"Then don't try. I know that hotel and it lets Dublin down," said Nuala. "We'll visit some of the better sights in the city and you'll forget your first impression. In any case, we wanted to have you here and we like people."

Emma turned to look at the small hurricane that came through the doorway, followed closely by Patrick. "I *did* wash my hands," Liam said. "He made me do them again with a brush and I got all wet!" Paul glanced across at his wife and they both laughed. Liam was small for his age and his manner was so like Mark Miller's that it was amusing.

Rose was entranced and wide-eyed as she listened to the family teasing as they sat down to dinner. Tara sat with Rose and the boys were separated by their parents and Mary, who ate with them. The food was well cooked and appetising but simple: Irish stew, mashed potatoes and green vegetables, soda bread and butter and local cheeses, ice cream and stewed fruit.

"We'll have coffee once the children are upstairs," Nuala said, and Mary took Rose by the hand and led her away with the others. "You can go up to say good-night to Rose later," Nuala went on. "She'll be fine, just fine with Mary and Tara."

Ten

Emma woke to a fine day and Paul humming softly as he came out of the shower. "Your face is cold," she said sleepily when he bent over the bed to kiss her.

"Wake up, lazy-bones. Breakfast as soon as you've showered and dressed."

"I'd better see Rose first. She was fast asleep when I came up to say good-night."

"Too late. Tara helped her dress half an hour ago and they're in the garden."

"Ever felt unwanted?" Emma smiled. "I still can't believe this is happening. Everything is so casual, and yet it's all organised and in many ways very disciplined."

Paul held her hands and pulled her from the bed. He held her close, her body soft and as yielding as it had been last night when they made love. "Get dressed before I seduce you," Paul said huskily.

"Again?" she asked and escaped into the shower room.

"The children have had breakfast," Mary said later when Emma joined Paul downstairs. "Liam wanted to show Rose his rabbits and Patrick's gone along to his friend next door to exercise the ponies. I'll make more coffee as Nuala said she'll join you for breakfast."

"Tara seems to like younger children," Emma said. "Is she always as good with them as she was with Rose last night?"

"I think you ought to know." Mary looked back at the doorway to make sure she wasn't overheard. "Tara has a small problem. Sure it's nothing at all, but she loves children a little too much for her age. She's protective of them because her mother lost a child of one year and Tara has not forgotten." She paused, and seemed on the point of tears. "It was a little boy, and we all loved him. I came here to be nanny to the family when Liam was born and when the baby was expected I was kept on here, but he died of meningitis the week after his first birthday and it made us all sad, God help us."

"How terrible." Emma was shocked: her impression of Nuala was of a calm, happy mother with no tragedy in her background.

"It's been said now, and she will not talk of it to anyone, but you have to know as you have Rose and Tara can be possessive at times."

"Thank you for telling me."

"We fill her time with the animals and she likes school and the nuns who teach her, but there are times when she stops eating and mopes and wants only her dolls."

"This seems such a happy home."

"It is that. Make no mistake, we are all happy here and Tara is very fond of the horses, so she will give her love to them."

"I have a good breakfast because I often forget to eat lunch," Nuala said as she sat down and they began to eat the eggs and bacon that Myra put before them. "Michael had to leave early as he has students today and you have a lecture to give this afternoon, Paul, don't you?"

"Less fraught than yesterday but of value, I think. I was asked to include a talk on child psychology so that's what I'm talking about today." He avoided looking directly at Nuala but Emma noticed that she was suddenly tense. "Emma sometimes sits in on my lectures as it helps in our clinics if she knows the score."

Emma remained silent. It had been a long time since she had listened to one of the lectures, and she wondered why he mentioned it now.

"Could I come to hear you?" Nuala looked at Emma. "Could we both go, and leave the children to Mary?"

"Of course. I want to see what the university is like inside and Rose seems very happy with Tara and Liam."

"Rose is very self-contained and confident," Nuala said. "I was glad to see that Liam won't have everything his own way there. She doesn't mind saying what she thinks."

"Our housekeeper has a little girl and she and Rose play together but they have separate lives," Paul said. "America was an education for Rose as she had three lively children in the Miller family who were just what she needed. Liam is like Mark, who she adored."

"I'm glad she prefers Liam to Tara. I noticed Rose shrugged away from Tara when she tried to lift her up as if she was a baby."

"Tara is so sweet with her," Emma replied. "But after America and lovely naughty little Mark and her big cousin Clive who has been staying with us in London,

116

she prefers boys. She'll be a tomboy if we don't civilise her!"

Nuala smiled and seemed pleased. "Come down to the paddock and meet Kavanagh and Sligo. I think Rose might be there now."

The broad field was roughly mown but full of thistles and Emma was glad to be wearing flat shoes that covered her feet well. Clumps of fading field daisies and trampled buttercups showed where animals had moved about the area and on the far side were two donkeys held on halters by Rose and Liam.

"Look, Mummy! Sligo is just like the donkey at the stables in Washington."

"Be careful. Remember that Mark was butted when he slapped him and annoyed him."

Rose laughed. "Liam said Sligo kicks, so I stay by his head."

Tara sat on a log and looked disapproving. She held two dolls on her lap and watched the children, but when Liam slipped on the moist grass she ignored him; he sat up and rubbed his bruised leg as if it hurt. Nuala ran forward to pick up the rope that he had dropped and to see that no real harm had been done.

"He's showing off, Ma," Tara said. "He thinks Rose wants to play with smelly donkeys, when I have my nice babies to show her."

"Babies?" Rose stared at her. "Those are dolls." She looked at Tara indulgently. "At the hotel I saw some leppercorns and thought they were real but Mummy said they were only dolls, and so are those." She sighed deeply. "I wish they *were* real. I want to have a leppercorn of my very own; a real one with green clothes and a funny hat and he'll give me wishes if I'm good."

Tara snatched up her dolls and stamped her foot. "Leprechauns are wicked. They took away my baby brother and if I see one I'll kill him!"

Paul sat on the log and looked up at her and Nuala turned pale. Tara saw the calm face and sympathetic eyes and moved closer to him. "How do you know?" he asked.

"My baby brother was in bed and they came and took him away and he never came back."

"Did you see them?"

Tara stared at him as if he wanted her to tell a lie. "They came," she insisted.

"You saw them?"

"No, they don't let many people see them," she said.

Rose was puzzled. "I've seen pictures of leppercorns and you *can* see them on the pictures so there must have been some at some time. How can I have one of my own if I can't see him?" Paul paused while Rose's logic seeped in. "How do you know it was a leppercorn if you didn't see him? They give wishes and are kind, unless you're naughty, and I am a good girl," Rose added piously. "Were you very naughty?" she said as an afterthought.

"No, I was good and the leprechauns were bad," Tara said passionately. "Bad, bad, bad!"

Rose looked abashed at the outburst and backed away, finding comfort in the rough warm coat of the donkey; Emma held her hand.

"If you didn't see the leprechauns, who told you they'd taken your baby away?" Paul asked seriously.

Tara eyed him rebelliously but refused to answer, and Nuala whisered to Emma that this was what happened every time they mentioned the baby.

"Did you dream that a little man in green clothes took away your baby?"

"No, I had no dream," Tara admitted.

"Then someone must have talked about it and told you what happened."

"I think you're silly," Rose said. "My mummy said they're like fairies and if you believe in them they are kind unless you do wrong and I shall find one and take him home to give me wishes. They don't steal babies," she added scornfully. "I expect the lady leppercorns have babies of their own."

"Come on, Rose, let's run with the donkeys to the hedge over there," Liam said. "I bet I can run faster than you. And when the donkeys are tired, Patrick will put them to the bridle and we can ride them."

Rose pulled on the halter and Sligo reluctantly followed her. "I still think you're silly, Tara," she called, and ran off with Liam.

"I'm not silly," Tara said and began to cry. "Rose doesn't know. She can't!"

"Rose is not a baby," Paul said quietly. "She's much older than your baby was, so we never treat her as a baby, and when we explain things to her she understands and knows what is the truth. She believes in fairies and Santa Claus, but only as a kind of dream, and the idea of leprechauns is fun just as fairies are."

"Rose does believe in them so what will happen if they take her away?"

119

"If they tried, I think she'd object very strongly and scream," Paul said, laughing. "As they're only a kind of dream in the mind, they'd find her very heavy to carry. Even a baby would be hard to take away and what would they do with one if they did take him from a cot?"

Tara muttered something and Paul looked alarmed. "Who told you that, Tara? Answer me," he said firmly, and she looked up through her tears. "Tell me," he said more gently. "They can't hurt you, Tara."

"They will," she wailed. "I've said it and I shall be taken away to be punished."

"Who told you that? It was someone in the house, wasn't it?" She nodded and seemed unable to take her eyes off his stern but kind face. "Was it Mary?" Tara shook her head vigorously and Emma sensed Nuala's relief. "Was it one of your family?" She shook her head again, and Paul glanced at Nuala for help as he had no idea who else was in the household but the woman who had silently served them with breakfast.

Nuala mouthed the name "Myra", but shrugged as if that was impossible.

"It was Myra, wasn't it?"

Tara gave a muffled scream and clung to her mother, the two dolls falling unheeded to the ground.

Nuala gently put her away to sit on the log and said quietly, "Tell Paul, darling. We will all protect you."

Paul waited until the sobs subsided and Tara wiped away the tears with a handkerchief that Nuala handed to her. "What did she say?"

As if released, Tara said, "I asked Myra where the baby was, as he wasn't in the nursery and Mummy had told me not to go in there in case I caught something. Myra said the baby had been taken away." A shuddering sigh and a residual moan made way for a clearer voice. "Mummy came back from somewhere and was crying. I asked where Baby had gone and she said Baby was with Mary and Jesus, but after she'd left me alone, Myra came and said the leprechauns had taken Baby and would eat him for supper as they liked boy babies, but as I knew what had happened, I must never tell anyone or they'd come and get me and kill me and all the family. Myra laughed as if it was a joke, but I couldn't talk about it with Mummy or Daddy. Myra frightened me so much."

"The wickedness of it!" Nuala said.

"Listen to me," Paul said quietly. "Your baby had a nasty infectious disease called meningitis and had to be taken to hospital, where he died. Mummy came back very sad and thought you were too young to understand what had happened. She was so upset she couldn't talk about it, so she said what you heard in church, that the baby had gone to Jesus and Mary his mother, which means he had died."

"I didn't see him when he was dead." Tara sounded as if she didn't believe him. "I saw my grandad after *he* died, and we all had a party."

"He died of old age," Nuala said. "Baby couldn't be put in an open coffin for people to see and touch as he had a bad infectious disease. They had to bury him quickly."

"You have wakes for the dead?" Paul asked. "I often think we should do more like that. It shows everyone that the person really is dead and the family can say goodbye but the dead person is still loved and life goes on."

"That's what I thought, until Baby died," Nuala said. "I blame myself for not talking about him to Tara. I was suffering too but as usual had to be strong for the rest of the family and thought Tara had got over it quickly even though she was quiet. Why didn't you tell me, Tara?" she asked bitterly.

"You were too close, and she was afraid for you and what would happen if she told anyone what Myra had said." Paul smiled. "That's what doctors like me are for, Nuala. People talk to us and we listen," he said simply.

"She'll have to go! I have had an evil woman cooking for us and being with my children."

"Is that necessary? I had the impression she's simple-minded, and maybe her head is full of old folklore. Has she ever hurt anyone except for this unfortunate happening?"

Nuala sighed. "We'll let Tara decide. It was very wicked of Myra to say those things to you and she must be told, but do you want her to leave?"

"No, Mummy. If she can say to me that she told lies, I want her to stay. She makes very nice barmbrack and washes my dolls' clothes." Tara was very calm now, she began to smile and looked at Paul with shining eyes. "Are you magic? I feel better."

"You're not just magic, you're an angel," Nuala said.

"Do you still want to hear my lecture on child psychology?" he said and laughed.

"More than ever. I want to know what I'm doing wrong!"

"Not a lot," Paul said softly. "You have a wonderful family and a bright future." He watched Tara walk away to see the other children. "Michael is an anthropologist and Tara is a very intelligent child. She could learn about local folklore from him, and be objective about it at an early age. It would stop her taking on half-baked ideas from people like Myra who almost believe what they say."

Nuala stood up and braced herself to see Myra. "She's a poor thing and we feel responsible for her as she has nobody of her own, but she must be told that if she ever frightens one of mine again she can go to the gypsies or Old Nick!"

"It's soup and sandwiches for lunch," Nuala said later. "I told Myra to stay away from me for the rest of the day and so I'm doing the cooking while she says her prayers, goes to confession and cries her eyes out! Sure it will do us all a power of good!"

"Let me help," Emma said.

"Can you make colcannon?"

"My Aunt Emily makes it and we often have it at home. She's half Irish and remembers what her mother taught her."

"We'll bring lamb chops back after the lecture and there's salad in the garden so we won't let them starve."

"Let me cut sandwiches," Emma said, and Nuala hugged her.

"It's like having a sister come home," she said. "It was a blessing from above when you and Paul came to Ireland."

123

"It's wonderful to be here," Emma said warmly. "You make us feel at home, and I know that Rose will hate to leave."

She buttered slices of bread and Nuala filled the sandwiches with ham and tomatoes, and put duck pâté and biscuits on a glass dish that looked as if it was a valuable antique. The Waterford glasses gleamed and made the simple cider and fruit juices look important.

"We must go to Waterford and buy glasses," Emma said. "It's time we had some decent glassware as we are entertaining more now."

"I'll come with you. I haven't been there for years." Nuala shrugged. "We had no need, as a lot of china and glass came to me with this house and Michael's family also left him many antiques and more glassware." She smiled. "We take it all for granted – nothing is made of the fact that we belong to very old Irish families." She sighed. "We still feel obligations to our tenants and people we employ, just as our ancestors did, which is why we put up with Myra. A lot of it goes back to the famine years when Ireland's potato crops failed and many starved or emigrated to escape it all. My family nearly starved with them as we gave what we had to our people and suffered with them, even if many believe that all the landowners turned their backs on the workers and their families."

"You still have land," Emma said.

"Only as far as the river on that side and the hill on the other; but it's enough, and we needed to sell a lot in my great-grandfather's time." She laughed. "We're well off by today's standards and we still have one racehorse which costs a fortune as he is stabled with the trainer."

"You must give me details, as Bea will be interested. You met her at Harvard, didn't you?"

"I met Dwight and Bea but not the children, as they were in Washington, but when we go over again I hope to visit them."

"Bea's father is thinking of buying a racehorse but it's a status symbol for him – he knows nothing about horses and would be scared to ride one."

"Why are you laughing, Mummy?" Liam held up grubby hands. "If I wash can I have something to eat? I'm starving."

"Lunch is ready," Nuala said and looked at the two flushed faces. "Aren't you a pair! Go and clean up and put on clean shirts. Do you need help, Rose?"

"I'll see to them," Emma said as Nuala put the food on the table. Tara walked in slowly. "I'm glad you know, Mummy. I was frightened you'd be taken away but I'm better now."

Nuala hugged her daughter and then asked what she wanted to drink, as if what had happened that morning was of no importance.

"Where's Myra?"

"I gave her time off," Nuala said shortly. "I sent her off to the priest for confession."

"Good. I hope he makes her say a hundred Hail Marys." Tara helped herself to a piece of cheese from the platter with more eagerness than she'd shown for weeks. "I'm hungry," she said, and Nuala saw the soft eyes and the smooth untroubled face that she'd thought were lost, and was glad to the point of tears.

Eleven

"I feel like celebrating," Nuala said. She smiled at Paul with real affection. "I loved your lecture and I shall never forget what you've done for Tara. Already she's the child I once knew and it's a miracle. I feel better myself, too, and know now that I should have seen what was happening to her and made sure she told me why she was withdrawn and frightened. I failed her because I was too involved with my own grief. Shall we have champagne tonight, Michael?"

"Anything you like, darling," Michael said. "Unless Paul has other ideas? We could eat out if that would help."

"What I'd really like, if it isn't a bore for you, is to go to a real Irish pub, drink Guinness and listen to a fiddle or two."

Emma recalled the intriguing sounds she had heard when she was too shy to go into the pub in Dublin. "Could we?" she asked eagerly.

"It's something we once did a lot but recently we just haven't seemed to get round to it, but it's a good idea. They serve food in Murphy's Barn and have good musicians, but there'll be no champagne, Nuala."

"A long cool glass of really good Guinness will do

nicely," Nuala said. She called for Mary and asked her if she would sit in for the children and give them supper, then suggested that Emma change into jeans and a light top and sweater. "They have a mixed bunch in Murphy's and we don't want to appear too dressed up. You'll like it," she added, as if Emma might be put off and expect a rough crowd in the bar.

"We couldn't do this if we were in a hotel with Rose," Paul pointed out as they changed for the evening. "You seem to be very much at home with Nuala, and Michael's a very interesting guy. I hope they visit us in London and stay for a while."

"Rose would like that – if Liam is invited too. It's strange but I feel as if Bea should be with us now, with her brood. They're so much alike. I hope we shall see more of this family in the future."

But when they sat on wooden chairs on the upper floor of the old pub to eat supper, looking down on the crowded bar and the group of musicians as if looking down from a minstrels' gallery, it was not Bea and her children who filled Emma's mind. A sensation of *déjà vu* that was completely unrealistic made her feel that Aunt Emily was just over there, out of sight, and Jane, her grandmother, was watching with the wry smile she had in her picture.

Emma sipped the smooth black stout and ate her seafood salad and soda bread while the musicians tuned up their fiddles and a few notes emerged from tin whistles and an old piano. A girl in a green skirt and white blouse sat on a stool and strummed gently on a washboard and as if they knew by instinct when to begin, the lively music came up to the gallery in perfect time and yet seeming to fit no time or pattern, but was almost hypnotic in its intensity and rhythm.

Paul looked at her and raised his glass. "To Emily and Janey," he said.

"And my grandmother," Emma whispered. "We came to the right place, Paul. I feel her here and the others are close."

"Sure it's the black stuff talking," he said in an exaggerated Irish accent.

"I love this place," Nuala said. "After a while I have enough of the fiddles but for an hour or so it's good and speaks of the past to me. It's very old and goes back beyond earlier troubles but thank God we are at peace here now and there is enough to eat in the villages. You said your grandmother was Irish, and tonight I see the touch of it in your face. You mentioned two aunts; they must have even more of the same look about them."

"They have dark hair and dark eyes and Aunt Emily is a bit fey."

"You're very lucky. That gift passed us by years ago; they said the gypsies stole it away." Nuala stopped. "I'm as bad as Myra! I must never say that in front of the children but it affects us all, Emma. We all have some regard for and slight fear of the little people. They were our fairy stories, told to us by sometimes ignorant servants and nannies whose whole lives were ruled by handed-down tales of what would happen if we displeased the little people. If we lose something, we say it was a gremlin who took it. It's handy to blame someone else for our own carelessness."

"With Aunt Emily and her family, it was the threat of being given to the gypsies that made them behave." Emma laughed. "It didn't work as they knew a family of Romanies who were highly respectable and my grand-mother knew one woman very well, so that threat was no good. One uncle said he wanted to go with the gypsies, and he wore a red scarf at his throat as their boys did. He was a wild one."

Empty glasses were whisked away from the band and full glasses replaced them as they took a break and ate the food provided. The people in the gallery were in a cloud of cigarette smoke, loud laughter and incessant chatter, made gentle by the fumes of the cold black stout that was so easy to drink.

"This has been a wonderful experience," Paul said as they walked back to the house in the cool damp evening.

"I wish we could do more for you," Nuala said, almost tearfully. "Tara is a different girl, as if you released her from something evil."

"I did nothing," Paul insisted. "I was a strange but sympathetic face who asked the right questions. It's my job," he added flatly as he saw that Nuala was becoming maudlin.

"Some coffee, I think," Michael said and put an arm round his wife's shoulders. "Come along now, you never could drink enough to make a night of it. She didn't dance on the table but let's get some coffee into her," he added and laughed. "*In vino veritas*," he said softly. "We are for ever in your debt, Paul."

"No problems?" Nuala asked when a sleepy Mary opened the door to them.

"All asleep, but Liam had to be promised that he could take Rose to see the racehorse. I can do that with them on the bus, but you might like the outing too?"

"We'll all go tomorrow and you can visit your cousin. We'll drop you off in the village and you can take her some fruit."

"Not me, I'm afraid, as they want me tomorrow to see a couple of patients," Paul said. "I know," he added when he saw Emma's disapproval. "It isn't on my lecturing schedule and I didn't agree to see patients here but I'm interested, and I'm not exactly overworked."

"Men!" Nuala said. "Michael is taping songs in Gaelic and when he gets into the encampments, he's there all day." She laughed. "I tell him it isn't necessary to ask them to cook in the old ways just to please him, but he has eaten hedgehog baked in a mud coating and squirrel stewed in a pot with rabbit, potatoes and herbs, and vegetables that I probably pass every day of my life but would never pick to eat."

"You miss a lot." Michael poured more coffee. "Stick by me when we're stranded on a desert island. You might survive if you eat what I do."

"I'd want my coffee," Nuala replied.

"That's easy. During the war we had coffee made from dandelion roots and many people found a taste for it and still use it."

"I prefer a good recognisable brand of strong black coffee with no chicory added to make it go further." She yawned. "Dear God, I'm tired. See you tomorrow . . . or is it today?"

*　　*　　*

"It's blessedly quiet here after Dublin," Emma said at breakfast. "After all that music and the coffee late at night I thought I'd never sleep, but I went out like a light."

"A pure heart and a contented mind," Paul said.

"Is that your message for your patients today?"

"A contented mind, certainly, but the other is more difficult. I leave that to the priest to sort out if they are very wicked!"

"You are almost a confessor," Emma pointed out. "You often hear more about them than the priest will ever be told."

"I'm not with somebody for longer than the treatment and I'm not involved in their private lives, but a priest is always in the community and takes confession from families he sees every day. I have a feeling that not every small sin is confessed, though, and they tell more to a stranger. In a way it is like a confessional, as we do keep patient-doctor confidentiality."

"When I travelled on a slow train during the war, the carriage was often crammed with soldiers going on leave and it's amazing what they told me: things they said they'd not told to anyone but wanted to get off their chests. They knew they'd never see me again and it was a release." She shrugged. "I suppose I have a sympathetic face."

Paul laughed. "Did it really stop there?"

"What do you mean?"

"Did they never offer to carry your bags and suggest you met again? You have a very pretty face, not just a sympathetic one."

The dimples in her cheeks gave away her amusement under her regal stare. "That had nothing to do with it."

"But it happened?"

"It happened." She laughed. "It was impossible to know what they were really like. I saw the uniform and the worried expression, but who was to say if one man was more honest than another? I took the coward's way out and said I'd love to see them again but my boyfriend was meeting me and I couldn't let him down."

"I'm glad you were cautious, or who knows? We wouldn't have met and you might be married to someone you found you didn't like."

"A ward full of lusty men with broken limbs, otherwise good health but lots of testosterone floating about soon taught me caution! In bed, in hospital pyjamas, they often showed very little outward sign of what they did and who they were in civvy life and I had a few shocks when I saw men who came to say goodbye on the day they were discharged as fit. They dressed in their own clothes, somehow taking on a personality with which they were more comfortable. Sometimes it was horrific. I never did like oxblood suits and winklepicker shoes. Often the quiet ones dressed well, and I could imagine them holding down responsible jobs before they were called up. A hospital ward is a great leveller, though, and most of them got along well together."

"Must go." Paul kissed her and picked up his briefcase. "Nuala said she'll take you in the Land Rover, so I can use the car. I should be back by dinnertime."

"Don't promise to see more cases than you want to

do," Emma warned. "Even *you* can't sort out the minds of the whole nation!"

"Patrick Hanratty wants me to hold his hand while he uses Thiopentone on two men who have shown little sign of recovery under conventional physiotherapy and tranquilliser drugs. Not many doctors here use hypnosis, and in cases of battle fatigue it's sometimes necessary to unlock the causes of things like functional paralysis. Patients often labelled malingerers are really ill. If I'd seen my best friend killed by a sniper and was knee-capped in a revenge attack, I think my mind would refuse to let me function properly even after the wounds healed, so I might convince myself that I was unable to walk just to avoid more conflict."

"You're getting enthusiastic," she warned him. "Have a good day, but make no other promises – we leave for Belfast next week, and you have more lectures to give."

"Everything is under control! I worry more about you. We have no room in Kensington for a thoroughbred racehorse and, dare I say it, we can't afford one."

Rose wanted to wear trousers as they were going to the stables. "It isn't like the one in America," Emma told her. "We're going to see horses in clean, neat racing stables and we'll have lunch in the country."

Nuala laughed. "Rose can wear a pair of jeans that no longer fit Liam. I can't imagine them coming back here without dirtying their clothes, so we might as well expect the worst."

"What is your horse called?"

"Tyrone of Ballykelly."

Rose wrinkled her nose. "When I have a horse I shall call him Max."

"Just Max?" asked Nuala. "That wouldn't look very impressive in the stud book."

"Max is a good name. He'd come if I called him that."

"We call ours Ty for short," Nuala admitted. "Are you coming with us, Tara?"

"I'm all ready, Ma, but Patrick is staying to meet Dermot from the farm. He said he'll wear a hard hat if he rides, so don't worry."

Nuala put extra sweaters in the Land Rover. "I remember being frozen the last time we went there as the wind sometimes sweeps over the hill. We'll take anoraks too and a change of clothes for the children: the restaurant is more formal than most and won't welcome children smelling of horses. We shall be warm once we go in for lunch."

The racing stables were quiet, and Nuala was told that the horses were out on the hill being exercised but were due back soon. Another family sat waiting for the string to return and Liam called out to the boy: "Play five stones?"

"No, you beat me the last time," protested the other child. He took a ball from his pocket and Liam wandered off with him to throw it against a stable wall.

"That boy's American," Rose said. "I wonder if he knows Mark?"

"America is a very big place," Emma reminded her. "We don't know everyone in London, and America is much bigger."

Rose went closer to the two boys but stood back when they started wrestling. Liam was laughing so Nuala shrugged and let them play.

"I hate rough boys," Rose said. "I don't want to play with them. That boy is spotty."

"Sam!" His father called him over and told him not to play with the other children. He smiled at Emma almost guiltily and sent a very sulky boy to sit in the car.

"I thought the boys were playing well for once," Nuala said. "That couple were quite friendly when we met them at the races, but maybe they think Liam is too rough."

"Sam has spots," Rose said again and Emma was alarmed.

"How many? Just a few on his face?"

"Lots and lots," Rose said with satisfaction.

Nuala walked over to the American couple and smiled. "Is something wrong?" she asked.

Sam's father looked very embarrassed. "We thought it would be fine out here in the fresh air with nobody about, then you turned up and Sam wanted to play. It was OK until they started on a tussle so I don't know what to say."

"Just tell me what the spots are," Nuala said sweetly, but her expression told him she needed a truthful answer.

"It's what all children have and it's nothing," he said defensively, then lowered his voice and said, "It's chickenpox."

"Praise be for that. It would be different if it was German measles."

"What's the difference?"

"My guest has to go back to England into a house where there's a pregnant girl."

135

He looked puzzled, and his wife stared at Nuala and lit a cigarette.

"You do know that if a pregnant woman is exposed to German measles, she might have a deformed baby?" Nuala said bluntly. "Are you sure it's only chickenpox?"

"Yes, we took him to the doctor and he told us," Sam's mother said.

"It could be worse," Nuala said with an air of resignation. "We'll look for spots in a week or so, after they were in such close contact just now."

"Sam isn't feeling ill and he has fewer spots today."

Nuala took Liam into the clubhouse and made him take off his jacket and change his jeans. "Maybe all the germs are on his clothes," she said hopefully and wrapped his top clothes in a towel, separate from the other things in the boot of the Land Rover.

The horses circled the yard, ridden by slender lads who had the same easy, almost casual manner as the ones they'd seen in the gypsy camp. "They all have the same ambition," Nuala said. "They want to ride a winner in a big race; and this is the best way to get on the books as a jockey after an apprenticeship here."

Rose stayed close to her mother, and even Liam seemed daunted by the tall sleek animals who bore no similarity to the sturdy ponies and donkeys he had ridden. "That's ours," he said at last and a stable boy nodded.

"The one with the white flash is it? He's a fine ride."

"I want to be a jockey." Liam looked at the lad with admiration.

"Don't get too big, or the horses won't take you,"

136

he was told. "How will you like mucking out for many months before you ever get to ride one of these?" He winked at Nuala.

Liam turned down his mouth. "I hate doing that," he said.

Nuala laughed. "Another career abandoned before it started. 'We've thought of being a train driver, a fireman and now a jockey, but Liam doesn't like hard work or getting up early." She rumpled his hair. "But he does like eating. Now what's it to be, Liam?"

In the restaurant they were served with watercress soup and roast duck, but Liam asked for bacon and scrambled eggs and Rose copied him. "He's a pain," Nuala said. "We bring him out for a treat and he has what he can have any day at home. This is delicious. Myra has no hand for duck. She overcooks it no matter how often I tell her to leave it pink in the middle, so we hardly ever eat it at home unless I cook it."

They watched a horse being exercised in the pool and when Nuala persuaded Liam that it was a pool for horses and not for little boys he lost interest. "Where's Sam?" he asked.

Emma told him she'd seen a car driven away by Sam's father, who had said they would stop off at a pub and eat out of doors away from people and go back to their rented apartment. "Kids!" he'd said. "This was supposed to be a holiday to take in a race or two, check on our horse and see Ireland, but Sam has ruined it. We feel like lepers and he gets tetchy in the evenings. I hope Liam doesn't pick it up," he added.

Twelve

"I'll have to go soon," Paul said. "I've stayed much longer here than I'd planned, but some of the work is relevant to Belfast as well as Dublin, and we've been in contact on the telephone. Connor was due to lecture in Belfast after me but he's changed round and that's given me a bit more time here."

"I shall be sorry to leave," Emma admitted. "Fortunately Nuala seems to want us to stay as long as we can, and the children get on very well, but we have been here for at least a week longer than anticipated, so Belfast, here we come."

"I'll ring about accommodation tomorrow," Paul said. "They offered me rooms in the university but I doubt if it would be private enough for three of us there, and it could be noisy."

"Nuala made me promise to come back for a few days on our way home, so we could leave some luggage here and pick it up on our return."

"You can pack later. Let's walk over to the paddock and say hello and goodbye to Sligo and Kavanagh." Paul grinned. "It's a pity we can't take a donkey home with us but we have no stable and I think Mrs Coster would object to dirty hooves on her nice hall floor!"

Emma raised an eyebrow. "A house-trained donkey? I don't believe there is such an animal."

"Rose? Liam? Anyone coming for a walk?"

Liam sidled into the room. "I'm not feeling well."

"We're going to see Kavanagh."

"Go on then," he said sulkily.

Emma bent down and looked at him more closely. The day before he'd been tired and wanted lots of cool drinks, yet had eaten well and played snap with Rose, but now he did look unwell. "Have you a pain?" she asked. He shook his head and rubbed his eyes. Emma unbuttoned the collar of his shirt and knew what to expect before she saw the spots. It was about right for the incubation period – there was no doubt that Liam had chickenpox.

"No walk now," she said to Paul. "I'd better see if Rose is all right."

Rose was asleep on the huge settee and Emma looked down at her flushed cheeks. "I don't think we can go to Belfast."

"Rose too?"

"A couple of spots on her face, which means there are many more on her body, and I think a raised temperature. I thought both the children were off colour a few days ago but hoped it was just because they were dashing about so much."

"Those Americans are not the most popular people I've met over here," Paul said grimly. "What are we to do? I shall have to go to Belfast alone, which is no problem, but we have a sick child who can't travel home on crowded ferries."

"And I must stay with her," Emma said.

"I hear you've seen Liam?" Nuala asked cheerfully. "He's very proud of his spots and says that Rose has them too, all over her back and tummy." She laughed. "A bit early to play doctors and nurses, but once again they have something in common . . . chickenpox."

"I can't take Rose to Belfast," Emma began, but Nuala shrugged aside her problem.

"I've asked Mary to make up the two small beds in the big room overlooking the garden. It will give us more space to look after them and they can compare spots to their hearts' content."

"I don't know what to say."

"The less said the better. It was our fault for letting Liam play with Sam, and this is easier if they have each other's company. Tara and Patrick had it when they were quite small so Tara can read to them if they feel a bit limp. I'll see what I have in the medicine chest. There should be some calamine lotion if it isn't all dried up, and we can get that easily from the local chemist."

"Do we have to call the doctor?"

"I'll ask him to look in. He enjoys a sherry before lunch so he'll be here about twelve if his past routine is anything to go by."

Mary put the two children to bed and gave them drinks. For once, neither of them wanted to play, soon drifting off to sleep. Emma packed a bag for Paul and decided rather guiltily that she would rather be with Rose and Nuala's family than kicking her heels in Belfast while she waited for Paul to finish lectures.

140

She glanced at the local newspaper and saw that another bomb had been set off in the Shankhill Road in Northern Ireland. She prayed that Paul would be safe.

"If I stay on the university campus I shall be away from any violence," he reassured her later. "These incidents make it even more essential for me to talk about stress and battle fatigue: some people still believe that there is no such malady, so people suffering are getting no help. Their attitude is as bad as that in the First World War, when men were hounded and sometimes shot for malingering."

"Be very careful," Emma said with vehemence. "Come back soon as we shall miss you. This is the first time we've been separated in a strange country and I hate it."

"The separation or the country?" he asked lightly.

She kissed his cheek. "The separation of course. I still love Ireland."

"Why do I feel a sense of relief that you aren't coming to Belfast? I suppose, in the back of my mind, I worry we could be taking Rose into danger. I shall give my lectures and maybe take a few sessions and come back as soon as I can, then we must go home."

"The spots are out" – Emma returned to the subject of Rose – "which means that they were infectious for a few days before that, so who knows how many local people they've infected?"

"Nuala hasn't had small children in the house lately, and we kept Liam and Rose out of the village because people who Nuala knows insisted on giving them too many sweets, so I can't think they've spread their little gift to anyone. I'm a bit rusty on infectious diseases. How long is the quarantine period after the spots are out?"

"A week after the spots have turned to little blisters and dried out," Emma said. "Most of the infection is spread before the spots appear but after that they recover fast. At least they don't have more serious symptoms like pain in the legs and muscles and very high temperatures."

Emma helped Mary give the children cool sponge baths and anointed them with calamine lotion until they looked like clowns in pinky-white make-up, which caused a lot of amusement. "You look like two ghosts," Tara said. "Ghosts with little red spots in the white make-up."

The doctor came and went, spending more time over his two large glasses of sherry than with the children. Nuala was relieved. "It's nothing, nothing at all," she asserted firmly.

"He hardly looked at them!"

"Don't underestimate him, Emma. He's a marvellous doctor if something is really bad, but he took one look at those two and said it was a mild infection. With you here, he was confident that we were doing all the right things and he might pop in to see them in a few days' time . . . when it will all be over and the sherry decanter will be topped up," Nuala added, with a laugh.

Paul telephoned every night and sounded bored with life in student accommodation, although he had dinner each evening with the professors in their more sumptuous dining room.

"Is it a busy hospital?" Emma asked when he told her he'd treated two patients who were recovering from bullet wounds but showed no signs of taking an interest in life.

"One advantage of a busy hospital is that they want to discharge patients as quickly as possible to make way for more urgent cases, so the ones I'm seeing will go to a convalescent hospital outside Belfast, with lovely views of the mountains. There's growing concern about the psychological harm done by violence and I hope I'm making sure that more doctors see what can be done by analysis under hypnosis."

"Surely the convalescent home is the place to do such work, in peaceful surroundings."

"I hope to go there for two days and do just that, starting tomorrow," Paul said. "I'm trying to collect a team to carry on after I leave, and there've been all the right murmurings, so after my visit to the Mountains of Mourne I shall be back with you and Rose."

"Buy some cards of local views. I envy you that visit: I wanted to go there, but I know it's impossible as according to Rose we have a very sick child. She tells me that when she wants something! I think she could have a career as an actress. I am a bit bored: all I do is stay here, dab on pink lotion and read the same books endlessly when Tara says she's had enough."

"Not long now, darling. I'm bored too. Suddenly, I want to see the London streets and have Mick tell me off for spending too much time with certain patients."

"We can go home at any time now. The vesicles have almost dried up and Rose and Liam are playing normally, but we still keep them in one room," Emma said. "I'll go into Dublin for last-minute shopping and be ready whenever you say we can leave."

With Mary in charge of the children, Nuala said she'd take Emma out to lunch in Dublin. "We deserve it, and the children are almost well, so let's make the most of this spell of fine weather and forget calamine lotion and Beatrix Potter books for a couple of hours."

"I feel almost civilised," Emma said as she pushed aside her depleted lobster and drank the last of her glass of white wine.

"I'm sorry you have to go back," Nuala said. "It's as if I'd found a long-lost sister."

"I feel the same. I wish we lived closer to each other. Rose will miss Liam, too, and I don't think Jean will fill that gap. However, I've bought toys for both of them and that will make their next meeting easy. It's a pity Clive's left, as Rose adores him, but Margaret wanted to get the apartment in Hampshire ready for the baby and for George to have a good welcome home when the Navy sends him back. She sounded very excited when I got through eventually on the phone last night and I think she's very happy and healthy."

"She's lucky to be pregnant," Nuala said wistfully. "I wanted more children, but after the last one I was advised to forget that and concentrate on the family I have."

"You have three healthy children." Emma tried to

sound objective. "I have one and hope for more but as yet we haven't been lucky."

Nuala smiled. "And what has that fey aunt of yours to say about that? I envy you such a relative. I can imagine her sitting with her feet on the fender round the fire, drinking strong tea laced with whiskey and sharing her gift of second sight."

"She doesn't do that all the time. She's a very shrewd woman and half of what she tells people is plain common sense." Emma laughed. "She has never been to Ireland and has no desire to do so but she was excited when I said we were coming here, as if the visit would be good for me in many ways."

"It has been for me," Nuala said. "Michael and I will never forget that in half an hour Paul released Tara from fear and made her glow again. You may shake your head and smile but it's true. One thing is true of the Irish, we never forget a good deed done to us and never forget a bad one." She sighed. "That may account for the troubles here."

"Back to Beatrix Potter, unless there's something more interesting in that bookshop."

"Too young, too old, and I'm not reading that one out loud or I'll weep," Nuala said dismissively as they looked through the stock.

"And this one would bring leprechauns back into the conversation again, so not that one," Emma added. They bought picture books of horses and farm animals and *The Wind in the Willows* for reading aloud and went home refreshed.

Rose was playing with Plasticine and showed Emma

a deformed animal, bright green with one leg shorter than the others as she had run out of green. "It's Sligo," she explained. "Can we go and see the donkeys?"

"I don't see why not. You could do with some fresh air, and a short walk will be fine, but no riding today as you both have a few drying spots."

"We'll take them some carrots," Liam said. "We won't ride them and we won't give them spots."

"A spotty donkey would be very strange," Emma replied, and dressed the two children warmly as there was a chill in the air that hinted at the coming autumn.

A few yellow leaves fluttered slowly down as they reached the paddock and Emma felt a pang of loss at the thought of autumn, the end of growth and the release of summer leaves. Who knew what might be in store? She remembered crunching dry leaves underfoot as she walked from the villa where the nurses lived to the main hospital when she was nursing wounded soldiers in Surrey. Autumn had always been a poignant time for her. It was in autumn that she'd braved the home on the Downs in Bristol and begun her nursing career, which turned her entire world upside-down.

She shook off the sudden depression, convinced that she was merely sad at the thought of leaving Nuala and the warm, intimate life of the family in Ireland. She held out a carrot to Kavanagh.

Rose watched her face and said, "Why are you sad, Mummy?"

"Not really sad, but we'll be sorry to leave Liam and the others when Daddy finishes teaching in Belfast."

"I don't want you to go!" Liam shouted and Sligo bucked away from the noise.

"You'll be coming to London to see us, and we can go to some lovely places," Emma said hastily.

"Promise?"

"Your mummy will come too and we'll all have a great time."

"You can get chocolate from a machine on the boat and write your name," Rose said, "and when we get home you can see the Changing of the Guard just like Christopher Robin did, and feed the ducks."

"Goodbye, donkeys," Emma said. "You've had all the carrots and now it's time for our elevenses."

"There's been a call from Paul," Nuala said when they got indoors. "It's nothing to worry you but he wanted you to hear it from him and not from the news."

"Is he all right?"

"Sure and he's fine, but a bomb dropped close to the university and destroyed a few walls. Paul's now on his way to the other hospital where, please God, they will not hurt him or the poor men already damaged," Nuala said fervently.

"Did he say when he'd be back here?"

"The day after tomorrow. We'll have a farewell dinner at Murphy's Barn and shed a few tears at your leaving us."

"I'd better pack a few things. It's amazing what I've bought since we came here."

"A few sweeteners for your staff," Nuala said shrewdly. "Do they expect so much?"

147

"I know I may have overdone that part, but Eileen and Mick are very precious, both as employees and as friends, and I hope that when we're home again the girls will find what they once had in common. After all, they will share memories of Ireland," she added hopefully.

"Don't push it. They're obviously different in many ways and you must accept it. Rose likes the boys best and I think Jean might be happier with girls and dolls."

"You're right, and when they go to school they will both make other friends."

Emma glanced at her watch for the third time. "You can't wait to set eyes on him, can you?" Nuala said and laughed.

Emma blushed. "It's ridiculous to feel like this after being married for so long, but the bomb scare made me want to gather him up and make sure he was safe."

"You can do that tonight," Nuala said mischievously. "Not now! I hear the car, so we can eat before I starve. Paul said he'd be here by lunchtime and he just made it."

"I smell Irish stew," Paul said after he'd kissed Emma.

"And I smell chocolate," Rose said hopefully.

"After lunch when I unpack my bag," Paul promised, and hugged her. "No spots?" he asked.

"All gone, and we're clear to go home according to the doctor."

"You just missed him, but he did leave enough sherry for us to have a glass before lunch," Nuala said.

148

"We do have spots," Liam said firmly. "Lots and lots and you can't go home."

"You will see us again soon," Emma said.

"You can't go! I'll never come to your house, and you'll forget all about me."

Paul took him by the hand. "There's a big calendar in Daddy's study. Let's make a mark on it to show when you will be coming to London. That mark will make it certain and you can see how quickly the time goes before you do come to us."

He glanced at Nuala, who nodded and suggested a date in about a month's time. Liam went off happily with Paul to ruin his father's neat calendar with crayon smudges.

"Can you manage that date?" asked Emma.

"My time is flexible, and Mary can cope while we're away. I doubt if Patrick would want to leave just now as he's helping to gentle a foal and thinks he's the world's best trainer." She sighed. "The summer goes too fast. I was forgetting that they'll both be at school and not have time to come to England, but Liam and I can come."

Paul telephoned Mick to make sure that a car would be ready to pick them up from the ferry port for the long drive home, and suddenly London seemed very near. "We can leave this hire car at the ferry terminal so our luggage will be easy to manage there; we'll take our time to drive back from Wales to London." He grinned. "Time enough for us to get used to the idea of going back to work."

Dinner in Murphy's Barn was as good as the first time and the fiddles and tin whistles were in great form, but the party in the gallery didn't stay late and went back to the house in a sober frame of mind.

"Don't be sad," Paul said when they were ready for bed. "Ireland isn't far away and you have a real bond now. Nuala will be in London before you know it and even Rose is looking forward to showing off to Jean."

"I know, but I shall miss Nuala very much. It's almost like being with Bea, but different."

"That's a bit Irish!"

"You know what I mean."

"Come to bed. Our last night in Ireland and our last night with nothing on our minds but each other and the way we are in love."

"It's wonderful to have you back," Emma whispered. "I was frightened when I heard of the bomb and wanted to hold you close to protect you."

"You can do that now," he said.

Thirteen

"I contacted Mick and explained that we're staying the night at a hotel halfway between the ferry and home as Rose is still a little fragile and weepy after leaving Liam and Tara, and the journey seems to be worrying her more than usual."

"Everything under control at home?" Emma asked.

Paul laughed. "It's just as well Rose had chickenpox in Ireland, as there's an epidemic in London and the Home Counties and Jean came out in spots yesterday."

"That's a relief. I thought we were safe to go home, but there was a niggling doubt about Rose being able to pass it on even though the doctor said she was well over the infection. I would hate Jean to have caught it from Rose."

"I bet she doesn't have as many spots as we did," Rose said.

"I should keep quiet about that. She may have lots more than you," Paul replied. He eyed her quizzically. "Don't you like Jean any more?"

"I do like her, but she can get anything she wants if she cries and you don't let me have as much as that." Rose went red. "I do like her but I hate her when she cries for things and tries to take mine."

"Does she do that?" Emma was worried.

"She tries, but I stop her and then we quarrel."

"Are the things that Jean cries for what you want?" Paul asked.

"No, they're silly things like dolls' clothes which I don't really want," Rose admitted.

"I don't see that you have a problem," Paul said. "You have lots of things that Jean doesn't have and you don't care for dolls."

Rose laughed. "It's fun making her cross, Daddy. She didn't like me playing with Clive or talking about Mark, and her friends aren't nice so she tries to take my things."

Paul looked serious. "Remember this, Rose. Jean didn't go to America and you did, Jean didn't have Mark and the other two children to play with and you did, Jean didn't have a lot of treats that you had when Clive and his mummy were here, and Jean doesn't have Aunt Emily and you have. She feels left out, so you must be nice to her. You are the lucky one." He ruffled her hair. "Maybe if we left you to stay with Mick and Eileen and Jean you could ask for whatever you wanted."

"No, Daddy. I want to stay with you. You wouldn't give me to them, would you?" she asked anxiously.

He hugged her tightly. "Never. We love our naughty, nice little girl and we want to keep her, but you must learn to share more with Jean. If she tries to be silly, just walk away and do something else."

"I can tell her nicely about Ireland and the donkeys. She doesn't like donkeys so she won't want one," Rose said, as if making a concession. She looked up slyly.

"What have you bought for us when we get home? I felt two parcels but couldn't see inside and I know they are for us."

"Miss Fiddle Fingers must wait," Paul said. "I might have bought some things, but they might be for Christmas," he teased.

Rose flung her arms round him. "Now I *know* they're for us."

"At least she seems to want to go home now," Emma said. "I do too. Having got this far away from Ireland, I look forward to seeing old friends and we shall see Nuala and Liam again very soon."

"You may have to take over from Eileen for a while if Jean is very demanding," Paul pointed out.

"Good. I shall enjoy that, but I shall never take over her place in the household again. I can relieve her for breaks, and Rose need not be isolated from Jean as it's unlikely that she'll be infected again."

Kensington was quiet and the leaves on the trees lining the streets sighed softly as if nothing was urgent. The two bay trees guarding the entrance to the house and clinic were freshly trimmed into elegant round shapes on slender trunks, and it was evident that Mrs Coster had given the steps an extra special welcoming scrub.

"Dwight and Bea made sure we would never forget them," Paul said when he saw the bay trees. "Remember the day when Dwight staggered in with those trees? They were terribly expensive but he insisted they added a lot of tone to the house, to impress private patients, and so they have."

153

"I think of Bea each time I come through that doorway," Emma agreed, and hurried into the hall.

Rose ran up the stairs into her bedroom and put her small case on the bed. "Can I see Jean now, Mummy?"

"Not yet. I'll go down to their flat and see if Eileen is there and ask her if Jean is ready for visitors. I don't think Eileen is in the kitchen." Emma walked slowly down the side staircase. The kitchen was not as tidy as usual and there was dirty washing-up left on the draining board. Of course, she told herself. Robert was now living in the house and he might have had a meal at an odd time between cases. If Eileen was busy with Jean she would leave such minor details until she was free.

"Oh, sister! You're back!" Eileen burst into tears.

Emma was alarmed. "What's wrong? How is Jean?"

"She's so difficult, and I've never had to nurse a very sick child in my whole life," Eileen said, dramatically.

"She's very ill?"

"The doctor says not, and hints that she's shamming, but they aren't always right. Jean says she feels ill and wants me here all the time. I can't get on with my work until she drops off to sleep. Last night I was up until midnight polishing the sitting room ready for you today."

"If you aren't used to illness it is very confusing," Emma agreed tactfully. "Is she really feeling ill or is she enjoying the time you give to her?"

"She wouldn't put it on," Eileen said, in a shocked voice.

"Oh yes she would," Mick said from the doorway. "Eileen spoils her something rotten and then wonders why Jean plays up."

"That's not true, Mick Grade." Eileen was close to tears again, so Mick shrugged and went back up to the office to brief Paul on what had been happening while he was away.

"Let me see her," Emma said. She opened the bedroom door and stood by the bed, smiling at Jean, who was sitting up surrounded by toys. "Hello, spotty," she said cheerfully.

Jean looked annoyed as she detected the lack of awe that a sick child should generate.

"I'm very ill," she muttered.

"Then all you'll want to do is sleep and have drinks," Emma said kindly. "I'll tell Rose that you're too sick to have visitors. If you sleep now, your mummy can get on with her work; you'll soon be better and then you can play."

"I want . . ." began Jean, then stopped before her mother could rush to her side, as Emma was in the way.

"You seem to have everything there," Emma said firmly. "Toys and books and a drink on the table, and you can take yourself to the lavatory."

"I want to see Rose," she whined in a plaintive little-girl voice.

"When you're better and not needing to have your mother with you all the time," Emma said firmly. "We all have work to do and I need Mummy upstairs, so be quick and ask for anything you *really* need now, and she will bring you your supper after you've had a nap."

Jean gave her an angry look and sank into the bedclothes with the sheet over her head.

"She's upset," Eileen said accusingly.

"Yes, I think she is," Emma said in a clear voice that penetrated the bedclothes. "She'll be fine alone until suppertime. I'll explain to Rose that she can't see Jean until she's better and not making such a fuss over a few spots. She'll be disappointed, as she wants to show what we bought in Ireland, but she'll have to wait." She paused as if turning to Eileen, speaking in a lower voice. "It's not much fun for Rose if Jean whines all the time and doesn't play nicely, so I'll keep her upstairs until Jean's feeling brighter. Come along, Eileen, I want to hear all about what's been happening while we were away, and we must arrange a rota of work that I can share with you until Jean is up and about." She shepherded the reluctant Eileen out of the room and closed the door behind her.

"What if she needs something?"

"She doesn't need anything but a good rest," Emma said firmly; and when Eileen crept down half an hour later, Jean was fast asleep and soon Eileen was laughing with Emma about the many good moments they had enjoyed in Ireland.

"Mick loved the stout," Eileen said. "We met some nice people and I liked the music in the pubs. Mick won fifty pounds at the races and he's put that aside towards our next holiday, whenever that may be. We might be able to go to a really nice hotel."

"We started out in a good hotel but we were very bored. I was so glad to go to a private house and have the company of the family there. Rose made friends with Liam, the smallest child of the family, and they

156

rode donkeys and did a lot of things they couldn't do in a hotel."

"Jean doesn't like boys," Eileen said. "Clive teased her and said that dolls were silly."

"Clive is old enough to know better. I'm sure he didn't mean to be unkind."

"What really upset her was that you took him and Rose to see the Changing of the Guard without her."

"Has she ever said she wanted to go there?"

"Well, no," Eileen admitted. "Mick tried to take her once but she began to cry and said she didn't want to see big rough men marching." Eileen looked thoughtful. She put away a couple of casserole dishes and dried some plates. "Mick says Jean is getting to be a pain in the neck and must come to terms with the fact that she can't have everything. But when I was little I had nothing much, and so I suppose I do spoil her."

"That's understandable, but if you spoil a child, the real treats mean nothing," Emma pointed out. "Obviously you want the best for Jean, but she will value occasional gifts more than if she asks for something and has it straight away."

"She keeps on about a leppercorn," Eileen said. "She said that Rose is bringing one home and she gets upset when she thinks she isn't going to have one."

Emma laughed. "We had a problem there. Rose was convinced that leprechauns were real and could grant her wishes, but we have managed to show her that they are just imaginary, like fairies, and that the dolls they make dressed in green are just toys."

"Jean did want one." Eileen sounded almost frightened of what the child would say or do if thwarted, and Emma made a mental note to hold the dolls in reserve until Jean's outlook was less anti-social.

Emma cooked dinner for Robert, Paul, Rose and herself; Mick and Eileen went down to their own apartment. Rose nodded with sleepiness and went to bed without fuss while the adults sat talking over glasses of wine.

"Joan's working this evening," Robert said.

"I'm looking forward to seeing her again," Emma assured him. "She's made the spare room very comfortable, and the sooner you get married the sooner you can move in together, except when you want to stay in Covent Garden."

"We want to have a very private ceremony, with only about a dozen guests including you and Paul. Joan doesn't want a white wedding in church, so I thought a civil ceremony sometime next month might be suitable."

"That's wonderful. If it's such a small party, we can have the reception here. It will be fun," Emma stated firmly when she saw his doubtful expression.

"What time off do you want?" Paul asked. "Take what you need: the clinic's running smoothly and we can cut down on appointments for non-urgent cases for a week or so."

"We thought we could go to Cornwall for a week, but we both want to come back after that and settle down to living together. Joan can take leave and come back to work in casualty on a part-time basis."

"Gradually the house is filling up, but we still have

room for guests," Paul said. "You'll like Nuala and her small dynamo, Liam."

"Will all this be too much for Eileen? She has her hands full with Jean and seems unsettled."

"She will be fine. As the spots disappear and Jean gets bored with being an invalid, Eileen can get back to work and leave Jean to play alone, or with Rose when I allow it."

Robert looked impressed. "You've managed to keep Rose away from the flat?" He grinned. "A brilliant psychological move, Emma. I can't imagine Jean staying in bed now, if she thinks she may be missing something."

Paul frowned. "It's difficult to undo the damage to a spoiled child, but we can't risk Rose becoming like her. I think she realised that we wouldn't let her be as bad as Jean when we were in Ireland. A healthy, selfish boy did wonders for her and she is very reasonable now."

"I feel sorry for Mick and Eileen," Emma said. "Tomorrow, I shall send them off to the pictures together after they've given Jean her supper, and I'll keep an eye on her." She stood up and sighed. "I'm sleepy, but I must unpack more of the clothes or they'll be a mass of creases."

"We'll do the washing-up," Robert promised. "That is if we have the energy after that lovely meal."

The cases, open on the bed, looked formidable but Emma sorted out clothes for washing and pressing and hung the rest away. She brought a black suit out of the closet and wondered if it needed dry-cleaning. It was a suit she'd bought at the height of the popularity of clothes worn by Jacqueline Kennedy. Every other girl with a reasonable figure had worn the smartly cut jackets and pencil-slim skirts topped by the Jacqui pillbox hat, and Emma had discarded the outfit as she hated to be one of a crowd; but now, with other accessories, it might be useful.

She slipped out of her dress and pulled the skirt on, then found the zip was difficult to do up and the waist button was impossible. "Damn!" she said softly.

The food in Ireland and the additional leisure had not been exactly slimming, but she had no idea she'd added so much to her waistline. She thought back. The suit had been close-fitting and she had always changed out of it as soon as she came home from meeting friends as the waistband was tight, but this was more than that. Slowly she put it back on the hanger and found that her heart was beating fast.

She opened her handbag and took out her diary. The visit to Ireland was clearly marked and so were the usual circles indicating her periods. She had been so busy and involved with other matters that she'd forgotten to check – she hadn't had a period for over two months!

Emma sat on the bed, not knowing if she wanted to laugh or cry. She ran her fingers over her breasts and found them slightly fuller than usual. Her face in the mirror seemed the same, but pale, and her excitement grew, then faded. It must be a false alarm. She had no morning sickness and felt fine.

"Finished?" Paul asked and looked up from his book. "What's wrong?" He put the book down and stood up. "You look pale. Was the journey so bad? We've been

160

selfish. I should have taken you out for a meal instead of you having to cook for all of us."

"It isn't that." She buried her face in his jacket and he had to bend over her to hear the words. "I think I'm pregnant, Paul." She raised her face to his and he was almost overwhelmed by her sudden serene beauty and his own elation. "Tell me it's true," she whispered. "I'm a month overdue but I've had no sickness, so is it a false alarm? If it is I don't think I can bear it."

"Do you feel as you did when you were expecting Rose?"

"No, I feel wonderful."

"We can't diagnose you tonight as obstetrics is not my subject, but I'll ring Stella in the morning and you can see her as soon as possible. She will tell you the truth and not make half-baked assumptions." He laughed. "Unless you want to consult Mrs Coster first? She has all the experience in the world after her brood and must have known people with pregnancies without sickness."

"I'll stick to Stella," Emma said firmly, but her colour returned and she smiled normally. "I mustn't think of it yet, but this convinces me how much I want another baby."

"We'll keep this to ourselves until we know if it's certain," Paul said. "Just make sure you lift no heavy weights or strain yourself in any way."

He made her sit down in an armchair and brought her hot milk with chocolate powder in it, her favourite treat when she was tired or overworked.

"Biscuit? I found some in a tin that Bea left here and they seem to be OK. What's the matter? Too hot?"

A seraphic smile as she thrust the hot drink away was full of triumph. "That tastes horrible," she said. "I fancy some Bovril."

"We're not going through that again, are we?" he asked in mock despair.

"It was tea the last time," she said complacently. "I really do think I *am*!"

The phone rang and Paul answered it. "We were going to ring you tomorrow but it's lovely to hear from you," he said warmly. "Here she is."

"Aunt Emily?"

"Who else? You sound in good form." Emily giggled. "How are you? Was it very good in Ireland? I had your card and it's time you came down here for a few days to be fed and rested. Rose too, after her chickenpox."

"I may do that, but Jean has chickenpox now and Eileen isn't very good at dealing with her as she's very spoiled and demanding."

"All the more reason for you to come away. You don't want to do much just now. Think of yourself for once and let them sort out their own affairs."

"It was Rose who had chickenpox, not me! I'm fine."

"Good. I'll expect you next week, and I expect Margaret will come over for a day to see you." She chuckled. "You have things in common."

"Aunt Emily! How can you possibly know? I only found out this evening and I haven't been seen by Stella yet!"

"I saw it before you went to Ireland. I knew it would happen there and I was right, wasn't I?"

"Yes," Emma said softly. "I'm glad it started there."

"Does Rose know?"

"Not yet. I have to get used to the idea first and choose the time carefully – after I've seen Stella to confirm it."

"It's different this time."

"What do you mean?"

"You sound very well and you aren't being sick," Emily said.

"Is that all you can tell me?" Emma tried to hide her disappointment.

"Margaret asked me if her baby would be a boy or a girl; I said I didn't like to forecast such things and she must wait and be thankful for what she is given."

"And that's what you want to say to me?" Emma asked drily. "All right, I can wait. I don't care what it is if it's healthy and has the right number of fingers and toes."

"There will be the right number," Emily said quietly. "Just rest well and come to see me soon. See Stella and leave the housekeeping to Eileen."

"You will be here when it comes?" Emma felt a pang of apprehension.

"If you need me, but that's a long way off."

"I'll need you," Emma said softly. "I'll always need you."

"You have your own strength, but I'll be there," Emily promised. She chuckled. "Look out those maternity clothes and tell me if you want anything. Let me know what Stella says."

Fourteen

"It was nice to get out with Mick," Eileen said.

Mick grinned and eyed his wife with tolerant humour. "She managed to forget Jean for two hours," he said, "and even suggested that we stop to buy fish and chips on the way home, like we used to do."

Emma laughed. "And when you got back, Jean was still alive and fast asleep."

Eileen busied herself in the kitchen with more energy than she'd shown since Jean had contracted chickenpox. "It was a lovely evening. We saw the news too and a bit about the Eurovision Song Contest they had some time ago. They said they might have it every year, with lots of countries taking part, but I couldn't understand a word the singer said. Where's Lugano?"

"Switzerland," Paul said. "Is that where they had it?"

"A girl called Lys Assid won with a song called 'Refrain'. Let's hope a British singer wins next time," Mick said. "I thought it a bit soppy but Eileen liked the clothes everyone wore. Some were a bit . . . you know . . . and I don't want you wearing anything like it," he said sternly. "Some of them showed more than you'd see in an underwear advert."

164

"And you didn't enjoy that, I suppose?" Eileen said.

"Not on my wife," Mick said. "They showed a lot about show business. I liked the bit about Elvis Presley. Now there's a *real* singer." Mick danced a few steps and intoned the only words he knew from the song. "You can do most anything but don't tread on my blue suede shoes."

"If I can't have pretty clothes like the film stars, you can't have suede shoes," Eileen said. "Do you know, I caught him looking at a pair in that shop down the road? Mrs Coster says that only pimps and swindlers wear them, so you can polish up your old brown brogues or buy some soft slip-ons."

"They were plain brown," Mick protested. "I think they're very smart."

Emma and Paul left them happily wrangling and went into the consulting room. Rose was in her bedroom doing a puzzle that Emma had found in the collection of toys they had bought in Ireland and Jean was dressing her dolls. She was quiet and less demanding now, and her spots were fading, but she wasn't allowed out of her own home until there was no possibility of her passing on any infection to Paul's patients.

"I think the evening out did a lot for them," Paul remarked. He grinned. "Mick seems to have had more than fish and chips when he got home. He hasn't had that light in his eyes for some time."

Emma laughed. "Whatever it was, Eileen looks happier and she has decided that Jean can't have everything she wants and have her dancing attendance all the time."

"*You* convinced her of that: Jean takes notice of what you say," Paul remarked. "By the way, I organised a session with Stella this afternoon, so be ready at two and I'll drive you there."

"I can manage it alone," Emma began.

"I'll take you. This concerns me too, and I shall take you to have tea afterwards if it's good news."

"What if it isn't?"

"It will be, but if it isn't, I'll still take you to tea at the Ritz."

"Aren't you forgetting something?"

"I can forget patients. Robert will take over."

"Not that. A full cream tea would be wasted. I shall have Marmite sandwiches and an apple for lunch, and possibly a boiled egg for dinner."

"What do I have? *I'm* not pregnant!"

"You won't starve," Emma said unsympathetically. "I think you have a patient now. I hear Mrs Coster in her royal mode showing someone upstairs. We should have bought more than one really pretty apron. She's wearing that one to death."

"Ask Bea to send another. I take it you'll be phoning her today?"

"Whatever the news." She smiled. "Aunt Emily saw no hitches and wants me to take Rose there for a day or so. It's a bit soon to be going there again, but I think it's a good idea."

"I do, too. Now, work," he said softly. "Good morning, Mrs Mortimer."

Emma took her jacket and settled her comfortably on the couch. Mrs Mortimer sighed. "I feel better just coming into this room." Her scars were fading but her hand was held awkwardly and seemed to have lost its function. Emma touched it and the skin was cold.

"How has it been?" Paul asked. He consulted her notes. "It's two months since the car accident, but Dr Forsyth wanted me to see you. He says you look a lot better than when you came here first but I am the one who uses hypnosis, and that may ease your mind about what happened. Do you use that hand yet?"

She shook her head but said nothing. Paul looked at the notes again. "Sister, will you ask Mr Grade to take over from you? I want him to make notes."

Emma looked surprised but left the room and asked Mick to take over.

"I expect you're busy," he assumed. "Straightforward hypnosis, is it?"

"Paul has the Thiopentone and there's everything he might need. Call me when she's ready to get off the couch and I'll bring her a cup of tea."

She was puzzled. The housekeeping was under control and the two girls were playing happily, so there was no need for Paul to send her away from what seemed like a routine consultation.

Robert put this head round the kitchen door. "Is Mrs Mortimer in there?" he asked. "I thought she must have gone, as you aren't with Paul."

"I was dismissed," Emma said shortly.

"Maybe I'll look in," he said. "Paul must have thought you had other things to do."

After half an hour of mixing a cake that they didn't

really need, Emma put it in the oven and read the daily paper, feeling unwanted.

At last Mick came out of the consulting room. "She's all yours, sister. If there's tea going, Himself can do with a cup, too." He shook his head. "Shocking business."

Emma made tea and carried the tray into the consulting room. She helped Mrs Mortimer into her jacket and shoes and poured tea. Paul looked tense, as if the session had drained him, but the patient was relaxed and drank her tea eagerly. Emma noticed that the hand that had been so limp was now able to hold a cup.

"Why did you push me out?" Emma asked as soon as Mrs Mortimer had left.

Paul eyed her with caution. "I didn't want you to hear what she'd say under hypnosis."

"She didn't seem all that ill, and her scars had faded almost completely – or so Robert said."

"She had malfunction of one hand that didn't respond to physio," Paul said.

"I noticed it was better when she took her cup," Emma recalled.

Paul sat down and took a deep breath. "The examination wasn't as bad as I thought, but even so, you would have found it traumatic just now. When the car crashed she was in the passenger seat with a baby who was wearing no restraint, although Mrs Mortimer was wearing a seatbelt. The baby was thrown out of her control and her hand was trapped when she tried to clutch the child."

"So she felt it was her fault that the baby was hurt?"

"Yes. Fortunately no real harm was done and the

child is fine, but each night Mrs Mortimer dreams that the child died; and the hand that failed to hold the baby refuses to work, or it did until today. She will need further analysis but she'll be well soon," he added with a reassuring smile.

"I'm glad to hear about it after your session and not while I was there," Emma admitted. "Thank you, Paul. I'm not really ready to face an account of harm to a baby. You know me too well, but it couldn't have been easy for you either, now that there may be a baby for us on the way."

"Well, this afternoon Stella can make sure that we're right," Paul said cheerfully. "We can eat at Mario's tonight and you can have plain spaghetti while I have a decent meal."

"I may be hungry and eat more than you do," she said.

He kissed her. "Be as difficult as you like. I still love you."

A jacket that Emma had discarded months ago as being too loose now seemed the perfect comfortable garment to wear when she saw Stella, and a long loose shirt and baggy trousers completed the picture of easy acceptance of the fact that she was not quite as lissom as usual.

Paul smiled and said nothing, but drove carefully as if the car contained a precious box of cut glass.

"I hoped I'd see you soon," Stella said as soon as Emma was sitting by the examination couch and had removed her jacket. She made a few notes and cast a practised gaze over Emma's figure and breasts. She took a blood-pressure reading and counted her pulse. "Fine," she said and chewed the end of her pen.

"You sounded surprised," Emma remarked.

"Not really. I saw that you're healthy as soon as you came in here, but you seem further on than I thought possible from your dates. Hop on the scales. I have a note of what you weighed the last time you came here for an examination, so let's compare. You've put on weight, I think."

"Too much good Irish food," Emma suggested.

"Maybe." Stella sounded pensive and checked the reading on the scales a second time. "No swollen ankles, and your specimen is clear, and you think you are two months pregnant."

"Perhaps three months," Emma said.

"On the couch." Stella felt the rising fundus of the uterus just behind the rigid pubic bone and smiled. "Three months, I think."

"I've had no sickness," Emma said as if she disbelieved Stella's words.

"Aren't you the lucky one! You may escape that and just bloom happily. It must have been the Guinness or the seafood!"

"Why is it so amusing? Are you sure everything's all right?"

"I don't need to do an internal today. It's quite, quite positive without me interfering at this stage."

"You're sure?"

"Sure and doubly sure." Stella gave a delighted laugh. "As far as I can tell, and I'm pretty sure even now, I think you may have twins in there."

"I can't believe it!" Tears of shock rolled down Emma's cheeks but she felt calm and happy. She began to giggle. "Bea will be thrilled. She'll say that I try to outdo her even now, and pretend to be jealous, then probably make an excuse to come over to see for herself how I am."

Stella wagged an admonishing finger at her. "You will now vegetate and do exactly as you are told."

"Yes, ma'am," Emma said humbly. "May I go now and tell Paul?"

"I suppose that aunt of yours knows?"

"How can she? Oh, dear, she does! When I said I didn't mind what it was so long as it was healthy and had all its fingers and toes, she said something about there being the right number of everything."

"Twenty tiny fingers and twenty tiny toes . . . as the song says. I could use her in the clinic."

"She's promised to be here when it happens and she doesn't seem worried," Emma said slowly. "I don't know why I feel so calm, but I trust her almost as much as I trust you. I know I shall be fine."

"I'm proud to be included with your diagnosing aunt," Stella said, and laughed. "Make sure you rest and eat sensibly and have lots of friends visiting you – if you don't have to work hard entertaining them – and see me in two weeks' time."

Paul was waiting by the desk in reception, talking to an old friend who was still working at Beattie's as an anaesthetist. The two men stopped talking and eyed Emma with speculation. "Well?" asked Paul.

"Very well," Stella said. "Emma, meet Martin and

smile at him. We might need an anaesthetist who can help you without making you sick. No, don't be alarmed, Paul. Just looking ahead at all contingencies. Some women *do* have a caesarean for twins, but I doubt if Emma will need that." She chuckled. "Ask her Aunt Emily and let me know what to expect."

"Twins?" For a moment Paul completely lost his calm and held Emma's hands in his. "Really twins?"

"I don't think it's more than two," Stella said. "Come into my sitting room and have coffee before you drive anywhere, Paul. It's quite a shock, isn't it?"

She showed them where her room was and asked the ward maid to take in coffee, then pleaded pressure of work and left them alone.

"It's wonderful," Paul said with a note of awe.

Emma said shakily, "I feel rather like a brood mare, and Stella wants me to become a calm fat cow!"

"Not both," he said in mock alarm. "But you will have to take everything slowly and rest a lot. No alarming tales from the clinic, and Maureen will have to look after Rose."

"Paul! This is *me*. I am fit and must have exercise as well as rest and Rose is very good now, so please don't smother me with care, much as I enjoy it," she said and kissed him. "No coffee for me, just water from that jug, and I must buy some fruit juice. What I'd like now is a mint humbug and a banana."

"Not at the same time?"

"Possibly," she replied, teasing him. "You look terrible, darling. I'll ask Robert to have you in for a session to iron out your hang-ups and anxieties. Ready? I have letters to write and calls to make. Can't waste time here." It was as if a niggling veil was lifted away, revealing the blue sky again, and she was full of excited energy.

"Do we tell her?" Paul asked when they opened the front door and met Mrs Coster, who was wiping her hands on her scrubbing-apron.

"How can we avoid it? She's lying in wait for the news."

"What did she tell you that we didn't know already?" Mrs Coster asked in a superior voice. "I've had enough babies, I ought to know. I said to Maureen I thought you'd got your dates wrong. That jacket will soon be too tight."

"I know," Emma said. "We did get one thing wrong. I might have twins."

"Just wait until I tell Maureen! You'll really need a full-time nanny when they come," she announced with satisfaction. Mrs Coster dried her hands and picked up her bucket. "You're healthy so it should be as easy as shelling peas from a pod," she said.

"First I'm a brood mare and now I'm a pea pod," Emma whispered. "What next, when I tell Bea? But first there's Eileen and Mick, otherwise Mrs Coster will tell them and they'll be hurt."

"Why not post a bulletin in the hall and let the whole of Kensington into the secret?" Paul said drily. "Oh, here's Robert; I think I can just beat Mrs Coster to it. See you at lunch, if we're eating. You'd better get to Eileen now. Mrs Coster has *important news* in her eyes."

173

"Rose has to know," Emma said, biting her lip. "How will she react?"

"I'll tell her that when you saw the children in Ireland you thought it would be a good idea to have a baby brother or sister for her to play with and look after. I don't think it's a good idea to say the leprechauns gave you a wish, or she might wish too hard and we'll find ourselves with quads!"

"Are you going to be faddy over food?" was Eileen's first reaction. She seemed on edge, and when Emma added that she was not only pregnant but it might be twins, Eileen burst into tears. "It's not fair," she sobbed.

"I thought you didn't want another baby."

"I don't know. Sometimes I do, and then I think of being fat again and hate the idea. Jean wants a sister and Mick keeps on about us having another and now he'll be mad at me for not copying you."

"If it's important to either of you there's plenty of time," Emma suggested.

"I like my job and I like being slim again," Eileen said with a toss of her head. "I didn't have much before I married Mick and now I feel . . . important." She blushed. "The butcher down the road calls me madam and the postman acts as if I'm mistress of the house. It may not be much to you, but it is to me."

Emma smiled. "You are mistress of the household. A skilled housekeeper rules her own little kingdom and you look after us very well."

"That's nice to know," Eileen said. "What do you want for lunch?"

"The same as Paul and Robert. It's soup and sandwiches today, isn't it?"

Mick looked bleak when he met her, then turned away at the office door. Emma wondered what he thought about the news, and when Eileen brought the soup into the dining room she noticed that she had a very red face and had been crying. She piled rolls on to a dish and made sure there were plates for the sandwiches and cheese.

Emma noticed that Paul had seen the tears too but neither of them mentioned it to Eileen or Mick.

A crash from the kitchen and a muffled expletive told them that Mick was not his usual calm self and was very annoyed.

"And our next patient will be . . ." whispered Robert.

"It could happen when Nuala and Liam come to stay," Paul said. "Mick has always wanted a boy and Liam is such a little tough guy he'd fit into his scheme of what a son should be and bring Mick a lot of joy."

"They do say that pregnancy is catching," Emma reminded them. "Perhaps this will happen to them and everyone will be happy. I can't bear to see such good people upset."

Paul saw her yawn. "You have to have a nap each afternoon," he told her. "Stella was firm about that."

Emma tried to look stubborn. "Doesn't the brood mare have an opinion?"

"No," both men said together.

She sighed and picked up her jacket. "See you later. I ought to look at my wardrobe again. I feel a bit

175

bloated and I can't think of much that will fit me in a few weeks' time."

"Joan will help you," Robert assured her. Emma looked at the two men and smiled. It was wonderful to have such care.

"I'll leave it until she comes here," she said. "At least I shall be fine for your wedding," she added, and gave them a look that forbade any disagreement. "Nothing has changed. I have the reception all planned and Maureen is coming in for a whole day to help with the children."

Mick was loitering outside the kitchen when she went out to go to her room. He grinned apologetically. "I haven't said congratulations."

"No need, Mick. We both know how you feel about us and I know that you will have another baby one day, so don't be too hurt that Eileen wants a breathing space."

He looked ashamed. "I went spare when the doc told me, and took it out on her. First time I've made her cry for ages."

"I think Eileen realises that Jean needs a brother or a sister, so go carefully and don't make her stubborn just for the sake of paying you out." Her dimples appeared mischievously. "Say you're sorry you were upset but that you were disappointed for her, as it's not fair that we should have all the fun and she would feel left out!"

Mick laughed. "Too many shrinks round here, but I see what you mean. I'll be as nice as pie and once Jean starts whining that she wants a baby too, I think that will settle that old lark."

Fifteen

"Have you something I can take with me to read?" Margaret looked along the bookshelves and picked out a light novel, then put it back. "I've gone off romantic novels and I'm not up to more serious books since Alistair was born. I think he fancies himself as a tub-thumper. He makes enough very determined noise for a Member of Parliament!"

"Wind," Emma said firmly.

"Too much spoiling," replied Margaret. "Janey can't resist him and picks him up as soon as he starts whimpering."

"Does it bother you?" Emma shifted into a more comfortable position in the deep armchair and winced when her sciatic nerve pointed out that a couple of babies was a burden that wasn't natural, especially when they kicked.

"Not at all, I love it, but coming to London was a very good idea. George will be off his ship today and we can go home together after he's been debriefed at the Admiralty. He can hold his son when he bawls and I can look on indulgently."

"You look very happy."

"I'm so happy I could burst, and I want to make George happy too."

"You've already done that, and he'll come back to a slim and beautiful wife with a baby boy who looks like him." Emma smoothed her heavy lump and sighed. "You give me courage. It *will* be over and I *might* get my figure back."

"Aunt Emily said she'll be with you in a day or so and stay for a while." Margaret laughed. "She's such a wonderful person. She told me that Alistair would be delivered quickly and without fuss and he was. He couldn't wait to get into the world and fight for his place in it!"

"Clive seems pleased."

"He sees another sailor coming into the family. And he's so busy at school that he hasn't really had time to be jealous."

"Paul is taking you to the Admiralty to pick up George, and the powers that be will take you to Hampshire, so I shan't see you or George again this time." She laughed. "In fact, I shall be having a nap, as befits a wallowing whale!"

"She's got over the brood-mare stage," Paul said. He grinned. "I wouldn't dare call her a whale but I do see her point."

"I almost wish I knew what to expect," Emma said with a frown. "Maybe it's as well that I can't even guess, but two of the same sex might be nice, or then one of each might be even better."

"Whatever they are will be welcome," Paul said warmly.

"At least I can't complain of the care I'm having," Emma said. "Bea was here last week and brought a lot of lovely baby things, plus her own brand of caustic humour which put me in my place when I moaned about my lump and did a lot of good. She has a lot in common with Aunt Emily and sneaked off to see her for a day, to Emily's delight."

"What about your friends in Ireland?"

Emma sighed. "They couldn't come because Patrick fell off a horse and spent a week in hospital, but they will come later."

"Why are you laughing?" Margaret asked.

"You haven't asked about the help I have *here*."

"Why? Is there a problem?"

"Eileen has watched with ill-concealed horror as my girth extended rapidly and remembers when she was carrying Jean."

"Has it put her off having another?"

"Too late!"

"What do you mean?"

"I don't know what went on downstairs, but Eileen was very cross for a week or so recently, as if she'd been made to do something she wanted to avoid."

Margaret giggled. "You think Mick had his evil unprotected way with her?"

"It would be more polite to say he exerted his lawful conjugal rights," Paul said.

"And has anything happened?"

"Nothing, apart from morning sickness," Emma said with an innocent air. "I shall have to spoil her a little as soon as I've got over this. I didn't show her the

179

baby clothes that Bea brought over, but some will go to Eileen. Most of the girls' things are very pretty and I hope she has a girl as she doesn't care for boys."

"For the first few months it doesn't matter if a boy wears skirts. It's easier to keep clean."

"Is that the reason? In Ireland they say that all babies should wear girls' clothes for the first two years or so in case the leprechauns steal the boy babies."

"You don't believe that?"

"Of course not – and Aunt Emily is a match for any old leprechaun – but I'm glad we didn't give the girls the dolls we brought back from Ireland. It might give Eileen ideas!"

"Alistair is yelling his little head off," Mick said complacently from the doorway. "What a lovely sound."

"I'll remind you of that remark very soon, Mick, and when ours are a bit more civilised, it will be your turn."

Mick blushed. "You heard Eileen in the loo?"

"Several times, so there can be no mistake. Have you taken her for a check?"

"Today. She has come to terms with it now, and is better than I thought possible."

"As soon as you tell us the news officially, I have some clothes she might like. I kept that rather nice silk suit that I wore during the early part of my pregnancy. She admired it so she can wear that."

"And I suggest that, as soon as she's eating more, you take her to Mario's in her best clothes for a celebration meal. That will do a lot for her morale. Mario has this fixation with pregnant women and thinks they are all beautiful and precious! He'll kiss her hand and make you jealous and she'll love it, as Emma did," Paul added drily.

Mick laughed. "Know what, doc? You'd make a good shrink!"

Margaret came back carrying her son. "A nice full nappy," she said happily. "With any luck he won't do it when George first sees him. "Shall we go now?"

She kissed Emma and held her tenderly. "I'll be with you in spirit, and Emily will tell me what is happening."

Paul packed the car with the bundles of nappies and other paraphernalia that small babies acquire, and Emma waved goodbye from a window.

She turned away and tried to read the newspaper but she was restless. Paul was busy with a patient and Robert was away for the day sorting out the flat in Covent Garden which was still convenient for him and his wife when they were in the West End or when Joan was working in casualty after their brief honeymoon.

Emma heaved her bulk out of the chair and went into the kitchen. She strained the chicken broth and added parsley and potato-flour thickener, making enough for Eileen, Mick and Jean as well as her own family and checking that there was enough bread for toast to go with it. Rose was helping Mrs Coster turn out a cupboard that gave up several lost toys and a few cobwebs, and Jean was playing with a friend in the basement.

Eileen sniffed and smiled. "I was coming to do that, sister. It does smell good. I'll take Jean's friend

181

home and call Mick as we have to go out this afternoon."

"It's good to see you hungry again," Emma said. "I heard you being sick a few times and asked Mick about it. He said you're going for a check today, so come back and tell me all about it. I'll lay the kitchen table and we can eat together."

Eileen came back after taking the little girl home and tidying Jean. Mrs Coster brushed Rose's hair and washed her hands, promising to wipe the dust from the long-lost toys before they went up to the nursery.

"The dolls can go to Jean," Rose said. "I'll keep the puzzles and the books."

"What if your mummy has a baby girl? You'll need dolls for her."

Rose shrugged. "She'll be like me and want a donkey," she replied. "And the boy will be like Mark and Liam and want a donkey too."

"It may be two girls," Emma said from the top of the stairs.

Rose wrinkled her nose. "No, I asked the leppercorns to send one of each."

"They can't do that. They are only fairy creatures."

"They like me," Rose said. "When I was down with Aunt Emily, I had a dream and they were very nice."

Emma took her into the kitchen where Paul was waiting for lunch. "Tell Daddy about it while I get the soup," she said with a warning glance at Paul.

Rose looked stubborn. "You told me there are no leppercorns but I saw them in my dream at Aunt Emily's and I talked to them and they told me about the babies."

"What if they were wrong, Rose?"

"They tell the truth."

"Not all the time," Paul said.

Rose darted away to fetch a book that Emma had overlooked when she wanted to remove anything about leprechauns and she showed them a picture of a leprechaun peeping round a large milk jug in a kitchen. "See!" Rose said triumphantly. "There are some."

"I didn't see it when I looked at that book."

Rose giggled. "The ones in my dream said he hid until you closed the book and then came out again."

"They may be wrong about the babies," Emma said again.

Rose took the book away and Paul said softly, "I'd be more worried if they were right. Do we have another Emily in the family?"

Mick answered the phone and called Emma. "It's your aunt," he said.

"Aunt Emily?"

"Just to say I shall be with you tomorrow, if that's all right? My doctor friend has to go to London and Surrey and said he'll bring me to you before he goes off to Reigate."

"That's wonderful. Tell him to be here for lunch," Emma said.

She walked back to the kitchen feeling pensive. Emily had mentioned that she might have to hire a car to bring her to London as the doctor would be unavailable in two weeks' time and she didn't want to have to twiddle her thumbs waiting for the birth for several days before it was due. She shrugged. Maybe

Emily was ready for a holiday and wanted to come early after all.

Emma put the remains of the chicken soup in a jug for Eileen to use and made a large Cornish pasty for lunch the next day. Stewed fruit would be enough for pudding, and she had ordered bread from the shop down the road. She went to sleep on the bed and woke feeling energetic enough to check over the case containing the clothes and toilet things that she'd want in the private wing of Beattie's when she needed to be admitted. She smiled. Silly me, she thought. I have another two weeks to wait, so nothing is urgent.

Rose came into the bedroom and sat on the bed. "Daddy said he'd help me write a letter to Liam when the babies have come." She leaned across nearer to Emma and put a hand on the swollen abdomen. She squealed with laughter. "That boy kicked me," she said.

"Not the girl?"

"She doesn't kick as hard," Rose said calmly. "See you soon," she said as she left the room; once again Emma felt that Emily was close.

Paul brought her hot lemon and a biscuit and drank his tea with her in the bedroom. "Everything all right?" he asked.

"I think so, but it will happen earlier than I imagined. Emily wouldn't come here before she had to, and even Rose seems to expect something soon."

"Shall I ring Stella and tell her your psychic aunt is on her way here, so clear the decks for action?"

"Of course not. She'd think we were crazy. You don't

think we are, do you? I haven't even a twinge. By the way, I've baked a pasty while you were out, for Emily and Dr Sutton tomorrow."

Paul could almost hear Stella's voice: "Let her do what she can and don't try to make her rest when she doesn't need it. She's strong and healthy but as soon as she gets restless and starts to make a nest – looking ahead and baking, tidying drawers and seeming to expect something to happen – ring me and we'll have her in before she goes into labour. Twins can make a few problems that can be avoided if we keep an eye on her."

He closed the door to the office while he called Beattie's.

"I was about to ring you," Stella said. "Emma has two more weeks to go but I would like her here tomorrow. A pity her aunt isn't coming to you until the dates we suggested, but never mind."

"When my wife does as you said, works to get everything ready, and then Emily announces that she's coming here tomorrow, two weeks early, I thought it was time I rang you," he said and laughed.

"Bring her in tomorrow afternoon," Stella said. "I never argue with witches. We may induce or it may be a caesarean."

"I brought you some rabbits from the farm," Emily said as soon as she'd said hello and asked if Emma was all right. "I'll cook them, as Eileen may be squeamish just now."

Paul grinned and kissed her cheek. "You bring an

equal quantity of sanity and madness to this house, and I know that everything will be fine."

"Did you doubt it?" Her eyes were full of the tenderness she hardly ever showed in physical contact, but she allowed Paul to hug her. "Janey sends her love," she said brusquely. "I'd better see Emma now if you'll take my bag up."

"Lunch as soon as Dr Sutton's ready, and a nice cup of tea afterwards," Paul said with a grin.

"Aunt Emily!" Emma and Rose converged on her and Rose clung to her coat.

"Are you staying to look after me while Mummy is away?"

"I thought you were going to look after *me*," Emily said. "I dare say we'll get on." She looked at Emma. "So you're going in today." She seemed pleased. "I did wonder."

"It's too early, but Stella is a bit fussy over twins."

"I told her you'd be here," Paul said. "That made up her mind to admit Emma now."

Emily looked embarrassed. "Nothing to do with me."

"It's going to be one of each, Aunt Emily."

"Is it, Rose? We'll wait and see." But she eyed the child with slight concern and changed the subject.

"If we are going, I'd rather be there or I'll need a nap," Emma said later. Paul took her case and extra jacket and a packet of fruit sweets, and Rose and Emily waved them off in the car.

"I'll ring this evening to say good-night," Paul said as soon as Emma was shown into her comfortable room.

"Yes, darling, do that," Emma said as if indulging a child.

Paul left, feeling excluded from the ancient feminine rites of new life, and Emma almost forgot her family for a while.

"A lot of hard work, but I think you can manage, Emma," Stella said. "I'll induce now and see what happens."

The injection to dilate the opening to the womb made Emma sleepy. She woke feeling as if she had a bad stomachache, then slept again until it was worse and Stella was examining her.

"Good girl. You can push gently now."

Emma tried to concentrate through the clouds of gas and air but was glad to leave everything to skilful hands. She heard a short laugh from the nurse giving her gas and air and felt the slippery baby released over her abdomen, then a pause. More gas and air gave her respite during the next contractions and she was suddenly free.

A nurse wiped her wet brow and Stella smiled her satisfaction over the white mask. "One of each, you clever girl," she said. "No stitches and everything complete including fingers and toes. We'll clean you up and then you must sleep. You'll see the babies soon but they need a bath, too."

Sleep came deeply and covered her mind. The muted sounds of clearing up the room and the small sounds of babies crying didn't disturb her until dawn. Her abdomen was flat but soggy and her body felt light as air. "Is it all over?" she asked in wonder.

"All over," said Paul. "Or all beginning," he added and yawned, but his happiness glowed through the exhaustion of a sleepless night.

"Go to bed," she told him. "I want to see them and then I shall have another nap."

"I'll bring the family this evening," he said. "Stella will let you see the twins later and said you must rest."

"Are they all right?"

"They're gorgeous! Now go back to sleep."

Emily put her head round the door and laughed. "We came just for five minutes," she said. "But I must say you look fine, just fine."

"Is Rose there?"

"She's being shown the babies and is coming with Paul."

"Mummy, they are small!" Rose tried to be calm.

"Not small for babies," Emma said.

"I said we'd have one of each," Rose said proudly.

"So you did," said Emily and eyed her great-niece with a quizzical gaze. "So you did."

"Five more minutes," the nurse said. "Have you everything you want, Mrs Sykes?"

Emma looked at the loving eager faces round her. "I have everything I shall ever want. My family is complete," she said.